Nick of the Woods
Or, Adventures of Prairie Life

by

Robert Montgomery Bird

Double 9 BOOKS

Nick of the Woods
Or, Adventures of Prairie Life
by Robert Montgomery Bird

ISBN: 978-93-62205-75-9

Published by

DOUBLE 9 BOOKS
2/13-B, Ansari Road
Daryaganj, New Delhi – 110002
info@double9books.com
www.double9books.com
Tel. 011-40042856

ABOUT THE AUTHOR

Robert Montgomery Bird was an American author, playwright, and doctor. He was born on February 5, 1806, and died on January 23, 1854. Bird was born on February 5, 1806, in New Castle, Delaware. He was born into a family of pioneers. His father was a wealthy partner in the firm of Navy agents Bird and Riddle. When Bird was four years old, his father died. His mother and brothers moved to Philadelphia, but his rich uncle, Nicholas Van Dyke, took him in. Then Bird went to New Castle Academy, where he was encouraged to get better at music. He later wrote that school was not fun for him. After going to the New Castle Academy and the Germantown Academy, he got his degree in 1824 from the University of Pennsylvania. Bird began to write about Latin, American, and English literature, especially the playwrights of the Elizabethan era. Then, while he was in medical school, he began to write short poems and stories. He wasn't very interested in medicine. By 1827, he had written for the Philadelphia Monthly Magazine and written two comedies, 'Twas All for the Best and News of the Night. After he graduated from medical school, he tried to start his own medical practice, but after a year, he gave up and went into writing instead.

CONTENTS

PREFACE

At the period when "Nick of the Woods" was written, the genius of Chateaubriand and of Cooper had thrown a poetical illusion over the Indian character; and the red men were presented—almost stereotyped in the popular mind—as the embodiments of grand and tender sentiment—a new style of the beau-ideal—brave, gentle, loving, refined, honourable, romantic personages—nature's nobles, the chivalry of the forest. It may be submitted that such are not the lineaments of the race—that they never were the lineaments of any race existing in an uncivilised state—indeed, could not be—and that such conceptions as *Atala* and *Uncas* are beautiful unrealities and fictions merely, as imaginary and contrary to nature as the shepherd swains of the old pastoral school of rhyme and romance; at all events, that one does not find beings of this class, or any thing in the slightest degree resembling them, among the tribes now known to travellers and legislators. The Indian is doubtless a gentleman; but he is a gentleman who wears a very dirty shirt, and lives a very miserable life, having nothing to employ him or keep him alive except the pleasures of the chase and of the scalp-hunt—which we dignify with the name of war. The writer differed from his critical friends, and from many philanthropists, in believing the Indian to be capable—perfectly capable, where restraint assists the work of friendly instruction—of civilisation: the Choctaws and Cherokees, and the ancient Mexicans and Peruvians, prove it; but, in his natural barbaric state, he is a barbarian—and it is not possible he could be anything else. The purposes of the author, in his book, confined him to real Indians. He drew them as, in his judgment, they existed—and as, according to all observation, they still exist wherever not softened by cultivation,—ignorant, violent, debased, brutal; he drew them, too, as they appeared, and still appear, in war—or the scalp-hunt—when all the worst deformities of the savage temperament receive their strongest and fiercest development.

Having, therefore, no other, and certainly no worse, desire than to make his delineations in this regard as correct and true to nature as he could, it was with no little surprise he found himself taken to account by some of the critical gentry, on the charge of entertaining the humane design of influencing the passions of his countrymen against the remnant of an unfortunate race, with a view of excusing the wrongs done to it by the whites, if not of actually hastening the period of that "final destruction" which it pleases so many men, against all probability, if not against all possibility, to predict as a certain future event. Had the accusation been confined to the reviewers, he might not, perhaps, have thought it safe to complain; but currency was given to it in a quarter which renders a disclaimer the more reasonable or the less presumptuous. One may contend with a brother author who dares not resist the verdict of the critics. In the English edition of the novel, published at the same time as the American, in a preface furnished by Mr. Ainsworth, the distinguished author of "Rookwood," "Crichton," &c. &c., to whom he is indebted for many polite and obliging expressions respecting it, it is hinted, hypothetically, that the writer's views were "coloured by national antipathy, and by a desire to justify the encroachments of his countrymen upon the persecuted natives, rather than by a reasonable estimate of the subject." The accused notices this fancy, however injurious he first felt it to be, less to refute than to smile at it. He prefers to make a more philosophic and practical application. The real inference to be drawn is, that he has succeeded very ill in this, somewhat essential, portion of his plan,—on the principle that the composition must be amiss, the design of which is so readily misapprehended. He may plead guilty to the defect; but he cannot admit the charge to have had any foundation in truth.

The writer confesses to have felt a little concern at an imputation, which was once faintly attempted to be made, he scarcely now remembers by whom, that in the character of Nathan Slaughter he intended to throw a slur upon the peaceful Society of Friends, of which Nathan is described as having been an unworthy member. This notion is undeserving of serious challenge. The whole object was here to portray the peculiar characteristics of a class of men, very limited, of course, in number, but found, in the old Indian days, scattered, at intervals, along the extreme frontier of every State, from New York to Georgia; men in whom the terrible barbarities of the savages, suffered through their families, or their friends and neighbours, had wrought a change of temper as strange as fearful. That passion is the mightiest which overcomes the most powerful restraints and prostrates the strongest barriers; and there was a dramatic propriety, at least, in associating with such a character as Nathan's, obstacles of faith and habit, which gave the greater force to his deeds and a deeper mystery to his story. No one conversant with the history of border affairs can fail to recollect some one or more instances of solitary men, bereaved fathers or orphaned sons, the sole survivors, sometimes, of exterminated households, who remained only to devote themselves to lives of vengeance; and "Indian-hating" (which implied the fullest indulgence of a rancorous animosity no blood could appease) was so far from being an uncommon passion in some particular districts, that it was thought to have infected, occasionally, persons, otherwise of good repute, who ranged the woods, intent on private adventures, which they were careful to conceal from the public eye. The author remembers, in the published journal of an old traveller—an Englishman, and, as he thinks, a Friend; but he cannot be certain of this fact, the name having escaped him, and the loose memorandum he made at the time, having been mislaid—who visited the region of the upper Ohio towards the close of the last century, an observation on this subject, which made too deep an impression to be easily forgotten. It was stated, as the consequence of the Indian atrocities, that such were the extent and depth of the vindictive feeling throughout the community, that it was suspected in some cases to have reached men whose faith was opposed to warfare and bloodshed. The legend of Wandering Nathan is, no doubt, an idle and unfounded one, although some vague notions touching the existence of just such a personage, whose habitat was referred to Western Pennsylvania, used to prevail among the cotemporaries, or immediate successors, of Boone and Kenton, M'Colloch and Wetzel. It is enough, however, for the author to be sustained in such a matter by poetical possibility; and he can afford to be indifferent to a charge which has the scarce consistent merit of imputing to him, at one and the same time, hostility towards the most warlike and the most peaceable of mankind.

CHAPTER I

The sun of an August afternoon, 1782, was yet blazing upon the rude palisades and equally rude cabins of one of the principal stations in Lincoln county, when a long train of emigrants, issuing from the southern forest, wound its way over the clearings, and among the waving maize-fields that surrounded the settlement, and approached the chief gate of its enclosure.

The party was numerous, consisting perhaps of seven or eight score individuals in all, men, women, and children, the last bearing that proportion to the others in point of numbers usually found in a borderer's family, and thus, with the help of pack-horses, cattle, and a few negroes, the property of the more wealthy emigrants, scattered here and there throughout the assemblage, giving to the whole train the appearance of an army, or moving village, of Vandals in quest of some new home to be won with the edge of the sword. Of the whole number there were at least fifty well-armed; some of these, however, being striplings of fourteen, and, in one or two instances, even of twelve, who balanced the big rifle on their shoulders, or sustained it over their saddle-bows, with all the gravity and dignity of grown warriors; while some few of the negroes were provided with the same formidable weapons. In fact, the dangers of the journey through the wilderness required that every individual of a party should be well armed, who was at all capable of bearing arms; and this was a kind of capacity which necessity instilled into the American frontiersman in the earliest infancy.

Of this armed force, such as it was, the two principal divisions, all well mounted, or at least provided with horses, which they rode or not as the humour seized them, were distributed in military order on the front and in the rear; while scouts, leading in the van, and flanking parties beating the woods on either side, where the nature of the country permitted, indicated still further the presence of a martial spirit on the part of the leaders. The women and children, stowed carefully away, for the most part with other valuable chattels, on the backs of pack-horses, were mingled with droves of cattle in the centre, many of which were made to bear burdens as well as the horses. Of wheeled carriages there was not a single one in the whole train, the difficulties of the road, which was a mere bridle-path, being such that they were never, at that early day, attempted to be brought into the country, unless when wafted in boats down the Ohio.

Thus marshalled, and stealing from the depth of the forest into the clearings around the Station, there was something in the appearance of the train—wild, singular, and striking. The tall and robust frames of the men, wrapped in blanket coats and hunting-frocks,—some of which, where the wearers were young and of gallant tempers, were profusely decked with fringes of yellow, green, and scarlet; the gleam of their weapons, and the tramp of their horses, gave a warlike air to the whole, typical, it might be supposed, of the sanguinary struggle by which alone the desert was to be wrung from the wandering barbarian; while the appearance of their families, with their domestic beasts and the implements of husbandry, was in harmony with what might be supposed the future destinies of the land, when peaceful labour should succeed to the strife of conquest.

The exiles were already in the heart of their land of promise, and many within view of the haven where they were to end their wanderings. Smiles of pleasure lighted their wayworn countenances, as they beheld the waving fields of maize and the gleam of the distant cabins; and their satisfaction was still further increased when the people of the Station, catching sight of them, rushed out, some mounted and others on foot, to meet them, uttering loud shouts of welcome, such as, in that day, greeted every band of new comers; and adding to the clamour of the reception a *feu-de-joie*, which they fired in honour of the numbers and martial appearance of the present company. The salutation was requited, and the stirring hurrahs returned, by the travellers, most of whom pressed forward to the van in disorder, eager to take part in the merry-making ere it was over, or perhaps to seek for friends who had preceded them in the journey through the wilderness. Such friends were, in many instances, found, and their loud and affectionate greetings were mingled with the scarce less cordial welcomes extended by the colonists, even to the unknown stranger. Such was the reception of the emigrants at that period and in that country, where men were united together by a sense of common danger; and where every armed visitor, besides being an accession to the strength of the colonists, brought with him such news of absent friends and still remembered homes as was sure to recommend him to favour.

The only individual who, on this occasion of rejoicing, preserved a melancholy countenance, and who, instead of riding forward, like the others, to shake hands with the people of the Station, betrayed an inclination to avoid their greetings altogether, was a young man, who, from the position he occupied in the band, and from other causes, was entitled to superior attention. With the rank and nominal title of second-captain,—a dignity conferred upon him by his companions, he was, in reality, the commander of the party, the ostensible leader being, although a man of good repute on the Virginia border, entirely wanting in the military reputation and skill which the other had acquired in the armies of the Republics, and of which the value was fully appreciated, when danger first seemed to threaten the exiles on their march. He was a youth of scarce twenty-three years of age; but five of those years had been passed in camps and battles; and the labours, passions, and privations of his profession had antedated the period of manhood. A frame tall and athletic, a countenance which, although retaining the smoothness and freshness of youth, was yet marked with the manly gravity and decision of mature life, added, in appearance, at least six years to his age. He wore a hunting-frock of the plainest green colour, with cap and leggings of leather, such as were worn by many of the poorest or least pretending exiles; like whom also he bore a rifle on his shoulder, with the horn and other equipments of a hunter. There was little, therefore, to distinguish him at the first view, from among his companions; although his erect military bearing, and the fine blooded bay horse which he rode, would have won him more than a passing look. The holsters at his saddle-bow, and the sabre at his side, were weapons not indeed very generally worn by frontiersmen, but still common enough to prevent their being regarded as badges of rank.

With this youthful officer the rear-guard, which he commanded, having deserted him, to press forward to the van, there remained only three persons, two of whom were negro slaves, both mounted and armed, that followed at a little distance behind, leading thrice their number of pack-horses. The third was a female, who rode closely at his side, the rein of her pony being, in fact, grasped in his hand; though he looked as if scarce conscious that he held it,—a degree of insensibility that would have spoken little in his favour to an observer; for his companion was both young and beautiful, and watched his moody countenance on her part with looks of the most anxious and affectionate interest. Her riding-habit, chosen, like his own garments, with more regard to usefulness than beauty, and perhaps somewhat the worse for its encounters with the wind and forest, could not conceal the graceful figure it defended; nor had the sunbeam, though it had darkened the bright complexion exposed to its summer fury, during a journey of more than six weeks, robbed her fair visage of a single charm. There was, in the general cast of features, a sufficient resemblance between the two to indicate near relationship; although it was plain that the gloom seated upon the brow of her kinsmen, as if a permanent characteristic, was an unwelcome and unnatural visitant on her own. The clear blue eye, the golden locks floating over her temples, the ruddy cheek and look of seventeen, and, generally, the frank and open character of her expression, betokened a spirit too joyous and elastic to indulge in those dark anticipations of the future or mournful recollections of the past, which clouded the bosom of her relative. And well for her that such was the cheerful temper of her mind; for it was manifest, from her whole appearance, that her lot, as originally cast, must have been among the gentle, the refined, and the luxurious, and that she was now, for the first time, exposed to discomfort, hardship, and suffering, among companions, who, however kind and courteous of conduct, were unpolished in their habits, conversation, and feelings, and, in every other respect, unfitted to be her associates.

She looked upon the face of her kinsman, and seeing that it grew the darker and gloomier the nearer they approached the scene of rejoicing, she laid her hand upon his arm, and murmured softly and affectionately—

"Roland,—cousin,—brother!—what is it that disturbs you? Will you not ride forward, and salute the good people that are making us welcome?"

"Us!" muttered the young man, with a bitter voice; "who is there on earth, Edith, to welcome us? Where shall *we* look for the friends and kinsfolk, that the meanest of the company are finding among yonder noisy barbarians?"

"You do them injustice, Roland," said the maiden. "Yesternight we had experience at the Station we left, that these wild people of the woods do not confine their welcomes to kinsmen. Kinder and more hospitable people do not exist in the world."

"It is not that, Edith," said the young man; "I were but a brute to doubt their hospitality. But look, Edith; we are in Kentucky, almost at our place of refuge. Yonder hovels, lowly, mean, and wretched—are they the mansions that should shelter the child of my father's brother? Yonder people, the outcasts of our borders, the poor, the rude, the savage—but one degree elevated above the Indians, with whom they contend,—are they the society from whom Edith Forrester should choose her friends?"

"They are," said Edith, firmly; "and Edith Forrester asks none better. In such a cabin as these, and, if need be, in one still more humble, she is content to pass her life, and dream that she is still in the house of her fathers. From such people, too, she will choose her friends, knowing that, even among the humblest of them, there are many worthy of her regard and affection. What have we to mourn in the world we have left behind us? We are the last of our name and race; fortune has left us nothing to regret. My only relative on earth, saving yourself, Roland,—saving yourself, my cousin, my brother,"—her lip quivered, and, for a moment her eyes were filled with tears,—"my only other living relation resides in this wilderness-land; and she, tenderly nurtured as myself, finds in it enough to engage her thoughts and secure her happiness. Why, then, should not I? Why should not *you*? Trust me, dear

Roland, I should myself be as happy as the day is long, could I only know that you did not grieve for me."

"I cannot but choose it," said Roland. "It is to me you owe the loss of fortune and your present banishment from the world."

"Say not so, Roland, for it is not true; no! I never can believe that our poor uncle would have carried his resentment, for such a cause, so far. But supposing that he could, and granting that all were as you say, I am prouder to be the poor cousin of Roland Forrester, who has bled in the battles of his country, than if I were the rich and courted kinswoman of one who had betrayed the memory of his father."

"You are, at least, an angel," said the youth; "and I am but a villain to say or do anything to give you pain. Farewell then to Fell-hallow, to old James River, and all! If you can forget these things, Edith, so will I; at all events, I will try."

"Now," said Edith, "you talk like my true cousin."

"Well, Edith, the world is before us; and shame be upon me, if I, who have health, strength, and youth to back my ambition, cannot provide you a refuge and a home. I will leave you for a while in the hands of this good aunt at the Falls; and then, with old Emperor there for my adjutant, and Sam for my rank and file, I will plunge into the forest, and scatter it as I have seen a band of tories scattered by my old major (who, by the bye, is only three years older than myself), Henry Lee, not many years back. Then, when I have built me a house, furrowed my acres with my martial plough-share (for to that, it appears, my sword must come), and reaped my harvest with my own hands (it will be hard work to beat my horse-pistols into a sickle), then, Edith—"

"Then, Roland," said the maiden, with a smile and a tear, "if you should still remember your poor cousin, it will not be hard to persuade her to follow you to your retreat, to share your fortunes of good and of evil, and to love you better in your adversity than she ever expected to love you in your prosperity."

"Spoken like my true Edith!" said the young officer, whose melancholy fled before her soft accents, as the evil spirit of Saul before the tinklings of the Jewish harp,—"spoken like my true Edith; for whom I promise, if fate smile upon my exertions, to rear a new Fell-hallow on the banks of the Ohio, in which I will be, myself, the first to forget that on James River. And now, Edith, let us ride forward and meet yon gay looking giant, whom, from his bustling demeanour, and fresh jerkin, I judge to be the commander of the Station, the redoubtable Colonel Bruce himself."

As he spoke the individual thus alluded to, separating himself from the throng, galloped up to the speaker, and displayed a person which excited the envy even of the manly looking Forrester. He was a man of at least fifty years, but as hale as one of thirty, without a single gray hair to deform the beauty of his raven locks, which fell down in masses nearly to his shoulders. His stature was colossal, and the proportions of his frame as just as they were gigantic; so that there was much in his appearance of real native majesty. Nothing, in fact, could be well imagined more truly striking and grand than his appearance, as seen at the first glance; though the second revealed a lounging indifference of carriage, amounting, at times, to something like awkwardness and uncouthness, which a little detracted from the effect. Such men were oft-times, in those days, sent from among the mountain counties of Virginia, to amaze the lesser mortals of the plains, who regarded them as the genii of the forest, and almost looked, as was said of the victor of the Kenhawa,[1] himself of the race, to see the earth tremble beneath their footsteps. With a spirit corresponding to his frame, he would have been the Nimrod that he seemed. But nature had long before extinguished the race of demigods; and the worthy Commander of the Station was not of them. He was a mortal man, distinguished by little, save his exterior, from other mortal men, and from the crowd of settlers who had followed him from the fortress. He wore, it is true, a new and jaunty hunting-shirt of dressed deer-skin, as yellow as gold, and fringed and furbelowed with shreds of the same substance, dyed as red as blood-root could make them; but was otherwise, to the view, a plain yeoman, endowed with those gifts of mind only which were necessary to his station, but with the virtues which are alike common to forest and city. Courage and hospitality, however, were then hardly accounted virtues, being too universal to be distinguished as such; and courtesy was equally native to the independent borderer.

[Footnote 1: Gen. Andrew Lewis.]

He shook the young officer heartily by the hand, a ceremony which he instantly repeated with the fair Edith; and giving them to understand that he claimed them as his own especial guests, insisted with much honest warmth, that old companionship in arms with one of their late nearest and dearest kinsmen had given him a double right to do so:—

"You must know," said he, "the good old Major your uncle, the brave old Major Roly, as we called him, Major Roland Forrester: well, K'-yaptin,—well, young lady,—my first battle war fought under his command; and an excellent commander he war; it war on the bloody Monongahela, whar the Frenchmen and Injuns trounced us so promiskous. Perhaps you've h'ard him tell of big Tom Bruce,—for so they called me then? I war a copporal in the first company of Rangers that crossed the river. Lord! how the world is turning upside down! I war a copporal then, and now I'm a k'-yunnel; a greater man in commission than war ever my old Major; and the Lord, he nows, I thought my old Major Forrester war the greatest man in all Virginnee, next to the G'-yovernor and K'-yunnel George Washington! Well, you must know, we marched up the g'yully that runs from the river; and bang went the savages' g'-yuns, and smash went their hatchets; and it came to close quarters, a regular rough-and-tumble, hard scratch! And so I war a-head of the Major, and the Major war behind, and the fight had made him as vicious as a wild cat, and he war hungry for a shot; and so says he to me, for I war right afore him, 'Git out of my way, you damned big rascal, till I git a crack at 'em!' And so I got out of his way, for I war mad at being called a damned big rascal, especially as I war doing my best, and covering him from mischief besides. Well! as soon as I jumped out of his way, bang went his piece, and bang went another, let fly by an Injun;—down went the Major, shot right through the hips, slam-bang. And so said I, 'Major,'—for I warn't well over my passion,—'if you'd 'a' taken things easy, I'd 'a' a stopped that slug for you.' And so says he, 'Bang away you big fool, and don't stand talking.' And so he swounded away; and that made me vicious, too, and I killed two of the red niggurs, before you could say Jack Robinson, just by way of satisfaction for the Major; and then I helped to carry him off to the tumbrels. I never see'd my old Major from that day to this; and it war only a month ago that I h'ard of his death. I honour his memory; and so, K'-yaptin, you see, thar's a sort of claim to old friendship between us."

To this characteristic speech, which was delivered with great earnestness, Captain Forrester made a suitable response; and intimating his willingness to accept the proffered hospitality of his uncle's companion in arms, he rode forward with his host and kinswoman towards the Station, of which, when once fairly relieved of the forest, he had a clear view.

It seemed unusually populous, as indeed it was; but Roland, as he rode by, remarked, on the skirts of the village, a dozen or more shooting-targets set up on the green, and perceived it was a gala-day which had drawn the young men from a distance to the fort. This, in fact, he was speedily told by a youth, whom the worthy Bruce introduced to him as his eldest son and namesake, "big Tom Bruce,—the third of that name; the other two Toms,—for two others he had had,—having been killed by the Injuns, and he having changed the boy's name, that he might have a Tom in the family." The youth was worthy of his father, being full six feet high, though scarcely yet out of his teens, and presented a visage of such serene gravity and good-humoured simplicity as won the affections of the soldier in a moment.

"Thar's a boy now, the brute," said Colonel Bruce, sending him off to assist in the distribution of the guests among the settlers, "that comes of the best stock for loving women and fighting Injuns in all Kentucky! And so, captain, if young madam, your sister h'yar, is for picking a husband out of Kentuck, I'll say it, and stand to it, thar's not a better lad to be found than Tom Bruce, if you hunt the district all over. You'd scarce believe it, mom," he continued, addressing Edith herself, "but the young brute did actually take the scalp of a full-grown Shawnee before he war fourteen y'ar old, and that in fa'r fight, whar thar war none to help him. The way of it war this: Tom war out in the range, looking for a neighbour's horse; when what should he see but two great big Shawnees astride of the identicular beast he war hunting! Away went Tom, and away went the bloody villians hard after, one of 'em afoot, the other on the horse. 'Now,' said Tom, this won't do, no how;' and so he let fly at the mounted feller; but being a little skeary, as how could he help it, the young brute, being the first time he ever banged at an Injun, he hit the horse, which dropped down in a flurry; and away comes the red devil over his head, like a rocket, end on to a sapling. Up jumps Tom and picks up the Injun's gun; and bang goes the other Shawnee at him, and jumps to a tree. 'A bird in the hand,' said Tom, 'is worth two in a bush;' and with that he blows out the first feller's brains, just as he is gitting up, and runs into the fort, hard chased by the other. And then to see the fellers, when I asked him why he didn't shoot the Injun that had fired at him, and so make sure of both, the other being in a sort of swound-like from the tumble, and ready to be knocked on the head at any moment? 'Lord!' said Tom, 'I never thought of it, I war such a fool!' and with that he blubbered all night, to think he had not killed them both. Howsomever, I war always of opinion that what he had done war good work for a boy of fourteen.—But, come now, my lovely young mom; we are entering the Station. May you never enter a house where you are less welcome."

CHAPTER II

Men and boys had rushed from the fortress together, to greet the new comers, and few remained save the women; of whom not a few, particularly of the younger individuals, were as eager to satisfy their curiosity as their fathers and brothers. The disorderly spirit had spread even among the daughters of the commandant, to the great concern of his spouse; who, although originally of a degree somewhat humbler even than his own, had a much more elevated sense of the dignity of his commission as a colonel of militia, and a due consciousness of the necessity of adapting her manners to her rank. She stood on the porch of her cabin, which had the merit of being larger than any other in the fort, maintaining order among some half dozen or more lasses, the eldest scarce exceeding seventeen, whom she endeavoured to range in a row, to receive the expected guests in state, though every moment some one or other might be seen edging away from her side, as if in the act of deserting her altogether.

"Out on you, you flirting critturs!" said she, her indignation provoked, and her sense of propriety shocked by such unworthy behaviour:—"Stop thar, you Nell! whar you going? You Sally, you Phoebe, you Jane, and the rest of you! ha'nt you no better idea of what's manners for a Cunnel's daughters? I'm ashamed of you,—to run ramping and tearing after the strange men thar, like tom-boys, or any common person's daughters! Laws! *do* remember your father's a Cunnel in the milishy, and set down in the porch here on the bench, like genteel young ladies; or stand up, if you like that better, and wait till your father, Cunnel Bruce that is, brings up the captains: one of 'em's a rale army captain, with epaulets and broad-sword, with a chance of money, and an uncommon handsome sister,—rale genteel people from old Virginnee: and I'm glad of it,—it's so seldom you sees any body but common persons come to Kentucky. Do behave yourselves: thar's Telie Doe thar at the loom don't think so much as turning her eyes around; she's a pattern for you."

"Law, mother!" said the eldest of the daughters, bridling with disdain, "I reckon I know how to behave myself as well as Telie Doe, or any other girl in the settlement;"—a declaration echoed and re-echoed by her sisters, all of whom bent their eyes towards a corner of the ample porch, where, busied with a rude loom, fashioned perhaps by the axe and knife of the militia colonel himself, on which she was weaving a coarse cloth from the fibres of the flax-nettle, sat a female somewhat younger than the eldest of the sisters, and doubtless of a more humble degree, as was shown by the labour in which she was engaged, while the others seemed to enjoy a holiday, and by her coarse brown garments, worn at a moment when the fair Bruces were flaunting in their best bibs and tuckers, the same having been put on not more in honour of the exiles, whose coming had been announced the day before, than out of compliment to the young men of the settlement, who were wont to assemble on such occasions to gather the latest news from the States.

The pattern of good manners thus referred to, was as unconscious of the compliment bestowed upon her by the worthy Mrs. Bruce as of the glances of disdain it drew from the daughters, being apparently at that moment too much occupied with her work to think of anything else; nor did she lift up her eyes until, the conversation having been resumed between the mother and daughters, one of the latter demanded "what was the name of that army captain, that was so rich and great, of whom her mother had been talking?"

"Captain Roland Forrester," replied the latter; at the sound of which name the maiden at the loom started and looked up with an air of fright, that caused exceeding diversion among the others. "Look at Telie Doe!" they cried, laughing: "you can't speak above your breath but she thinks you are speaking to her; and, sure, you can't speak to her, but she looks as if she would jump out of her skin, and run away for her dear life!"

And so, indeed, the girl did appear for a moment, looking as wild and terrified as the animal whose name she bore, when the first bay of the deer-hound startles her in the deep woodland pastures, rolling her eyes, catching her breath convulsively, shivering, and, in short, betraying a degree of agitation; that would have appeared unaccountable to a stranger; though, as it caused more amusement than surprise among the merry Bruces, it was but fair to suppose that it sprung from constitutional nervousness, or the sudden interruption of her meditations. As she started up in her confusion, rolling her eyes from one laughing maiden to another, her very trepidation imparted an interest to her features, which were in themselves pretty enough, though not so much as to attract observation, when in a state of rest. Then it was that the observer might see, or fancy he saw, a world of latent expression in her wild dark eyes, and trace the workings of a quick and sensitive spirit, whose existence would have been otherwise unsuspected, in the tremulous movement of her lips. And then, too, one might have been struck with the exquisite contour of a slight figure, which even the coarse garments, spun, and perhaps shaped, by her own hands, could not entirely conceal. At such times of excitement, there was something in her appearance both striking and singular—Indian-like, one might almost have said. Such an epithet might have been borne out by the wildness of her looks, the darkness of her eyes, the simple arrangement of her coal-black hair—which instead of being confined by comb or fillet, was twisted round a thorn cut from the nearest locust-tree—and by the smallness of her stature, though the lightness and European tinge of her complexion must have instantly disproved the idea.

Her discomposure dispelled from the bosoms of her companions all the little resentment produced by the matron's invidious comparison; and each now did her best to increase it by cries of "Jump, Telie, the Indians will catch you!" "Take care, Telie, Tom Bruce will kiss you!" "Run, Telie, the dog will bite you!" and other expressions, of a like alarming nature, which, if they did not augment her terror, divided and distracted her attention, till quite bewildered, she stared now on one, now on the other, and at each mischievous assault, started, and trembled, and gasped for breath, in inexpressible confusion. It was fortunate for her that this species of baiting, which from the spirit and skill with which her youthful tormentors pursued it, seemed no uncommon infliction, the reforming mother considered to be, at least at that particular moment, unworthy the daughters of a colonel in the militia.

"Do behave yourselves, you ungenteel critturs," said she; "Phoebe Bruce, you're old enough to know better; don't expose yourself before strannger. Thar they come now; thar's Cunnel Bruce that is, talking to Captain Forrester that is, and a right-down soldier-looking captain he is, too. I wonder whar's his cocked hat, and feather, and goold epaulets? Thar's his big broad-sword, and—but, Lord above us, ar'nt his sister a beauty! Any man in Kentucky will be proud of her; but, I warrant me, she'll take to nothing under a cunnel!"

The young misses ceased their sport to stare at the strangers, and even Telie Doe, pattern of propriety as she was, had no sooner recovered her equanimity than she turned her eyes from the loom and bent them eagerly upon the train now entering through the main gate, gazing long and earnestly upon the young captain and the fair Edith, who with the colonel of militia, and a fourth individual, parted from it, and rode up to the porch. The fourth person, a sober, and substantial-looking borderer, in a huge blanket-coat and slouched hat, the latter stuck round with buck's tails, was the nominal captain of the party. He conversed a moment with Forrester and the commandant, and then, being given in charge by the latter to his son Tom, who was hallooed from the crowd for this purpose, he rode away, leaving the colonel to do the honours to his second in command. These the colonel executed with much courtesy and gallantry, if not with grace, leaping from his horse with unexpected activity, and assisting Edith to dismount, which he effected by taking her in his arms and whisking her from the saddle with as little apparent effort as though he were handling an infant.

"Welcome, my beautiful young lady," said he, giving her another hearty shake of the hand: "H'yar's a house that shall shelter you; though thar's not much can be said of it, except that it is safe and wholesome. H'yar's my old lady too, and my daughters, that will make much of you; and as for my sons, thar's not a brute of 'em that won't fight for you; but th' ar' all busy stowing away the stranngers; and, I reckon, they think it ar'nt manners to show themselves to a young lady, while she's making acquaintance with the women."

With that the gallant colonel presented the fair stranger to his wife and daughters, the latter of whom, a little daunted at first by her appearance, as a being superior in degree to the ordinary race of mortals, but quickly re-assured by her frank and easy deportment, loaded her with caresses, and carried her into the house, to improve the few hours allowed to make her acquaintance, and to assist her in changing her apparel, for which the means were furnished from sundry bags and packages, that the elder of the two negromen, the only immediate followers of her kinsmen, took from the back of a pack-horse. The mother of the Bruces thought it advisable to follow them, to see, perhaps, in person, that they conducted themselves towards their guest as a colonel's daughter should.

None of the females remained on the porch save Telie, the girl of the loom, who, too humble or too timid to seek the acquaintance of the stranger lady, like the others, had been overlooked in the bustle, and now pursued her labour with but little notice from those who remained.

"And now, Colonel," said the young officer, declining the offer of refreshments made by his host, "allow me, like a true soldier, to proceed to the business with which you heard our commander, Major Johnson, charge me. To-morrow we resume our journey to the Falls. I should gladly myself, for Miss Forrester's sake, consent to remain with you a few days, to recruit our strength a little. But that cannot be. Our men are resolved to push on without delay; and as I have no authority to restrain them, I must e'en accompany them."

"Well," said Colonel Bruce, "if it must be, it must, and I'm not the brute to say 'No' to you. But lord, Captain, I should be glad to have you stay a month or two, war it only to have a long talk about my old friend, the brave old major. And thar's your sister, Captain,—lord, sir, she would be the pet of the family, and would help my wife teach the girls manners. Lord!" he continued, laughing, "you've no idea what grand notions have got into the old woman's head about the way of behaving, ever since it war that the Governor of Virginnie sent me a cunnel's commission. She thinks I ought to w'ar a cocked hat and goold swabs, and put on a blue coat instead of a leather shirt; but I wonder how soon I'd see the end of it, out h'yar in the bushes? And then, as for the girls, why thar's no end of the lessons she gives them;—and thar's my Jenny,—that's the youngest,—came blubbering up the other day, saying, 'she believed mother intended even to stop their licking at the sugar-troughs, she was getting so great and so proud!' Howsomever, women will be women, and thar's the end of it."

To this philosophic remark the officer of inferior degree bowed acquiescence, and recalling his host's attention to the subject of most interest to himself, requested to be informed what difficulties or dangers might be apprehended on the further route to the Falls of Ohio.

"Why, none on 'arth that I know of," said Bruce; "you've as cl'ar and broad a trace before you as man and beast could make—a buffalo-street,[2] through the canes; and, when thar's open woods, blazes as thick as stars, and horse-tracks still thicker: thar war more than a thousand settlers have travelled it this year already. As for danngers, Captain, why I reckon thar's none to think on. Thar war a good chance of whooping and howling about Bear's Grass, last year, and some hard fighting; but I h'ar nothing of Injuns thar this y'ar. But you leave some of your people h'yar: what force do you tote down to the Falls to-morrow?"

[Footnote 2: The bison-paths when very broad, were often thus called.]

"Twenty-seven guns in all: but several quite too young to face an enemy."

"Thar's no trusting to years in a matter of fighting!" said the Kentuckian. "Thar's my son Tom, that killed his brute at fourteen; but, I remember, I told you that story. Howsomever, I hold thar's no Injuns on the road; and if you should meet any, why, it will be down about Bear's Grass, or the Forks of Salt, whar you can keep your eyes open, and whar the settlements are so thick, it is easy taking cover. No, no, Captain, the fighting this year is all on the north side of Kentucky."

"Yet, I believe," said Roland, "there have been no troubles there since the defeat of Captain Estill on Little Mountain, and of Holder at that place,—what do you call it?"

"Upper Blue Licks of Licking," said Bruce; "and war'nt they troubles enough for a season? Two Kentucky captains (and one of them a south-side man, too,) whipped in fa'r fight, and by nothing better than brutish Injuns!"

"They were sad affairs, indeed; and the numbers of white men murdered made them still more shocking."

"The murdering," said the gallant Colonel Bruce, "is nothing, sir: it is the shame of the thumping that makes one feel vicious; thar's the thing no Kentuckian can stand, sir. To be murdered, whar thar's ten Injuns to one white man, is nothing; but whar it comes to being trounced by equal numbers, why thar's the thing not to be tolerated. Howsomever, Captain, we're no worse off in Kentucky than our neighbours. Thar's them five hundred Pennsylvanians that went out in June, under old Cunnel Crawford from Pittsburg, agin the brutes of Sandusky, war more ridiculously whipped by old Captain Pipe, the Delaware, thar's no denying."

"What!" said Roland, "was Crawford's company beaten?"

"Beaten!" said the Kentuckian, opening his eyes; "cut off the *b*, and say the savages made a dinner of 'em, and you'll be nearer the true history of the matter. It's but two months ago; and so I suppose the news of the affa'r hadn't got into East Virginnie when you started. Well, Captain, the long and short of it is,—the cunnel *war* beaten and exterminated, and that on a hard run from the fight he had hunted hard after. How many ever got back safe agin to Pittsburg, I never could rightly h'ar, but what I know is, that thar war dozens of prisoners beaten to death by the squaws and children, and that old Cunnel Crawford himself war put to the double torture and roasted alive; and, I reckon, if he war'nt eaten, it war only because he war too old to be tender."

"Horrible!" said the young soldier, muttering half to himself, though not in tones so low but that the Kentuckian caught their import; "and I must expose my poor Edith to fall into the power of such fiends and monsters!"

"Ay, Captain," said Bruce, "thar's the thing that sticks most in the heart of them that live in the wilderness and have wives and daughters;—to think of *their* falling into the hands of the brutes, who murder and scalp a woman just as readily as a man. As to their torturing them, that's not so certain, but the brutes arn't a bit too good for it; and I did h'ar of their burning one poor woman at Sandusky. But now, Captain, if you are anxious to have the young lady, your sister, in safety, h'yar's the place to stick up your tent-poles, h'yar, in this very settlement, whar the Injuns never trouble us, never coming within ten miles of us. Thar's as good land here as on Bear's Grass; and we shall be glad of your company. It is not often we have a rich man to take luck among us. Howsomever, I won't deceive you, if you will go to the Ohio; I hold, thar's no danger on the trace for either man or woman."

"My good friend," said Roland, "you seem to labour under two errors in respect to me which it is fitting I should correct. In the first place, the lady whom you have several times called, I know not why, my sister, claims no such near relationship, being only my cousin."

"Why, sure!" said the colonel, "someone told me so, and thar's a strong family likeness."

"There should be," said the youth, "since our fathers were twin brothers, and resembled each other in all particulars, in body, in mind, and, as I may say, in fortune. They were alike in their lives, alike also in their deaths: they fell together, struck down by the same cannon-ball, at the bombardment of Norfolk, seven years ago."

"May I never see a scalp," said the Kentuckian, warmly grasping the young man's hand, "if I don't honour you the more for boasting such a father and such uncles! You come of the true stock, captain, thar's no denying; and my brave old major's estates have fallen into the right hands; for, if thar's any believing the news the last band of emigrants brought of you h'yar, thar war no braver officer in Lee's corps, nor in the whole Virginnee line, than young Captain Forrester."

"Here," said Roland, looking as if what he said cost him a painful effort, "lies the second error,—your considering me, as you manifestly do, the heir of your old major, my uncle Roland,—which I am not."

"Lord!" said the worthy Bruce, "he was the richest man in Prince-George, and he had thousands of fat acres in the Valley, the best in all Fincastle, as I know very well, for I war a Fincastle man myself; and thar war my old friend Braxley,—he war a lieutenant under the major at Braddock's, and afterwards his steward, and manager, and lawyer-like,—who used to come over the Ridge to see after them. But I see how it is; he left all to the young lady?"

"Not an acre," said Roland.

"What!" said the Kentuckian: "he left no children of his own. Who then is the heir?"

"Your old friend, as you call him, Richard Braxley. And hence you see," continued the youth, as if desirous to change the conversation, "that I come to Kentucky, an adventurer and fortune-hunter, like other emigrants, to locate lands under proclamation-warrants and bounty-grants, to fell trees, raise corn, shoot bisons and Indians, and, in general, do any thing else that can be required of a good Virginian or good Kentuckian."

It was evidently the captain's wish now to leave altogether the subject on which he had thought it incumbent to acquaint his host with so much; but the worthy Bruce was not so easily satisfied; and not conceiving there was any peculiar impropriety in indulging curiosity in matters relating to his old major, however distasteful that curiosity might prove to his guest, he succeeded in drawing from the reluctant young man many more particulars of his story; which, as they have an important connection with the events it is our object to narrate, we must be pardoned for briefly noticing.

Major Roland Forrester, the uncle and godfather of the young soldier, and the representative of one of the most ancient and affluent families on James River (for by this trivial name Virginians are content to designate the noble *Powhatan*), was the eldest of three brothers, of whom the two younger, as was often the case under the *ancien regime* in Virginia, were left, at the death of their parent, to shift for themselves; while the eldest son inherited the undivided princely estate of his ancestors. This was at the period when that contest of principle with power, which finally resulted in the separation of the American Colonies from the parent State, first began to agitate the minds of the good planters of Virginia, in common with the people of all the other colonies. Men had already begun to take sides, in feeling as in argument; and, as usual, interest had, no doubt, its full share in directing and confirming the predilections of individuals. These circumstances,—the regular succession of the eldest-born to the paternal estate, and the necessity imposed on the others of carving out their own fortunes,—had, perhaps, their influence in determining the political bias of the brothers, and preparing them for contention when the increase of party feeling, and the clash of interests between the government abroad and the colonies at home, called upon all men to avow their principles and take their stands. It was as natural that the one should retain affection and reverence for the institutions which had made him rich and distinguished, as that the younger brothers, who had suffered under them a deprivation of their natural rights, should declare for a system of government and laws more liberal and equitable in their character and operation. At all events, and be the cause of difference what it might, when the storm of the Revolution burst over the land, the brothers were found arrayed on opposite sides—the two younger, the fathers of Roland and Edith, instantly taking up arms in the popular cause, while nothing, perhaps, but helpless feebleness and bodily infirmities, the results of wounds received in Braddock's war, throughout which he had fought at the head of a battalion of "Buckskins," or Virginia Rangers, prevented the elder brother from arming as zealously in the cause of his king. Fierce, uncompromising, and vindictive, however, in his temper, he never forgave his brothers the bold and active part they both took in the contest; and it was his resentment, perhaps, more than natural affection for his neglected offspring, that caused him to defeat his brothers' hopes of succession to his estates, (he being himself unmarried), by executing a will in favour of an illegitimate child, an infant daughter, whom he drew from concealment and acknowledged as his offspring. This child, however, was soon removed, having being burned to death in the house of its foster-mother. But its decease effected little or no change in his feelings towards his brothers, who, pursuing the principles they had so early avowed, were among the first to take arms among the patriots of Virginia, and fell, as Roland had said, at Norfolk, leaving each an orphan child—Roland, then a youth of fifteen, and Edith, a child of ten, to the mercy of the elder brother. Their death effected what perhaps their prayers never would have done. The stern loyalist took the orphans to his bosom, cherished and loved them, or at least appeared to do so, and often avowed his intention to make them his heirs. But it was Roland's ill fate to provoke his ire, as Roland's father had done before him. The death of that father, one of the earliest martyrs to liberty, had created in his youthful mind a strong abhorrence of everything British and loyal; and after presuming a dozen times or more to disclose and defend his hatred, he put the coping-stone to his audacity, by suddenly leaving his uncle's house, two years after he had been received into it, and galloping away, a cornet in one of the companies of the first regiment of horse which Virginia sent to the armies of Congress. He never more saw his uncle. He cared little for his wrath or its effects; if disinherited himself, it pleased his imagination to think he had enriched his gentle cousin. But his uncle carried his resentment further than he had dreamed, or indeed any one else who had beheld the show of affection he continued to the orphan Edith up to the last moment of his existence. He died in October of the preceding year, a week before the capitulation at York-town, and almost within the sound of the guns that proclaimed the fall of the cause he had so loyally espoused. From this place of victory Roland departed to seek his kinswoman. He found her in the house—not of his fathers, but of a stranger—herself a destitute and homeless orphan. No will appeared to pronounce her the mistress of the wealth he had himself rejected; but, in place of it, the original testament in favour of Major Forrester's own child was produced by Braxley, his confidential friend and attorney, who, by it, was appointed both executor of the estate and trustee to the individual in whose favour it was constructed.

The production of such a testament, so many years after the death of the girl, caused no little astonishment; but this was still further increased by what followed, the aforesaid Braxley instantly taking possession of the whole estate in the name of the heiress, who, he made formal deposition, was, to the best of his belief, yet alive, and would appear to claim her inheritance. In support of this extraordinary averment, he produced, or professed himself ready to produce, evidence to show that Forrester's child, instead of being burned to death as was believed, had actually been trepanned and carried away by persons to him unknown, the burning of the house of her foster-mother having been devised and executed merely to give colour to the story of her death. Who were the perpetrators of such an outrage, and for what purpose it had been devised, he affected to be ignorant; though he threw out many hints and surmises of a character more painful to Edith and Roland than even the loss of the property. These hints Roland could not persuade himself to repeat to the curious Kentuckian, since they went, in fact, to charge his own father, and Edith's, with the crime of having themselves concealed the child, for the purpose of removing the only bar to their expectations of succession.

Whatever might be thought of this singular story, it gained some believers, and was enough in the hands of Braxley, a man of great address and resolution, and withal, a lawyer, to enable him to laugh to scorn the feeble efforts made by the impoverished Roland to bring it to the test of legal arbitrament. Despairing, in fact, of his cause, after a few trials had convinced him of his impotence, and perhaps himself almost believing the tale to be true, the young man gave up the contest, and directed his thoughts to the condition of his cousin Edith; who, upon the above circumstances being made known, had received a warm invitation to the house and protection of her only female relative, a married lady, whose husband had, two years before, emigrated to the Falls of Ohio, where he was now a person of considerable importance. This invitation determined the course to be pursued. The young man instantly resigned his commission, and converting the little property that remained into articles necessary to the emigrant, turned his face to the boundless West, and with his helpless kinswoman at his side, plunged at once into the forest. A home for Edith in the house of a relative was the first object of his desires; his second, as he had already mentioned, was to lay the foundation for the fortunes of both.

There was something in the condition of the young and almost friendless adventurers to interest the feelings of the hardy Kentuckian; but they were affected still more strongly by the generous self-sacrifice, as it might be called, which the young soldier was evidently making for his kinswoman, for whom he had given up an honourable profession and his hopes of fame and distinction, to live a life of inglorious toil in the desert. He gave the youth another energetic grasp of hand, and said, with uncommon emphasis,—

"Hark'ee, Captain, my lad, I love and honour ye; and I could say no more, if you war my own natteral born father! As to that 'ar' Richard Braxley, whom I call'd my old friend, you must know, it war an old custom I have of calling a man a friend who war only an acquaintance; for I am for being friendly to all men that ar' white and honest, and no Injuns. Now, I do hold that Braxley to be a rascal,—a precocious rascal, sir! and, I rather reckon, thar war lying and villiany at the bottom of that will; and I hope you'll live to see the truth of it."

The sympathy felt by the Kentuckian in the story was experienced in a still stronger degree by Telie Doe, the girl of the loom, who, little noticed, if at all, by the two, sat apparently occupied with her work, yet drinking in every word uttered by the young soldier with a deep and eager interest, until Roland by chance looking round, beheld her large eyes fastened upon him, with a wild, sorrowful look, of which, however, she herself seemed quite unconscious, that greatly surprised him. The Kentuckian observing her at the same time, called to her,—"What, Telie, my girl, are you working upon a holiday? You should be dressed like the others, and making friends with the stranger lady. And so git away with you now, and make yourself handsome, and don't stand thar looking as if the gentleman would eat you."

"A qu'ar crittur she, poor thing!" said Bruce, looking after her commiseratingly; "and a stranger might think her no more nor half-witted. But she has sense enough, poor crittur! and, I reckon, is just as smart, if she war not so humble and skittish, as any of my own daughters."

"What," said Roland, "is she not then your child?"

"No, no," replied Bruce, shaking his head; "a poor crittur, of no manner of kin whatever. Her father war an old friend, or acquaintance-like; for, rat it, I won't own friendship for any such apostatised villians, no how:—but the man war taken by the Shawnees; and so as thar war none to befriend her, and she war but a little chit no bigger nor my hand, I took to her myself and raised her. But the worst of it is, and that's what makes her so wild and skeary, her father, Abel Doe, turned Injun himself, like Girty, Elliot, and the rest of them refugee scoundrels you've h'ard of. Now *that's* enough, you see, to make the poor thing sad and frightful; for Abel Doe is a rogue, thar's no denying, and everybody hates and cusses him, as is but his due; and it's natteral, now she's growing old enough to be ashamed of him, she should be ashamed of herself too,—though thar's nothing but her father to charge against her, poor creatur'. A bad thing for her to have an Injunised father;

for if it war'nt for him, I reckon, my son Tom, the brute, would take to her, and marry her."

"Poor creature, indeed!" muttered Roland to himself, contrasting in thought the condition of this helpless and deserted girl with that of his own unfortunate kinswoman, and sighing to acknowledge that it was still more forlorn and pitiable.

His sympathy was, however, but short-lived, being interrupted on the instant by a loud uproar of voices from the gate of the stockade, sounding half in mirth, half in triumph; while the junior Bruce was seen approaching the porch, looking the very messenger of good news.

CHAPTER III

"What's the matter, Tom Bruce?" said the father, eyeing him with surprise.

"Matter enough," responded the young giant, with a grin of mingled awe and delight; "the Jibbenainosay is up again!"

"Whar?" cried the senior, eagerly,—"not in our limits?"

"No, by Jehoshaphat," replied Tom; "but nigh enough to be neighbourly,—on the north bank of Kentuck, whar he has left his mark right in the middle of the road, as fresh as though it war but the work of the morning!"

"And a clear mark, Tom?—no mistake in it?"

"Right to an iota!" said the young man;—"a reggelar cross on the breast, and a good tomahawk dig right through the skull; and a long-legg'd fellow, too, that looked as though he might have fou't old Sattan himself?"

"It's the Jibbenainosay, sure enough; and so good luck to him!" cried the commander: "thar's a harricane coming!"

"Who is the Jibbenainosay?" demanded Forrester.

"Who?" cried Tom Bruce: "Why, Nick,—Nick of the Woods."

"And who, if you please, is Nick of the Woods?"

"Thar," replied the junior, with another grin, "thar, strannger, you're too hard for me. Some think one thing, and some another; but thar's many reckon he's the devil."

"And his mark, that you were talking of in such mysterious terms,—what is that?"

"Why, a dead Injun, to be sure, with Nick's mark on him,—a knife-cut, or a brace of 'em, over the ribs in the shape of a cross. That's the way the Jibbenainosay marks all the meat of his killing. It has been a whole year now since we h'ard of him."

"Captain," said the elder Bruce, "you don't seem to understand the afta'r altogether; but if you were to ask Tom about the Jibbenainosay till doomsday, he could tell you no more than he has told already. You must know, thar's a creatur' of some sort or other that ranges the woods round about our station h'yar, keeping a sort of guard over us like, and killing all the brute Injuns that ar' onlucky enough to come in his way, besides scalping them and marking them with his mark. The Injuns call him *Jibbenainosay*, or a word of that natur', which them that know more about the Injun gabble than I do, say, means the *Spirit-that-walks*; and if we can believe any such lying devils as Injuns (which I am loath to do, for the truth ar'nt in 'em), he is neither man nor beast, but a great ghost or devil that knife cannot harm nor bullet touch; and they have always had an idea that our fort h'yar in partickelar, and the country round about, war under his friendly protection—many thanks to him, whether he be a devil or not; for that whar the reason the savages so soon left off a worrying of us."

"Is it possible," said Roland, "that any one can believe such an absurd story?"

"Why not?" said Bruce, stoutly. "Thar's the Injuns themselves, Shawnees, Hurons, Delawares, and all,—but partickelarly the Shawnees, for he beats all creation a-killing of Shawnees,—that believe in him, and hold him in such eternal dread, that thar's scarce a brute of 'em has come within ten miles of the station h'yar this three y'ar; because as how, he haunts about our woods h'yar in partickelar, and kills 'em wheresomever he catches 'em,—especially the Shawnees, as I said afore, against which the creatur' has a most butchering spite; and there's them among the other tribes that call him *Shawneewannaween*, or the Howl of the Shawnees, because of his keeping them ever a-howling. And thar's his marks, captain,—what do you make of *that*? When you find an Injun lying scalped and tomahawked, it stands to reason thar war something to kill him?"

"Ay, truly," said Forrester; "but I think you have human beings enough to give the credit to, without referring it to a supernatural one."

"Strannger," said Big Tom Bruce the younger, with a sagacious nod, "when you kill an Injun yourself, I reckon,—meaning no offence—you will be willing to take all the honour that can come of it, without leaving it to be scrambled after by others. Thar's no man 'arns a scalp in Kentucky, without taking great pains to show it to his neighbours."

"And besides, captain," said the father, very gravely, "thar are men among us who have *seen* the creatur'!"

"*That*," said Roland, who perceived his new friends were not well pleased with his incredulity, "is an argument I can resist no longer."

"Thar war Ben Jones, and Samuel Sharp, and Peter Small-eye, and a dozen more, who all had a glimpse of him stalking through the woods, at different times; and, they agree, he looks more like a devil nor a mortal man,—a great tall fellow, with horns and a hairy head like a buffalo-bull, and a little devil that looks like a black b'ar, that walks before him to point out the way. He war always found in the deepest forests, and that's the reason we call him Nick of the Woods; wharby we mean *Old* Nick of the Woods; for we hold him to be the devil, though a friendly one to all but Injuns. Now, captain, I war never superstitious in my life,—but I go my death on the Jibbenainosay! I never seed the creatur' himself, but I have seen, in my time, two different savages of his killing. It's a sure sign, if you see him in the woods, that thar's Injuns at hand: and it's a good sign when you find his mark without seeing himself, for then you may be sure the brutes are off,—for they can't stand old Nick of the Woods no how! At first, he war never h'ard of afar from our station; but he has begun to widen his range. Last year he left his marks down Salt River in Jefferson; and now, you see, he is striking game north of the Kentucky; and I've h'ard of them that say he kills Shawnees even in their own country; though consarning *that* I'll not be so partickelar. No, no, Captain, thar's no mistake in Nick of the Woods; and if you are so minded, we will go and h'ar the whole news of him. But, I say, Tom," continued the Kentuckian, as the three left the porch together, "who brought the news?"

"Captain Ralph,—Roaring Ralph Stackpole," replied Tom Bruce, with a knowing and humorous look.

"What!" cried the father, in sudden alarm; "Look to the horses, Tom!"

"I will," said the youth, laughing: "it war no sooner known that Captain Ralph war among us than it was resolved to have six Regulators in the range all night! Thar's some of these new colts (not to speak of our own creaturs), and especially that blooded brown beast of the captain's, which the nigger calls Brown Briery, or some such name, would set a better man than Roaring Ralph Stackpole's mouth watering."

"And who," said Roland, "is Roaring Ralph Stackpole? and what has he to do with Brown Briarens?"

"A proper fellow as ever you saw," replied Tom, approvingly;—"killed two Injuns once, single-handed, on Bear-Grass, and has stolen more horses from them than ar' another man in Kentucky. A prime creatur'! but he has his fault, poor fellow, and sometimes mistakes a Christian's horse for an Injun's, thar's the truth of it!"

"And such scoundrels you make officers of?" demanded the soldier, indignantly.

"Oh," said the elder Bruce, "thar's no reggelar commission in the case. But whar thar's a knot of our poor folks out of horses, and inclined to steal a lot from the Shawnees (which is all fa'r plundering, you see, for thar's not a horse among them, the brutes, that they did not steal from Kentucky), they send for Roaring Ralph and make him their captain; and a capital one he is, too, being all fight from top to bottom; and as for the stealing part, thar's no one can equal him. But, as Tom says, he sometimes *does* make mistakes, having stolen horses so often from the Injuns, he can scarce keep his hands off a Christian's, and that makes us wrathy."

By this time the speakers had reached the gate of the fort, and passed among the cabins outside, where they found a throng of the villagers, surrounding the captain of horse-thieves, and listening with great edification to, and deriving no little amusement from, his account of the last achievement of the Jibbenainosay. Of this, as it related no more than the young Bruce had already repeated,—namely, that, while riding that morning from the north side, he had stumbled upon the corse of an Indian, which bore all the marks of having been a late victim to the wandering demon of the woods,—we shall say nothing; but the appearance and conduct of the narrator, one of the first, and perhaps the parent, of the race of men who have made Salt River so renowned in story, were such as to demand a less summary notice. He was stout, bandy-legged, broad-shouldered, and bull-headed, ugly, and villanous of look; yet with an impudent, swaggering, joyous self-esteem traced in every feature and expressed in every action of body, that rather disposed the beholder to laugh than to be displeased at his appearance. An old blanket-coat, or wrap-rascal, once white, but now of the same muddy brown hue that stained his visage—and once also of sufficient length to defend his legs, though the skirts had long since been transferred to the cuffs and elbows, where they appeared in huge patches—covered the upper part of his body; while the lower boasted a pair of buckskin breeches and leather wrappers, somewhat its junior in age, but its rival in mud and maculation. An old round fur hat, intended originally for a boy, and only made to fit his head by being slit in sundry places at the bottom, thus leaving a dozen yawning gaps, through which, as through the chinks of a lattice, stole out as many stiff bunches of black hair, gave to the capital excrescence an air as ridiculous as it was truly uncouth; which was not a little increased by the absence on one side of the brim, and by a loose fragment of it hanging down on the other. To give something martial to an appearance in other respects so outlandish and ludicrous, he had his rifle, and other usual equipments of a woodsman, including the knife and tomahawk, the first of which he carried in his hand, swinging it about at every moment, with a vigour and apparent carelessness well fitted to discompose a nervous person, had any such happened among his auditors. As if there was not enough in his figure, visage, and attire to move the mirth of beholders, he added to his other attractions a variety of gestures and antics of the most extravagant kinds, dancing, leaping, and dodging about, clapping his hands and cracking his heels together, with the activity, restlessness, and, we may add, the grace, of a jumping-jack. Such was the worthy, or unworthy, son of Salt River, a man wholly unknown to history, though not to local and traditionary fame, and much less to the then inhabitants of Bruce's Station, to whom he related his news of the Jibbenainosay with that emphasis and importance of tone and manner which are most significantly expressed in the phrase of "laying down the law."

As soon as he saw the commander of the station approaching, he cleared the throng around him by a skip and a hop, seized the colonel by the hand, and doing the same with the soldier, before Boland could repel him, as he would have done, exclaimed, "Glad to see you, cunnel;—same to you, strannger—What's the news from Virginnie? Strannger, my name's Ralph Stackpole, and I'm a ring-tailed squealer!"

"Then, Mr. Ralph Stackpole, the ring-tailed squealer," said Roland, disengaging his hand, "be so good as to pursue your business, without regarding or taking any notice of me."

"'Tarnal death to me!" cried the captain of horse-thieves, indignant at the rebuff, "I'm a gentleman, and my name's *Fight*! Foot and hand, tooth and nail, claw and mudscraper, knife, gun, and tomahawk, or any other way you choose to take me, I'm your man! Cock-a-doodle-doo!" And with that the gentleman jumped into the air, and flapped his wings, as much to the amusement of the provoker of his wrath as of any other person present.

"Come, Ralph," said the commander of the Station, "whar'd' you steal that brown mar' thar?"—a question whose abruptness somewhat quelled the ferment of the man's fury, while it drew a roar of laughter from the lookers-on.

"Thar it is!" said he, striking an attitude and clapping a hand on his breast, like a man who felt his honour unjustly assailed. "Steal! *I* steal any horse but an Injun's! Whar's the man dar's insinivate that? Blood and massacree-ation! whar's the man?"

"H'yar," said Bruce, very composedly. "I know that old mar' belongs to Peter Harper, on the north side."

"You're right, by Hooky!" cried Roaring Ralph; at which seeming admission of his knavery the merriment of the spectators was greatly increased; nor was it much lessened when the fellow proceeded to aver that he had borrowed it, and that with the express stipulation that it should be left at Bruce's Station, subject to the orders of its owner. "Thar, cunnel," said he, "thar's the beast; take it; and just tell me whar's the one you mean to lend me,—for I must be oft afore sunset."

"And whar are you going?" demanded Bruce.

"To St. Asaphis,"—which was a Station some twenty or thirty miles off,—replied Captain Stackpole.

"Too far for the Regulators to follow, Ralph," said Colonel Bruce; at which the young men present laughed louder than ever, and eyed the visitor in a way that seemed both to disconcert and offend him.

"Cunnel," said he, "you're a man in authority, and my superior officer; wharfo' thar' can be no scalping between us. But my name's Tom Dowdle, the ragman!" he screamed, suddenly skipping into the thickest of the throng, and sounding a note of defiance; "my name's Tom Dowdle, the ragman, and I'm for any man that insults me! log-leg or leather-breeches, green-shirt or blanket-coat, land-trotter or river-roller,—I'm the man for a massacree!" Then giving himself a twirl upon his foot that would have done credit to a dancing-master, he proceeded to other antic demonstrations of hostility, which when performed in after years on the banks of the Lower Mississippi, by himself and his worthy imitators, were, we suspect, the cause of their receiving the name of the mighty alligator. It is said, by naturalists, of this monstrous reptile, that he delights, when the returning warmth of spring has brought his fellows from their holes, and placed them basking along the banks of a swampy lagoon, to dart into the centre of the expanse, and challenge the whole field to combat. He roars, he blows the water from his nostrils, he lashes it with his tail, he whirls round and round, churning the water into foam; until, having worked himself into a proper fury, he darts back again to the shore, to seek an antagonist. Had the gallant captain of horse-thieves boasted the blood, as he afterwards did the name, of an "alligator half-breed," he could have scarce conducted himself in a way more worthy of his parentage. He leaped into the centre of the throng, where, having found elbow-room for his purpose, he performed the gyration mentioned before, following it up by other feats expressive of his hostile humour. He flapped his wings and crowed, until every chanticleer in the settlement replied to the note of battle; he snorted and neighed like a horse; he bellowed like a bull; he barked like a dog; he yelled like an Indian; he whined like a panther; he howled like a wolf; until one would have thought he was a living managerie, comprising within his single body the spirit of every animal noted for its love of conflict. Then, not content with such a display of readiness to fight the field, he darted from the centre of the area allowed him for his exercise, and invited the lookers-on individually to battle. "Whar's your buffalo-bull," he cried, "to cross horns with the roarer of Salt River? Whar's your full-blood colt that can shake a saddle off? h'yar's an old nag can kick off the top of a buck-eye! Whar's your cat of the Knobs? your wolf of the Rolling Prairies? h'yar's the old brown b'ar can claw the bark off a gum tree! H'yar's a man for you, Tom Bruce! Same to you, Sim Roberts! to you, Jimmy Big-nose! to you, and to you, and to you! Ar'n't I a ring-tailed squealer? Can go down Salt on my back, and swim up the Ohio! Whar's the man to fight Roaring Ralph Stackpole?"

Now, whether it happened that there were none present inclined to a contest with such a champion, or whether it was that the young men looked upon the exhibition as a mere bravado meant rather to amuse them than irritate, it so occurred that not one of them accepted the challenge; though each, when personally called on, did his best to add to the roarer's fury, if fury it really were, by letting off sundry jests in relation to borrowed horses and Regulators.[3] That the fellow's rage was in great part assumed, Roland, who was, at first, somewhat amused at his extravagance, became soon convinced; and growing at last weary of it, he was about to signify to his host his inclination to return into the fort, when the appearance of another individual on the ground suddenly gave promise of new entertainment.

[Footnote 3: It is scarce necessary to inform the reader that by this term must be understood those public-spirited citizens, amateur jack-ketches, who administer Lynch-law in districts where regular law is but inefficiently, or not at all, established.]

CHAPTER IV

"If you're ralely ripe for a fight, Roaring Ralph," cried Tom Bruce the younger, who had shown, like the others, a greater disposition to jest than to do battle with the champion, "here comes the very man for you. Look, boys, thar comes Bloody Nathan!" At which formidable name there was a loud shout set up, with an infinite deal of laughing and clapping of hands.

"Whar's the fellow?" cried Captain Stackpole, springing six feet into the air, and uttering a whoop of anticipated triumph. "I've heerd of the brute, and, 'tarnal death to me, but I'm his super-superior! Show me tho critter, and let me fly! Cock-a-doodle-doo!"

"Hurrah for Roaring Ralph Stackpole!" cried the young men, some of whom proceeded to pat him on the back in compliment to his courage, while others ran forward to hasten the approach of the expected antagonist.

The appearance of the comer, at a distance, promised an equal match to tho captain of horse-thieves; but Roland perceived, from the increase of merriment among the Kentuckians, and especially from his host joining heartily in it, that there was more in Bloody Nathan than met the eye. And yet there was enough in his appearance to attract attention, and to convince the soldier that if Kentucky had shown him, in Captain Stackpole, one extraordinary specimen of her inhabitants, she had others to exhibit not a whit less remarkable. It is on the frontiers, indeed, where adventurers from every corner of the world, and from every circle of society are thrown together, that we behold the strongest contrasts, and the strangest varieties, of human character.

Casting his eyes down the road, or street (for it was flanked by the outer cabins of the settlement, and perhaps deserved the latter name), which led, among stumps and gullies, from the gate of the stockade to the bottom of the hill, Forrester beheld a tall man approaching, leading an old lame white horse, at the heels of which followed a little silky haired black or brown dog, dragging its tail betwixt its legs, in compliment to the curs of the Station, which seemed as hospitably inclined to spread a field of battle for the submissive brute, as their owners were to make ready another for its master. The first thing that surprised the soldier in the appearance of the person bearing so formidable a name, was an incongruity which struck others as well as himself, even the colonel of militia exclaiming, as he pointed it out with his finger, "It's old Nathan Slaughter, to the backbone! Thar he comes, the brute, leading a horse in his hand, and carrying his pack on his own back! But he's a marciful man, Old Nathan, and the horse thar, old White Dobbin, war foundered and good for nothing ever since the boys made a race with him against Sammy Parker's jackass."

As he approached yet higher, Roland perceived that his tall, gaunt figure was arrayed in garments of leather from top to toe, even his cap, or hat (for such it seemed, having several broad flaps suspended by strings, so as to serve the purpose of a brim), being composed of fragments of tanned skins rudely sewed together. His upper garment differed from a hunting shirt only in wanting the fringes usually appended to it, and in being fashioned without any regard to the body it encompassed, so that in looseness and shapelessness, it looked more like a sack than a human vestment; and, like his breeches and leggings, it bore the marks of the most reverend antiquity, being covered with patches and stains of all ages, sizes, and colours.

Thus far Bloody Nathan's appearance was not inconsistent with his name, being uncommonly wild and savage; and to assist in maintaining his claims to the title, he had a long rifle on his shoulder, and a knife in his belt, both of which were in a state of dilapidation worthy of his other equipments; the knife, from long use and age, being worn so thin that it seemed scarce worthy the carrying, while the rifle boasted a stock so rude, shapeless, and, as one would have judged from its magnitude and weight, so unserviceable, that it was easy to believe it had been constructed by the unskilful hands of Nathan himself. His visage, seeming to belong to a man of at least forty-five or fifty years of age, was hollow, and almost as weather-worn as his apparel, with a long hooked nose, prominent chin, a wide mouth exceedingly straight and pinched, with a melancholy or contemplative twist at the corners, and a pair of black staring eyes, that beamed a good-natured, humble, and perhaps submissive, simplicity of disposition. His gait, too, as he stumbled along up the hill, with a shuffling, awkward, hesitating step, was like that of a man who apprehended injury and insult, and who did not possess the spirit to resist them. The fact, moreover, of his sustaining on his own shoulders a heavy pack of deer and other skins, to relieve the miserable horse which he led, betokened a merciful temper, scarce compatible with the qualities of a man of war and contention. Another test and criterion by which Roland judged his claims to the character of a roarer, he found in the little black dog; for the Virginian was a devout believer, as we are ourselves, in that maxim of practical philosophers, namely, that by the dog you shall know the master, the one being fierce, magnanimous, and cowardly, just as his master is a bully, a gentleman, or a dastard. The little dog of Nathan was evidently a coward, creeping along at White Dobbin's heels, and seeming to supplicate with his tail, which now draggled in the mud, and now attempted a timid wag, that his fellow-curs of the Station should not be rude and inhospitable to a peaceful stranger.

On the whole, the appearance of the man was anything in the world but that of the ferocious ruffian whom the nick-name had led Roland to anticipate; and he scarce knew whether to pity him, or to join in the laugh with which the young men of the settlement greeted his approach. Perhaps his sense of the ridiculous would have disposed the young soldier to merriment; but the wistful look with which, while advancing, Nathan seemed to deprecate the insults he evidently expected, spoke volumes of reproach to his spirit, and the half-formed smile faded from his countenance.

"Thar!" exclaimed Tom Bruce, slapping Stackpole on the shoulder, with great glee, "thar's the man that calls himself Dannger! At him, for the honour of Salt River; but take care of his forelegs, for, I tell you, he's the Pennsylvany war-horse!"

"And arn't I the ramping tiger of the Rolling Fork?" cried Captain Ralph; "and can't I eat him, hoss, dog, dirty jacket, and all? Hold me by the tail while I devour him!"

With that, he executed two or three escapades, demivoltes curvets, and other antics of a truly equine character, an galloping up to the amazed Nathan, saluted him with a neigh so shrill and hostile that even White Dobbin pricked up his ears, and betrayed other symptoms of alarm.

"Surely, Colonel," said Roland, "you will not allow that mad ruffian to assail the poor man?"

"Oh," said Bruce, "Ralph won't hurt him; he's never vicious, except among Injuns and horses. He's only for skearing the old feller."

"And who," said Forrester, "may the old fellow be? and why do you call him Bloody Nathan?"

"We call him Bloody Nathan," replied the commander, "because he's the only man in all Kentucky that *won't fight*! and thar's the way he beats us all hollow. Lord, Captain, you'd hardly believe it, but he's nothing more than a poor Pennsylvany Quaker; and what brought him out to Kentucky, whar thar's nar another creatur' of his tribe, thar's no knowing. Some say he war dishonest, and so had to cut loose from Pennsylvany; but I never heerd of his stealing anything in Kentucky; I reckon thar's too much of the chicken about him for that. Some say he is hunting rich lands; which war like enough for anybody that war not so poor and lazy. And some say his wits are unsettled, and I hold that that's the truth of the creatur'; for he does nothing but go wandering up and down the country, now h'yar and now thar, hunting for meat and skins; and that's pretty much the way he makes a living: and once I see'd the creatur' have a fit—a right up-and-down touch of the falling-sickness, with his mouth all of a foam. Thar's them that's good-natur'd that calls him Wandering Nathan, because of his being h'yar and thar, and every whar. He don't seem much afear'd of the Injuns; but, they say, the red brutes never disturbs the Pennsylvany Quakers. Howsomever, he makes himself useful; for sometimes he finds Injun sign whar thar's no Injuns thought of, and so he gives information; but he always does it, as he says, to save bloodshed, not to bring on a fight. He comes to me once, thar's more than three years ago, and instead of saying, 'Cunnel, thar's twenty Injuns lying on the road at the lower ford of Salt, whar you may nab them,' says he, says he, 'Friend Thomas, thee must keep the people from going nigh the ford, for thar's Injuns thar that will hurt them;' and then he takes himself off; whilst I rides down thar with twenty-five men and exterminates them, killing six, and driving the others the Lord knows whar. He has had but a hard time of it amongst us, poor creatur'; for it used to make us wrathy to find thar war so little fight in him that he wouldn't so much as kill a murdering Injun. I took his gun from him once; for why, he wouldn't attend muster when I had enrolled him. But I pitied the brute; for he war poor, and thar war but little corn in his cabin, and nothing to shoot meat with; and so I gave it back, and told him to take his own ways for an old fool."

While Colonel Bruce was thus delineating the character of Nathan Slaughter, the latter found himself surrounded by the young men of the Station, the butt of a thousand jests, and the victim of the insolence of the captain of horse-thieves. It is not to be supposed that Roaring Ralph was really the bully and madman that his extravagant freaks and expressions seemed to proclaim him. These, like any other "actions that a man might play," were assumed, partly because it suited his humour to be fantastic, and partly because the putting of his antic disposition on, was the only means which he, like many of his betters, possessed of attracting attention, and avoiding the neglect and contempt to which his low habits and appearance would have otherwise justly consigned him. There was, therefore, little really hostile in the feelings with which he approached the non-combatant; though it was more than probable, the disgust he, in common with the other warlike personages, entertained toward the peaceable Nathan, might have rendered him a little more malicious than usual.

"Nathan!" said he, as soon as he had concluded his neighing and curvetting, "if you ever said your prayers, now's the time. Down with your pack—for I can't stand deer's ha'r sticking in my swallow, no how!"

"Friend," said Nathan, meekly, "I beg thee will not disturb me. I am a man of peace and quiet."

And so saying, he endeavoured to pass onwards, but was prevented by Ralph, who, seizing his heavy bundle with one hand, applied his right foot to it with a dexterity that not only removed it from the poor man's back, but sent the dried skins scattering over the road. This feat was rewarded by the spectators with loud shouts, all which, as well as the insult itself, Nathan bore with exemplary patience.

"Friend," he said, "what does thee seek of me, that thee treats me thus?"

"A fight!" replied Captain Stackpole, uttering a war-whoop; "a fight, strannger, for the love of heaven!"

"Thee seeks it of the wrong person," said Nathan; "and I beg thee will get thee away,"

"What!" said Stackpole, "arn't thee the Pennsylvanny war-horse, the screamer of the meeting-house, the ba'r of Yea-Nay-and-Verily?"

"I am a man of peace," said the submissive Slaughter.

"Yea verily, verily and yea!" cried Ralph, snuffling through the nostrils, but assuming an air of extreme indignation: "Strannger, I've heerd of you! You're the man that holds it agin duty and conscience to kill Injuns, the redskin screamers—that refuses to defend the women, the splendiferous creatur's! and the little children, the squall-a-baby d'avs! And wharfo'? Bec'ause as how you're a man of peace and no fight, you superiferous, long-legged, no-souled crittur! But I'm the gentleman to make a man of you. So down with your gun, and 'tarnal death to me, I'll whip the cowardly devil out of you."

"Friend," said Nathan, his humility yielding to a feeling of contempt, "thee is theeself a cowardly person, or thee wouldn't seek a quarrel with one thee knows can't fight thee Thee would not be so ready with thee match."

With that, he stooped to gather up his skins, a proceeding that Stackpole, against whom the laugh was turned by this sally of Nathan's, resisted by catching him by the nape of the neck, twirling him round, and making as if he really would have beaten him.

Even this the peaceful Nathan bore without anger or murmuring; but his patience fled, when Stackpole, turning to the little dog, which was bristling its back and growling, expressed a half inclination to take up its master's quarrel, applied his foot to its ribs with a violence that sent it rolling some five or six yards down the hill, where it lay for a time yelping and whining with pain.

"Friend!" said Nathan, sternly, "thee is but a dog theeself, to harm the creature! What will thee have with me?"

"A fight! a fight, I tell thee!" replied Captain Ralph, "till I teach thy leatherified conscience the new doctrines of Kentucky."

"Fight thee I cannot and dare not," said Nathan; and then added, much to the surprise of Forrester, who, sharing, his indignation at the brutality of his tormentor, had approached to drive the fellow off,—"But if thee must have thee deserts, thee *shall* have them.—Thee prides theeself upon thee courage and strength—will thee adventure with me a friendly fall?"

"Hurrah for Nathan!" cried the young men, vastly delighted at his unwonted spirit, while Captain Ralph himself expressed his pleasure, by leaping into the air, crowing, and dashing off his hat, which he kicked down the hill with as much good will as he had previously bestowed upon the little dog.

"Off with your leather night-cap, and down with your rifle," he cried, giving his own weapon into the hands of a looker-on, "and scrape some of the grease off your jacket; for, 'tarnal death to me, I shall give you the Virginny lock, fling you head-fo'most, and you'll find yourself, in a twinkling, sticking fast right in the centre of the 'arth!"

"Thee may find theeself mistaken," said Nathan, giving up his gun to one of the young men, but instead of rejecting his hat, pulling it down tight over his brows. "There is locks taught among the mountains of Bedford that may be as good as them learned on the hills of Virginia.—I am ready for thee."

"Cock-a-doodle-doo!" cried Ralph Stackpole, springing towards his man, and clapping his hands, one on Nathan's left shoulder, the other on his right hip: "Are you ready?"

"I am," replied Nathan.

"Down, then, you go, war you a buffalo!" And with that the captain of the horse-thieves put forth his strength, which was very great, in an effort that appeared to Roland quite irresistible; though, as it happened, it scarce moved Nathan from his position.

"Thee is mistaken, friend!" he cried, exerting his strength in return, and with an effect that no one had anticipated. By magic, as it seemed, the heels of the captain of the horse-thieves were suddenly seen flying in the air, his head aiming at the earth, upon which it as suddenly descended with the violence of a bomb-shell; and there it would doubtless have burrowed, like the aforesaid implement of destruction, had the soil been soft enough for the purpose, or exploded into a thousand fragments, had not the shell been double the thickness of an ordinary skull.

"Huzza! Bloody Nathan for ever!" shouted the delighted villagers.

"He has killed the man," said Forrester; "but bear witness, all, the fellow provoked his fate."

"Thanks to you, strannger! but not so dead as you reckon," said Ralph, rising to his feet, and scratching his poll, with a stare of comical confusion. "I say, strannger, here's my shoulders,—but whar's my head?—Do you reckon I had the worst of it?"

"Huzza for Nathan Slaughter! He has whipped the ramping tiger of Salt River!" cried the young men of the Station.

"Well, I reckon he has," said the magnanimous Captain Ralph, picking up his hat: then walking up to Nathan, who had taken his dog into his arms, to examine into the little animal's hurts, he cried, with much good-humoured energy,—"Thar's my fo'paw, in token I've had enough of you and want no mo'. But I say, Nathan Slaughter," he added, as he grasped the victor's hand, "it's no thing you can boast of, to be the strongest man in Kentucky, and the most sevagarous at a tussel,—h'yar among murdering Injuns and scalping runnegades,—and keep your fists off their top-knots. Thar's my idear: for I go for the doctrine that every able-bodied man should sarve his country and his neighbours, and fight their foes; and them that does is men and gentlemen, and them that don't is cowards and rascals, that's my idear. And so, fawwell."

Then, executing another demivolte or two, but with much less spirit than he had previously displayed, he returned to Colonel Bruce, saying, "Whar's that horse you promised me, cunnel? I'm a licked man, and I can't stay here no longer, no way no how. Lend me a hoss, cunnel, and trust to my honour."

"You shall have a beast," said Bruce, coolly; "but as to trusting your honour, I shall do no such thing, having something much better to rely on. Tom will show you a horse; and, remember, you are to leave him at Logan's. If you carry him a step further, captain, you'll never carry another. Judge Lynch is looking at you; and so bewar'."

Having uttered this hint, he left the captian of horse-thieves to digest it as he might, and stepped up to Nathan, who had seated himself on a stump, where, with his skins at his side, his little dog and his rifle betwixt his legs, he sat enduring a thousand sarcastic encomiums on his strength and spirit, with as many sharp denunciations of the peaceful principles that robbed the community of the services he had shown himself so well able to render. The doctrine, so eloquently avowed by Captain Ralph, that it was incumbent upon every able-bodied man to fight the enemies of their little state, the murderers of their wives and children, was a canon of belief imprinted on the heart of every man in the district; and Nathan's failure to do so, however caused by his conscientious aversion to bloodshed, no more excused him from contempt and persecution in the wilderness, than it did others of his persuasion in the Eastern republics, during the war of the revolution. His appearance, accordingly, at any Station, was usually the signal for reproach and abuse; the fear of which had driven him almost altogether from the society of his fellowmen, so that he was seldom seen among them, except when impelled by necessity, or when his wanderings in the woods had acquainted him with the proximity of the foes of his persecutors. His victory over the captain of horse-thieves exposed him, on this occasion, to ruder and angrier remonstrances than usual; which having sought in vain to avert, he sat down in despair, enduring all in silence, staring from one to another of his tormentors with lack-lustre eyes, and playing with the silken hair of his dog. The approach of the captain of the Station procured him an interval of peace, which he, however, employed only to communicate his troubles to the little cur, that, in his perplexity, he had addressed pretty much as he would have addressed a human friend and adviser: "Well, Peter," said he, abstractedly, and with a heavy sigh, "what does *thee* think of matters and things!" To which question, the ridiculousness of which somewhat mollified the anger of the young men, Peter replied by rubbing his nose against his master's hand, and by walking a step or two down the hill, as if advising an instant retreat from the inhospitable Station.

"Ay, Peter," muttered Nathan, "the sooner we go the better; for there are none that makes us welcome. But nevertheless, Peter, we must have our lead and our powder; and we must tell these poor people the news."

"And pray, Nathan," said Colonel Bruce, rousing him from his meditations, "what may your news for the poor people be? I reckon it will be much wiser to tell it to me than that 'ar brute dog. You have seen the Jibbenainosay, perhaps, or his mark thar-away on the Kentucky?"

"Nay," said Nathan. "But there is news from the Injun towns of a great gathering of Injuns with their men of war in the Miami villages, who design, the evil creatures, marching into the district of Kentucky with a greater army than was ever seen in the land before."

"Let them come, the brutes," said the Kentuckian, with a laugh of scorn; "it will save us the trouble of hunting them up in their own towns."

"Nay," said Nathan, "but perhaps they *have* come; for the prisoner who escaped, and who is bearing the news to friend Clark, the General at the Falls, says they were to march two days after he fled from them."

"And whar did you learn this precious news?"

"At the lower fort of Kentucky, and from the man himself," said Nathan. "He had warned the settlers at Lexington—"

"That's piper's news," interrupted one of the young men. "Captain Ralph told us all about that; but he said thar war nobody at Lexington believed the story."

"Then," said Nathan, meekly, "it may be that the man was mistaken. Yet persons should have a care, for there is Injun sign all along the Kentucky. But that is my story. And now, friend Thomas, if thee will give me lead and powder for my skins, I will be gone, and trouble thee no longer."

"It's a sin and a shame to waste them on a man who only employs them to kill deer, b'ar, and turkey," said Bruce, "yet a man musn't starve, even whar he's a quaker. So go you along with my son Dick thar, to the store, and he'll give you the value of your plunder. A poor, miserable brute, thar's no denying," he continued, contemptuously, as Nathan, obeying the direction, followed Bruce's second son into the fortress. "The man has some spirit now and then; but whar's the use of it, while he's nothing but a no-fight quaker? I tried to reason him out of his notions; but thar war no use in trying, no how I could work it. I have an idea about these quakers—"

But here, luckily, the worthy Colonel's idea was suddenly put to flight by the appearance of Telie Doe, who came stealing through the throng, to summon him to his evening meal,—a call which neither he nor his guest was indisposed to obey; and taking Telie by the hand in a paternal manner, he ushered the young soldier back into the fort.

The girl, Roland observed, had changed her attire at the bidding of her protector, and now, though dressed with the greatest simplicity, appeared to more advantage than before. He thought her, indeed, quite handsome, and pitying her more than orphan condition, he endeavoured to show her such kindness as was in his power, by addressing to her some complimentary remarks, as he walked along at her side. His words, however, only revived the terror she seemed really to experience, whenever any one accosted her; seeing which, he desisted, doubting if she deserved the compliment the benevolent Bruce had so recently paid to her good sense.

CHAPTER V

The evening meal being concluded, and a few brief moments devoted to conversation with her new friends, Edith was glad, when, at a hint from her kinsman as to the early hour appointed for setting out on the morrow, she was permitted to seek the rest of which she stood in need. Her chamber—and, by a rare exercise of hospitality, the merit of which she appreciated, since she was sensible it could not have been made without sacrifice, she occupied it alone—boasted few of the luxuries, few even of the comforts, to which she had been accustomed in her native land, and her father's house. But misfortune had taught her spirit humility; and the recollection of nights passed in the desert, with only a thin mattress betwixt her and the naked earth, and a little tent-cloth and the boughs of trees to protect her from inclement skies, caused her to regard her present retreat with such feelings of satisfaction as she might have indulged if in the chamber of a palace.

She was followed to the apartment by a bevy of the fair Bruces, all solicitous to render her such assistance as they could, and all, perhaps, equally anxious to indulge their admiration, for the second or third time, over the slender store of finery, which Edith good-naturedly opened to their inspection. In this way the time fled amain until Mrs. Bruce, more considerate than her daughters, and somewhat scandalised by the loud commendations which they passed on sundry articles of dress such as were never before seen in Kentucky, rushed into the chamber, and drove them manfully away.

"Poor, ignorant critturs!" said she, by way of apology, "they knows no better: thar's the mischief of being raised in the back-woods. They'll never l'arn to be genteel, thar's so many common persons comes out here with their daughters. I'm sure, I do my best to l'arn 'em."

With these words she tendered her own good offices to Edith, which the young lady declining with many thanks, she bade her good-night, and, to Edith's great relief, left her to herself. A few moments then sufficed to complete her preparations for slumber, which being effected, she threw herself on her knees, to implore the further favour of the orphan's Friend, who had conducted her so far in safety on her journey.

Whilst thus engaged, her mind absorbed in the solemn duty, she failed to note that another visitor had softly stolen into the apartment; and accordingly, when she rose from her devotions, and beheld a female figure standing in the distance, though regarding her with both reverence and timidity, she could not suppress an exclamation of alarm.

"Do not be afraid,—it is only Telie Doe," said the visitor, with a low and trembling voice: "I thought you would want some one to—to take the candle."

"You are very good," replied Edith, who, having scarcely before observed the humble and retiring maid, and supposing her to be one of her host's children, had little doubt she had stolen in to indulge her curiosity, like the others, although at so late a moment as to authorise a little cruelty on the part of the guest. "I am very tired and sleepy," she said, creeping into bed, hoping that the confession would be understood and accepted as an apology. She then, seeing that Telie did not act upon the hint, intimated that she had no further occasion for the light, and bade her good-night. But Telie, instead of departing, maintained her stand at the little rude table, where, besides the candle, were several articles of apparel that Edith had laid out in readiness for the morning, and upon which she thought the girl's eyes were fixed.

"If you had come a little earlier," said Edith, with unfailing good-nature, "I should have been glad to show you anything I have. But now, indeed, it is too late, and all my packages are made up—"

"It is not *that*," interrupted the maiden hastily, but with trepidation. "No, I did not want to trouble you. But—"

"But what?" demanded Edith, with surprise, yet with kindness, for she observed the agitation of the speaker.

"Lady," said Telie, mustering resolution, and stepping to the bed-side, "if you will not be angry with me, I would, I would—"

"You would ask a favour, perhaps," said Edith, encouraging her with a smile.

"Yes, that is it," replied the girl, dropping on her knees, not so much, however, as it appeared, from abasement of spirit, as to bring her lips nearer to Edith's ear, that she might speak in a lower voice. "I know, from what they say, you are a great lady, and that you once had many people to wait upon you; and now you are in the wild woods, among strangers, and none about you but men." Edith replied with a sigh, and Telie, timorously grasping at the hand lying nearest her own, murmured eagerly, "If you would but take *me* with you, I am used to the woods, and I would be your servant."

"*You*!" exclaimed Edith, her surprise getting the better of her sadness. "Your mother would surely never consent to your being a servant?"

"My mother?" muttered Telie,—"I have no mother,—no relations."

"What! Mr. Bruce is not then your father?"

"No,—I have no father. Yes,—that is, I have a father; but he has,—he has turned Indian."

These words were whispered rather than spoken, yet whispered with a tone of grief and shame that touched Edith's feelings. Her pity was expressed in her countenance, and Telie, reading the gentle sympathy infused into every lovely feature, bent over the hand she had clasped, and touched it with her lips.

"I have told you the truth," she said, mournfully: "one like me should not be ashamed to be a servant. And so, lady, if you will take me, I will go with you and serve you; and poor and ignorant as I am, I *can* serve you,—yes, ma'am," she added, eagerly, "I can serve you more and better than you think,—indeed, indeed I can."

"Alas, poor child," said Edith, "I am one who must learn to do without attendance and service. I have no home to give you."

"I have heard it all," said Telie; "but I can live in the woods with you, till you have a house; and then I can work for you, and you'll never regret taking me,—no, indeed, for I know all that's to be done by a woman in a new land, and you don't; and, indeed, if you have none to help you, it would kill you, it would indeed: for it is a hard, hard time in the woods, for a woman that has been brought up tenderly."

"Alas, child," said Edith, perhaps a little pettishly, for she liked not to dwell upon such gloomy anticipations, "why should you be discontented with the home you have already? Surely, there are none here unkind to you?"

"No," replied the maiden, "they are very good to me, and Mr. Bruce has been a father to me. But then I am *not* his child, and it is wrong of me to live upon him, who has so many children of his own. And then my father—all talk of my father; all the people here hate him, though he has never done them harm, and I know,—yes, I know it well enough, though they won't believe it,—that he keeps the Indians from hurting them; but they hate him and curse him; and oh! I wish I was away, where I should never hear them speak of him more. Perhaps they don't know anything about him at the Falls, and then there will be nobody to call me the white Indian's daughter."

"And does Mr. Bruce, or his wife, know of your desire to leave him?"

"No," said Telie, her terrors reviving; "but if you should ask them for me, then they would agree to let me go. He told the Captain,—that's Captain Forrester,—he would do any thing for him; and indeed he would, for he is a good man, and he will do what he says."

"How strange, how improper, nay, how ungrateful then, if he be a good man," said Edith, "that you should wish to leave him and his kind family, to live among persons entirely unknown. Be content, my poor maid. You have little save imaginary evils to affect you. You are happier here than you can be among strangers."

Telie clasped her hands in despair: "I shall never be happy here, nor anywhere. But take me," she added eagerly, "take me for your own sake;—for it will be good for you to have me with you in the woods,—it will, indeed it will."

"It cannot be," said Edith, gently. But the maiden would scarce take a refusal. Her terrors had been dissipated by her having ventured so far on speech, and she now pursued her object with an imploring and passionate earnestness that both surprised and embarrassed Edith, while it increased her sympathy for the poor bereaved pleader. She endeavoured to convince her, if not of the utter folly of her desires, at least of the impossibility there was on her part of granting them. She succeeded, however, in producing conviction only on one point. Telie perceived that her suit was not to be granted; of when, as soon as she was satisfied, she left off entreaty, and rose to her feet with a saddened and humbled visage, and then, taking up the candle, she left the fair stranger to her repose.

In the meanwhile, Roland also was preparing for slumber; and finding, as indeed he could not avoid seeing, that the hospitality of his host had placed the males of the family under the necessity of taking their rest in the open air on the porch, he insisted upon passing the night in the same place in their company. In fact, the original habitation of the back-woodsman seldom boasted more than two rooms in all, and these none of the largest; and when emigrants arrived at a Station, there was little attempt made to find shelter for any save their women and children, to whom the men of the settlement readily gave up their own quarters, to share those of their male visitors under the blanket-tents which were spread before the doors. This, to men who had thus passed the nights for several weeks in succession, was anything but hardship; and when the weather was warm and dry, they could congratulate themselves on sleeping in greater comfort than, their sheltered companions. Of this Forrester was well aware, and he took an early period to communicate his resolution of rejecting the unmanly luxury of a bed, and sleeping like a soldier, wrapped in his cloak, with his saddle for a pillow. In this way, the night proving unexpectedly sultry, he succeeded in enjoying more delightful and refreshing slumbers than blessed his kinswoman in her bed of down. The song of the katydid and the cry of the whippoorwill came more sweetly to his ears from the adjacent woods; and the breeze that had stirred a thousand leagues of forest in its flight, whispered over his cheek with a more enchanting music than it made among the chinks and crannies of the wall by Edith's bed-side. A few idle dreams,—recollections of home, mingled with the anticipated scenes of the future, the deep forest, the wild beast, and the lurking Indian,—amused, without harassing, his sleeping mind; and it was not until the first gray of dawn that he experienced any interruption. He started up suddenly, his ears still tingling with the soft tones of an unknown voice, which had whispered in them, "Cross the river by the Lower Ford,—there is danger at the Upper." He stared around, but saw nothing all was silent around him, save the deep breathing of the sleepers at his side. "Who spoke?" he demanded in a whisper, but received no reply. "River,—Upper and Lower Ford,—danger?—" he muttered: "now I would have sworn some one spoke to me; and yet I must have dreamed it. Strange things, dreams,—thoughts in freedom, loosed from the chains of association,—temporary mad-fits, undoubtedly: marvellous impressions they produce on the organs of sense; see, hear, smell, taste, touch, more exquisitely *without* the organs than *with* them—What's the use of organs? There's the poser—I think—I—" but here he ceased thinking altogether, his philosophy having served the purpose such philosophy usually does, and wrapped him a second time in the arms of Morpheus. He opened his eyes almost immediately, as he thought; but his morning nap had lasted half an hour; the dawn was already purple and violet in the sky, his companions had left his side, and the hum of voices and the sound of footsteps in and around the Station, told him that his fellow-exiles were already preparing to resume their journey.

"A brave morrow to you, captain!" said the commander of the fortress, the thunder of whose footsteps, as he approached the house with uncommonly fierce strides, had perhaps broken his slumbers. A frown was on his brow, and the grasp of his hand, in which every finger seemed doing the duty of a boa-constrictor, spoke of a spirit up in arms, and wrestling with passion.

"What is the matter?" asked Roland.

"Matter that consarns you and me more than any other two persons in the etarnal world!" said Bruce, with such energy of utterance as nothing-but rage could supply. "Thar has been a black wolf in the pin-fold,—*alias*, as they used to say at the court-house, Captain Ralph Stackpole; and the end of it is, war I never to tell another truth in my life, that your blooded brown horse has absquatulated!"

"*Absquatulated!*" echoed Forrester, amazed as much at the word as at the fierce visage of his friend,—"what is that? Is the horse hurt?"

"Stolen away, sir, by the etarnal Old Scratch! Carried off by Roaring Ralph Stackpole, while I, like a brute, war sound a-sleeping! And h'yar's the knavery of the thing; sir! the unpronounceable rascality, sir!—I loaned the brute one of my own critturs, just to be rid of him, and have him out of harm's way; for I had a forewarning, the brute, that his mouth war a-watering after the Dew beasts in the pinfold, and after the brown horse in partickelar! And so I loaned him a horse, and sent him off to Logan's. Well, sir, and what does the brute do but ride off, for a make-believe, to set us easy; for he knew, the brute, if he war in sight of us, we should have had guards over the cattle all night long; well, sir, down he sot in ambush, till all were quiet; and then he stole back, and turning my own horse among the others, as if to say, 'Thar's the beast that I borrowed,'—it war a wonder the brute war so honest!—picked the best of the gathering, your blooded brown horse, sir! and all the while, I war sleeping like a brute, and leaving the guest in my own house to be robbed by Captain Ralph Stackpole, the villian!"

"If it be possible to follow the rascal," said Roland, giving way to wrath himself, "I must do so, and without a moment's delay. I would to heaven I had known this earlier."

"Whar war the use," said Bruce; "whar was the use of disturbing a tired man in his nap, and he a guest of mine too?"

"The advantage would have been," said Roland, a little testily, "that the pursuit could have been instantly begun."

"And war it *not*?" said the colonel. "Thar war not two minutes lost after the horse war missing, afore my son Tom and a dozen more of the best woodsmen war mounted on the fleetest horses in the settlement, and galloping after, right on the brute's trail."

"Thanks, my friend," said Roland, with a cordial grasp of the hand. "The horse will be recovered?"

"Thar's no denying it," said Bruce, "if a fresh leg can outrun a weary one; and besides, the brute war not content with the best horse, but he must have the second best too, that's Major Smalleye's two-y'ar-old pony. He has an eye for a horse, the etarnal skirmudgeon! but the pony will be the death of him; for he's skeary, and will keep Ralph slow in the path. No, sir; we'll have your brown horse before you can say Jack Robinson. But the intolerability of the thing, sir, is that Ralph Stackpole should steal my guest's horse, sir! But it's the end of his thieving, the brute, or thar's no snakes! I told him Lynch war out, the brute, and I told the boys to take car' I war not found lying; and I reckon they won't forget me! I like the crittur, thar's no denying, for he's a screamer among the Injuns; but thar's no standing a horse-thief! No, sir, thar's no standing a horse-thief!"

The only consequence of this accident which was apprehended, was that the march of the exiles must be delayed until the soldier's horse was recovered, or Roland himself left behind until the animal was brought in; unless, indeed, he chose to accept another freely offered him by his gallant host, and trust to having his own charger restored on some future occasion. He was himself unwilling that the progress of more than a hundred human beings towards the long sighed for land of promise should be delayed a moment on his account; and for this reason he exhorted his nominal superior to hasten the preparations for departure, without thinking of him. His first resolution in relation to his own course, was to proceed with the company, leaving his horse to be sent after him, when recovered. He was loath, however, to leave the highly-prized and long-tried charger behind; and Colonel Bruce, taking advantage of the feeling, and representing the openness and safety of the road, the shortness of the day's journey (for the next Station at which the exiles intended lodging was scarce twenty miles distant), and above all, promising, if he remained, to escort him thither with a band of his young men, to whom the excursion would be but an agreeable frolic, the soldier changed his mind, and, in an evil hour, as it afterwards appeared, consented to remain until Brown Briareus was brought in,—provided this should happen before mid-day; at which time, if the horse did not appear, it was agreed he should set out, trusting to his good fortune and the friendly zeal of his host, for the future recovery and restoration of his charger. Later than mid-day he was resolved not to remain; for however secure the road, it was wiser to pursue it in company than alone; nor would he have consented to remain a moment, had there appeared the least impediment to his joining the companions of his exile before nightfall.

His measures were taken accordingly. His baggage-horses, under the charge of the younger of the two negroes, were sent on with the band; the other, an old and faithful slave of his father, being retained as a useful appendage to a party containing his kinswoman, from whom he, of course, saw no reason to be separated. To Edith herself, the delay was far from being disagreable. It promised a gay and cheerful gallop through the forest, instead of the dull, plodding, funeral-like march to which she had been day after day monotonously accustomed. She assented, therefore, to the arrangement, and, like her kinsman, beheld, in the fresh light of sun-rise, without a sigh, without even a single foreboding of evil, the departure of the train of emigrants, with whom she had journeyed in safety so many long and weary leagues through the desert.

They set out in high spirits, after shaking hands with their hosts at the gates, and saluting them with cheers, which they repeated in honour of their young captain; and, in a few moments, the whole train had vanished, as if swallowed up by the dark forest.

CHAPTER VI

Within an hour after the emigrants had set out, the sky, which had previously been clear and radiant, began to be overcast with clouds, dropping occasional rains, which Roland scarcely observed with regret, their effect on the sultry atmosphere being highly agreeable and refreshing. They continued thus to fall at intervals until nine o'clock; when Roland, as he sat on the porch debating with Bruce the probabilities of their continuance, was roused by a shout from the outer village; and looking up, he beheld, to his great delight, Richard Bruce, the second son of his host, a lad of sixteen, ride into the enclosure, leading in triumph his recovered charger.

"Thar's the brute, strannger!" said he, with uncommon glee: "he war too hard a horse for Ralph's riding; and, I reckon, if he hadn't been, you wouldn't have had him so easy, for he's a peeler at a run, trot, or gallop, he is, I tell you! It's bad luck for Stackpole to be flung by man and beast two days hand-running,—first by Bloody Nathan, then by a stolen crittur!"

"And whar *is* the brute, Stackpole? and what have you done with him?" demanded Bruce.

"Thar, father, you're too hard for me," replied the youth; "but I'll tell you all I know on it. You needn't look at his legs, Captain, for they're all as sound as hickory: the crittur's a bit worried with his morning's work; but that's nothing to speak on."

The lad's story was soon told. The track of the horse-thief had been followed through the woods; and it was soon seen, from its irregularity, that he had made an unlucky selection of beasts, both being so restive and rebellious, that, it was obvious, he had found it no easy matter to urge them along. A place was found where he appeared to have been thrown by the turbulent Briareus, which he seemed afterwards to have pursued, mounted on the pony, in the vain hope of retaking the mettlesome charger, until persuaded of his inability, or afraid, from the direction in which the animal had fled, of being led back again to the settlement. His track, after abandoning the chase, was as plain as that left by the war-horse, and was followed by the main body of pursuers, while Richard and two or three others, taking the latter, had the good fortune to find and recover the animal as he was solacing himself, after his morning adventures, in a grassy wood, scarce two miles from the Station. What had become of Stackpole the lad knew not, but had no doubt, as he added, with a knowing look, "that Lynch's boys would soon give a good account of him; for Major Smalleye war as mad as a beaten b'ar about the two-y'ar-old pony."

"Well," said the father, "I reckon the brute will deserve all he may come by; and thar's no use in mourning him. Thar's as good Injun-fighters as he, left in Kentucky, thar's the comfort; and thar's no denying, men will be much easier about their horses."

With this consoling assurance, in which Roland saw implied the visitation of the deadliest vengeance on the head of the offender, Bruce proceeded to congratulate him on the recovery of Brown Briareus, and to intimate his readiness, after the animal had been allowed a little rest, which it evidently needed, to marshal his band of young men, and conduct him on his way after the exiles. But fate willed that the friendly intention should never be put into execution, and that the young soldier should go forth on his pilgrimage unattended and unprotected.

Within the space of half an hour, the clouds, which seemed previously to have discharged all their moisture, collected into a dense canopy, darkening the whole heaven, and rumbling with thunder, that became every moment louder and heavier. Then came gusts of wind, groaning through the forest, rattling among the dead limbs of the girdled trees, and whistling over the palisades of the fort. These were succeeded by louder peals of thunder, and vivid flashes of lightning, which continued and increased, until the tempest, for such it was, burst in fury, discharging deluges of rain, that fell with unintermitting violence until an hour or more after mid-day.

This was a circumstance which, as it necessarily deferred the moment of his setting out, caused Forrester a little uneasiness; but he soon came to believe he had reason to congratulate himself on its occurrence, since it was scarce possible the band would continue their journey in such a storm; and, indeed, Bruce was of opinion that the day's march would be ended on the banks of the river,—one of the principal forks of the Salt,—but little more than ten miles from his Station; where, if the exiles were wise, they would pitch their camp, waiting for the subsidence of the waters. This was a point that Roland might be expected to reach in a ride of three or four hours at most; which consideration not only satisfied him under the delay, but almost made him resolve to defer his setting-out until the following morning, that his kinswoman might have the advantage of sleeping a second time under the shelter of a roof, rather than be compelled to exchange it for the chill and humid forest.

It was while he was balancing this thought in his mind, and watching with a gladdened eye the first flash of sunshine, breaking through the parted clouds, that a shout, louder than that which had proclaimed the recovery of his steed, but of a wild and mournful character, arose from the outer village, and a horseman, covered with mud, reeking with rain, and reeling in the saddle with fatigue and exhaustion, rode into the fort, followed by a crowd of men, women, and children, all testifying, by their looks and exclamations, that he was the bearer of alarming news. And such indeed he was, as was shown by the first words he answered in reply to Bruce's demand "what was the matter?"

"There are a thousand Indians," he said, "Shawnees, Delawares, Wyandots, Miamies,—all the tribes of the North,—laying siege to Bryant's Station, and perhaps at this moment they are burning and murdering at Lexington. Men, Colonel Bruce! send us all your men, without a moment's delay; and send off for Logan and his forces: despatch some one who can ride, for I can sit a horse no longer."

"Whar's Dick Bruce?" cried the Kentuckian; and the son answering, he continued, "Mount the roan Long-legs, you brute, and ride to St. Asaph's in no time. Tell Cunnel Logan what you h'ar; and add, that before he can draw girth, I shall be, with every fighting-man in my fort, on the north side of Kentucky. Ride, you brute, ride for your life; and do you take car' *you* come along with the Cunnel; for it's time you war trying your hand at an Injun top-knot. Ride, you brute, ride!"

"Wah—wah—wah—wah!" whooped the boy, like a young Indian, flying to obey the order, and exulting in the expectation of combat.

"Sound horn, you Samuel Sharp!" cried the father. "You, Ben Jones, and some more of you, ride out and rouse the settlement; and, some of you, hunt up Tom Bruce and the Regulators: it war a pity they hanged Ralph Stackpole; for he fights Injuns like a wolverine. Tell all them that ar'n't ready to start to follow at a hard gallop, and join me at the ford of Kentucky; and them that can't join me thar, let them follow to Lexington; and them that don't find me thar, let them follow to Bryant's, or to any-whar whar thar's Injuns! Hurrah, you brutes! whar's your guns and your horses? your knives and your tomahawks? If thar's a thousand Injuns, or the half of 'em, thar's meat for all of you. Whar's Ikey Jones, the fifer? Let's have Yankee-Doodle and the Rogue's March for, by the etarnal Old Scratch, all them white men that ar'n't a-horse-back in twenty-five minutes, are rogues worse than red Injuns!—Hurrah for Kentucky!"

The spirit of the worthy officer of militia infused animation into all bosoms; and, in an instant, the settlement, late so peaceful, resounded with the hum and uproar of warlike preparation. Horses were caught and saddled, rifles pulled from their perches, knives sharpened, ammunition-pouches and provender-bags filled, and every other step taken necessary to the simple equipment of a border army, called to action in an emergency so sudden and urgent.

In the meanwhile, the intelligence was not without its effects on Roland Forrester, who, seeing himself so unexpectedly deprived of the promised escort,—for he could scarce think, under such circumstances, of withdrawing a single man from the force called to a duty so important,—perceived the necessity of employing his own resources to effect escape from a position which he now felt to be embarrassing. He regretted, for the first time, his separation from the band of emigrants, and became doubly anxious to follow them: for, if it were true that so large a force of Indians was really in the District, there was every reason to suppose they would, according to their known system of warfare, divide into small parties, and scatter over the whole country, infesting every road and path; and he knew not how soon some of them might be found following on the heels of the messenger. He took advantage of the first symptom of returning serenity on the part of his host, to acquaint him with his resolution to set out immediately, the rains having ceased, and the clouds broken up and almost vanished.

"Lord, captain," said the Kentuckian, "I hoped you would have been for taking a brush with us; and it war my idea to send a messenger after your party, in hopes your men would join us in the rusty. Whar will they have such another chance? A thousand Injuns ready cut and dried for killing! Lord, what a fool I war for not setting more store by that tale of Nathan Slaughter's! I never knowed the brute to lie in such a case; for, as he is always ramping about the woods, he's as good as a paid scout. Howsomever, the crittur did'nt speak on his own knowledge; and that infarnal Stackpole was just ripe from the North side. But, I say, captain, if your men will fight, just tote 'em back, stow away the women behind the logs here, and march your guns after me; and, if thar's half the number of red niggurs they speak of to be found, you shall see an affa'r of a skrimmage that will be good for your wholesome,—you will, by the etarnal!"

"If the men are of that mind," said Roland, gallantly, "I am not the one to balk them. I will, at least, see whither their inclinations tend; and that the matter may the sooner be decided, I will set out without delay."

"And we who war to escort you, captain," said the Kentuckian, with some embarrassment: "you're a soldier, captain, and you see the case!"

"I do; I have no desire to weaken your force; and, I trust, no protection is needed."

"Not an iota; the road is as safe as the furrow of a Virginnee corn-field,—at least till you strike the lower Forks; and *thar* I've heard of no rampaging since last summer: I'll indamnify you against all loss and mischief,—I will, if it war on my salvation!"

"If you could but spare me a single guide," said Forrester.

"Whar's the use, captain? The road is as broad and el'ar as a turnpike in the Old Dominion; it leads you, chock up, right on the Upper Ford, whar thar's safe passage at any moment: but, I reckon, the rains will make it look a little wrathy a while, and so fetch your people to a stand-still. But it's a pot soon full and soon empty, and it will be low enough in the morning."

"The Upper Ford?" said Roland, his dream, for so he esteemed it, recurring to his mind: "is there then a Lower Ford?"

"Ay," replied Bruce; "but thar's no passing it in the freshes; and besides, the place has a bad name. It war thar old John Ashburn pitched his Station, in '78; but the savages made murdering work of him, taking every scalp in the company; and so it makes one sad-like to pass thar, and the more partickelarly that it's all natteral fine ground for an ambush. You'll see the road, when you're six mile deep in the forest, turning off to the right, under a shivered beech-tree. You are then four miles from the river, or tharabouts, and just that distance, I reckon, from your company. No, captain," he repeated, "the road is wide and open, and a guide war mere lumber on your hands."

This was a point, however, on which the young soldier, doubly solicitous on his kinswoman's account, to avoid mistake, was not so easily satisfied: seeing which, the Kentuckian yielded to his importunity,—perhaps somewhat ashamed of suffering his guests to depart entirely alone,—and began to cast about him for some suitable person who could be prevailed upon to exchange the privilege of fighting Indians for the inglorious duty of conducting wayfarers through the forest. This was no easy task, and it was not until he assumed his military authority, as commander of all the enrolled militia-men in his district, empowered to make such disposition of his forces as he thought fit, that he succeeded in compelling the service of one of his reluctant followers, under whose guidance Roland and his little party soon after set out. Their farewells were briefly said, the urgent nature of his duties leaving the hospitable Bruce little opportunity for superfluous speech. He followed them, however, to the bottom of the hill, grasped

Roland by the hand; and doing the same thing by Edith, as if his conscience smote him for dismissing her with so little ceremony and such insufficient attendance, he swore that if any evil happened to her on the road, he would rest neither night nor day until he had repaired it, or lost his scalp in the effort.

With this characteristic and somewhat ominous farewell, he took his leave; and the cousins, with their guide and faithful servant, spurred onwards at a brisk pace, until the open fields of the settlement were exchanged for the deep and gloomy woodlands.

CHAPTER VII

The sun shone out clearly and brilliantly, and the tree-tops, from which the winds had already shaken the rain, rustled freshly to the more moderate breezes that had succeeded them; and Roland, animated by the change, by the brisk pace at which he was riding, and by the hope of soon overtaking his fellow-exiles, met the joyous look of his kinswoman with a countenance no longer disturbed by care.

And yet there was a solemnity in the scene around them that might have called for other and more sombre feelings. The forest into which they had plunged, was of the grand and gloomy character which the fertility of the soil and the absence of the axe for a thousand years imprint on the western woodlands, especially in the vicinity of rivers. Oaks, elms, and walnuts, tulip-trees and beeches, with other monarchs of the wilderness, lifted their trunks like so many pillars, green with mosses and ivies, and swung their majestic arms, tufted with mistletoe, far over head, supporting a canopy,—a series of domes and arches without end,—that had for ages overshadowed the soil. Their roots, often concealed by a billowy undergrowth of shrubs and bushes, oftener by brakes of the gigantic and evergreen cane, forming fences as singular as they were, for the most part, impenetrable, were yet at times visible, where open glades stretched through the woods, broken only by buttressed trunks, and by the stems of colossal vines, hanging from the boughs like cables, or the arms of an oriental banyan; while their luxuriant tops rolled in union with the leafy roofs that supported them. The vague and shadowy prospects opened by these occasional glades stirred the imagination, and produced a feeling of solitude in the mind, greater perhaps than would have been felt had the view been continually bounded by a green wall of canes.

The road, if such it could be called, through this noble forest was, like that the emigrants had so long pursued through the wilderness, a mere path, designated, where the wood was open, by blazes, or axe-marks on the trees; and, where the undergrowth was dense, a narrow track cut through the canes and shrubs, scarce sufficient in many places to allow the passage of two horsemen abreast; though when, as was frequently the case, it followed the ancient routes of the bisons to fords and salt-licks, it presented, as Bruce had described, a wide and commodious highway, practicable even to wheeled carriages.

The gait of the little party over this road was at first rapid and cheery enough; but by and by, having penetrated deeper into the wood, where breezes and sunbeams were alike unknown, they found their progress impeded by a thousand pools and sloughs, the consequences of the storm, that stretched from brake to brake. These interruptions promised to make the evening journey longer than Roland had anticipated; but he caught, at intervals, the fresh foot-prints of his comrades in the soil where it was not exposed to the rains, and reflected with pleasure, that, travelling even at the slowest pace, he must reach the ford where he expected to find them encamped, long before dark. He felt, therefore, no uneasiness at the delay; nor did he think any of those obstacles to rapid progress a cause for regret that gave him the better opportunity to interchange ideas with his fair kinswoman.

His only concern arose from the conduct of his guide, a rough, dark-visaged man, who had betrayed, from the first moment of starting, a sullen countenance, indicative of his disinclination to the duty assigned him; which feeling evidently grew stronger the further he advanced, nowithstanding sundry efforts Forrester made to bring him to a better humour. He displayed no desire to enter into conversation with the soldier, replying to such questions as were directed at him with a brevity little short of rudeness; and his smothered exclamations of impatience, whenever his delicate followers slackened their pace at a bog or gully, which he had himself dashed through with a manly contempt of mud and mire, somewhat stirred the choler of the young captain.

They had, perhaps, followed him a distance of four miles into the forest, when the occurrence of a wider and deeper pool than ordinary producing a corresponding delay on the part of Roland, who was somewhat averse to plunging with Edith up to the saddle-girths in mire, drew from him a very unmannerly, though not the less hearty execration on the delicacy of "them thar persons who," as he expressed it, "stumped at a mud-hole as skearily as if every tadpole in it war a screeching Injun."

Of this explosion of ill-temper Roland took no notice, until he had, with the assistance of Emperor, the negro, effected a safe passage for Edith over the puddle; in the course of which he had leisure to observe that the path now struck into a wide buffalo-street, that swept away through a wilderness of wood and cane-brake, in nearly a straight line, for a considerable distance. He observed, also, that the road looked drier and less broken than usual; his satisfaction at which had the good effect of materially abating the rage into which he had been thrown by the uncivil bearing of the guide. Nevertheless, he had no sooner brought his kinswoman safely to land, than, leaving her in the charge of Emperor, he galloped up to the side of his conductor, and gave vent to his indignation in the following pithy query:—

"My friend," said he, "will you have the goodness to inform me whether you have ever lived in a land where courtesy to strangers and kindness and respect to women are ranked among the virtues of manhood?"

The man replied only by a fierce and angry stare; and plying the ribs of his horse with his heels, he dashed onwards. But Roland kept at his side, not doubting that a little more wholesome reproof would be of profit to the man, as well as advantageous to his own interests.

"I ask that question," he continued, "because a man from such a land, seeing strangers, and one of them a female, struggling in a bog, would, instead of standing upon dry land, making disrespectful remarks, have done his best to help them through it."

"Strannger," said the man, drawing up his horse, and looking, notwithstanding his anger, as if he felt the rebuke to be in a measure just, "I am neither hog nor dog, Injun nor outlandish niggur, but a man—a man, strannger! outside and inside, in flesh, blood, and spirit, jest as my Maker made me; though thar may be something of the scale-bark and parsimmon about me, I'll not deny; for I've heer'd on it before. I axes the lady's pardon, if I've offended: and thar's the eend on't."

"The end of it," said Forrester, "will be much more satisfactory, if you give no further occasion for complaint. But now," he continued, Edith drawing nigh, "let us ride on and as fast as you like; for the road seems both open and good."

"Strannger," said the guide, without budging an inch, "you have axed me a question; and, according to the fa'r rule of the woods, it's my right to ax you another."

"Very well," said Roland, assenting to the justice of the rule; "ask it, and he brief."

"What you war saying of the road is true; thar it goes, wide, open, cl'ar, and straight, with as good a fence on both sides of it to keep in stragglers, as war ever made of ash, oak, or chestnut rails,—though it's nothing but a natteral bank of cane-brake: and so it runs, jest as cl'ar and wide, all the way to the river."

"I am glad to hear it," was the soldier's reply; "but now for your question?"

"Hy'ar it is," said the man, flinging out his hand with angry energy; "I wants to ax of you, as a sodger, for I've heer'd you're of the reggelar sarvice, whether it's a wiser and more Christian affa'r, when thar's Injuns in the land a murdering of your neighbours' wives and children, and all the settlement's in a screech and a cry, to send an able-bodied man to fight them; or to tote him off, a day's journey thar and back ag'in, to track a road that a blind man on a blind horse could travel, without axing questions of anybody? Thar's my question," he added, somewhat vehemently; "and now let's have a sodger's answer!"

"My good friend," said Roland, a little offended, and yet more embarrassed, by the interrogatory, "none can tell better than yourself how much, or how little occasion I may have for a guide. Your question, therefore, I leave you to answer yourself. If you think your duty calls you to abandon a woman in the wild woods to such guidance as one wholly unacquainted with them can give, you can depart as soon as you think fit; for I cannot—"

The guide gave him no time to finish the sentence. "You're right, strannger," he cried; "thar is your road, as plain as the way up a hickory, b'aring to a camp of old friends and acquaintances,—and hy'ar is mine, running right slap among fighting Injuns!"

And with that he turned his horse's head, and flourishing his right hand, armed with the ever constant rifle, above his own, and uttering a whoop expressive of the wild pleasure he felt at being released from his ignoble duty, he dashed across the pool, and galloped in a moment out of sight, leaving Roland and his party confounded at the desertion.

"An outlandish niggur'!" muttered old Emperor, on whom this expression of the guide had produced no very favourable effect; "guess the gemman white man is a niggur himself, and a rogue, and a potater, or whatsomever you call 'em! Leab a lady and a gemman lost in the woods, and neither take 'em on nor take 'em back!—lor-a-massy!"

To this half-soliloquised expression of indignation the soldier felt inclined to add a few bitter invectives of his own; but Edith treating the matter lightly, and affecting to be better pleased at the rude man's absence than she had been with his company, he abated his own wrath, and acknowledged that the desertion afforded the best proof of the safety of the road; since he could not believe that the fellow, with all his roughness and inhumanity, would have been so base as to leave them while really surrounded by difficulties. He remembered enough of Bruce's description of the road, which he had taken care should be minute and exact, to feel persuaded that the principal obstructions were now over, and that, as the guide had said, there was no possibility of wandering from the path. They had already travelled nearly half the distance to the river, and to accomplish the remainder, they had yet four hours of day-light. He saw no reason why they should not proceed alone, trusting to their good fate for a fortunate issue to their enterprise. To return to the fort would be only to separate themselves further from their friends, without ensuring them a better guide, or, indeed, any guide at all, since it was highly probable they would find it only occupied by women and children. In a word, he satisfied himself that nothing remained for him but to continue his journey, and trust to his own sagacity to end it to advantage.

He set out accordingly, followed by Edith and Emperor, the latter bringing up the rear in true military style, and handling his rifle, as if almost desirous of finding an opportunity to use it in the service of his young mistress.

In this manner, they travelled onwards with but little interruption for more than a mile; and Roland was beginning anxiously to look for the path that led to the Lower Ford, when Emperor galloped to the van and brought the party to a halt by reporting that he heard the sound of hoofs following at a distance behind.

"Perhaps,—perhaps," said Edith, while the gleam of her eye, shining with sudden pleasure, indicated how little real satisfaction she had felt at the desertion of their conductor,—"perhaps it is the sour fellow, the guide, coming back, ashamed of his misconduct."

"We will soon see," said Roland, turning his horse to reconnoitre; a proceeding that was, however, rendered unnecessary by the hurried speed of the comer, who, dashing suddenly round a bend in the road, disclosed to his wondering eyes, not the tall frame and sullen aspect of the guide, but the lighter figure and fairer visage of the girl, Telie Doe. She was evidently arrayed for travel, having donned her best attire of blue cloth, with a little cap of the same colour on her head, under which her countenance, beaming with exercise and anxiety, looked, in both Roland's and Edith's eyes, extremely pretty; much more so, indeed, than either had deemed it to be; while, secured behind the cushion or pillion, on which she rode,—for not a jot of saddle had she,—was a little bundle containing such worldly comforts as were necessary to one seriously bent upon a journey. She was mounted upon a sprightly pony, which she managed with more address and courage than would have been augured from her former timorous demeanour; and it was plain that she had put him to his mettle through the woods, with but little regard to the sloughs and puddles which had so greatly embarrassed the fair Edith. Indeed, it appeared that the exercise which had infused animation into her countenance had bestowed a share also on her spirit:

for, having checked her horse an instant, and looked a little abashed at the sudden sight of the strangers, she recovered herself in a moment, and riding boldly up, she proceeded, without waiting to be questioned, to explain the cause of her appearance. She had met the deserter, she said, returning to the Station, and thinking it was not right the stranger lady should be left without a guide in the woods, she had ridden after her to offer *her* services.

"It was at least somewhat surprising," Roland could not avoid saying, "that the fellow should have found you already equipt in the woods?"

At this innuendo, Telie was somewhat embarrassed, but more so, when, looking towards Edith, as if to address her reply to her, she caught the inquiring look of the latter, made still more expressive by the recollection which Edith retained of the earnest entreaty Telie had made the preceding night, to be taken into her service.

"I will not tell you a falsehood, ma'am," she said at last, with a firm voice; "I was not on the road by chance; I came to follow you. I knew the man you had to guide you was unwilling to go, and I thought he would leave you, as he has done. And, besides, the road is not so clear as it seems; it branches off to so many of the salt-licks, and the tracks are so washed away by the rains, that none but one that knows it can be sure of keeping it long."

"And how," inquired Edith, very pointedly,—for, in her heart, she suspected the little damsel was determined to enter her service, whether she would or not, and had actually run away from her friends for the purpose,—"how, after you have led us to our party, do you expect to return again to your friends?"

"If you will let me go with you as far as Jackson's Station" (the settlement at which it was originally determined the emigrants should pass the night), said the maiden humbly, "I will find friends there who will take me home; and perhaps our own people will come for me, for they are often visiting about among the Stations."

This declaration, made in a tone that convinced Edith the girl had given over all hopes of being received into her protection, unless she could remove opposition by the services she might render on the way, pointed out also an easy mode of getting rid of her when a separation should be advisable, and thus removed the only objection she felt to accept her proffered guidance. As for Roland, however, he expressed much natural reluctance to drag a young and inexperienced female so far from her home, leaving her afterwards to return as she might. But he perceived that her presence gave courage to his kinswoman; he felt that her acquaintance with the path was more to be relied upon than his own sagacity; and he knew not, if he even rejected her offered services altogether, how he could with any grace communicate the refusal, and leave her abandoned to her own discretion in the forest. He felt a little inclined, at first, to wonder at the interest she seemed to have taken in his cousin's welfare; but, by and by, he reflected that perhaps, after all, her motive lay in no better or deeper feeling than a mere girlish desire to make her way to the neighbouring station (twenty miles make but a neighbourly distance in the wilderness), to enjoy a frolic among her gadding acquaintance. This reflection ended the struggle in his mind; and turning to her with a smiling countenance, he said, "If you are so sure of getting home, my pretty maid, you may be as certain we will be glad of your company and guidance. But let us delay no longer."

The girl, starting at these words with alacrity, switched her pony and darted to the head of the little party, as if addressing herself to her duty in a business-like way; and there she maintained her position with great zeal, although Roland and Edith endeavoured, for kindness' sake, to make her sensible they desired her to ride with them as a companion, and not at a distance, like a pioneer. The faster they spurred, however, the more zealously she applied her switch, and her pony being both spirited and fresh, while their own horses were both not a little the worse for their long journey, she managed to keep in front, maintaining a gait that promised in a short time to bring them to the banks of the river.

They had ridden perhaps a mile in this manner, when a sudden opening in the cane-brake on the right hand, at a place where stood a beech-tree, riven by a thunderbolt in former years, but still spreading its shattered ruins in the air, convinced Roland that he had at last reached the road to the Lower Ford, which Bruce had so strictly cautioned him to avoid. What, therefore, was his surprise, when Telie, having reached the tree, turned at once into the by-road, leaving the direct path which they had so long pursued, and which still swept away before them, as spacious and uninterrupted, save by occasional pools, as ever.

"You are wrong," he cried, checking his steed.

"This is the road, sir," said the girl, though in some trepidation.

"By no means," said Forrester, "that path leads to the Lower Ford; here is the shivered beech, which the colonel described to me."

"Yes, sir," said Telie, hurriedly; "it is the mark; they call it the Crooked Finger-post."

"And a crooked road it is like to lead us, if we follow it," said Roland. "It leads to the Lower Ford, and is not therefore *our* road. I remember the Colonel's direction."

"Yes, sir," said Telie, anxiously,—"to take the beech on the right shoulder, and then down four miles, to the water."

"Precisely so," said the soldier; "with only this difference (for, go which way we will, the tree being on the right side of each path, we must still keep it on the right shoulder), that the road to the Upper Ford, which I am now travelling, is the one for our purposes. Of this I am confident."

"And yet, Roland," said Edith, somewhat alarmed at this difference of opinion, where unanimity was so much more desirable, "the young woman should know best."

"Yes!" cried Telie, eagerly; "I have lived here almost seven years, and been across the river more than as many times. This is the shortest and safest way."

"It may be both the shortest and safest," said Forrester, whose respect for the girl's knowledge of the woods and ability to guide him through them, began to be vastly diminished; "but *this* is the road Mr. Bruce described. Of this I am positive; and to make the matter still more certain, if need be, here are horse-tracks, fresh, numerous, scarcely washed by the rain, and undoubtedly made by our old companions; whereas *that* path seems not to have been trodden for a twelve-month."

"I will guide you right," faltered Telie, with anxious voice.

"My good girl," said the soldier, kindly, but positively, "you must allow me to doubt your ability to do that,—at least, on that path. Here is our road; and we must follow it."

He resumed it, as he spoke, and Edith, conquered by his arguments, which seemed decisive, followed him; but looking back, after having proceeded a few steps, she saw the baffled guide still lingering on the rejected path, and wringing her hands with grief and disappointment.

"You will not remain behind us?" said Edith, riding back to her: "You see, my cousin is positive: you must surely be mistaken?"

"I am *not* mistaken," said the girl, earnestly; "and, oh! he will repent that ever he took his own way through this forest."

"How can that be? What cause have you to say so?"

"I do not know," murmured the damsel, in woeful perplexity; "but—but, sometimes, that road is dangerous."

"Sometimes all roads are so," said Edith, her patience failing, when she found Telie could give no better reason for her opposition. "Let us continue: my kinsman is waiting us, and we must lose no more time by delay."

With these words, she again trotted forward, and Telie, after hesitating a moment, thought fit to follow.

But now the animation that had, a few moments before, beamed forth in every look and gesture of the maiden, gave place to dejection of spirits, and even, as Edith thought, to alarm. She seemed as anxious now to linger in the rear as she had been before to preserve a bold position in front. Her eyes wandered timorously from brake to tree, as if in fear lest each should conceal a lurking enemy; and often, as Edith looked back, she was struck with the singularly mournful and distressed expression of her countenance.

CHAPTER VIII

These symptoms of anxiety and alarm affected Edith's own spirits; they did more,—they shook her faith in the justice of her kinsman's conclusions. His arguments in relation to the road were, indeed, unanswerable, and Telie had offered none to weaken them. Yet why should she betray such distress, if they were upon the right one? and why, in fact, should she not be supposed to know both the right and the wrong, since she had, as she said, so frequently travelled both?

These questions Edith could not refrain asking of Roland, who professed himself unable to answer them, unless by supposing the girl had become confused, as he thought was not improbable, or had, in reality, been so long absent from the forest as to have forgotten its paths altogether: which was likely enough, as she seemed a very simple-minded, inexperienced creature. "But why need we," he said, "trouble ourselves to find reasons for the poor girl's opposition? Here are the tracks of our friends, broader and deeper than ever: here they wind down into the hollow; and there, you may see where they have floundered through that vile pool, that is still turbid, where they crossed it. A horrible quagmire! But courage, my fair cousin: it is only such difficulties as these which the road can lead us into."

Such were the expressions with which the young soldier endeavoured to reassure his kinswoman's courage, his own confidence remaining still unmoved; although in secret he felt somewhat surprised at the coincidence between the girl's recommendations of the by-road and the injunctions of his morning dream. But while pondering over the wonder, he had arrived at the quagmire alluded to, through which the difficulties of conducting his cousin were sufficiently great to banish other matters for a moment from his mind. Having crossed it at last in safety, he paused to give such instructions or assistance as might be needed by his two followers; when Edith, who had halted at his side, suddenly laid her hand on his arm, and exclaimed, with a visage of terror,—"Hark, Roland! do you hear? What is that?"

"Heard him, massa!" ejaculated Emperor from the middle of the bog, with voice still more quavering than the maiden's, and lips rapidly changing from Spanish-brown to clayey-yellow; "heard him, massa! Reckon it's an Injun! lorra-massy!"

"Peace, fool," cried Forrester, bending his looks from the alarmed countenance of his kinswoman to the quarter whence had proceeded the sound which had so suddenly struck terror into her bosom.

"Hark, Roland! it rises again!" she exclaimed; and Roland now distinctly heard a sound in the depth of the forest to the right hand, as of the yell of a human being, but at a great distance off. At the place which they had reached, the canes and undergrowth of other kinds had disappeared, and a wide glade, stretching over hill and hollow, swept away from both sides of the road further than the eye could see. The trees, standing wider apart than usual, were, if possible, of a more majestic stature; their wide and massive tops were so thickly interlaced, that not a single sunbeam found its way among the gloomy arcades below. A wilder, more solitary, and more awe-inspiring spot Roland had not before seen; and it was peculiarly fitted to add double effect to sights and sounds of a melancholy or fearful character. Accordingly, when the cry was repeated, as it soon was, though at the same distance as before, it came echoing among the hollow arches of the woods with a wild and almost unearthly cadence, the utterance, as it-seemed, of mortal agony and despair, that breathed a secret horror through the breasts of all.

"It is the Jibbenainosay!" muttered the shivering Telie: "these are the woods he used to range in most; and they say he screams after his prey! It is not too late:—let us go back!"

"An Injun, massa!" said Emperor, stuttering with fright, and yet proceeding both to handle his arms and to give encouragement to his young mistress, which his age and privileged character, as well as the urgency of the occasion, entitled him to do: "don't be afraid, missie Edie; nebber mind;—ole Emperor will fight and die for missie, old massa John's daughter!"

"Hist!" said Roland, as another scream rose on the air, louder and more thrilling than before.

"It is the cry of a human being!" said Edith,—"of a man in distress!"

"It is, indeed," replied the soldier,—"of a man in great peril, or suffering. Remain here on the road; and if anything—Nay, if you will follow me, it may be better; but let it be at a distance. If anything happens to me, set spurs to your horses:—Telie here can at least lead you back to the fort."

With these words, and without waiting to hear the remonstrances, or remove the terrors of his companions, the young man turned his horse into the wood, and guided by the cries, which were almost incessant, soon found himself in the vicinity of the place from which they proceeded. It was a thick grove of beeches of the colossal growth of the west, their stems as tall and straight as the pines of the Alleghanies, and their boughs, arched and pendulous like those of the elm, almost sweeping the earth below, over which they cast shadows so dark that scarce anything was visible beneath them, save their hoary and spectral trunks.

As Roland, followed by his little party, approached this spot, the cries of the unknown, and as yet unseen, sufferer, fearful even at a distance, grew into the wildest shrieks of fear, mingled with groans, howls, broken prayers and execrations, and half-inarticulate expressions, now of fondling entreaty, now of fierce and frantic command, that seemed addressed to a second person hard by.

A thousand strange and appalling conceits had crept into Roland's mind, when he first heard the cries. One while he almost fancied he had stumbled upon a gang of savages, who were torturing a prisoner to death; another moment, he thought the yells must proceed from some unlucky hunter, perishing by inches in the grasp of a wild beast, perhaps a bear or panther, with which animals it was easy to believe the forest might abound. With such horrible fancies oppressing his mind, his surprise may be imagined, when, having cocked his rifle and thrown open his holsters, to be prepared for the worst, he rushed into the grove and beheld a spectacle no more formidable than was presented by a single individual,—a man in a shaggy blanket-coat,—sitting on horseback under one of the most venerable of the beeches, and uttering those diabolical outcries that had alarmed the party, for no imaginable purpose, as Roland was at first inclined to suspect, unless for his own private diversion.

A second look, however, convinced the soldier that the wretched being had sufficient cause for his clamour, being, in truth, in a situation almost as dreadful as any Roland had imagined. His arms were pinioned behind his back, and his neck secured in a halter (taken, as it appeared, from his steed), by which he was fastened to a large bough immediately above his head, with nothing betwixt him and death, save the horse on which he sat,—a young and terrified beast, at whose slightest start or motion, he must have swung off and perished, while he possessed no means of restraining the animal whatever, except such as lay in strength of leg and virtue of voice.

In this terrible situation, it was plain, he had remained for a considerable period, his clothes and hair (for his hat had fallen to the ground) being saturated with rain; while his face purple with blood, his eyes swollen and protruding from their orbits with a most ghastly look of agony and fear, showed how often the uneasiness of his horse, round whose body his legs were wrapped with the convulsive energy of despair, had brought him to the very verge of strangulation.

The yells of mortal terror, for such they had been, with which he had so long filled the forest, were changed to shrieks of rapture, as soon as he beheld help approach in the person of the astonished soldier. "Praised be the Etarnal!" he roared; "cut me loose, strannger!—Praised be the Etarnal, and this here dumb beast!—Cut me loose, strannger, for the love of God!"

Such was Roland's intention; for which purpose he had already clapped his hand to his sabre, to employ it in a service more humane than any it had previously known; when, unfortunately, the voice of the fellow did what his distorted countenance had failed to do, and revealed to Roland's indignant eyes the author of all his present difficulties, the thief of the pinfold, the robber of Brown Briareus,—in a word, the redoubtable Captain Ralph Stackpole.

In a moment, Roland understood the mystery which he had been before too excited to inquire into. He remembered the hints of Bruce, and he had learned enough of border customs and principles to perceive that the justice of the woods had at last overtaken the horse-thief. The pursuing party had captured him,—taken him in the very manner, while still in possession of the 'two-year-old pony,' and at once adjudged him to the penalty prescribed by the border code,—tied his arms, noosed him with the halter of the stolen horse, and left him to swing, as soon as the animal should be tired of supporting him. There was a kind of dreadful poetical justice in thus making the stolen horse the thief's executioner; it gave the animal himself an opportunity to wreak vengeance for all wrongs received, and at the same time allowed his captor the rare privilege of galloping on his back into eternity.

Such was the mode of settling such offences against the peace and dignity of the settlements; such was the way in which Stackpole had been reduced to his unenviable situation; and, that all passers-by might take note that the execution had not been done without authority, there was painted upon the smooth white bark of the tree, in large black letters, traced by a finger well charged with moistened gunpowder, the ominous name—JUDGE LYNCH,—the Rhadamanthus of the forest, whose decisions are yet respected in the land, and whose authority sometimes bids fair to supersede that of all erring human tribunals.

Thus tied up, his rifle, knife, and ammunition laid under a tree hard by, that he might have the satisfaction, if satisfaction it could be, of knowing they were in safety, the executioners had left him to his fate, and ridden away long since, to attend to other important affairs of the colony.

The moment that Roland understood in whose service he was drawing his sword, a change came over the spirit of his thoughts and feelings, and he returned it very composedly to its sheath,—much to the satisfaction of the negro, Emperor, who, recognising the unfortunate Ralph at the same instant, cried aloud, "'Top massa! 't ar Captain Stackpole, what stole Brown Briery! Reckon I'll touch the pony on the rib, hah! Hanging too good for him, white niggah t'ief, hah!"

With that, the incensed negro made as if he would have driven the pony from under the luckless Ralph; but was prevented by his master, who, taking a second survey of the spectacle, motioned to the horror-struck females to retire, and prepared himself to follow them.

"'Tarnal death to you, captain! you won't leave me?" cried Ralph, in terror. "Honour bright! Help him that needs help—that's the rule for a Christian!"

"Villain!" said Roland, sternly, "I have no help to give you. You are strung up according to the laws of the settlements, with which I have no desire to interfere. I am the last man you should ask for pity."

"I don't ax your pity, 'tarnal death to me,—I ax your *help*.'" roared Ralph; "Cut me loose is the word, and then sw'ar at me atter! I stole your hoss thar:—well, whar's the harm? Didn't he fling me, and kick me, and bite me into the bargain, the cursed savage? and ar'n't you got him ag'in as good as ever? And besides, didn't that etarnal old Bruce fob me off with a beast good for nothing, and talk big to me besides? and warn't that all fa'r provocation? An didn't you yourself sw'ar ag'in shaking paws with me, and treat me as if I war no gentleman? 'Tarnal death to me, cut me loose, or I'll haunt you, when I'm a ghost, I will, 'tarnal death to me!"

"Cut him down, Roland, for Heaven's sake!" said Edith, whom the surprise and terror of the spectacle at first rendered speechless: "you surely,—no, Roland, you surely can't mean to leave him to perish?"

"Upon my soul," said the soldier, and we are sorry to record a speech representing him in a light so unamiable, "I don't see what right I have to release him; and I really have not the least inclination to do so. The rascal is the cause of all our difficulties; and, if evil should happen us, he will be the cause of that too. But for him, we should be now safe with our party. And besides, as I said before, he is hanged according to Kentucky law; a very good law, as far as it regards horse-thieves, for whom hanging is too light a punishment."

"Nevertheless, release him,—save the poor wretch's life," reiterated Edith, to whom Stackpole, perceiving in her his only friend, now addressed the most piteous cries and supplications: "the law is murderous, its makers and executioners barbarians. Save him, Roland, I charge you, I entreat you!"

"He owes his life to your intercession," said the soldier; and drawing his sabre again, but with no apparent good will, he divided the halter by which Ralph was suspended, and the wretch was free.

"Cut the tug, the buffalo-tug!" shouted the culprit, thrusting his arms as far from his back as he could, and displaying the thong of bison-skin, which his struggles had almost buried in his flesh. A single touch of the steel, rewarded by such a yell of transport as was never before heard in those savage retreats, sufficed to sever the bond; and Stackpole, leaping on the earth, began to testify his joy in modes as novel as they were frantic. His first act was to fling his arms round the neck of his steed, which he hugged and kissed with the most rapturous affection, doubtless in requital of the docility it had shown when docility was so necessary to its rider's life; his second, to leap half a dozen times into the air, feeling his neck all the time, and uttering the most singular and vociferous cries, as if to make double trial of the condition of his windpipe; his third, to bawl aloud, directing the important question to the soldier, "How many days has it been since they hanged me? War it to-day, or yesterday, or the day before? or war it a whole year ago? for may I be next hung to the horn of a buffalo, instead of the limb of a beech tree, if I didn't feel as if I had been squeaking thar ever since the beginning of creation! Cock-a-doodle-doo! him that ar'nt born to be hanged, won't be hanged, no-how!" Then running to Edith, who sat watching his proceedings with silent amazement, he flung himself on his knees, seized the hem of her riding-habit, which he kissed with the fervour of an adorer, exclaiming with a vehement sincerity, that made the whole action still more strangely ludicrous, "Oh! you splendiferous creatur'! you angeliferous anngel! here am I, Ralph Stackpole the Screamer, that can whip all Kentucky, white, black, mixed, and Injun; and I'm the man to go with you to the ends of the 'arth, to fight, die, work, beg, and steal bosses for you! I am, and you may make a little dog of me; you may, or a niggur, or a boss, or a door-post, or a back-log, or a dinner,—'tarnal death to me, but you may *eat* me! I'm the man to feel a favour, partickelarly when it comes to helping me out of a halter; and so jist say the word who I shall lick, to begin on; for I'm your slave jist as much as that niggur, to go with you, as I said afore, to the ends of the 'arth, and the length of Kentucky over?"

"Away with you, you scoundrel and jackanapes," said Roland, for to this ardent expression of gratitude Edith was herself too much frightened to reply.

"Strannger!" cried the offended horse-thief, "you cut the tug, and you cut the halter; and so, though you did it only on hard axing, I'd take as many hard words of you as you can pick out of a dictionary,—I will, 'tarnal death to me. But as for madam thar, the anngel, she saved my life, and I go my death in her sarvice; and now's the time to show sarvice, for thar's danger abroad in the forest."

"Danger!" echoed Roland, his anxiety banishing the disgust with which he was so much inclined to regard the worthy horse-thief; "what makes you say that?"

"Strannger," replied Ralph, with a lengthened visage and a gravity somewhat surprising for him, "I seed the Jibbenainosay! 'tarnal death to me, but I seed him as plain as ever I seed old Salt! I war a-hanging thar, and squeaking and cussing, and talking soft nonsense to the pony, to keep him out of his tantrums, when what should I see but a great crittur come tramping through the forest, right off yander by the fallen oak, with a big b'ar before him—"

"Pish!" said the soldier, "what has this to do with danger?"

"Beca'se and because," said Ralph, "when you see the Jibbenainosay, thar's always abbregynes[4] in the cover. I never seed the crittur before, but I reckon it war he, for thar's nothing like him in natur'. And so I'm for cutting out of the forest jist on the track of a streak of lightning,—now hy'yar, now thar, but on a full run without stopping. And so, if anngeliferous madam is willing, thump me round the 'arth with a crab-apple, if I don't holp her out of the bushes, and do all her fighting into the bargain,—I will, 'tarnal death to me!"

[Footnote 4: *Abbregynes*—aborigines.]

"You may go about your business," said Roland, with as much sternness as contempt. "We will have none of your base company."

"Whoop! whoo, whoo, whoo! don't rifle[5] me, for I'm danngerous!" yelled the demibarbarian, springing on his stolen horse, and riding up to Edith. "Say the word, marm," he cried; "for I'll fight for you, or run for you, take scalp or cut stick, shake fist or show leg, anything in reason or out of reason. Strannger thar's as brash[6] as a new hound in a b'ar fight, or a young boss in a corn-field, and no safe friend in a forest. Say the word, marm,—or if you think it ar'nt manners to speak to a strannger, jist shake your little finger, and I'll follow like a dog, and do you dog's sarvice. Or, if you don't like me, say the word, or shake t'other finger, and 'tarnal death to me, but I'll be off like an elk of the prairies!"

[Footnote 5: To *rifle*—to ruffle.]

[Footnote 6: *Brash*—rash, head-strong, over-valiant.]

"You may go," said Edith, not at all solicitous to retain a follower of Mr. Stackpole's character and conversation: "we have no occasion for your assistance."

"Farewell!" said Ralph; and turning, and giving his pony a thump with his fist and a kick with each heel, and uttering a shrill whoop, he darted away through the forest, and was soon out of sight.

CHAPTER IX

The course of Stackpole was through the woods, in a direction immediately opposite to that by which Roland had ridden to his assistance.

"He is going to the Lower Ford," said Telie, anxiously. "It is not too late for us to follow him. If there are Indians in the wood, it is the only way to escape them!"

"And why should we believe there *are* Indians in the wood?" demanded Roland; "because that half-mad rogue, made still madder by his terrors, saw something which his fancy converted into the imaginary Nick of the Woods? You must give me a better reason than that, my good Telie, if you would have me desert the road. I have no faith in your Jibbenainosays."

But a better reason than her disinclination to travel it, and her fears lest, if Indians were abroad, they would be found lying in ambush at the upper and more frequented pass of the river, the girl had none to give; and, in consequence, Roland (though secretly wondering at her pertinacity, and still connecting it in thought with his oft-remembered dream), expressing some impatience at the delays they had already experienced, led the way back to the buffalo-road, resolved to prosecute it with vigour. But fate had prepared for him other and more serious obstructions.

He had scarce regained the path, before he became sensible, from the tracks freshly printed in the damp earth, that a horseman, coming from the very river towards which he was bending his way, had passed by whilst he was engaged in the wood liberating the horse-thief. This was a circumstance that both pleased and annoyed him. It was so far agreeable, as it seemed to offer the best proof that the road was open, with none of those dreadful savages about it, who had so long haunted the brain of Telie Doe. But what chiefly concerned the young soldier was the knowledge that he had lost an opportunity of inquiring after his friends, and ascertaining whether they had really pitched their camp on the banks of the river; a circumstance which he now rather hoped than dared to be certain of, the tempest not seeming to have been so violent in that quarter as, of a necessity, to bring the company to a halt. If they had *not* encamped in the expected place, but, on the contrary, had continued their course to the appointed Station, he saw nothing before him but the gloomy prospect of concluding his journey over an unknown road, after night-fall, or returning to the Station he had left, also by night; for much time had been lost by the various delays, and the day was now declining fast.

These considerations threw a damp over his spirits, but taught him the necessity of activity; and he was, accordingly, urging his little party forward with such speed as he could, when there was suddenly heard at a distance on the rear the sound of fire-arms, as if five or six pieces were discharged together, followed by cries not less wild and alarming than those uttered by the despairing horse-thief.

These bringing the party to a stand, the quick ears of the soldier detected the rattling of hoofs on the road behind, and presently their came rushing towards them with furious speed a solitary horseman, his head bare, his locks streaming in the wind, and his whole appearance betraying the extremity of confusion and terror; which was the more remarkable, as he was well mounted and armed with the usual rifle, knife, and hatchet of the back-woodsman. He looked as if flying from pursuing foes, his eyes being cast backwards, and that so eagerly that he failed to notice the party of wondering strangers drawn up before him on the road, until saluted by a halloo from Roland; at which he checked his steed, looking for an instant ten times more confounded and frightened than before.

"You tarnation critturs!" he at last bawled, with the accents of one driven to desperation, "if there a'n't no dodging you, then there *a'n't*. Here's for you, you everlasting varmints—due your darndest!"

With that he clubbed his rifle, and advanced towards the party in what seemed a paroxysm of insane fury, brandishing the weapon and rolling his eyes with a ferocity that could have only arisen from his being in that happy frame of mind which is properly termed "frightened out of fear."

"How, you villain!" said Roland, in amazement, "do you take us for wild Indians?"

"What, by the holy hokey, and *a'n't* you?" cried the stranger, his rage giving way to the most lively transports; "Christian men!" he exclaimed in admiration, "and one of 'em a niggur, and two of em wimming! oh hokey! You're Capting Forrester, and I've heerd on you! Thought there was nothing in the wood but Injuns, blast their ugly picturs! and blast him, Sy Jones, as was, that brought me among 'em! And now I'm talking of 'em, Capting, don't stop to ax questions, but run,—cut and run, Capting, for there's an everlasting sight of 'em behind me!—six of 'em, Capting, or my name a'n't Pardon Dodge,—six of 'em,—all except one, and *him* I shot, the blasted crittur! for, you see, they followed me behind, and they cut me off before: and there was no dodging 'em,—(Dodge's my name, and dodging's my natur')—without getting lost in the woods; and it was either losing myself or my scalp; and so that riz my ebenezer, and I banged the first of 'em all to smash—if I didn't, then it a'n't no matter!"

"What, in Heaven's name," said Roland, overcome by the man's volubility and alarm together,—"what means all this? Are there Indians behind us?"

"Five of 'em, and the dead feller,—shocking long-legged crittur he was; jumped out of a bush, and seized me by the bridle—hokey! how he skeared me!—Gun went off of her own accord, and shot him into bits as small as fourpence-ha'pennies. Then there was a squeaking and squalling, and the hull of e'm let fly at me; and then, I cut on the back track, and they took and took atter; and I calculate, if we wait here a quarter of a minute longer, they will be on us jist like devils and roaring lions.—But where shall we run? You can't gin us a hint how to make way through the woods?—Shocking bad woods to be lost in! Bad place here for talking, Capting,—right 'twixt two fires,—six Injuns behind (and one of 'em dead), and an almighty passel before,—the Ford's full on 'em!"

"What!" said Roland, "did you pass the Ford? and is not Colonel Johnson, with his emigrants, there?"

"Not a man on 'em; saw 'em streaking through the mud, half way to Jackson's. Everlasting lying critturs, them emigrants! told me there was no Injuns on the road! when what should I do but see a hull grist on 'em dodging among the bushes at the river, to surround me, the tarnation critturs. But I kinder had the start on 'em, and I whipped, and I cut, and I run, and I dodged. And so says I, 'I've beat you, you tarnation scalping varmints!' when up jumps that long-legged feller, and the five behind him; and, blast 'em, that riz my corruption. And I—"

"In a word," said Roland, impatiently, and with a stern accent, assumed perhaps to reassure his kinswoman, whom the alarming communications of the stranger, uttered in an agony of terror and haste, filled with an agitation which she could not conceal, "you have seen Indians, or you say you have. If you tell the truth, there is no time left for deliberation; if a falsehood—"

"Why should we wait upon the road to question and wonder?" said Telie Doe, with a boldness and firmness that at another moment would have excited surprise; "why should we wait here, while the Indians may be approaching? The forest is open, and the Lower Ford is free."

"If you can yet lead us thither," said Roland, eagerly, "all is not yet lost. We can neither advance nor return. On, maiden, for the love of Heaven!"

These hasty expressions revealed to Edith the deep and serious light in which her kinsman regarded their present situation, though at first seeking to hide his anxiety under a veil of composure. In fact, there was not an individual present on whom the fatal news of the vicinity of the redman had produced a more alarming impression than on Roland. Young, bravo, acquainted with war, and accustomed to scenes of blood and peril, it is not to be supposed that he entertained fear on his own account; but the presence of one whom he loved, and whom he would have rescued from danger, at any moment, at the sacrifice of his own life thrice over, was enough to cause, and excuse, a temporary fainting of spirit, and a desire to fly the scene of peril, of which, under any other circumstances, he would have been heartily ashamed. The suddenness of the terror—for up to the present moment he had dreamed of no difficulty comprising danger, or of no danger implying the presence of savages in the forest—had somewhat shocked his mind from its propriety, and left him in a manner unfitted to exercise the decision and energy so necessary to the welfare of his feeble and well-nigh helpless followers. The vastness of his embarrassment, all disclosed at once,—his friends and fellow-emigrants now far away; the few miles which he had, to the last, hoped separated him from them, converted into leagues; Indian enemies at hand; advance and retreat both alike cut off; and night approaching fast, in which, without a guide, any attempt to retreat through the wild forest would be as likely to secure his destruction as deliverance;—these were circumstances that crowded into his mind with benumbing effect, engrossing his faculties, when the most active use of them was essential to the preservation of his party.

It was at this moment of weakness and confusion, while uttering what was meant to throw some little discredit over the story of Dodge, to abate the terrors of Edith, that the words of Telie Doe fell on his ears, bringing both aid and hope to his embarrassed spirits. *She*, at least, was acquainted with the woods; she, at least, could conduct him, if not to the fortified Station he had left (and bitterly now did he regret having left it), to the neglected ford of the river, which her former attempts to lead him thither, and the memory of his dream, caused him now to regard as a city of refuge pointed out by destiny itself.

"You shall have your way, at last, fair Telie," he said, with a laugh, but not with merriment: "Fate speaks for you; and whether I will or not, we must go to the Lower Ford"

"You will never repent it," said the girl, the bright looks which she had worn for the few moments she was permitted to control the motions of the party, returning to her visage, and seeming to emanate from a rejoicing spirit;—"they will not think of waylaying us at the Lower Ford."

With that, she darted into the wood, and, followed by the others, including the new-comer, Dodge, was soon at a considerable distance from the road.

"Singular," said Roland to Edith, at whose rein he now rode, endeavouring to remove her terrors, which, though she uttered no words, were manifestly overpowering,—"singular that the girl should look so glad and fearless, while we are, I believe, all horribly frightened. It is, however, a good omen. When one so timorous as she casts aside fear, there is little reason for others to be frighted."

"I hope,—I hope so," murmured Edith. "But—but I have had my omens, Roland, and they were evil ones. I dreamed—You smile at me!"

"I do," said the soldier, "and not more at your joyless tones, my fair cousin, than at the coincidence of our thoughts. *I* dreamed (for I also have had my visions) last night, that some one came to me and whispered in my ear to 'cross the river at the Lower Ford, the Upper being dangerous.' Verily, I shall hereafter treat my dreams with respect. I suppose,—I hope, were it only to prove we have a good angel in common,—that you dreamed the same thing."

"No,—it was not that," said Edith, with a sad and anxious countenance. "It was a dream that has always been followed by evil. I dreamed—. But it will offend you, cousin?"

"What!" said Roland, "a dream? You dreamed perhaps that I forgot both wisdom and affection, when, for the sake of this worthless beast, Briareus, I drew you into difficulty and peril?"

"No, no," said Edith, earnestly, and then added in a low voice, "I dreamed of Richard Braxley!"

"Curse him!" muttered the youth, with tones of bitter passion: "it is to him we owe all that now afflicts us,—poverty and exile, our distresses and difficulties, our fears and our dangers. For a wooer," he added, with a smile of equal bitterness, "methinks he has fallen on but a rough way of proving his regard. But you dreamed of him. Well, what was it? He came to you with the look of a beaten dog, fawned at your feet, and displaying that infernal will, 'Marry me,' quoth he, 'fair maid, and I will be a greater rascal than before,—I will burn this will, and consent to enjoy Roland Forrester's lands and houses in right of my wife, instead of claiming them in trust for an heir no longer in the land of the living.' Cur!—and but for you, Edith, I would have repaid his insolence as it deserved. But you ever intercede for your worst enemies. There is that confounded Stackpole, now: I vow to heaven,

I am sorry I cut the rascal down!—But you dreamed of Braxley! What said the villain?"

"He said," replied Edith, who had listened mournfully, but in silence, to the young man's hasty expressions, like one who was too well acquainted with the impetuosity of his temper to think of opposing him in his angry moments, or perhaps because her spirits were too much subdued by her fears to allow her to play the monitress,—"He said, and frowningly too, 'that soft words were with him the prelude to hard resolutions, and that where he could not win as the turtle, he could take his prey like a vulture;'—or some such words of anger. Now, Roland, I have twice before dreamed of this man, and on each occasion a heavy calamity ensued, and that on the following day. I dreamed of him the night before our uncle died. I dreamed a second time, and the next day he produced and recorded the will that robbed us of our inheritance. I dreamed of him again last night; and what evil is now hovering over us I know not;—but, it is foolish of me to say so,—yet my fears tell me it will be something dreadful."

"Your fears, I hope, will deceive you," said Roland, smiling in spite of himself at this little display of weakness on the part of Edith. "I have much confidence in this girl, Telie, though I can scarce tell why. A free road and a round gallop will carry us to our journey's end by nightfall; and, at the worst, we shall have bright starlight to light us on. Be comforted, my cousin. I begin heartily to suspect yon cowardly Dodge, or Dodger, or whatever he calls himself, has been imposed upon by his fears, and that he has actually seen no Indians at all. The springing up of a bush from under his horse's feet, and the starting away of a dozen frighted rabbits, might easily explain his conceit of the long-legged Indian, and his five murderous accomplices; and as for the savages seen in ambush at the Ford, the shaking of the cane-brake by the breeze, or by some skulking bear, would as readily account for them. The idea of his being allowed to pass a crew of Indians in their lair, without being pursued, or even fired upon, is quite preposterous."

These ideas, perhaps devised to dispel his kinswoman's fears, were scarce uttered before they appeared highly reasonable to the inventor himself; and he straightway rode to Dodge's side, and began to question him more closely than he had before had leisure to do, in relation to those wondrous adventures, the recounting of which had produced so serious a change in the destination of the party. All his efforts, however, to obtain satisfactory confirmation of his suspicion were unavailing. The man, now in a great measure relieved of his terrors, repeated his story with a thousand details, which convinced Roland that it was, in its chief features, correct. That he had actually been attacked, or fired upon by some persons, Roland could not doubt, having heard the shots himself. As to the ambush at the

Ford, all he could say was, that he had actually seen several Indians,—he knew not the number,—stealing through the wood in the direction opposite the river, as if on the outlook for some expected party,—Captain Forrester's, he supposed, of which he had heard among the emigrants; and that this giving him the advantage of the first discovery, he had darted ahead with all his speed, until arrested at an unexpected moment by the six warriors, whose guns and voices had been heard by the party.

Besides communicating all the information which he possessed on these points, he proceeded, without waiting to be asked, to give an account of his own history; and a very lamentable one it was. He was from the Down-East country, a representative of the Bay State, from which he had been seduced by the arguments of his old friend Josiah Jones, to go "a pedlering" with the latter to the new settlements in the West; where the situation of the colonists, so far removed from all markets, promised uncommon advantages to the adventurous trader. These had been in a measure realised on the Upper Ohio; but the prospect of superior gains in Kentucky had tempted the two friends to extend their speculations further; and in an evil hour they embarked their assorted notions and their own bodies in a flatboat on the Ohio; in the descent of which it was their fortune to be stripped of every thing, after enduring risks without number, and daily attacks from, Indians lying in wait on the banks of the river, which misadventures had terminated in the capture of their boat, and the death of Josiah, the unlucky projector of the expedition. Pardon himself barely escaping with his life. These calamities were the more distasteful to the worthy Dodge, whose inclinations were of no warlike cast, and whose courage never rose to the fighting point, as he freely professed, until goaded into action by sheer desperation. He had "got enough," as he said, "of the everlasting Injuns, and of Kentucky, where there was such a shocking deal of 'em that a peaceable trader's scalp was in no more security than a rambling scout's;" and cursing his bad luck, and the memory of the friend who had cajoled him into ruin, difficulty, and constant danger, his sole desire was now to return to the safer lands of the East, which he expected to effect most advantageously by advancing to some of the South-eastern stations, and throwing himself in the way of the first band of militia whose tour of duty in the district was completed, and who should be about to return to their native state. He had got enough of the Ohio as well as the Indians; the wilderness-road possessed fewer terrors, and therefore appeared to his imagination the more eligible route of escape.

CHAPTER X

Dodge's story, which was not without its interest to Roland, though the rapidity of their progress through the woods, and the constant necessity of being on the alert, kept him a somewhat inattentive listener, was brought to an abrupt close by the motions of Telie Doe, who, having guided the party for several miles with great confidence, began at last to hesitate, and betray symptoms of doubt and embarrassment, that attracted the soldier's attention. There seemed some cause for hesitation: the glades, at first broad and open, through which they had made their way, were becoming smaller and more frequently interrupted by copses; the wood grew denser and darker; the surface of the ground became broken by rugged ascents and swampy hollows, the one encumbered by stones and mouldering trunks of trees, the other converted by the rains into lakes and pools, through which it was difficult to find a path; whilst the constant turning and winding to right and left, to avoid such obstacles, made it a still greater task to preserve the line of direction which Telie had intimated was the proper one to pursue. "Was it possible," he asked of himself, "the girl could be at fault?" The answer to this question, when addressed to Telie herself, confirmed his fears. She was perplexed, she was frightened; she had been long expecting to strike the neglected road, with which she professed to be so well acquainted, and, sure she was, they had ridden far enough to find it. But the hills and swamps had confused her; she was afraid to proceed,—she knew not where she was.

This announcement filled the young soldier's mind with alarm; for upon Telie's knowledge of the woods he had placed his best reliance, conscious that his own experience in such matters was as little to be depended on as that of any of his companions. Yet it was necessary he should now assume the lead himself, and do his best to rescue the party from its difficulties; and this, after a little reflection, he thought he could scarce fail in effecting. The portion of the forest through which he was rambling was a kind of triangle, marked by the two roads on the east, with its base bounded by the long looked for river; and one of these boundaries he must strike, proceed in whatsoever direction he would. If he persevered in the course he had followed so long, he must of necessity find himself, sooner or later, in the path which Telie had failed to discover, and failed, as he supposed, in consequence of wandering away to the west, so as to keep it constantly on the right hand, instead of in front. To recover it, then, all that was necessary to be done was to direct his course to the right, and to proceed until the road was found.

The reasoning was just, and the probability was that a few moments would find the party on the recovered path. But a half-hour passed by, and the travellers, all anxious and doubting, and filled with gloom, were yet stumbling in the forest, winding amid labyrinths of bog and brake, hill and hollow, that every moment became wilder and more perplexing. To add to their alarm, it was manifest that the day was fast approaching its close. The sun had set, or was so low in the heavens that not a single ray could be seen trembling on the tallest tree; and thus was lost the only means of deciding towards what quarter of the compass they were directing their steps. The mosses on the trees were appealed to in vain,—as they will be by all who expect to find them pointing like the mariner's needle to the pole. They indicate the quarter from which blow the prevailing humid winds of any region of country; but in the moist and dense forests of the interior, they are often equally luxuriant on every side of the tree. The varying shape and robustness of boughs are thought to offer a better means of finding the points of the compass; but none but Indians and hunters grown gray in the woods, can profit by *their* occult lessons. The attempts of Roland to draw instruction from them served only to complete his confusion; and, by and by, giving over all hope of succeeding through any exercise of skill or prudence, he left the matter to fortune and his good horse, riding, in the obstinacy of despair, withersoever the weary animal chose to bear him, without knowing whether it might be afar from danger, or backwards into the vicinity of the very enemies whom he had laboured so long to avoid.

As he advanced in this manner, he was once or twice inclined to suspect that he was actually retracing his steps, and approaching the path by which he had entered the depths of the wood; and on one occasion he was almost assured that such was the fact by the peculiar appearance of a brambly thicket, containing many dead trees, which he thought he had noticed while following in confidence after the leading of Telie Doe. A nearer approach to the place convinced him of his error, but awoke a new hope in his mind, by showing him that he was drawing nigh the haunts of men. The blazes of the axe were seen on the trees, running away in lines, as if marked by the hands of the surveyor; those trees that were dead, he observed, had been destroyed by girdling; and on the edge of the tangled brake where they were most abundant, he noticed several stalks of maize, the relics of some former harvest, the copse itself having once been, as he supposed, a corn-field,

"It is only a tomahawk-improvement," said Telie Doe, shaking her head, as he turned towards her a look of joyous inquiry; and she pointed towards what seemed to have been once a cabin of logs of the smallest size—too small indeed for habitation—but which, more than half fallen down, was rotting away, half hidden under the weeds and brambles that grew, and seemed to have grown for years, within its little area; "there are many of them in the woods, that were never settled."

Roland did not require to be informed that a "tomahawk-improvement," as it was often called in those days, meant nothing more than the box of logs in form of a cabin, which the hunter or land-speculator could build with his hatchet in a few hours, a few girdled trees, a dozen or more grains of corn from his pouch-thrust into the soil, with perhaps a few poles laid along the earth to indicate an enclosed field; and that such improvements, as they gave pre-emption rights to the maker, were often established by adventurers, to secure a claim in the event of their not lighting on lands more to their liking. Years had evidently passed by since the maker of this neglected improvement had visited his territory, and Roland no longer hoped to discover such signs about it as might enable him to recover his lost way. His spirits sunk as rapidly as they had risen, and he was preparing to make one more effort to escape from the forest, while the daylight yet lasted, or to find some stronghold in which to pass the night; when his attention was drawn to Telie Doe, who had ridden a little in advance, eagerly scanning the trees and soil around, in the hope that some ancient mark or footstep might point out a mode of escape. As she thus looked about her, moving slowly in advance, her pony on a sudden began to snort and prance, and betray other indications of terror, and Telie herself was seen to become agitated and alarmed, retreating back upon the party, but keeping her eyes wildly rolling from bush to bush, as if in instant expectation of seeing an enemy.

"What is the matter?" cried Roland, riding to her assistance. "Are we in enchanted land, that our horses must be frightened, as well as ourselves?"

"He smells the war-paint," said Telie, with a trembling voice;—"there are Indians near us."

"Nonsense!" said Roland, looking around, and seeing, with the exception of the copse just passed, nothing but an open forest, without shelter or harbour for an ambushed foe. But at that moment Edith caught him by the arm, and turned upon him a countenance more wan with fear than that she had exhibited upon first hearing the cries of Stackpole. It expressed, indeed, more than alarm,—it was the highest degree of terror, and the feeling was so overpowering that her lips, though moving as in the act of speech, gave forth no sound whatever. But what her lips refused to tell, her finger, though shaking in the ague that convulsed every fibre of her frame, pointed out; and Roland, following it with his eyes, beheld the object that had excited so much emotion. He started himself, as his gaze fell upon a naked Indian stretched under a tree hard by, and sheltered from view only by a dead bough lately fallen from its trunk, yet lying so still and motionless that he might easily have been passed by without observation in the growing dusk and twilight of the woods, had it not been for the instinctive terrors of the pony, which, like other horses, and, indeed, all other domestic beasts in the settlements, often thus pointed out to their masters the presence of an enemy.

The rifle of the soldier was in an instant cocked and at his shoulder, while the pedler and Emperor, as it happened, were too much discomposed at the spectacle to make any such show of battle. They gazed blankly upon the leader, whose piece, settling down into an aim that must have been fatal, suddenly wavered, and then, to their surprise, was withdrawn.

"The slayer has been here before us," he exclaimed,—"the man is dead and scalped already!"

With these words he advanced to the tree, and the others following, they beheld with horror the body of a savage, of vast and noble proportions, lying on its face across the roots of the tree, and glued, it might almost be said, to the earth by a mass of coagulated blood, that had issued from the scalp and axe-cloven skull. The fragments of a rifle shattered, as it seemed, by a violent blow against the tree under which he Jay, were scattered at his side, with a broken powder-horn, a splintered knife, the helve of a tomahawk, and other equipments of a warrior, all in like manner shivered to pieces by the unknown assassin. The warrior seemed to have perished only after a fearful struggle; the earth was torn where he lay, and his hands, yet grasping the soil, were dyed a double red in the blood of his antagonist, or perhaps in his own.

While Roland gazed upon the spectacle, amazed, and wondering in what manner the wretched being had met his death, which must have happened very recently, and whilst his party was within the sound of a rifle-shot, he observed a shudder to creep over the apparently lifeless frame; the fingers relaxed their grasp of the earth, and then clutched it again with violence; a broken, strangling rattle came from the throat; and a spasm of convulsion seizing upon every limb, it was suddenly raised a little upon one arm, so as to display the countenance, covered with blood, the eyes retroverted into their orbits, and glaring with the sightless whites. It was a horrible spectacle,—the last convulsion of many that had shaken the wretched and insensible, yet still suffering clay, since it had received the death-stroke. The spasm was the last, and but momentary; yet it sufficed to raise the body of the mangled barbarian, so far that, when the pang that excited it suddenly ceased, and, with it, the life of the sufferer, the body rolled over on the back, and thus lay, exposing to the eyes of the lookers-on two gashes, wide and gory, on the breast, traced by a sharp knife and a powerful hand, and, as it seemed, in the mere wantonness of a malice and lust of blood which even death could not satisfy. The sight of these gashes answered the question Roland had asked of his own imagination; they were in the form of a *cross;* and as the legend, so long derided, of the forest-fiend recurred to his memory, he responded, almost with a feeling of superstitious awe, to the trembling cry of Telie Doe:—

"It is the Jibbenainosay!" she exclaimed, staring upon the corse with mingled horror and wonder:—"Nick of the Woods is up again in the forest!"

CHAPTER XI

There was little really superstitious in the temper of Captain Forrester; and however his mind might be at first stirred by the discovery of a victim of the redoubted fiend so devoutly believed in by his host of the preceding evening, it is certain that his credulity was not so much excited as his surprise. He sprang from his horse and examined the body, but looked in vain for the mark of the bullet that had robbed it of life. No gun-shot wound, at least none of importance, appeared in any part. There was, indeed, a bullet-hole in the left shoulder, and, as it seemed, very recently inflicted: but it was bound up with leaves and vulnerary herbs, in the usual Indian way, showing that it must have been received at some period anterior to the attack which had robbed the warrior of life. The gashes across the ribs were the only other wounds on the body; that on the head, made by a hatchet, was evidently the one that had caused the warrior's death.

If this circumstance abated the wonder the soldier had at first felt on the score of a man being killed at so short a distance from his own party, without any one hearing the shot, he was still more at a loss to know how one of the dead man's race, proverbial for wariness and vigilance, should have been approached by any merely human enemy so nigh as to render fire-arms unnecessary to his destruction. But that a human enemy had effected the slaughter, inexplicable as it seemed, he had no doubt; and he began straightway to search among the leaves strewn over the ground, for the marks of his foot-steps; not questioning that, if he could find and follow them for a little distance, he should discover the author of the deed, and, which was of more moment to himself, a friend and guide to conduct his party from the forest.

His search was, however, fruitless; for, whether it was that the shadows of the evening lay too dark on the ground, or that eyes more accustomed than his own to such duties were required to detect a trail among dried forest leaves, it was certain that he failed to discover a single foot-step, or other vestige of the slayer. Nor were Pardon Dodge and Emperor, whom he summoned to his assistance, a whit more successful; a circumstance, however, that rather proved their inexperience than the supernatural character of the Jibbenainosay, whose foot-prints, as it appeared, were not more difficult to find than those of the dead Indian, for which they sought equally in vain.

While they were thus fruitlessly engaged, an exclamation from Telie Doe drew their attention to a spectacle, suddenly observed, which, to her awe-struck eyes, presented the appearance of the very being, so truculent yet supernatural, whose traces, it seemed, were to be discovered only on the breasts of his lifeless victims; and Roland, looking up, beheld with surprise, perhaps even for a moment with the stronger feeling of awe, a figure stalking through the woods at a distance, looking as tall and gigantic in the growing twilight, as the airy demon of the Brocken, or the equally colossal spectres seen on the wild summits of the Peruvian Andes. Distance and the darkness together rendered the vision indistinct; but Roland could see that the form was human, that it moved onwards with rapid strides, and with its countenance bent upon the earth, or upon another moving object, dusky and of lesser size, that rolled before it, guiding the way, like the bowl of the dervise in the Arabian story; and, finally, that it held in its hands, as if on the watch for an enemy, an implement wondrously like the fire-lock of a human fighting-man. At first, it appeared as if the figure was approaching the party, and that in a direct line; but presently Roland perceived it was gradually bending its course away to the left, its eyes still so closely fixed on its dusky guide,—the very bear, as Roland supposed, which was said so often to direct the steps of the Jibbenainosay,—that it seemed as if about to pass the party entirely without observation.

But this it made no part of the young soldier's resolutions to permit; and, accordingly, he sprang upon his horse, determined to ride forwards and bring the apparition to a stand, while it was yet at a distance.

"Man or devil, Jibbenainosay or rambling settler," he cried, "it is, at least, no Indian, and therefore no enemy. Holla, friend!" he exclaimed aloud, and dashed forward, followed, though not without hesitation, by his companions.

At the sound of his voice the spectre started and looked up; and then, without betraying either surprise or a disposition to beat a mysterious retreat, advanced to meet the soldier, walking rapidly, and waving his hand all the while with an impatient gesture, as if commanding the party to halt;—a command which was immediately obeyed by Roland and all.

And now it was, that, as it drew nigh, its stature appeared to grow less and less colossal, and the wild lineaments with which fancy had invested it, faded from sight, leaving the phantom a mere man, of tall frame indeed, but without a single characteristic of dress or person to delight the soul of wonder. The black bear dwindled into a little dog, the meekest and most insignificant of his tribe, being nothing less or more, in fact, than the identical Peter, which had fared so roughly in the hands, or rather under the feet, of Roaring Ralph Stackpole, at the Station, the day before; while the human spectre, the supposed fiend of the woods, sinking from its dignity in equal proportion of abasement, suddenly presented to Roland's eyes the person of Peter's master, the humble, peaceful, harmless Nathan Slaughter.

The transformation was so great and unexpected, for even Roland looked to find in the wanderer, if not a destroying angel, at least some formidable champion of the forest, that he could scarce forbear a laugh, as Nathan came stalking up, followed by little Peter, who stole to the rear, as soon as strangers were perceived, as if to avoid the kicks and cuffs which his experience had, doubtless, taught him were to be expected on all such occasions. The young man felt the more inclined to indulge his mirth, as the character which Bruce had given him of Wandering Nathan, as one perfectly acquainted with the woods, convinced him that he could not have fallen upon a better person to extricate him from his dangerous dilemma, and thus relieved his breast of a mountain of anxiety and distress. But the laugh with which he greeted his approach found no response from Nathan himself, who, having looked with amazement upon Edith and Telie, as if marvelling what madness had brought females at that hour into that wild desert, turned at last to the soldier, demanding, with inauspicious gravity,—

"Friend! does thee think thee is in thee own parlour with thee women at home, that thee shouts so loud and laughs so merrily? or does thee know thee is in a wild Kentucky forest, with murdering Injuns all around thee?"

"I trust not," said Roland, much more seriously; "but, in truth, we all took you for Nick of the Woods, the redoubtable Nick himself; and you must allow that our terrors were ridiculous enough, when they could convert a peaceful man like you into such a blood-thirsty creature. That there are Indians in the wood I can well believe, having the evidence of Dodge, here, who professes to have seen six, and killed one, and of my own eyes into the bargain.—Yonder lies one, dead, at this moment, under the walnut-tree, killed by some unknown hand,—Telie Doe says by Nick of the Woods himself—"

"Friend," said Nathan, interrupting the young man, without ceremony, "thee had better think of living Injuns than talk of dead ones; for, of a truth, thee is like to have trouble with them!"

"Not now, I hope, with such a man as you to help me out of the woods. In the name of heaven, where am I, and whither am I going?"

"Whither thee is going," replied Nathan, "it might be hard to say, seeing that thee way of travelling is none of the straightest: nevertheless, if thee continues thee present course, it is my idea, thee is travelling to the Upper Ford of the river, and will fetch it in twelve minutes, or thereabouts, and, in the same space, find theeself in the midst of thirty ambushed Injuns."

"Good heavens!" cried Roland, "have we then been labouring only to approach the cut-throats? There is not a moment, then, to lose, and your finding us is even more providential than I thought. Put yourself at our head, lead us out of this den of thieves,—conduct us to the Lower Ford,—to our companions, the emigrants; or, if that may not be, take us back to the Station,—or any where at all, where I may find safety for these females.—For myself, I am incapable of guiding them longer."

"Truly," said Nathan, looking embarrassed, "I would do what I could for thee, but—"

"*But!* Do you hesitate?" cried the Virginian, in extreme indignation: "will you leave us to perish, when you, and you alone, can guide us from the forest?"

"Friend," said Nathan, in a submissive, deprecating tone, "I am a man of peace: and paradventure, the party being so numerous, the Injuns will fall upon us: and, truly, they will not spare me any more than another: for they kill the non-fighting men, as well as them that fight. Truly, I am in much fear for myself: but a single man might escape."

"If you are such a knave, such a mean-spirited, unfeeling dastard, as to think of leaving these women to their fate," said Roland, giving way to rage, "be assured that the first step will be your last;—I will blow your brains out, the moment you attempt to leave us!"

At these ireful words, Nathan's eyes began to widen.

"Truly," said he, "I don't think thee would be so wicked! But thee takes by force that which I would have given with good will. It was not my purpose to refuse thee assistance; though it is unseemly that one of my peaceful faith should go with fighting-men among men of war, as if to do battle. But, friend, if we should fall upon the angry red-men, truly, there will bloodshed come of it; and thee will say to me, 'Nathan, lift up thee gun and shoot;' and peradventure, if I say 'Nay,' thee will call me hard names, as thee did before, saying, 'If thee don't, I will blow thee brains out!'—Friend, I am a man of peace; and if—"

"Trouble yourself no longer on that score," said the soldier, who began to understand how the land lay, and how much the meek Nathan's reluctance to become his guide was engendered by his fears of being called on to take a share in such fighting as might occur: "trouble yourself no longer; we will take care to avoid a contest."

"Truly," said Nathan, "that may not be as thee chooses, the Injuns being all around thee."

"If a rencontre should be inevitable," said Roland, with a smile, mingling grim contempt of Nathan's pusillanimity with secret satisfaction at the thought of being thus able to secure the safety of his kinswoman, "all that I shall expect of you will be to decamp with the females, whilst we three, Emperor, Pardon Dodge, and myself, cover your retreat: we can, at least, check the assailants, if we die for it!"

This resolute speech was echoed by each of the other combatants, the negro exclaiming, though with no very valiant utterance, "Yes, massa! no mistake in ole Emperor;—will die for missie and massa,"—while Pardon, who was fast relapsing into the desperation that had given him courage on a former occasion, cried out, with direful emphasis, "If there's no dodging the critturs, then there a'n't; and if I must fight, then I *must*; and them that takes my scalp must gin the worth on't, or it a'n't no matter!"

"Truly," said Nathan, who listened to these several outpourings of spirit with much complacency, "I am a man of peace and amity, according to my conscience; but if others are men of wrath and battle, according to theirs, I will not take it upon me to censure them,—nay, not even if they should feel themselves called upon by hard necessity to shed the blood of their Injun fellow-creatures,—who, it must be confessed, if we should stumble on the same, will do their best to make that necessity as strong as possible. But now let us away, and see what help there is for us; though whither to go, and what to do, there being Injuns before, and Injuns behind, and Injuns all around, truly, truly, it doth perplex me."

And so, indeed, it seemed; for Nathan straightway fell into a fit of musing, shaking his head, and tapping his finger contemplatively on the stock of that rifle, terrible only to the animals that furnished him subsistence, and all the while in such apparent abstraction, that he took no notice of a suggestion made by Roland,—namely, that he should lead the way to the deserted Ford, where, as the soldier said, there was every reason to believe there were no Indians,—but continued to argue the difficulty in his own mind, interrupting the debate only to ask counsel where there seemed the least probability of obtaining it:—

"Peter!" said he, addressing himself to the little dog, and that with as much gravity as if addressing himself to a human adviser, "I have my thoughts on the matter,—what does *thee* think of matters and things?"

"My friend," cried Roland, impatiently, "this is no affair to be entrusted to the wisdom of a brute dog!"

"If there is any one here whose wisdom can serve us better," said Nathan, meekly, "let him speak. Thee don't know Peter, friend, or thee would use him with respect. Many a long day has he followed me through the forest; and many a time has he helped me out of harm and peril from man and beast, when I was at sore shifts to help myself. For, truly, friend, as I told thee before, the Injuns have no regard for men, whether men of peace or war; and an honest, quiet, peace-loving man can no more roam the wood, hunting for the food that sustains life, without the fear of being murdered, than a fighting-man in search of his prey.—Thee sees now what little dog Peter is doing? He runs to the tracks, and he wags his tail;—truly I am of the same way of thinking!"

"What tracks are they?" demanded Roland, as he followed Nathan to the path which the latter had been pursuing, when arrested by the soldier, and where the little cur was now smelling about, occasionally lifting his head and wagging his tail, as if to call his master's attention.

"*What* tracks!" echoed Nathan, looking on the youth first with wonder, and then with commiseration, and adding,—"It was a tempting of Providence, friend, for *thee* to lead poor helpless women into a wild forest. Does thee not know the tracks of thee own horses?"

"'Sdeath!" said Roland, looking on the marks, as Nathan, pointed them out in the soft earth, and reflecting with chagrin how wildly he had been rambling, for more than an hour, since they had been impressed on the soil.

"Thee knows the hoof-marks," said Nathan, now pointing with a grin, at other tracks of a different appearance among them; "perhaps thee knows *these* foot-prints also?"

"They are the marks of footmen," said the soldier, in surprise; "but how came they there I know not, no footmen being of our party."

The grin that marked the visage of the man of peace widened almost into a laugh, as Roland spoke. "Verily," he cried, "thee is in the wrong place, friend, in the forest! If thee had no footmen with thee, could thee have none *after* thee? Look, friend, here are tracks, not of one man, but of five, each stepping on tiptoe, as if to tread lightly and look well before him,—each with a moccasin on,—each with a toe turned in; each—"

"Enough,—they were Indians!" said Roland, with a shudder, "and they must have been close behind us!"

"Now, friend," said Nathan, "thee will have more respect for Peter; for, truly, it was Peter told me of these things, when I was peaceably hunting my game in the forest. He showed me the track of five ignorant persons rambling through the wood, as the hawk flies in the air,—round, round,

round, all the time,—or like an ox that has been browsing on the leaves of the buck-eye;[7] and he showed me that five evil-minded Shawnees were pursuing in their trail. So thinks I to myself, 'these poor creatures will come to mischief, if no one gives them warning of their danger;' and therefore I started to follow, Peter showing me the way. And truly, if there can any good come of me finding thee in this hard ease, thee must give all the thanks and all the praise to poor Peter!"

> [Footnote 7: The buck-eye, or American horse-chestnut, seems to be universally considered, in the West, a mortal poison, both fruit and leaves. Cattle affected by it are said to play many remarkable antics, as if intoxicated—turning, twisting, and rolling about and around, until death closes their agonies]

"I will never more speak ill of a dog as long as I live," said Roland. "But let us away. I thought our best course was to the Lower Ford; but, I find, I am mistaken. We must away in the opposite direction."

"Not so," said Nathan, coolly; "Peter is of opinion that we must run the track over again; and, truly, so am I. We must follow these, same five Injuns: it is as much as our lives are worth."

"You are mad!" said Roland. "This will be to bring us right upon the skulking cut-throats. Let us fly in another direction: the forest is open before us."

"And how long does thee think it will keep open? Friend, I tell thee, thee is surrounded by Injuns. On the south, they lie at the Ford; on the west, is the river rolling along in a flood; and at the east, are the roads full of Shawnees on the scout. Verily, friend, there is but little comfort to think of proceeding in any direction, even to the north, where there are five murdering creatures full before us. But this is my thought, and, I rather think, it is Peter's: if we go to the north, we know pretty much all the evil that lies before us, and how to avoid it; whereas, by turning in either of the other quarters, we go into danger blindfold."

"And how shall we avoid these five villains before us?" asked Roland, anxiously.

"By keeping them before us," replied Nathan; "that is, friend, by following *them*, until such time as they turn where thee turned before them, (and, I warrant me, the evil creatures will turn wheresoever thee trail does); when we, if we have good luck, may slip quietly forward, and leave them, to follow us, after first taking the full swing of all thee roundabout vagaries."

"Take your own course," said Roland; "it may be the best. We can, at the worst, but stumble upon these five; and then (granting that you can, in the meanwhile, bear the females off), I will answer for keeping two or three of the villains busy. Take your own course," he repeated; "the night is darkening around us; we must do something."

"Thee says the truth," cried Nathan. "As for stumbling unawares on the five evil persons thee is in dread of, trust Peter for that; thee shall soon see what a friend thee has in little dog Peter. Truly, for a peaceful man like me, it is needful I should have some one to tell me when dangerous persons are nigh."

With these words, which were uttered with a good countenance, showing how much his confidence in the apparently insignificant Peter preserved him from the fears natural to his character and situation, the man of peace proceeded to marshal the company in a line, directing them to follow him in that order, and earnestly impressing upon all the necessity of preserving strict silence upon the march. This being done, he boldly strode forwards, taking a post at least two hundred paces in advance of the others, at which distance, as he gave Roland to understand, he desired the party to follow, as was the more necessary, since their being mounted rendered them the more liable to be observed by distant enemies. "If thee sees me wave my hand above my head," were his last instructions to the young soldier, who began to be well pleased with his readiness and forecast, "bring thee people to a halt; if thee sees me drop upon the ground, lead them under the nearest cover, and keep them quiet; for thee may then be certain there is mischief, or mischievous people nigh at hand. But verily, friend, with Peter's help, we will circumvent them all."

With this cheering assurance, lie now strode forward to his station, and coming to a halt with his dog Peter, Roland immediately beheld the latter run to a post forty or fifty paces further in advance, when he paused to receive the final orders of his master, which were given with a motion of the same hand that a moment after beckoned the party to follow. Had Roland been sufficiently nigh to take note of proceedings, he would have admired the conduct of the little brute, the unerring accuracy with which he pursued the trail, the soft and noiseless motion with which he stepped from leaf to leaf, casting his eyes ever and anon to the right and left, and winding the air before him, as if in reality conscious of peril, and sensible that the welfare of the six mortals at his heels depended upon the faithful exercise of all his sagacity. These things, however, from the distance, Roland was unable to observe; but he saw enough to convince him that the animal addressed itself to its task with as much zeal and prudence as its master. A sense of security, the first felt for several hours, now began to disperse the gloom that had oppressed his spirits; and Edith's countenance, throughout the whole of the adventure a faithful, though doubtless somewhat exaggerated reflection of his own, also lost much of its melancholy and terror, though without at any moment regaining the cheerful smiles that had decked it at the setting out. It was left for Roland alone, as his mind regained its elasticity, to marvel at the motley additions by which his party had increased in so short a time to twice its original numbers, and to speculate on the prospects of an expedition committed to the guidance of such a conductor as little Peter.

CHAPTER XII

The distance at which Roland with his party followed the guides, and the gloom of the woods, prevented his making any close observations upon their motions, unless when some swelling ridge, nearly destitute of trees, brought them nearer to the light of the upper air. At other times he could do little more than follow with his eye the tall figure of Nathan, plunging from shadow to shadow, and knoll to knoll, with a pace both free and rapid, and little resembling the shambling, hesitating step with which he moved among the haunts of his contemners and oppressors. As for the dog, little Peter, he was only with difficulty seen when ascending some such illuminated knoll as has been mentioned, when he might be traced creeping along with unabated vigilance and caution.

It was while ascending one of these low, and almost bare swells of ground, that the little animal gave the first proof of that sagacity or wisdom, as Nathan called it, on which the latter seemed to rely for safety so much more than on his own experience and address. He had no sooner reached the summit of the knoll than he abruptly came to a stand, and by and by cowered to the earth, as if to escape the observation of enemies in front, whose presence he indicated in no other way, unless by a few twitches and flourishes of his tail, which, a moment after, became as rigid and motionless as if, with his body, it had been suddenly converted into stone. The whole action, as far as Roland could notice it was similar to that of a well-trained spaniel marking game, and such was the interpretation the soldier put upon it, until Nathan, suddenly stopping, waved his hand as a signal to the party to halt, which was immediately obeyed. The next moment Nathan was seen creeping up the hill, to investigate the cause of alarm, which he proceeded to do with great caution, as if well persuaded there was danger at hand. Indeed, he had not yet reached the brow of the eminence, when Roland beheld him suddenly drop upon his face, thereby giving the best evidence of the existence of peril of an extreme and urgent character.

The young Virginian remembered the instructions of his guide, to seek shelter for his party the moment this signal was given; and, accordingly, he led his followers without delay into a little tangled brake hard by, where he charged them to remain in quiet until the cause of the interruption should be ascertained and removed. From the edge of the brake he could see the guide, still maintaining his position on his face, yet dragging himself upward like a snake, until he had reached the top of the hill and looked over into the maze of forest beyond. In this situation he lay for several moments, apparently deeply engaged with the scene before him; when Forrester, impatient of his silence and delay, anxiously interested in every turn of events, and perhaps unwilling, at a season of difficulty, to rely altogether on Nathan's unaided observations, gave his horse in charge of Emperor, and ascended the eminence himself; taking care, however, to do as Nathan had done, and throw himself upon the ground, when near its summit. In this way, he succeeded in creeping to Nathan's side, when the cause of alarm was soon made manifest.

The forest beyond the ridge was, for a considerable distance, open and free from undergrowth, the trees standing wide apart, and thus admitting a broad extent of vision, though now contracted by the increasing dusk of evening. Through this expanse, and in its darkest corner, flitting dimly along, Roland's eyes fell upon certain shadows, at first vague and indistinct, but which soon assumed the human form, marching one after the other in a line, and apparently approaching the very ridge on which he lay, each with the stealthy yet rapid pace of a wild cat. They were but five in number; but the order of their march, the appearance of their bodies seemingly half naked, and the busy intentness with which they pursued the trail left so broad and open by the inexperienced wanderers, would have convinced Roland of their savage character, had he possessed no other evidence than that of his own senses.

"They are Indians;" he muttered in Nathan's ear.

"Shawnee creatures," said the latter, with edifying coolness;—"and will think no more of taking the scalps of thee two poor women than of digging off thee own."

"There are but five of them, and—" The young man paused, and the gloom that a spirit so long harassed by fears, though fears for another, had spread over his countenance, was exchanged for a look of fierce decision that better became his features. "Harkee, man," he abruptly resumed, "we cannot pass the ridge without being seen by them; our horses are exhausted, and we cannot hope to escape them by open flight."

"Verily," said Nathan, "thee speaks the truth."

"Nor can we leave the path we are now pursuing, without fear of falling into the hands of a party more numerous and powerful. Our only path of escape, you said, was over this ridge, and towards yonder Lower Ford?"

"Truly," said Nathan, with a lugubrious look of assent,—"what thee says is true: but how we are to fly these evil-minded creatures, with poor frightened women hanging to our legs—"

"We will not fly them!" said Roland, the frown of battle gathering on his brows. "Yonder crawling reptiles,—reptiles in spirit as in movement,—have been dogging our steps for hours, waiting for the moment when to strike with advantage at my defenceless followers; and they will dog us still, if permitted, until there is no escape from their knives and hatchets for either man or woman. There is a way of stopping them,—there is a way of requiting them!"

"Truly," said Nathan, "there is no such way; unless we were wicked men of the world and fighting men, and would wage battle with them!"

"Why not meet the villains in their own way? There are but five of them,—and footmen too! By heavens, man, we will charge them,—cut them to pieces, and so rid the wood of them! Four strong men like us, fighting, too, in defence of women,"

"*Four!*" echoed Nathan, looking wonder and alarm together: "does thee think to have *me* do the wicked thing of shedding blood? Thee should remember, friend, that I am a follower of peaceful doctrines, a man of peace and amity."

"What!" said Roland, warmly, "would you not defend your life from the villains? Would you suffer yourself to be tomahawked, unresisting, when a touch of the trigger under your finger, a blow of the knife at your belt, would preserve the existence nature and heaven alike call on you to protect? Would you lie still, like a fettered ox, to be butchered?"

"Truly," said Nathan, "I would take myself away; or, if that might not be, why then, friend,—verily, friend, if I could do nothing else,—truly, I must then give myself up to be murdered,"

"Spiritless, mad, or hypocritical!" cried Roland, with mingled wonder and contempt. Then grasping his strange companion by the arm, he cried, "Harkee, man, if you would not strike a blow for yourself,—would you not strike it for another? What if you had a wife, a parent, a child, lying beneath the uplifted hatchet, and you with these arms in your hands,—what! do you tell me you would stand by and see them murdered?—I say, a wife or child!—the wife of your bosom,—the child of your heart? would you see *them* murdered?"

At this stirring appeal, uttered with indescribable energy and passion, though only in a whisper, Nathan's countenance changed from dark to pale, and his arm trembled in the soldier's grasp. He turned upon him also a look of extraordinary wildness, and muttered betwixt his teeth an answer that betokened as much confusion of mind as agitation of spirits: "Friend," he said, "whoever thee is, it matters nothing to thee what might happen, or has happened, in such case made and provided. I am a man, thee is another; thee has thee conscience, and I have mine. If thee will fight, fight; settle it with thee conscience. If thee don't like to see thee kinswoman murdered, and thee thinks thee has a call to battle, do thee best with sword and pistol, gun and tomahawk; kill and slay to thee liking: if thee conscience finds no fault with thee, neither will I. But as for me, let the old Adam of the flesh stir me as it may, I have no one to fight for,—wife or child, parent or kinsman, I have none: if thee will hunt the world over, thee will not find one in it that is my kinsman or relative."

"But I ask you," said Roland, somewhat surprised at the turn of Nathan's answer, "I ask you, if you *had* a wife or child—"

"But I have *not*," cried Nathan, interrupting him vehemently; "and therefore, friend, why should thee speak of them? Them that are dead, let them rest: they can never cry to me more.—Think of thee own blood, and do what seems best to thee for the good thereof."

"Assuredly I would," said Roland, who, however much his curiosity was roused by the unexpected agitation of his guide, had little time to think of any affairs but his own,—"Assuredly I would, could I only count upon your hearty assistance. I tell you, man, my blood boils to look at yonder crawling serpents, and to think of the ferocious object with which they are dogging at my heels; and I would give a year of my life,—ay, if the whole number of years were but ten,—one whole year of all,—for the privilege of paying them for their villany beforehand."

"Thee has thee two men to back thee," said Nathan, who had now recovered his composure; "and with these two men, if thee is warlike enough, thee might do as much mischief as thee conscience calls for. But, truly, it becomes not a man of peace like me to speak of strife and bloodshed—Yet, truly," he added, hastily, "I think there must mischief come of this meeting; for, verily, the evil creatures are leaving thee tracks, and coming towards us!"

"They stop!" said Forrester, eagerly,—"they look about them,—they have lost the track,—they are coming this way! You will not fight, yet you may counsel.—What shall I do? Shall I attack them? What *can* I do?"

"Friend," replied Nathan, briskly, "I can't tell what thee can do; but I can tell thee what a man of Kentucky, a wicked fighter of Injuns, would do in such a case made and provided. He would betake him to the thicket where he had hidden his women and horses, and he would lie down with his fighting men behind a log; and truly, if these ill-disposed Injun-men were foolish enough to approach, he would fire upon them with his three guns, taking them by surprise, and perhaps, wicked man, killing the better half of them on the spot: and then—"

"And then," interrupted Roland taking fire at the idea, "he would spring on his horse, and make sure of the rest with sword and pistol?"

"Truly," said Nathan, "he would do no such thing, seeing that, the moment he lifted up his head above the log, he would be liker to have an Injun bullet through it than to see the wicked creature that shot it. Verily, a man of Kentucky would be wiser. He would take the pistols thee speaks of, supposing it were his good luck to have them, and let fly at the evil-minded creatures with them also; not hoping, indeed, to do any execution with such small ware, but to make the Injuns believe there were as many enemies as fire-arms: and, truly, if they did not take to their heels after such a second volley, they would be foolisher Injuns than were ever before heard of in Kentucky."

"By Heaven," said Forrester, "it is good advice: and I will take it!"

"Advice, friend! I don't advise thee," said Nathan, hastily: "truly, I advise to nothing but peace and amity. I only tell thee what a wicked Kentucky fighting-man would do,—a man that might think it, as many of them do, as lawful to shoot a prowling Injun as a skulking bear."

"And I would to Heaven," said Roland, "I had but two,—nay, but one of them with me this instant. A man like Bruce were worth the lives of a dozen such scum.—I must do my best."

"Truly, friend," said Nathan, who had listened to the warlike outpourings of the young soldier with a degree of complacency and admiration one would have scarce looked for in a man of his peaceful character, "thee has a conscience of thee own, and if thee will fight these Injun-men from an ambush, truly, I will not censure nor exhort thee to the contrary. If thee can rely upon thee two men, the coloured person and the other, thee may hold the evil creatures exceeding uneasy."

"Alas," said Roland, the fire departing from his eyes, "you remind me of my weakness. My men will *not* fight, unless from sheer desperation. Emperor I know to be a coward, and Dodge, I fear, is no braver."

"Verily," said Nathan, bluffly, "it was foolish of thee to come into the woods in such company, foolisher still to think of fighting five Injun-men with such followers to back thee; and truly," he added, "it was foolishest of all to put the safe-keeping of such helpless creatures into the hands of one who can neither fight for them nor for himself. Nevertheless, thee is as a babe and suckling in the woods, and Peter and I will do the best we can for thee. It is lucky for thee, that as thee cannot fight, thee has the power to fly; and, truly, for the poor women's sake, it is better thee should leave the woods in peace."

With that, Nathan directed the young man's attention to the pursuing foes, who, having by some mischance, lost the trail, had scattered about in search of it, and at last recovered it; though not before two of them had approached so nigh the ridge on which the observers lay as to give just occasion for fear lest they should cross it immediately in front of the party of travellers. The deadly purpose with which the barbarians were pursuing him Roland could infer from the cautious silence preserved while they were searching for the lost tracks; and even when these were regained, the discovery was communicated from one to another merely by signs, not a man uttering so much as a word. In a few moments, they were seen again, formed in a single file, stealing through the woods with a noiseless but rapid pace, and, fortunately, bending their steps towards a distant part of the ridge, where Roland and his companions had so lately crossed it.

"Get thee down to thee people," said Nathan; "lead them behind the thicket, and when thee sees me beckon thee, carry them boldly over the hill. Thee must pass it, while the Shawnee-men are behind yonder clump of trees, which is so luckily for thee on the very comb of the swell. Be quick in obeying, friend, or the evil creatures may catch sight of thee: thee has no time to lose."

The ardour of battle once driven from his mind, Roland was able to perceive the folly of risking a needless contest betwixt a superior body of wild Indian warriors and his own followers. But had his warlike spirit been at its height, it must have been quelled in a moment by the appearance of his party, left in the thicket, during his brief absence on the hill, to feed their imaginations with terrors of every appalling character; in which occupation, as he judged at a glance, the gallant Dodge and Emperor had been even more industrious than the females, the negro looking the very personification of mute horror, and bending low on his saddle as if expecting every instant a shower of Indian bullets to be let fly into the thicket; while Pardon expressed the state of his feelings by trying aloud, as soon as Rowland appeared, "I say, Capting, if you seed 'em, a'nt there no dodging of 'em no how?"

"We can escape, Roland!" exclaimed Edith, anticipating the soldier's news from his countenance; "the good man can save us?"

"I hope, I trust so," replied the kinsman: "we are in no immediate danger. Be composed, and for your lives, all now preserve silence."

A few words served to explain the posture of affairs, and a few seconds to transfer the party from its ignoble hiding-place to the open wood behind it; when Roland, casting his eyes to where Nathan lay motionless on the hill, awaited impatiently the expected signal. Fortunately, it was soon given; and, in a few moments more, the party, moving briskly but stealthily over the eminence, had plunged into the dark forest beyond, leaving the baffled pursuers to follow afterwards as they might.

"Now," said Nathan, taking post at Roland's side, and boldly directing his course across the track of the enemy, "we have the evil creatures behind us, and, truly, there we will keep them. And now, friend soldier, since such thee is, thee must make thee horses do duty, tired or not; for if we reach not the Old Ford before darkness closes on us, we may find but ill fortune crossing the waters. Hark, friend! does thee hear?" he exclaimed, coming to a pause, as a sudden and frightful yell suddenly rose in the forest beyond the ridge, obviously proceeding from the five foes, and expressing at once surprise, horror, and lamentation: "Did thee not say thee found a dead Injun in the wood?"

"We did," replied the soldier, "the body of an Indian horribly mangled; and, if I am to believe the strange story I have heard of the Jibbenainosay, it was some of his bloody work."

"It is good for thee, then, and the maidens that is with thee," said Nathan; "for, truly, the evil creatures have found that same dead man, being doubtless one of their own scouting companions; and, truly, they say the Injuns, in such cases made and provided, give over their evil designs in terror and despair; in which case, as I said, it will be good for thee and thee companions. But follow, friends, and tarry not to ask questions. Thee poor women shall come to no harm, if Nathan Slaughter or little Dog Peter can help them."

With these words of encouragement, Nathan, bounding along with an activity that kept him ever in advance of the mounted wanderers, led the way from the open forest into a labyrinth of brakes and bogs, through paths traced rather by wolves and bears than any nobler animals, so wild, so difficult, and sometimes, in appearance, so impracticable to be pursued, that Roland, bewildered from the first, looked every moment to find himself plunged into difficulties from which neither the zeal of Nathan nor the sagacity of the unpretending Peter could extricate his weary followers. The night was coming fast, and coming with clouds and distant peals of thunder, the harbingers of new tempests; and how the journey was to be continued, when darkness should at last invest them, through the wild mazes of vine and brake in which they now wandered, was a question which he scarce durst answer. But night came, and still Nathan led the way with unabated confidence and activity, professing a very hearty contempt for all perils and difficulties of the woods, except such as proceeded from "evil-minded Shawnee creatures;" and, indeed, averring that there was scarce a nook in the forest, for miles around, with which he was not as well acquainted as with the patches of his own leathern garments. "Truly," said he, "when I first came to this land, I did make me a little cabin in a place hard by; but the Injuns burned the same; and, verily, had it not been for little Peter, who gave me a hint of their coming, I should have been burned with it. Be of good heart, friend: if thee will keep the ill-meaning Injun-men out of my way, I will adventure to lead thee anywhere thee will, within twenty miles of this place, on the darkest night, and that through the thickest cane, or deepest swamp, thee can lay eyes on,—that is, if I have but little dog Peter to help me. Courage, friend; thee is now coming fast to the river; and, if we have but good luck in crossing it, thee shall, peradventure, find theeself nearer thee friends than thee thinks for."

This agreeable assurance was a cordial to the spirits of all, and the travellers now finding themselves, though still in profound darkness, moving through the open woodlands again, instead of the maze of copses that had so long confined them, Roland took advantage of the change to place himself at Nathan's side, and endeavour to draw from him some account of his history, and the causes that had brought him into a position and way of life so ill suited to his faith and peaceful habits. To his questions, however, Nathan seemed little disposed to return satisfactory answers, except in so far as they related to his adventures since the period of his coming to the frontier; of which he spoke very freely, though succinctly. He had built him cabins, like other lonely settlers, and planted cornfields, from which he had been driven, time after time, by the evil Shawnees, incurring frequent perils and hardships; which, with the persecutions he endured from his more warlike and intolerant neighbours, gradually drove him into the forest to seek a precarious subsistence from the spoils of the chase. As to his past life, and the causes that had made him a dweller of the wilderness, he betrayed so little inclination to satisfy the young man's curiosity, that Roland dropped the subject entirely, not however without suspecting, that the imputations Bruce had cast upon his character might have had some foundation in truth.

But while conning these things over in his mind, on a sudden the soldier stepped from the dark forest into a broad opening, canopied only by the sky, sweeping like a road through the wood, in which it was lost behind him; while, in front, it sank abruptly into a deep hollow or gulf, in which was heard the sullen rush of an impetuous river.

CHAPTER XIII

The roar of the moving flood, for such, by its noise, it seemed, as they descended the river-bank, to which Nathan had so skilfully conducted them, awoke in Roland's bosom a feeling of dismay.

"Fear not," said the guide, to whom he imparted his doubts of the safety of the ford; "there is more danger in one single skulking Shawnee than ten thousand such sputtering brooks. Verily, the ford is good enough, though deep and rough; and if the water should soil thee young women's garments a little, thee should remember it will not make so ugly a stain as the bood-mark of a scalping-savage."

"Lead on," said Pardon Dodge, with unexpected spirit; "I am not one of them 'ere fellers as fears a big river; and my hoss is a dreadful fine swimmer."

"In that case," said Nathan, "if thee consents to the same; I will get up behind thee, and so pass over dry-shod; for the feel of wet leather-breeches is quite uncomfortable."

This proposal, being reasonable enough, was readily acceded to, and Nathan was in the act of climbing to the crupper of Dodge's horse, when little Peter began to manifest a prudent desire to pass the ford dry-shod also, by pawing at his master's heels, and beseeching his notice with sundry low but expressive whinings. Such, at least, was the interpretation which Roland, who perceived the animal's motions, was inclined to put upon them. He was, therefore, not a little surprised when Nathan, starting from the stirrup into which he had climbed, leaped again to the ground, staring around him from right to left with every appearance of alarm.

"Right, Peter!" he at last muttered, fixing his eye upon the further bank of the river, a dark mass of hill and forest that rose in dim relief against the clouded sky, overshadowing the whole stream, which lay like a pitchy abyss betwixt it and the travellers,—"right, Peter! thee eyes is as good as thee nose—thee is determined the poor women shall not be murdered!"

"What is it you see?" demanded Forrester, "and why do you talk of murdering?"

"Speak low, and look across the river," whispered the guide, in reply; "does thee see the light glimmering among the rocks by the roadside?"

"I see neither rocks nor road—all is to my eyes confused blackness; and as for a light, I see nothing—stay! No; 'tis the gleam of a fire-fly."

"The gleam of a fire-fly!" murmured Nathan, with tones that seemed to mingle wonder and derision with feelings of a much more serious character; "it is such a fire-fly as might burn a house, or roast a living captive at the stake:—it is a brand in the hands of a 'camping Shawnee! Look, friend, he is blowing it into a flame; and presently thee will see the whole bank around it in a glow."

It was even as Nathan said. Almost while he was yet speaking, the light, which all now clearly beheld, at first a point as small and faint as the spark of a lampyris, and then a star scarce bigger or brighter than the torch of a jack-o'-lantern, suddenly grew in magnitude, projecting a long and lance-like, though broken, reflection over the wheeling current, and then as suddenly shot into a bright and ruddy blaze, illumining hill and river, and even the anxious countenances of the travellers. At the same time, a dark figure, as of a man engaged feeding the flame with fresh fuel, was plainly seen twice or thrice to pass before it. How many others, his comrades, might be watching its increasing blaze, or preparing for their wild slumbers, among the rocks and bushes where it was kindled, it was impossible to divine. The sight of the fire itself in such a solitary spot, and under such circumstances, even if no attendant had been seen by it, would have been enough to alarm the travellers, and compel the conviction that their enemies had not forgotten to station a force at this neglected ford, as well as at the other more frequented one above, and thus to deprive them of the last hope of escape.

This unexpected incident, the climax of a long series of disappointments, all of a character so painful and exciting, drove the young soldier again to despair; which feeling the tantalising sense that he was now within but a few miles of his companions in exile, and separated from them only by the single obstruction before him, exasperated into a species of fury bordering almost upon frenzy.

"There is but one way of escape," he exclaimed, without venturing even a look towards his kinswoman, or seeking by idle words to conceal the danger of their situation: "we must pass the river, the roar of the water will drown the noise of our foot-steps; we can cross unheard and unlooked for; and then, if there be no way of avoiding them, we can pour a volley among the rascals at their fire, and take advantage of their confusion to gallop by. Look to the women, Nathan Slaughter; and you, Pardon Dodge, and Emperor, follow me, and do as you see me do."

"Truly," said Wandering Nathan, with admirable coolness and complacency, "thee is a courageous young man, and a young man of sense and spirit,—that is to say, after thee own sense of matters and things: and, truly, if it were not for the poor women, and for the blazing fire, thee might greatly confound and harmfully vanquish the evil creatures, there placed so unluckily on the bank, in the way and manner which thee thinks of. But, friend, thee plan will not do: thee might pass unheard indeed, but not unseen. Does thee not see how brightly the fire blazes on the water? Truly, we should all be seen and fired at, before we reached the middle of the stream; and, truly, I should not be surprised if the gleam of the fire on the pale faces of thee poor women should bring a shot upon us where we stand; and, therefore, friend, the sooner we get us out of the way, the better."

"And where shall we betake us?" demanded Roland, the sternness of whose accents but ill-disguised the gloom and hopelessness of his feelings.

"To a place of safety and of rest," replied the guide, "and to one that is nigh at hand; where we may lodge us, with little fear of Injuns, until such time as the waters shall bate a little, or the stars give us light to cross them at a place where are no evil Shawnees to oppose us. And then, friend as to slipping by these foolish creatures who make such bright fires on the public highway, truly, with little Peter's assistance, we can do it with great ease."

"Let us not delay," said Roland; and added sullenly, "though where a place of rest and safety can be found in these detestable woods, I can no longer imagine."

"It is a place of rest, at least for the dead," said Nathan, in a low voice, at the same time leading the party back again up the bank, and taking care to shelter them as he ascended, as much as possible, from the light of the fire, which was now blazing with great brilliancy: "nine human corpses,—father and mother, grandam and children,—sleep under the threshold at the door; and there are not many, white men or Injuns, that will, of their free will, step over the bosoms of the poor murdered creatures, after nightfall; and, the more especially, because there are them that believe they rise at midnight, and roam round the house and the clearings, mourning. Yet it is a good hiding-place for them that are in trouble; and many a night have little Peter and I sheltered us beneath the ruined roof, with little fear of either ghosts or Injuns; though, truly, we have sometimes heard strange and mournful noises among the trees around us. It is but a poor place and a sad one; but it will afford thee weary women a safe resting-place till such time as we can cross the river."

These words of Nathan brought to Roland's recollection the story of the Ashburns, whom Bruce had alluded to, as having been all destroyed at their

Station in a single night by the Indians, and whose tragical fate, perhaps, more than any other circumstance, had diverted the course of travel from the ford, near to which they had seated themselves, to the upper, and, originally, less frequented one.

It was not without reluctance that Roland prepared to lead his little party to this scene of butchery and sorrow; for, though little inclined himself to superstitious feelings of any kind, he could easily imagine what would be the effect of such a scene, with its gloomy and blood-stained associations, on the harassed mind of his cousin. But suffering and terror, even on the part of Edith, were not to be thought of, where they could purchase escape from evils far more real and appalling; and he therefore avoided all remonstrance and opposition, and even sought to hasten the steps of his conductor towards the ruined and solitary pile.

The bank was soon re-ascended; and the party, stealing along in silence, presently took their last view of the ford, and the yet blazing-fire that had warned them so opportunely from its dangerous vicinity. In another moment they had crept a second time into the forest, though in the opposite quarter from that whence they had come; making their way through what had once been a broad path, evidently cut by the hands of man, through a thick cane-brake, though long disused, and now almost choked by brambles and shrubs; and, by and by, having followed it for somewhat less than half a mile, they found themselves on a kind of clearing, which, it was equally manifest, had been once a cultivated field of several acres in extent. Throughout the whole of this space, the trunks of the old forest-trees, dimly seen in the light of a clouded sky, were yet standing, but entirely leafless and dead, and presenting such an aspect of desolation as is painful to the mind, even when sunshine, and the flourishing maize at their roots, invest them with a milder and more cheerful character. Such prospects are common enough in all new American clearings, where the husbandman is content to deprive the trees of life, by *girdling*, and then leave them to the assaults of the elements and the natural course of decay; and where a thousand trunks, of the gigantic growth of the West, are thus seen rising together in the air, naked and hoary with age, they impress the imagination with such gloom as is engendered by the sight of ruined colonnades.

Such was the case with the present prospect; years had passed since the axe had sapped the strength of the mighty oaks and beeches; bough after bough, and limb after limb, had fallen to the earth, with here and there some huge trunk itself, overthrown by the blast, and now rotting among weeds on the soil which it cumbered. At the present hour, the spectacle was peculiarly mournful and dreary. The deep solitude of the spot,—the hour itself,—the gloomy aspect of the sky veiled in clouds,—the occasional rush of the wind sweeping like a tempest through the woods, to be succeeded by a dead and dismal calm,—the roll of distant thunder reverberating among- the hills,—but, more than all, the remembrance of the tragical event that had consigned the ill-fated settlement to neglect and desolation, gave the deepest character of gloom to the scene.

As the travellers entered upon the clearing, there occurred one of those casualties which so often increase the awe of the looker-on, in such places. In one of the deepest lulls and hushes of the wind, when there was no apparent cause in operation to produce such an effect, a tall and majestic trunk was seen to decline from the perpendicular, topple slowly through the air, and then fall to the earth with a crash like the shock of an earthquake.

The poet and the moralising philosopher may find food for contemplation in such a scene and such a catastrophe. He may see, in the lofty and decaying trunks, the hoary relics and representatives of a generation of better and greater spirits than those who lead the destinies of his own,—spirits, left not more as monuments of the past than as models for the imitation of the present; he may contrast their majestic serenity and rest, their silence and immovableness, with the turmoil of the greener growth around, the uproar and collision produced by every gust, and trace the resemblance to the scene where the storms of party, rising among the sons, hurtle so indecently around the gray fathers of the republic, whose presence should stay them; and, finally, he may behold in the trunks, as they yield at last to decay, and sink one by one to the earth, the fall of each aged parent of his country,—a fall, indeed, as of an oak of a thousand generations, shocking the earth around, and producing for a moment, wonder, awe, grief, and then a long forgetfulness.

But men in the situation of the travellers have neither time nor inclination for moralising. The fall of the tree only served to alarm the weaker members of the party, to some of whom, perhaps, it appeared as an inauspicious omen. Apparently, however, it woke certain mournful recollections in the brains of both little Peter and his master, the former of whom, as he passed it by, began to snuffle and whine in a low and peculiar manner; while Nathan immediately responded, as if in reply to his counsellor's address, "Ay, truly, Peter!—thee has a good memory of the matter; though five long years is a marvellous time for thee little noddle to hold things. It was under this very tree they murdered the poor old granny, and brained the innocent, helpless babe. Of a truth, it was a sight that made my heart sink within me."

"What!" asked Roland, who followed close at his heels, and over heard the half-soliloquised expressions; "were *you* present at the massacre!"

"Alas, friend," replied Nathan, "it was neither the first nor last massacre that I have seen with these eyes. I dwelt, in them days, in a cabin a little distance down the river; and these poor people, the Ashburns, were my near neighbours; though, truly, they were not to me as neighbours should be, but held me in dis-favour because of my faith, and ever repelled me from their doors with scorn and ill-will. Yet was I sorry for them, because of the little children they had in the house, the same being far from succour; and when I found the tracks of the Injun party in the wood, as it was often my fate to do, while rambling in search of food, and saw that they were bending their way towards my own little wigwam, I said to myself, 'Whilst they are burning the same, I will get me to friend Ashburn, that he may be warned and escape to friend Brace's Station in time, with his people and cattle.' But, verily, they held my story light, and laughed and derided me: for, in them days, the people hardened their hearts and closed their ears against me, because I held it not according to conscience to kill Injuns as they did, and so refused. And so, friend, they drove me from their doors; seeing which, and perceiving the poor creatures were in a manner besotted, and bent upon their own destruction, and the night coming on fast, I turned my steps and ran with what speed I could to friend Bruce's, telling him the whole story, and advising that he should despatch a strong body of horsemen to the place, so as to frighten the evil creatures away; for, truly, I did not hold it right that there should be bloodshed. But, truly and alas, friend, I fared no better, and perhaps a little worse, at the Station than I had fared before at Ashburn's; wherefore, being left in despair, I said to myself, I will go into the woods, and hide me away, not returning to the river, lest I should be compelled to look upon the shedding-of the blood of the women and little babes, which I had no power to prevent. But it came into my mind, that, perhaps, the Injuns, not finding me in the wigwam, might lie in wait round about it, expecting my return, and so delay the attack upon friend Ashburn's house; whereby I might have time to reach him, and warn him of his danger again; and this idea prevailed with me, so that I rose me up again, and, with little Peter at my side, I ran back again, until I had reached this very field; when Peter gave me to know the Injuns were hard by. Thee don't know little Peter, friend; truly, he has the strongest nose for an Injun thee ever saw. Does thee not fear how he whines and snuffs along the grass? Now, friend, were it not that this is a bloody spot that Peter remembers well, because of the wicked deeds he saw performed, I would know by his whining, as truly as if he were to open his mouth and say as much in words, that there were evil Injuns nigh at hand, and that it behooved me to be up and a-doing. Well, friend, as I was saying,—it was with such words as these that little Peter told me that mischief was nigh; and, truly, I had scarce time to hide me in the corn, which was then in the ear, before I heard the direful yells with which the bloodthirsty creatures, who were then round about the house, woke up its frighted inmates. Verily, friend, I will not shock thee by telling thee what I heard and saw. There was a fate on the family, and even on the animals that looked to it for protection. Neither horse nor cow gave them the alarm; and even the house-dog slept so soundly, that the enemies dragged loose brush into the porch and fired it, before any one but themselves dreamed of danger. It was when the flames burst out that the warwhoop was sounded; and when the eyes of the sleepers opened, it was only to see themselves surrounded by flames and raging Shawnees. Then, friend," continued Nathan, speaking with a faltering and low voice, graduated for the ears of Roland, for whom alone the story was intended, though others caught here and there some of its dismal revealments, "then, thee may think, there was rushing out of men, women, and children, with the cracking of rifles, the crashing of hatchets, the plunge of knives, with yells and shrieks such as would turn thee spirit into ice and water to hear. It was a fearful massacre; but, friend, fearful as it was, these eyes of mine had looked on one more dreadful before: thee would not believe it, friend, but thee knows not what them see who have spent their lives on the Injun border.—Well, friend," continued the narrator, after this brief digression, "while they were murdering the stronger, I saw the weakest of all,—the old grandam, with the youngest babe in her arms, come flying into the corn; and she had reached this very tree that has fallen but now, as if to remind me of the story, when the pursuer,—for it was but a single man they sent in chase of the poor feeble old woman, caught up with her, and struck her down with his tomahawk. Then, friend,—for, truly, I saw it all in the light of the fire, being scarce two rods off,—he snatched the poor babe from the dying woman's arms, and struck it with the same bloody hatchet,—"

"And you!" exclaimed Roland, leaning from his horse and clutching the speaker by the collar, for he was seized with ungovernable indignation, or rather fury, at what he esteemed the cold-blooded cowardice of Nathan, "*You*!" he cried, grasping him as if he would have torn him to pieces, "You, wretch! stood by and saw the child murdered!"

"Friend!" said Nathan, with some surprise at the unexpected assault, but still with great submissiveness, "thee is as unjust to me as others. Had I been as free to shed blood as thee theeself, yet could I not have saved the babe in that way, seeing that my gun was taken from me, and I was unarmed. Thee forgets,—or rather I forgot to inform thee,—how, when I told friend Bruce my story, he took my gun from me, saying that 'as I was not man enough to use it, I should not be allowed to carry it,' and so turned me out naked from the fort. Truly, it was an ill thing of him to take from me that which gave me my meat; and truly too, it was doubly ill of him, as it concerned the child; for I tell thee, friend, when I stood in the corn and saw the great brutal Injun raise the hatchet to strike the little child, had there been a gun in my hand, I should—I can't tell thee, friend, what I might have done; but, truly, I should not have permitted the evil creature to do the bloody deed!"

"I thought so, by Heaven!" said Roland, who had relaxed his grasp the moment Nathan mentioned the seizure of the gun, which story was corroborated by the account Bruce had himself given of that stretch of authority,—"I thought so: no human creature, not an Indian, unless the veriest dastard and dog that ever lived, could have had arms in his hand, and, on such an occasion, failed to use them! But you had humanity,—you did something?"

"Friend," said Nathan, meekly, "I did what I could,—but, truly, what could I? Nevertheless, friend, I did, being set beside myself by the sight, snatch the little babe out of the man's hands, and fly to the woods, hoping, though it was sore wounded, that it might yet live. But, alas, before I had run a mile, it died in my arms, and I was covered from head to foot with its blood. It was a sore sight for friend Bruce, whom I found with his people galloping to the ford, to see what there might be in my story: for, it seems, as he told me himself, that after he had driven me away, he could not sleep for thinking that perhaps I had told the truth. And truth enough, he soon found, I had spoken; for galloping immediately to Ashburn's house, he found nothing there but the corses of the people, and the house partly consumed,—for, being of green timber, it could not all burn. There was not one of the poor family that escaped."

"But they were avenged?" muttered the soldier.

"If thee calls killing the killers avenging," replied Nathan, "the poor deceased people had vengeance enough. Of the fourteen murderers, for that was the number, eleven were killed before day-dawn, the pursuers having discovered where they had built their fire, and so taken them by surprise; and of the three that escaped, it was afterwards said by returning captives, that only one made his way home, the other two having perished in the woods, in some way unknown.—But, truly," continued Nathan, suddenly diverting his attention from the tragic theme to the motions of his dog, "little Peter is more disturbed than is his wont. Truly, he has never had a liking to the spot: I have heard them that said a dog could scent the presence of spirits."

"To my mind," said Roland, who had not forgotten Nathan's eulogium on the excellence of the animal's nose for scenting Indians, and who was somewhat alarmed at what appeared to him the evident uneasiness of little

Peter, "he is more like to wind another party of cursed Shawnees than any harmless, disembodied spirits."

"Friend," said Nathan, "it may be that Injuns have trodden upon this field this day, seeing that the wood is full of them; and it is like enough that those very evil creatures at the ford hard by have stolen hither, before taking their post, to glut their eyes with the sight of the ruins, where the blood of nine poor white persons was shed by their brothers in a single night; though, truly, in that case, they must have also thought of the thirteen murderers that bled for the victims; which would prove somewhat a drawback to their satisfaction. No, friend; Peter has his likes and his dislikes, like a human being; and this is a spot he ever approaches with abhorrence,—as, truly, I do myself, never coming hither unless when driven, as now, by necessity. But, friend, if thee is in fear, thee shall be satisfied there is no danger before thee; it shall never be said that I undertook to lead thee poor women out of mischief only to plunge them into peril. I will go before thee to the ruin, which thee sees there by the hollow, and reconnoitre."

"It needs not," said Roland, who now seeing the cabin of which they were in search close at hand, and perceiving that Peter's uneasiness had subsided, dismissed his own as being groundless. But notwithstanding, he thought proper, as Nathan advanced, to ride forward himself, and inspect the condition of the building, in which he was about to commit the safety of the being he held most dear, and on whose account, only, he felt the thousand anxieties and terrors he never could have otherwise experienced.

The building was a low cabin of logs, standing, as it seemed, on the verge of an abyss, in which the river could be heard rushing tumultuously, as if among rocks and other obstructions. It was one of those double cabins so frequently found in the west; that is to say, it consisted of two separate cots, or wings, standing a little distance apart, but united by a common roof; which thus afforded shelter to the open hall, or passage, between them; while the roof, being continued also from the eaves, both before and behind, in pent-house fashion, it allowed space for wide porches, in which, and in the open passage, the summer traveller, resting in such a cabin, will almost always find the most agreeable quarters.

How little soever of common wisdom and discretion the fate of the builders might have shown them to possess, they had not forgotten to provide their solitary dwelling with such defences as were common to all others in the land at that period. A line of palisades, carelessly and feebly constructed indeed, but perhaps sufficient for the purpose intended, enclosed the ground on which the cabin stood; and this being placed directly in the centre, and joining the palisades at the sides, thus divided the enclosure into two little yards, one in front, the other in the rear, in which was space sufficient for horses and cattle, as well as for the garrison, when called to repel assailants. The space behind extended to the verge of the river-bank, which, falling down a sheer precipice of forty or fifty feet, required no defence of stakes, and seemed never to have been provided with them; while that in front circumscribed a portion of a cleared field entirely destitute of trees, and almost of bushes.

Such had been the original plan and condition of a fortified private-dwelling, a favourable specimen, perhaps, of the *family-forts* of the day, and which, manned by five or six active and courageous defenders, might have bidden defiance to thrice the number of barbarians that had actually succeeded in storming it. Its present appearance was ruinous and melancholy in the extreme. The stockade was in great part destroyed, especially in front, where the stakes seemed to have been rooted up by the winds, or to have fallen from sheer decay; and the right wing or cot, that had suffered most from the flames, lay a black and mouldering-pile of logs, confusedly heaped on its floor, or on the earth beneath. The only part of the building yet standing was the cot on the left hand, which consisted of but a single room, and that, as Roland perceived at a glance, almost roofless and ready to fall.

Nothing could be more truly cheerless and forbidding than the appearance of the ruined pile; and the hoarse and dismal rush of the river below, heard the more readily by reason of a deep rocky fissure, or ravine, running from the rear yard to the water's edge, through which the sound ascended in hollow echoes, added double horror to its appearance. It was, moreover, obviously insecure and untenable against any resolute enemy, to whom the ruins of the fallen wing and stockade and the rugged depths of the ravine offered much more effectual shelter, as well as the best place of annoyance. The repugnance, however, that Roland felt to occupy it even for a few hours, was combatted by Nathan, who represented that the ford at which he designed crossing the river, several miles farther down, could not be safely attempted until the rise of the waning moon, or until the clouds should disperse, affording them the benefit of the dim star-light; that the road to it ran through swamps and hollows, now submerged, in which could be found no place of rest for the females, exhausted by fatigue and mental suffering; and that the ruin might be made as secure as the Station the travellers had left; "for truly," said he, "it is not according to my ways or conscience to leave anything to chance or good luck, when there is Injun scent in the forest, though it be in the forest ten miles off. Truly, friend, I design, when thee poor tired women is sleeping, to keep watch round the ruin, with Peter to help me; and if theeself and thee two male persons have strength to do the same, it will be all the better for the same."

"It shall be done," said Roland, as much relieved by the suggestion as he was pleased by the humane spirit that prompted it: "my two soldiers can watch, if they cannot fight, and I shall take care they watch well."

Thus composing the difficulty, preparations were immediately made to occupy the ruin, into which Roland, having previously entered with the Emperor, and struck a light, introduced his weary kinswoman with her companion Telie; while Nathan and Pardon Dodge led the horses into the ravine, where they could be easily confined, and allowed to browse and drink at will, being at the same time beyond the reach of observation from any foe that might yet be prowling through the forest.

CHAPTER XIV

The light struck by the negro was soon succeeded by a fire, for which ample materials lay ready at hand among the ruins; and as it blazed up from the broken and long deserted hearth, the travellers could better view the dismal aspect of the cabin. It consisted, as has been mentioned, of but a single remaining apartment, with walls of logs, from whose chinks the clay, with which they had been originally plastered, had long since vanished, with here and there a fragment of a log itself, leaving a thousand gaps for the admission of wind and rain. The ceiling of poles (for it had once possessed a kind of garret) had fallen down under the weight of the rotting roof, of which but a small portion remained, and that in the craziest condition; and the floor of *puncheons*, or planks of split logs, was in a state of equal dilapidation, more than half of it having rotted away, and mingled with the earth on which it reposed. Doors and windows there were none; but two mouldering gaps in the front and the rear walls, and another of greater magnitude opening, from the side, into what had once been the hall or passage (though now a platform heaped with fragments of charred timber), showed where the narrow entrance and loop-hole windows had once existed. The former was without leaf or defence of any kind, unless such might have been found in three or four logs standing against the wall hard by, whence they could be easily removed and piled against the opening; for which purpose, Roland did not doubt they had been used, and by the houseless Nathan himself. But a better protection was offered by the ruins of the other apartment, which had fallen down in such a way as almost to block up the door, leaving a passage in and out, only towards the rear of the building; and, in case of sudden attack and seizure of this sole entrance, there were several gaps at the bottom of the wall, through one of which, in particular, it would be easy enough to effect a retreat. At this place, the floor was entirely wanting, and the earth below washed into a gully communicating with the rocky ravine, of which it might be considered the head.

But the looks of the soldier did not dwell long upon the dreary spectacle of ruin; they were soon cast upon the countenance of Edith, concealed so long by darkness. It was even wanner and paler than he feared to find it, and her eye shone with an unnatural lustre, as it met his own. She extended her hands and placed them in his, gazed upon him piercingly, but without speaking, or indeed seeming able to utter a single word.

"Be of good heart," he said, replying to the look of inquiry; "we are unfortunate, Edith, but we are safe."

"Thank Heaven!" she exclaimed, but more wildly than fervently: "I have been looking every moment to see you shot dead at my feet! Would I had died, Roland, my brother, before I brought you to this fatal land—But I distress you! Well, I will not be frightened more. But is not this an adventure for a woman that never before looked upon a cut finger without fainting? Truly, Roland,—'truly,' as friend Nathan says,—it is as ridiculous as frightful: and then this cabin, where they killed so many poor women and children,—is it not a ridiculous lodging place for Edith Forrester? a canopy of clouds, a couch of clay, with owls and snakes for my bed-fellows—truly, truly, truly, it is very ridiculous!"

It seemed, for a moment, as if the maiden's effort to exchange her melancholy and terror for a more joyous feeling, would have resulted in producing even greater agitation than before; but the soothing words of Roland, and the encouraging countenance maintained by Telie Doe, who seemed little affected by their forlorn situation, gradually tranquilised her mind, and enabled her the better to preserve the air of levity and mirthfulness, which she so vainly attempted at first to assume. This moment of calm Roland took advantage of to apprise her of the necessity of recruiting her spirits with a few hours' asleep; for which purpose he began to look about him for some suitable place in which to strew her a bed of fern and leaves.

"Why, here is one strewn for me already," she cried, with an affected laugh, pointing to a corner, in which lay a mass of leaves so green and fresh that they looked as if plucked but a day or two before: "truly, Nathan has not invited me to his hiding-place to lodge me meanly (Heaven forgive me for laughing at the poor man; for we owe him our lives!) nay, nor to send me supperless to bed. See!" she added, pointing to a small brazen kettle, which her quick eye detected among the leaves, and which was soon followed by a second that Emperor stirred up from its concealment, and both of them, as was soon perceived, still retaining the odour of a recent savoury stew: "Look well, Emperor: where the kitchen is, the larder cannot be far distant. I warrant we shall find that Nathan has provided us a good supper."

"Such, perhaps, as a woodman only can eat," said Roland, who, somewhat surprised at the superfluous number of Nathan's valuables (for to Nathan, he doubted not, they belonged), had begun stirring the leaves, and succeeded in raking up with his rifle, which he had not laid aside, a little earthen pouch, well stored with parched corn. "A strange fellow, this

Nathan," he muttered: "he really spoke as if he had not visited the ruin for a considerable period; whereas it is evident he must have slept here last night. But he seems to affect mystery in all that concerns his own private movements—it is the character of his persuasion."

While Roland, with the females, was thus laying hands, and speculating, upon the supposed chattels of their conductor, Nathan himself entered the apartment, betraying some degree of agitation in his countenance; whilst the faithful Peter, who followed at his side, manifested equal uneasiness, by snuffing the air, whining, and rubbing himself frequently against his master's legs.

"Friends," he cried, abruptly, "Peter talks too plainly to be mistaken: there is mischief nigh at hand, though where, or how it can be, sinner and weak foolish man that I am, I know not: we must leave warm fires and soft beds, and take refuge again in the woods."

This unexpected announcement again banished the blood from Edith's cheeks. She had, on his entrance, caught the pouch of corn from Roland's hands, intending to present it to the guide, with some such light expressions as should convince her kinsman of her recovered spirits; but the visage and words of Nathan struck her dumb, and she stood holding it in her hand, without speaking a word, until it caught Nathan's eye. He snatched it from her grasp, surveying it with astonishment and even alarm, and only ceased to look at it, when little Peter, who had run into the corner and among the bed of leaves, uttered a whine louder than before. The pouch dropped from Nathan's hand as his eye fell upon the shining-kettles, on which he gazed as if petrified.

"What, in Heaven's name, is the matter!" demanded Roland, himself taking the alarm: "are you frighted at your own kettles?"

"Mine!" cried Nathan, clasping his hands, and looking terror and remorse together—"If thee will kill me, friend, thee will scarce do amiss; for, miserable, blind sinner that I am, I have led thee poor luckless women into the very lion's den! into the hiding-place and head-quarters of the very cut-throats that is seeking to destroy thee! Up and away—does thee not hear Peter howling at the door? Hist! Peter, hist!—Truly, this is a pretty piece of business for thee, Nathan Slaughter!—Does thee not hear them close at hand?"

"I hear the hooting of an owl and the answer of his fellow," replied Roland; but his words were cut short by a second howl from Peter, and the cry of his master, "Up, if thee be not besotted; drag thee women by the hands and follow me."

With these words, Nathan was leaping towards the door, when a cry from Roland arrested him. He looked round and perceived Edith had fainted in the soldier's arms. "I will save the poor thing for thee—help thou the other," he cried, and snatching her up as if she had been but a feather, he was again in the act of springing to the door, when brought to a stand by a far more exciting impediment. A shriek from Telie Doe, uttered in sudden terror, was echoed by a laugh, strangely wild, harsh, guttural, and expressive of equal triumph and derision, coming from the door; looking to which the eyes of Nathan and the soldier fell upon a tall and naked Indian, shorn and painted, who, rifle in hand, the grim smile yet writhing on his features, and exclaiming with a mockery of friendly accost, "*Bo-zhoo*,[8] brudders,—Injun good friend!" was stepping that moment into the hovel; and as if that spectacle and those sounds were not enough to chill the heart's blood of the spectators, there were seen over his shoulders, the gleaming eyes, and heard behind his back, the malign laughter of three or four equally wild and ferocious companions.

[Footnote 8: *Bo-zhoo*—a corruption of the French *bon jour*, a word of salutation adopted by Western Indians from the *Voyageurs* of Canada, and used by them with great zeal by night as well as by day.]

"To the door, if thee is a man,—rush!" cried Nathan, with a voice more like the blast of a bugle than the tone of a frighted man of peace; and casting Edith from his arms, he set the example of attack or flight—Roland scarcely knew which,—by leaping against the breast of the daring intruder. Both fell together across the threshold, and Roland obeying the call with desperate and frantic ardour, stumbled over their bodies, pitching headlong into the passage, whereby he escaped the certain death that otherwise awaited him, three several rifle-shots having been that instant poured upon him from a distance of scarce as many feet.

"Strike, if thee conscience permits thee!" he heard the voice of Nathan cry in his ears, and the next moment, a shot from the interior of the hovel, heralded by a quavering cry from the faithful Emperor,—"Lorra-gor! nebber harm an Injun in my life!" struck the hatchet from the shattered hand of a foeman, who had taken advantage of his downfall to aim a fatal blow at him while rising. A yell of pain came from the maimed and baffled warrior, who, springing over the blackened ruins before the door, escaped the stroke of the clubbed rifle which the soldier aimed at him in return, the piece having been discharged by the fall. The cry of the flying assailant was echoed by what seemed in Roland's ears the yells of fifty supporters, two of whom he saw within six feet of him, brandishing their hatchets, as if in the act of flinging them at his almost defenceless person. It was at this moment that he experienced aid from a quarter whence it was almost least expected; a rifle was discharged from the ravine, and as one of the fierce foes suddenly dropped, mortally wounded upon the floor, he heard the voice of Pardon, the Yankee, crying in tones of desperation, "When there is no dodging 'em, then I'm the man for 'em, or it a'n't no matter!"

"Bravo! bravely done, Emperor and Dodge both!" cried Roland, to whom this happy and quite unexpected display of courage from his followers, and its successful results, imparted a degree of assurance and hope not before felt; for, indeed, up to this moment, his feeling had been the mere frenzy of despair—"Courage, and rush on!" And with these words, he did not hesitate to dash against the remaining foe, striking up the uplifted hatchet with his rifle, and endeavouring with the same effort to dash his weapon into the warrior's face. But the former part only of the manoeuvre succeeded; the tomahawk was indeed dashed aside, but the rifle was torn from his own grasp, and the next moment he was clutched as in the embrace of a bear, and pressed with suffocating force upon the breast of his undaunted adversary.

"Brudder!" growled the savage, and the foam flew from his grinning lips, advanced until they were almost in contact with the soldier's face—"Brudder!" he cried, as he felt his triumph, and twined his arms still more tightly around Roland's frame, "Long-knife nothing! hab a scalp, Shawnee!"

With these words, he sprang from the broken floor of the passage, on which the encounter began, and dragging the soldier along, made as if he would have carried him off alive. But although in the grasp of a man of much superior strength, the resolution and activity of Roland preserved him from a destiny at once so fearful and ignoble. He exerted the strength he possessed at the instant when the bulky captor was springing from the floor to the broken ground beneath, and with such effect, that, though it did not entirely release him from his grasp, it carried them headlong to the earth together; whence, after a brief and blind struggle, both rose together, each clutching at the weapon that promised soonest to terminate the contest. The pistols of the soldier, which, as well as Emperor's, the peaceful Nathan had taken the precaution to carry with him into the ruin, had been forgotten in the suddenness and hurry of the assault; his rifle had been wrested from his hands, and thrown he knew not where. The knife, which, like a true adventurer of the forest, he had buckled in his belt, was ready to be grasped; but the instinct of long habits carried his hand to the broad-sword, which was yet strapped to his thigh; and this, as he rose, he attempted to draw, not doubting that a single blow of the trusty steel would rid him of his brown enemy. But the Shawnee, as bold, as alert, and far more discreet, better acquainted, too, with those savage personal rencontres which, make up so large a portion of Indian warfare, had drawn his knife before he had yet regained his footing; and before the Virginian's sword was half unsheathed, the hand that tugged at it was again seized and held as in a vice, while the warrior, elevating his own free weapon above his head, prepared, with a laugh and whoop of triumph, to plunge it into the soldier's throat. His countenance, grim with warpaint, grimmer with ferocious exultation, was distinctly perceived, the bright blaze of the fire shining through the gaps of the hovel, so as to illuminate every feature; and Roland, as he strove in vain to clutch at the uplifted arm so as to avert the threatened blow, could distinguish every motion of the weapon, and every change of his foeman's visage. But he did not even then despair, for he was, in all circumstances affecting only himself, a man of true intrepidity; and it was only when, on a sudden, the light wholly vanished from the cabin, as if the brands had been scattered and trodden out, that he began to anticipate a fatal result from the advantage possessed by his opponent. But at that very instant, and while, blinded by the sudden darkness, he was expecting the blow which he no longer knew how to avoid, the laugh of the warrior, now louder and more exultant than before, was suddenly changed to a yell of agony. A jet of warm blood, at the same moment, gushed over Roland's right arm; and the savage, struck by an unknown hand, or by a random ball, fell a dead man at his feet, overwhelming the soldier in his fall.

"Up, and do according to thee conscience!" cried Nathan Slaughter; whose friendly arm, more nervous than that of his late foe, at this conjuncture jerked Roland from beneath the body: "for, truly, thee fights like unto a young lion, or an old bear; and, truly, I will not censure thee, if thee kills a whole dozen of the wicked cut-throats! Here is thee gun and thee pistols: fire and shout aloud with thee voice; for, of a verity, thee enemies is confounded by thee resolution: do thee make them believe thee has been reinforced by numbers."

And with that the peaceful Nathan, uplifting his voice, and springing among the ruins from log to log, began to utter a series of shouts, all designed to appear as if coming from different throats, and all expressing such manly courage and defiance, that even Pardon Dodge, who yet lay ensconced among the rocks of the ravine, and Emperor, the negro, who, it seems, had taken post behind the ruins at the door, felt their spirits wax resolute and valiant, and added their voices to the din, the one roaring, "Come on, ye 'tarnal critturs, if you *must* come!" while the other bellowed, with equal spirit, "Don't care for niggah Injun no way—will fight and die for massa and missie!"

All these several details, from the moment of the appearance of the warrior at the door until the loud shouts of the besieged travellers took the place of the savage whoops previously sounded, passed in fewer moments than we have taken pages to record them. The rush of Nathan against the leader, the discomfiture of one, and the death of his two comrades, were indeed the work of but an instant, as it seemed to Roland; and he was scarce aware of the assault, before he perceived that it was over. The successful, and, doubtless, the wholly unexpected resistance of the little party, resulting in a manner so fatal to the advanced guard of assailants, had struck terror and confusion into the main body, whose presence had been only made known by their yells, not a single shot having yet been fired by them.

It was in this moment of confusion that Nathan sprang to the side of Roland, who was hastily recharging his piece, and catching him by the hand, said, with a voice that betrayed the deepest agitation, though his countenance was veiled in night,—"Friend, I have betrayed thee poor women into danger, so that the axe and scalping-knife is now near their innocent poor heads."

"It needs not to speak of it," said Roland; adding hastily. "The miscreant that entered the cabin—did you kill him?"

"*Kill*, friend! *I* kill!" echoed Nathan, with accents more disturbed than ever; "would thee have me a murderer? Truly, I did creep over him, and leave the cabin."

"And left him in it alive!" cried Roland, who was about to rush into the hovel, when Nathan detained him, saying, "Don't thee be alarmed, friend. Truly, thee may think it was ill of me to fall upon him so violently; but, truly, be must have split his head upon a log, or wounded himself with a splinter;—or perhaps the coloured person stuck him with a knife; but, truly, as it happened his blood spouted on my hand, by reason of the hurt he got; so that I left him clean dead."

"Good!" said Roland; "but, by Heaven, I hoped and believed you had yourself finished him like a man. But time presses: we must retreat again to the woods,—they are yet open behind us."

"Thee is mistaken," said Nathan; and, as if to confirm his words, there arose at that moment a loud whooping, with the crack of a dozen or more rifles, let fly with impotent rage by the enemy, showing plainly enough that the ruin was already actually environed.

"The ravine,—the river!" cried Forrester; "we can swim it with the horses, if it be not fordable."

"It is a torrent that would sweep thee, with thee strongest war-horse, to perdition," muttered Nathan: "does thee not hear how it roars among the rocks and cliffs? It is here deep, narrow, and rocky; and, though, in the season of drought, a child might step across it from rock to rock, it is a cataract in the time of floods. No, friend; I have brought thee into a trap whence thee has no escape, unless thee would desert these poor helpless women."

"Put but them in safety," said Roland, "and care not for the rest.—And yet I do not despair: we have shown what we can do by resolution: we can keep the cut-throats at bay till the morning."

"And what will that advantage thee, except to see thee poor females murdered in the light of the sun, instead of having them killed out of thee sight in darkness? Truly, the first glimmer of dawn will be the signal of death to all; for then the Shawnees will find thee weakness, if indeed they do not find it before."

"Man!" said Roland, "why should you drive me to despair? Give me better comfort,—give me counsel, or say no more. You have brought us to this pass: do your best to save us, or our blood be upon your head!"

To these words of unjust reproach, wrung from the young soldier by the bitterness of his feelings, Nathan at first made no reply. Preserving silence for awhile, he said, at last:

"Well, friend, I counsel thee to be of good heart, and to do what thee can, making thee enemies, since thee cannot increase thee friends, as few in numbers as possible;—to do which, friend," he added, suddenly, "if thee will shoot that evil creature that lies like a log on the earth, creeping towards the ruin, I will have no objection!"

With these words, which were uttered in a low voice, Nathan, pulling the young man behind a screen of fallen timbers near to which they stood, endeavoured to point him out the enemy whom his eye had that moment detected crawling towards the hovel, with the subtle motion of a serpent. But the vision of Roland, not yet accustomed to trace objects in the darkness of a wood, failed to discover the approaching foe.

"Truly," said Nathan, somewhat impatiently, "if thee will not consider it as an evil thing of me, and a blood-guiltiness, I will hold thee gun for thee, and thee shall pull the trigger!" which piece of service the man of peace, having doubtless satisfied his conscience of its lawfulness, was actually about to render the soldier, when the good intention was set at naught by the savage suddenly leaping to his feet, followed by a dozen others, all springing, as it seemed, out of the earth, and rushing with wild yells against the ruin. The suddenness and fury of the attack struck dismay to the bosom of the soldier, who, discharging his rifle, and snatching up his pistols, already in imagination beheld the bloody fingers of a barbarian grasped among the bright locks of his Edith; when Nathan, crying, "Blood upon my hands, but not upon my head!—give it to them, murdering dogs!" let fly his own piece upon the throng; the effect of which, together with the discharge of Roland's pistols immediately after, was such as to stagger the assailants, of whom but a single one preserved resolution enough to advance upon the defenders, whooping to his companions in vain to follow. "Thee will remember I fight to save the lives of thee helpless women!" muttered Nathan, in Roland's ear; and then as if the first act of warfare had released him for ever from all peaceful obligations, awakened a courage and appetite for blood superior even to the soldier's, and, in other words, set him entirely beside himself, he rushed against the advancing Shawnee, dealing him a blow with the butt of his heavy stocked rifle that crushed through skull and brain as through a gourd, killing the man on the spot. Then leaping like a buck to avoid the shot of the others, he rushed back to the ruin, and grasping the hand of the admiring soldier, and wringing it with all his might, he cried, "Thee sees what thee has brought me to! Friend, thee has seen me shed a man's blood!—But, nevertheless, friend, the villains shall not kill thee poor women, nor harm a hair of their heads."

The valour of the man of peace was fortunately seconded on this occasion by Dodge and the negro, the former from his hiding place in the ravine, the latter from among the ruins; and the enemy, thus seriously warned of the danger of approaching too nigh a fortress manned by what very naturally appeared to them eight different persons,—for such, including the pistols, was the number of fire-arms,—retired precipitately to the woods, where they expressed their hostility only by occasional whoops, and now and then by a shot fired impotently against the ruins.

The success of this second defence, the spirited behaviour of Dodge and Emperor, but more than all the happy change in the principles and practice of Nathan, who seemed as if about to prove that he could deserve the nickname of Tiger so long bestowed upon him in derision, greatly relieved the spirits of the soldier, who was not without hopes of being able to maintain the contest until the enemy should be discouraged and driven off, or some providential accident bring him succour. He took advantage of the cessation of hostilities to creep into the hovel and whisper words of assurance to his feebler dependents, of whom indeed Telie Doe now betrayed the greatest distress and agitation, while Edith, on the contrary, maintained, as he judged—for the fire was extinguished, and he saw not her countenance—a degree of tranquillity he had not dared to hope. It was a tranquillity, however, resulting from despair and stupor,—a lethargy of spirit, resulting from overwrought feelings, in which she happily remained, more than half unconscious of what was passing around her.

CHAPTER XV

The enemy, twice repulsed, and on both occasions with severe loss, had been taught the folly of exposing themselves too freely to the fire of the travellers; but although driven back, they manifested little inclination to fly further than was necessary to obtain shelter, and as little to give over their fierce purposes. Concealing themselves severally behind logs, rocks, and bushes, and so disposing their force as to form a line around the ruin, open only towards the river, where escape was obviously impracticable, they employed themselves keeping a strict watch upon the hovel, firing repeated volleys, and as often uttering yells, with which they sought to strike terror into the hearts of the besieged. Occasionally some single warrior, bolder than the rest, would creep near the ruins, and obtaining such shelter as he could, discharge his piece at any mouldering beam, or other object, which his fancy converted into the exposed body of a defender. But the travellers had taken good care to establish themselves in such positions among the ruins as offered the best protection; and although the bullets whistled sharp and nigh, not a single one had yet received a wound; nor was there much reason to apprehend injury so long as the darkness of night befriended them.

Yet it was obvious to all that this state of security could not last long, and that it existed only because the enemy was not yet aware of his advantage. The condition of the ruins was such that a dozen men of sufficient spirit, dividing themselves, and creeping along the earth, might at any moment make their way to any and every part of the hovel without being seen, when a single rush must put it in their power. An open assault indeed from the whole body of besiegers, whose number was reckoned by Nathan at full fifteen or twenty, must have produced the same success, though with the loss of several lives. A random shot might at any moment destroy or disable one of the little garrison, and thus rob one important corner of the hovel, which, from its dilapidated state was wholly indefensible from within of defence. It was indeed, as Roland felt, more than folly to hope that all should escape unharmed for many hours longer. But the worst fear of all was that previously suggested by Nathan: all might survive the perils of the night; but what fate was to be expected when the coming of day should expose the party, in all its true weakness, to the eyes of the enemy? If relief came not before morning, Roland's heart whispered him, it must come in vain. But the probabilities of relief, what were they? The question was asked of Nathan, and the answer went like iron through Roland's soul. They were in the deepest and most solitary part of the forest, twelve miles from Bruce's Station, and at least eight from that at which the emigrants were to lodge; with no other places within twice the distance, from which help could be obtained. They had left, three or four miles behind, the main and only road on which volunteers, summoned from the Western Stations to repel the invasion, of which the news had arrived before Roland's departure from Bruce's village, could be expected to pass; if indeed the strong force of the enemy posted at the Upper Ford had not cut off all communication between the two districts. From Bruce's Station little or no assistance could be hoped, the entire strength of its garrison, as Roland well knew, having long since departed to share in the struggle on the north side of Kentucky. Assistance could be looked for only from his late companions, the emigrants, from whom he had parted in an evil hour. But how were they to be made acquainted with his situation?

The discussion of these questions almost distracted the young man. Help could only come from themselves. Would it not be possible to cut their way through the besiegers? He proposed a thousand wild schemes of escape; now he would mount his trusty steed, and dashing among the enemy, receive their fire, distract their attention, and perhaps draw them in pursuit, while Nathan and the others galloped off with the women in another quarter; and again, he would plunge with them into the boiling torrent below, trusting to the strength of the horses to carry them through in safety.

To these and other frantic proposals, uttered in the intervals of combat, which was still maintained, with occasional demonstrations on the part of the enemy of advancing to a third assault, Nathan replied only by representing the certain death they would bring upon all, especially "the poor helpless women," whose condition, with the reflection that he had brought them into it, seemed ever to dwell upon his mind, producing feelings of remorseful excitement not inferior even to the compunctions which he expressed at every shot discharged by him at the foe. Indeed his conscience seemed sorely distressed and perplexed; now he upbraided himself with being the murderer of the two poor women, and now of his Shawnee fellow-creatures; now he wrung the soldier by the hand, begging him to bear witness that he was shedding blood, not out of malice or wantonness, or even self-defence, but purely to save the innocent scalps of poor women, whose blood would be otherwise on his head; and now beseeching the young man with equal fervour to let the world know of his doings, that the blame might fall, not upon the faith of which he was an unworthy professor, but upon him, the evil-doer and backslider. But with all his remorse and contrition, he manifested no inclination to give over the work of fighting; but, on the contrary, fired away with extreme good-will at every evil Shawnee creature that showed himself, encouraging Roland to do the same, and exhibiting throughout the whole contest the most exemplary courage and good conduct.

But courage and good conduct, although so unexpectedly manifested in the time of need by all his companions, Roland felt could only serve to defer for a few hours the fate of his party. The night wore away fast, the assailants grew bolder; and from the louder yells and more frequent shots coming from them, it seemed as if their numbers, instead of diminishing under his own fire, were gradually increasing by the dropping in of their scouts from the forest. At the same time, he became sensible that his stores of ammunition were fast decreasing.

"Friend," said Nathan, wringing the soldier's hand for the twentieth time, when made acquainted with the deficiency, "it is written, that thee women shall be murdered before thee eyes! Nevertheless I will do my best to save them. Friend, I must leave thee! Thee shall have assistance. Can thee hold out the hovel till morning? But it is foolish to ask thee: thee *must* hold it out, and with none save the coloured person and the man Dodge to help thee; for I say to thee, it has come to this at last, as I thought it would: I must break through the lines of thee Injun foes, and find thee assistance."

"It is impossible," said Roland in despair; "you will only provoke your destruction."

"It may be, friend, as thee says," responded Nathan; "nevertheless, friend, for thee women's sake, I will adventure it; for it is I, miserable sinner that I am, that have brought them to this pass, and that must bring them out of it again, if man can do it."

At a moment of less grief and desperation, Roland would have better appreciated the magnitude of the service which Nathan thus offered to attempt, and even hesitated to permit what must have manifestly seemed the throwing away of a human life. But the emergency was too great to allow the operation of any but selfish feelings. The existence of his companions, the life of his Edith, depended upon procuring relief, and this could be obtained in no other way. If the undertaking was dangerous in the extreme, he saw it with the eyes of a soldier as well as a lover: it was a feat he would himself have dared without hesitation, could it have promised, in his hands, any relief to his followers.

"Go, then, and God be with you," he muttered, eagerly "you have our lives in your hand. But it will be long, long before you can reach the band on foot. Yet do not weary or pause by the way. I have but little wealth; but with what I have I will reward you."

"Friend," said Nathan proudly, "what I do I do for no lucre of reward, but for pity of thee poor women; for truly I have seen the murdering and scalping of poor women before, and the seeing of the same has left blood upon my head, which is a mournful thing to think of."

"Well, be not offended: do what you can—our lives may rest on a single minute."

"I *will* do what I can, friend," replied Nathan; "and if I can but pass safely through thee foes, there is scarce a horse in thee company, were it even thee war-horse, that shall run to thee friends more fleetly. But, friend, do thee hold out the house: use thee powder charily; keep up the spirits of thee two men, and be of good heart theeself, fighting valiantly, and slaying according to thee conscience; and then, friend, if it be Heaven's will, I will return to thee, and help thee out of thee troubles."

With these words, Nathan turned from the soldier, setting out upon his dangerous duty with a courage and self-devotion of which Roland did not yet know all the merit. He threw himself upon the earth, and muttering to little Peter, "Now, Peter, as thee ever served thee master well and truly, serve him well and truly now," began to glide away amongst the ruins, making his way from log to log, and bush to bush, close behind the animal, who seemed to determine the period and direction of every movement. His course was down the river, the opposite of that by which the party had reached the ruin, in which quarter the woods were highest, and promised the most accessible, as well as the best shelter; though that could be reached only in the event of his successfully avoiding the different barbarians hidden among the bushes on its border. He soon vanished, with his dog, from the eyes of the soldier; who now, in pursuance of instructions previously given him by Nathan, caused his two followers to let fly a volley among the trees, which had the expected effect of drawing another in return from the foes, accompanied by their loudest whoops of menace and defiance. In this manner Nathan, as he drew nigh the wood, was enabled to form correct opinions as to the different positions of the besiegers, and to select that point in the line which seemed the weakest; while the attention of the foe was in a measure drawn off, so as to give him the better opportunity of advancing on them unobserved. With this object in view, a second and third volley were fired by the little garrison; after which they ceased making such feints of hostility, and left him, as he had directed, to his fate.

It was then that, with a beating heart, Roland awaited the event; and as he began to figure to his imagination the perils which Nathan must necessarily encounter in the undertaking, he listened for the shout of triumph that he feared would, each moment, proclaim the capture or death of his messenger. But he listened in vain,—at least, in vain for such sounds as his skill might interpret into evidences of Nathan's fate: he heard nothing but the occasional crack of a rifle aimed at the ruin, with the yell of the savage that fired it, the rush of the breeze, the rumbling of the thunder, and the deep-toned echoes from the river below. There was nothing whatever occurred, at least for a quarter of an hour, by which he might judge what was the issue of the enterprise; and he was beginning to indulge the hope that Nathan had passed safely through the besiegers, when a sudden yell of a peculiarly wild and thrilling character was uttered in the wood in the quarter in which Nathan had fled; and this, exciting, as it seemed to do, a prodigious sensation among his foes, filled him with anxiety and dread. To his ears the shout expressed fury and exultation such as might well be felt at the sudden discovery and capture of the luckless messenger; and his fear that such had been the end of Nathan's undertaking was greatly increased by what followed. The shots and whoops suddenly ceased, and, for ten minutes or more, all was silent, save the roar of the river, and the whispering of the fitful breeze. "They have taken him alive, poor wretch!" muttered the soldier, "and now they are forcing from him a confession of our weakness!"

It seemed as if there might be some foundation for the suspicion; for presently a great shout burst from the enemy, and the next moment a rush was made against the ruin as if by the whole force of the enemy. "Fire!" shouted Roland to his companions: "if we must die, let it be like men;" and no sooner did he behold the dark figures of the assailants leaping among the ruins, than he discharged his rifle and a pair of pistols which he had reserved in his own hands, the other pair having been divided between Dodge and the negro, who used them with equal resolution, and with an effect that Roland had not anticipated; the assailants, apparently daunted by the weight of the volley, seven pieces having been discharged in rapid succession, instantly beat a retreat, resuming their former positions. From these, however, they now maintained an almost incessant fire; and by and by several of them, stealing cautiously up, effected a lodgment in a distant part of the ruins, whence, without betraying any especial desire to come to closer quarters, they began to carry on the war in a manner that greatly increased Roland's alarm, their bullets flying about and into the hovel so thickly that he became afraid lest some of them should reach its hapless inhabitants. He was already debating within himself the propriety of transferring Edith and her companion from this ruinous and now dangerous abode to the ravine, where they might be sheltered from all danger, at least for a time, when a bolt of lightning, as he at first thought it, shot from the nearest group of foes, flashed over his head, and striking what remained of the roof, stood trembling in it, an arrow of blazing fire. The appearance of this missile, followed, as it immediately was, by several others discharged from the same tow, confirmed the soldier's resolution to remove the females, while it greatly increased his anxiety; for although there was little fear that the flames could be communicated from the arrows to the roof so deeply saturated by the late rains, yet each, while burning, served, like a flambeau, to illuminate the ruins below, and must be expected before long to reveal the helplessness of the party, and to light the besiegers to their prey.

With such fears on his mind, he hesitated no longer to remove his cousin and her companion to the ravine; which was effected with but little risk or difficulty, the ravine heading, as was mentioned before, under the floor of the hovel itself, and its borders being so strewn with broken timbers and planks, as to screen the party from observation. He concealed them both among the rocks and brambles with which the hollow abounded, listened a moment to the rush of the flood as it swept the precipitous bank, and the roar with which it seemed struggling among rocky obstructions above, and smiling with the grim thought, that, when resistance was no longer availing, there was yet a refuge for his kinswoman within the dark bosom of those troubled waters, to which he felt, with the stern resolution of a Roman father rather than of a Christian lover, that he could, when nothing else remained, consign her with his own hands, he returned to the ruins, to keep up the appearance of still defending it, and to preserve the entrance of the ravine.

CHAPTER XVI

The flaming arrows were still shot in vain at the water-soaked roof, and the combustibles with which they were armed, burning out very rapidly, produced hut little of that effect in illuminating the ruins which Roland had apprehended, and for which they had been perhaps in part designed; and, in consequence, the savages soon ceased to shoot them. A more useful ally to the besiegers was promised in the moon, which was now rising over the woods, and occasionally revealing her wan and wasted crescent through gaps in the clouds. Waning in her last quarter, and struggling amid banks of vapour, she yet retained sufficient, magnitude and lustre, when risen a few more degrees, to dispel the almost sepulchral darkness that had hitherto invested the ruins, and thus proved a more effectual protection to the travellers than their own courage. Of this Roland was well aware; and he watched the increasing light with sullen and gloomy forebodings; though still exhorting his two supporters to hope and courage, and setting them a constant example of vigilance and resolution. But neither hope nor courage, neither vigilance nor resolution, availed to deprive the foe of the advantage he had gained in effecting a lodgment among the ruins, where four or five different warriors still maintained a hot fire upon the hovel, doing, of course, little harm, as it was entirely deserted, but threatening mischief enough, when it should fall into their hands,—a catastrophe that was deferred only in consequence of the extreme cautiousness with which they now conducted hostilities, the travellers making only a show of defending it, though sensible that it almost entirely commanded the ravine.

It was now more than an hour and a half since Nathan had departed, and Roland was beginning himself to feel the hope he encouraged in the others, that the man of peace had actually succeeded in effecting his escape, and that the wild whoop which he at first esteemed the evidence of his capture or death, and the assault that followed it, had been caused by some circumstance having no relation to Nathan whatever,—perhaps by the arrival of a reinforcement, whose coming had infused new spirit into the breasts of the so long baffled assailants. "If he *have* escaped," he muttered, "he must already be near the camp:—a strong man and fleet runner might reach it in an hour. In another hour,—nay, perhaps in half an hour, for there are good horses and bold hearts in the band,—I shall hear the rattle of their hoofs in the wood, and the yells of these cursed bandits, scattered like dust under their footsteps. If I can but hold the ravine for an hour! Thank Heaven, the moon is a second time lost in clouds, the thunder is again rolling through the sky! A tempest now were better than gales of Araby,—a thunder-gust were our salvation."

The wishes of the soldier seemed about, to be fulfilled. The clouds, which for half an hour had been breaking up, again gathered, producing thicker darkness than before; and heavy peals of thunder, heralded by pale sheets of lightning that threw a ghastly but insufficient light over objects, were again heard rattling at a distance over the woods. The fire of the savages began to slacken, and by and by entirely ceased. They waited perhaps for the moment when the increasing glare of the lightning should enable them better to distinguish between the broken timbers, the objects of so many wasted volleys, and the crouching bodies of the defenders.

The soldier took advantage of this moment of tranquillity to descend to the river to quench his thirst, and to bear back some of the liquid element to his fainting followers. While engaged in this duty he cast his eyes upon the scene, surveying with sullen interest the flood that cut off his escape from the fatal hovel. The mouth of the ravine was wide and scattered over with rocks and bushes, that even projected for some little space into the water, the latter vibrating up and down in a manner that proved the strength and irregularity of the current. The river was here bounded by frowning cliffs, from which, a furlong or two above, had fallen huge blocks of stone that greatly contracted its narrow channel; and among these the swollen waters surged and foamed with the greatest violence, producing that hollow roar, which was so much in keeping with the solitude of the ruin, and so proper an accompaniment to the growling thunder and the wild yells of the warriors. Below these massive obstructions, and opposite the mouth of the ravine, the channel had expanded into a pool; in which the waters might have regained their tranquillity and rolled along in peace, but for the presence of an island, which, growing up in the centre of the expanse, consolidated by the roots of a thousand willows and other trees that delight in such humid soils, and, in times of flood, covered by a raft of drift timber entangled among its trees, presented a barrier, on either side of which the current swept with speed and fury, though, as it seemed, entirely unopposed by rocks. In such a current, as Roland thought, there was nothing unusually formidable; a daring swimmer might easily make his way to the island opposite, where, if difficulties were presented by the second channel, he might as easily find shelter from enemies firing on him from the banks. He gazed again on the island, which, viewed in the gloom, revealed to his eyes only a mass of shadowy boughs, resting in peace and security. His heart beat high with hope, and he was beginning to debate the chances of success in an attempt to swim his party across the channel on the horses, when a flash of lightning, brighter than usual, disclosed the fancied island a cluster of shaking tree-tops, whose trunks as well as the soil that supported them, were buried fathoms deep in the flood. At the same moment, he heard coming on a gust that repelled and deadened for a time the louder tumult from the rocks above, other roaring sounds, indicating the existence of other rocky obstructions at the foot of the island, among which as he could now see, the same flash having shown him the strength of the current in the centre of the channel, the swimmer must be dashed, who failed to find footing on the island.

"We are imprisoned, indeed," he muttered, bitterly: "Heaven itself has deserted us."

As he uttered these repining words, stooping to dip the canteen with which he was provided, in the water, a little canoe, darting forward with a velocity that seemed produced by the combined strength of the current and the rower, shot suddenly among the rocks and bushes at the entrance of the ravine, wedging itself fast among them, and a human figure leaped from it to the shore. The soldier started back aghast, as if from a dweller of another world; but recovering his courage in an instant, and not doubting that he beheld in the unexpected visitor a Shawnee and foe, who had thus found means of assailing his party on the rear, he rushed upon the stranger with drawn sword, for he had laid his rifle aside, and taking him at a disadvantage, while stooping to drag the boat further ashore, he smote him such a blow over the head, as brought him instantly to the ground, a dead man to all appearance, since, while his body fell upon the earth, his head,—or at least a goodly portion of it, sliced away by the blow,—went skimming into the water.

"Die, dog!" said Roland, as he struck the blow; and not content with that, he clapped his foot on the victim's breast, to give him the *coup-de-grace* when, wonder of wonders, the supposed Shawnee and dead man opened his lips, and cried aloud, in good choice Salt-River English,—"'Tarnal death to you, white man! what are you after?"

It was the voice, the never-to-be-forgotten voice, of the captain of horse-thieves; and as Roland's sword dropped from his hand in the surprise, up rose Roaring Ralph himself, his eyes rolling, as Roland saw by a second flash of lightning, with thrice their usual obliquity, his left hand scratching among the locks of hair exposed by the blow of the sabre, which had carried off a huge slice of his hat, without doing other mischief, while his right brandished a rifle, which he handled as if about to repay the favour with interest. But the same flash that revealed his visage to the astonished soldier, disclosed also Roland's features to him, and he fairly yelled with joy at the sight. "'Tarnal death to me!" he roared, first leaping into the air and cracking' his heels together, then snatching at Roland's hand, which he clutched and twisted with the gripe of a bear, and then cracking his heels together again, "'tarnal death to me, sodger, but I know'd it war *you* war in a squabblification! I heard the cracking and the squeaking; "'Tarnal death to me!' says I, 'thar's Injuns!' And then I thought, and says I, '"Tarnal death to me, who are they after?' and then, 'tarnal death to me, it came over me like a strick of lightning, and says I, 'Tarnal death to me, but its anngelliferous madam that helped me out of the halter!' Strannger!" he roared, executing another demivolte, "h'yar am I, come to do anngelliferous madam's fighting ag'in all critturs human and inhuman, Christian and Injun, white, red, black, and party-coloured. Show me anngelliferous madam, and then show me the abbregynes; and if you ever seed fighting, 'tarnal death to me, but you'll say it war only the squabbling of seed-ticks and blue-bottle flies! I say, sodger, show me anngelliferous madam: you cut the halter, and you cut the tug; but it war madam the anngel that set you on: wharfo', I'm her dog and her niggur from now to etarnity, and I'm come to fight for her, and lick her enemies till you shall see nothing left of 'em but ha'rs and nails!"

Of these expressions, uttered with extreme volubility and the most extravagant gestures, Roland took no notice; his astonishment at the horse-thief's appearance was giving way to new thoughts and hopes, and he eagerly demanded of Ralph how he had got there.

"In the dug-out,"[9] said Ralph; "found her floating among the bushes, ax'd me out a flopper[10] with my tom-axe in no time, jumped in, thought of anngelliferous madam, and came down the falls like a cob in a corn-van—ar'n't I the leaping trout of the waters? Strannger, I don't want to sw'ar; but I reckon if there ar'n't hell up thar among the big stones, thar's hell no other whar all about Salt River! But I say, sodger, I came here not to talk nor cavort[11], but to show that I'm the man, Ralph Stackpole, to die dog for them that pats me. So, whar's anngelliferous madam? Let me see her, sodger, that I may feel wolfish when I jumps among the redskins; for I'm all for a fight, and thar ar'n't no run in me."

[Footnote 9: *Dug-out*—a canoe—because *dug out* or hollowed with the axe.]

[Footnote 10: *Flopper*—a flapper, a paddle.]

[Footnote 11: *Cavort*—to play pranks, to gasconade.]

"It is well, indeed, if it shall prove so," said Roland, not without bitterness; "for it is to you alone we owe all our misfortunes."

With these words, he led the way to the place, where, among the horses, concealed among brambles and stones, lay the unfortunate females, cowering on the bare earth. The pale sheets of lightning, flashing now with greater frequency, revealed them to Ralph's eyes, a ghastly and melancholy pair, whose situation and appearance were well fitted to move the feelings of a manly bosom; Edith lying almost insensible across Telie's knees, while the latter, weeping bitterly, yet seemed striving to forget her own distresses, while ministering to those of her companion.

"'Tarnal death to me!" cried Stackpole, looking upon Edith's pallid visage and rayless eyes with more emotion than would have been expected from his rude character, or than was expressed in his uncouth phrases, "if that don't make me eat a niggur, may I be tetotaciously chawed up myself! Oh, you anngelliferous madam! jist look up and say the word, for I'm now ready to mount a wild-cat: jist look up, and don't make a die of it, for thar's no occasion: for ar'n't I your niggur-slave, Ralph Stackpole? and ar'n't I come to lick all that's agin you, Mingo, Shawnee, Delaware, and all! Oh, you anngelliferous crittur! don't swound away, but look up, and see how I'll wallop 'em!"

And here the worthy horse-thief, seeing that his exhortations produced no effect upon the apparently dying Edith, dropped upon his knees, and began to blubber and lament over her, as if overcome by his feelings, promising her a world of Indian scalps, and a whole Salt River full of Shawnee blood, if she would only look up and see how he went about it.

"Show your gratitude by actions, not by words," said Roland, who, whatever his cause for disliking the zealous Ralph, was not unrejoiced at his presence, as that of a valuable auxiliary: "rise up, and tell me, in the name of heaven, how you succeeded in reaching this place, and what hope there is of leaving it?"

But Ralph was too much afflicted by the wretched condition of Edith, whom his gratitude for the life she had bestowed had made the mistress paramount of his soul, to give much heed to any one but herself; and it was only by dint of hard questioning that Roland drew from him, little by little, an account of the causes which had kept him in the vicinity of the travellers, and finally brought him to the scene of combat.

It had been, it appeared, an eventful and unlucky day with the horse-thief, as well as the soldier. Aside from his adventure on the beech-tree, enough in all truth to mark the day for him with a black stone, he had been peculiarly unfortunate with the horses to which he had so unceremoniously helped himself. The gallant Briareus, after sundry trials of strength with his new master, had at last succeeded in throwing him from his back; and the two-year-old pony, after obeying him the whole day with the docility of a dog, even when the halter was round his neck, and carrying him in safety until within a few miles of Jackson's Station, had attempted the same exploit, and succeeded, galloping off on the back track towards his home. This second loss was the more intolerable, since Stackpole, having endured the penalty for stealing him, considered himself as having a legal, Lynch-like right to the animal, which no one could now dispute. He therefore returned in pursuit of the pony, until night arrested his footsteps on the banks of the river, which, the waters still rising, he did not care to cross in the dark. He had, therefore, built a fire by the road-side, intending to camp-out till morning.

"And it was your fire, then, that checked us?" cried Roland, at this part of the story,—"it was *your* light we took for the watch-fire of Indians?"

"Injuns you may say," quoth Stackpole, innocently, "for thar war a knot of 'em I seed sneaking over the ford; and jist as I was squinting a long aim at 'em, hoping I might smash two of 'em at alick, slam-bang goes a feller that had got behind me, 'tarnal death to him, and roused me out of my snuggery. Well, sodger, then I jumps into the cane, and next into the timber; for I reckoned all Injun creation war atter me. And so I sticks fast in a lick; and then to sumtotalise, I wallops down a rock, eend foremost, like a bull-toad: and, 'tarnal death to me, while I war scratching my head, and wondering whar I came from, I heerd the crack of the guns across the river, and thought of anngelliferous madam. 'Tarnal death to me, sodger, it turned me wrong side out! and while I war axing all natur' how I war to get over, what should I do but see the old sugar-trough floating in the bushes,—I seed her in a strick of lightning. So pops I in, and paddles I down, till I comes to the rocks,—and ar'n't they beauties? 'H'yar goes for grim death and massacreation,' says I, and tuck the shoot; and if I didn't fetch old dug-out through slicker than snakes, and faster than a well-greased thunderbolt, niggurs ar'n't niggurs, nor Injuns Injuns: and, strannger, if you axes me why, h'yar's the wharfo'—'twar because I thought of anngelliferous madam! Strannger, I am the gentleman to see her out of a fight; and so jist tell her thar's no occasion for being uneasy; for, 'tarnal death to me, I'll mount Shawnees, and die for her, jist like nothing."

"Wretch that you are," cried Roland, whose detestation of the unlucky cause of his troubles, revived by the discovery that it was to *his* presence at the ford they owed their last and most fatal disappointment, rendered him somewhat insensible to the good feelings and courage which had brought the grateful fellow to his assistance,—"you were born for our destruction; every way you have proved our ruin: but for you my poor kinswoman would have been now in safety among her friends. Had she left you hanging on the beech, you would not have been on the river, to cut off her only escape, when pursued close at hand by murderous savages."

The reproach, now for the first time acquainting Stackpole with the injury he had, though so unintentionally and innocently, inflicted upon his benefactress; and the sight of her, lying apparently half-dead at his feet, wrought up the feelings of the worthy horse-thief to a pitch of desperate compunction, mingled with fury.

"If I'm the crittur that holped her into the fix, I'm the crittur to holp her out of it. 'Tarnal death to me, whar's the Injuns? H'yar goes to eat 'em!"

With that, he uttered a yell,—the first human cry that had been uttered for some time, for the assailants were still resting on their arms,—and rushing up the ravine, as if well acquainted with the localities of the Station, he ran to the ruin, repeating his cries at every step, with a loudness and vigour of tone that soon drew a response from the lurking enemy.

"H'yar you 'tarnal-temporal, long-legged, 'tater-headed paint-faces!" he roared, leaping from the passage floor to the pile of ruins before the door of the hovel (where Emperor yet lay ensconced, and whither Roland followed him), as if in utter defiance of the foemen whom he hailed with such opprobrious epithets,—"h'yar you bald head, smoke-dried, punkin-eating red-skins! you half-niggurs! you 'coon-whelps! you snakes! you varmints! you raggamuffins what goes about licking women and children, and scar'ring-anngelliferous madam! git up and show your scalp-locks; for 'tarnal death to me, I'm the man to take 'em—cock-a-doodle-doo!"

And the valiant horse-thief concluded his warlike defiance with such a crow as might have struck consternation to the heart not merely of the best game-cock in Kentucky, but of the bird of Jove itself. Great was the excitement it produced among the warriors. A furious hubbub was heard to arise among them, followed by many wrathful voices exclaiming in broken English, with eager haste, "Know him dah! cuss' rascal! Cappin Stackpole!—steal Injun hoss!" And the' "steal Injun hoss!" iterated and reiterated by a dozen voices, and always with the most iracund emphasis, enabled Roland to form a proper conception of the sense in which his enemies held that offence, as well as of the great merits and wide-spread fame of his new ally, whose mere voice had thrown the red-men into such a ferment.

But it was not with words alone they vented their displeasure. Rifle-shots and execrations were discharged together against the notorious enemy of their pinfolds; who nothing daunted, and nothing loath, let fly his own "speechifier," as he denominated his rifle, in return, accompanying the salute with divers yells and maledictions, in which latter he showed himself, to say the truth, infinitely superior to his antagonists. He would even, so great and fervent was his desire to fight the battles of his benefactress to advantage, have retained his exposed stand on the pile of ruins, daring every bullet, had not Roland dragged him down by main force, and compelled him to seek a shelter like the rest, from which, however, he carried on the war, loading and firing his piece with wonderful rapidity, and yelling and roaring all the time with triumphant fury, as if reckoning upon every shot to bring down an enemy.

It was not many minutes, however, before Roland began to fear that the fatality which had marked all his relations with the intrepid horse-thief, had not yet lost its influence, and that Stackpole's present assistance was anything but advantageous to his cause. It seemed, indeed, as if the savages had been driven to increased rage by the discovery of his presence; and that the hope of capturing *him*, the most daring and inveterate of all the hungerers after Indian horseflesh, and requiting his manifold transgressions on the spot, had infused into them new spirit and fiercer determination. Their fire became more vigorous, their shouts more wild and ferocious: those who had effected a lodgment among the ruins crept higher, while others appeared dealing their shots from other quarters close at hand; and in fine, the situation of his little party became so precarious, that Roland, apprehending every moment a general assault, and despairing of being again able to repel it, drew them secretly off from the ruin, which he abandoned entirely, and took refuge among the rocks at the head of the ravine.

It was then,—while unconscious of the sudden evacuation of the hovel, but not doubting they had driven the defenders into its interior, tho enemy poured in half a dozen or more volleys, as preliminaries to the assault which the soldier apprehended,—that he turned to the unlucky Ralph; and arresting him as he was about to fire upon the foe from his new cover, demanded, with much agitation, if it were not possible to transport the hapless females in the little canoe, which his mind had often reverted to as a probable means of escape, to a place of safety.

"'Tarnal death to me," said Ralph, "thar's a boiling-pot above and a boiling pot below; but ar'n't I the crittur to shake old Salt by the fo'-paw? Can take anngelliferous down 'ar a shoot that war ever seed!"

"And why, in Heaven's name," cried the Virginian, "did you not say so before, and relieve her from this horrible situation?"

"'Tarnal death to me, ar'nt I to do her fighting first?" demanded the honest Ralph. "Jist let's have another crack at the villians, jist for madam's satisfaction; and then, sodger, if you're for taking the shoot, I'm jist the salmon to show you the way. But I say, sodger, I won't lie," he continued, finding Roland was bent upon instant escape, while the savages were yet unaware of their flight from the hovel,—"I wont lie, sodger;—thar's rather a small trough to hold madam and the gal, and me and you and the nigger and the white man" (for Stackpole was already acquainted with the number of the party); "and as for the hosses, 'twill be all crucifixion to get 'em through old Salt's fingers."

"Think not of horses, nor of us," said Roland. "Save but the women, and it will be enough. For the rest of us, we will do our best. We can keep the hollow till we are relieved; for, if Nathan be alive, relief must be now on the way." And in a few hurried words, he acquainted Stackpole with his having despatched the man of peace to seek assistance.

"Thar's no trusting the crittur, Tiger Nathan," said Ralph; "though at a close hug, a squeeze on the small ribs, or a kick up of heels, he's all splendiferous. Afore you see his ugly pictur' ag'in, 'tarnal death to me, strannger, you'll be devoured; the red niggurs thar won't make two bites at you. No, sodger,—if we run, we run,—thar's the principle; we takes the water, the whole herd together, niggurs, hosses, and all, particularly the hosses; for, 'tarnal death to me, it's ag'in my conscience to leave so much as a hoof. And so, sodger, if you conscientiously thinks thar has been walloping enough done on both sides, I'm jist the man to help you all out of the bobbery;—though, cuss me, you might as well have cut me out of the beech without so much hard axing!"

These words of the worthy horse-thief, uttered as hurriedly as his own, but far more coolly, animated the spirits of the young soldier with double hope; and taking advantage of the busy intentness with which the enemy still poured their fire into the ruin, he despatched Ralph down the ravine, to prepare the canoe for the women, while he himself summoned Dodge and Emperor to make an effort for their own deliverance.

CHAPTER XVII

The roar of the river, alternating with peals of thunder, which were now loud and frequent, awake many an anxious pang in Roland's bosom, as he lifted his half-unconscious kinswoman from the earth, and bore her to the canoe; but his anxiety was much more increased when he came to survey the little vessel itself, which was scarce twelve feet in length, and seemed ill-fitted to sustain the weight of even half the party. It was, besides, of the clumsiest and worst possible figure, a mere log, in fact, roughly hollowed out, without any attempt having been made to point its extremities; so that it looked less like a canoe than an ox-trough; which latter purpose it was perhaps designed chiefly to serve, and intended to be used for the former only when an occasional rise of the waters might make a canoe necessary to the convenience of the maker. Such a vessel, managed by a skilful hand, might indeed bear the two females, with honest Ralph, through the foaming rapids below; but Roland felt, that to burden it with others would be to insure the destruction of all. He resolved, therefore, that no other should enter it; and, having deposited Telie Doe in it by the side of Edith, he directed Dodge and Emperor to mount their horses, and trust to their strength and courage for a safe escape. To Emperor, whatever distaste he might have for the adventure, this was an order, like all others, to be obeyed without murmuring; and, fortunately, Pardon Dodge's humanity, or his discretion, was so strongly fortified by his confidence in the swimming virtues of his steed, that he very readily agreed to try his fortune on horseback.

"Anything to git round them everlasting varmint,—though it a'n't no sich great circumstance to fight 'em neither, where one's a kinder got one's hand in," he cried, with quite a joyous voice; and added, as if to encourage the others,—"it's my idea, that, if such an old crazy boat can swim the river, a hoss can do it a mortal heap better."

"'Tarnal death to me," said Ralph Stackpole, "them's got the grit that'll go down old Salt on horseback! But it's all for the good of anngelliferous madam: and so, if thar's any hard rubbing, or drowning, or anything-of that synommous natur', to happen, it ar'n't a thing to be holped no how. But hand in the guns and speechifiers, and make ready for a go; for, 'tarnal death to me, the abbrygynes ar' making a rush for the cabin!"

There was indeed little time left for deliberation. While Ralph was yet speaking, a dozen or more flaming brands were suddenly seen flung into the air, as if against the broken roof of the cabin, through which they fell into the interior; and, with a tremendous whoop, the savages, thus lighting the way to the assault, rushed against their fancied prey. The next moment, there was heard a yell of disappointed rage and wonder, followed by a rush of men into the ravine.

"Now, sodger," cried Ralph, "stick close to the trough; and if you ever seed etarnity at midnight, you'll see a small sample now!"

With that, he pushed the canoe into the stream, and Roland, urging his terrified steed with voice and spur, and leading his cousin's equally alarmed palfrey, leaped in after him, calling to Dodge and Emperor to follow. But how they followed, or whether they followed at all, it was not easy at that moment to determine; for a bright flash of lightning, glaring over the river, vanished suddenly, leaving all in double darkness, and the impetuous rush of the current whirled him he knew not whither; while the crash of the thunder that followed, prevented his hearing any other noise, save the increasing and never absent roar of the waters. Another flash illuminated the scene, and during its short-lived radiance he perceived himself flying, as it almost seemed, through the water, borne along by a furious current betwixt what appeared to him two lofty walls of crag and forest, towards those obstructions in the channel, which, in times of flood, converted the whole river into a boiling caldron. They were masses of rock, among which had lodged rafts of drift timber, forming a dam or barrier on either side of the river, from which the descending floods were whirled into a central channel, ample enough in the dry season to discharge the waters in quiet, but through which they were now driven with all the hurry and rage of a torrent. The scene, viewed in the momentary glare of the lightning, was indeed terrific: the dark and rugged walls on either side, the ramparts of timber of every shape and size, from the little willow sapling to the full-grown sycamore piled high above the rocks, and the rushing gulf betwixt them, made up a spectacle sufficient to appal the stoutest heart; and Roland gasped for breath, as he beheld the little canoe whirl into the narrow chasm, and then vanish, even before the light was over, as if swallowed up in its boiling vortex.

But there was little time for fear or conjecture. He cast the rein of the palfrey from his hand, directed Briareus's head towards the abyss, and the next moment, sweeping in darkness and with the speed of an arrow, betwixt the barriers, he felt his charger swimming beneath him in comparatively tranquil waters. Another flash illumined hill and river, and he beheld the little canoe dancing along in safety, scarce fifty yards in advance, with

Stackpole waving the tattered fragments of his hat aloft, and yelling out a note of triumph. But the lusty hurrah was unheard by the soldier. A more dreadful sound came to his ears from behind, in a shriek that seemed uttered by the combined voices of men and horses, and was heard even above the din of the torrent. But it was as momentary as dreadful, and if a cry of agony, it was of agony that was soon over. Its fatal cause was soon exhibited, when Roland, awakened by the sound from the trance, which, during the brief moment of his passage through the abyss, had chained his faculties, turned, by a violent jerk, the head of his charger up the stream, in the instinctive effort to render assistance to his less fortunate followers. A fainter flash than before played upon the waters, and he beheld two or three dark masses, like the bodies of horses, hurried by among the waves, whilst another, of lesser bulk and human form, suddenly rose from the depth of the stream at his side. This he instantly grasped in his hand, and dragged half across his saddle-bow, when a broken, strangling exclamation, "Lorra-g-g-gor!" made him aware that he had saved the life of the faithful Emperor. "Clutch fast to the saddle," he cried; and the negro obeying with another ejaculation, the soldier turned Briareus again down the stream, to look for the canoe. But almost immediately his charger struck the ground; and Roland, to his inexpressible joy, found himself landed upon a projecting bank, on which the current had already swept the canoe, with its precious freight, unharmed.

"If that ar'n't equal to coming down a strick of lightning," cried Roaring Ralph, as he helped the soldier from the water, "thar's no legs to a jumping bull-frog! Smash away, old bait!" he continued, apostrophising with great exultation and self-admiration the river whose terrors he had thus so successfully defied; "ar'n't I the gentleman for you? Roar as much as you please;—when it comes to fighting for anngelliferous madam, I can lick you, old Salt, 'tarnal death to me! And so, anngelliferous madam, don't you car' a copper for the old crittur; for thar's more in his bark than his bite. And as for the abbregynes, if I've fout 'em enough for your satisfaction, we'll just say good-bye to 'em, and leave 'em to take the scalp off old Salt."

The consolation thus offered by the worthy captain of horse-thieves was lost upon Edith, who, locked in the arms of her kinsman, and sensible of her escape from the horrid danger that had so long surrounded her, sensible also of the peril from which he had just been released, wept her terrors away upon his breast, and for a moment almost forgot that her sufferings were not yet over.

It was only for an instant that the young soldier indulged his joy. He breathed a few words of comfort and encouragement, and then turned to inquire after Dodge, whose gallant hearing in the hour of danger had conquered the disgust he at first felt at his cowardice, and won upon his gratitude and respect. But the Yankee appeared not, and the loud calls Roland made for him were echoed only by the hoarse roar from the barriers, now left far behind, and the thunder that yet pealed through the sky. Nor could Emperor, when restored a little to his wits, which had been greatly disturbed by his own perils in the river, give any satisfactory account of his fate. He could only remember that the current had borne himself against the logs, under which he had been swept, and whirled he knew not whither until he found himself in the arms of his master; and Dodge, who had rushed before him into the flood, he supposed, had met a similar fate, but without the happy termination that marked his own.

That the Yankee had indeed found his death among the roaring waters, Roland could well believe, the wonder only being how the rest had escaped in safety. Of the five horses, three only had reached the bank, Briareus and the palfrey, which had fortunately followed Roland down the middle of the chasm, and the horse of the unlucky Pardon. The others had been either drowned among the logs, or swept down the stream.

A few moments sufficed to acquaint Roland with several losses; but he took little time to lament them. The deliverance of his party was not yet wholly effected, and every moment was to be improved, to put it, before daylight, beyond the reach of pursuit. The captain of horse-thieves avouched himself able to lead the way from the wilderness, to conduct the travellers to a safe ford below, and thence through the woods, to the rendezvous of the emigrants.

"Let it be anywhere," said Roland, "where there is safety; and let us not delay a moment longer. Our remaining here can avail nothing to poor Dodge."

With these words, he assisted his kinswoman upon her palfrey, placed Telie Doe upon the horse of the unfortunate Yankee, and giving up his own Briareus to the exhausted negro, prepared to resume his ill-starred journey on foot. Then, taking post on the rear, he gave the signal to his new guide; and once more the travellers were buried in the intricacies of the forest.

CHAPTER XVIII

It was at a critical period when the travellers effected their escape from the scene of their late sufferings. The morning was already drawing nigh, and might, but for the heavy clouds that prolonged the night of terror, have been seen shooting its first streaks through the eastern skies. Another half hour, if for that half hour they could have maintained their position in the ravine, would have seen them exposed in all their helplessness to the gaze, and to the fire of the determined foe. It became them to improve the few remaining moments of darkness, and to make such exertions as might get them, before dawn, beyond the reach of discovery or pursuit.

Exertions were, accordingly, made; and, although man and horse were alike exhausted, and the thick brakes and oozy swamps through which Roaring Ralph led the way, opposed a thousand obstructions to rapid motion, they had left the fatal ruin at least two miles behind them, or so honest Stackpole averred, when the day at last broke over the forest. To add to the satisfaction of the fugitives, it broke in unexpected splendour. The clouds parted, and, as the floating masses rolled lazily away before a pleasant morning breeze, they were seen lighted up and tinted with a thousand glorious dyes of sunshine.

The appearance of the great luminary was hailed with joy, as the omen of a happier fate than had been heralded by the clouds and storms of evening. Smiles began to beam from the haggard and care-worn visages of the travellers; the very horses seemed to feel the inspiring influence of the change; and as for Roaring Ralph, the sight of his beautiful benefactress recovering her good looks, and the exulting consciousness that it was *his* hand which had snatched her from misery and death, produced such a fever of delight in his brain as was only to be allayed by the most extravagant expressions and actions. He assured her a dozen times over, "he was her dog and her slave, and vowed he would hunt her so many Injun scalps, and steal her such a 'tarnal chance of Shawnee hosses, thar shorld'nt be a gal in all Kentucky should come up to her for stock and glory:" and, finally, not content with making a thousand other promises of an equally extravagant character, and swearing, that, "if she axed it, he would go down on his knees and say his prayers to her," he offered, as soon as he had carried her safely across the river, to "take the backtrack, and lick, single-handed, all the

Injun abbregynes that might be following." Indeed, to such a pitch did his enthusiasm run, that, not knowing how otherwise to give vent to his over-charged feelings, he suddenly turned upon his heel, and shaking his fist in the direction whence he had come, as if against the enemy who had caused his benefactress so much distress, he pronounced a formal and emphatic curse upon their whole race, "from the head-chief to the commoner, from the whisky-soaking warrior down to the pan-licking squall-a-baby," all of whom he anathematised with as much originality as fervour of expression; after which, he proceeded, with more sedateness, to resume his post at the head of the travellers, and conduct them onwards on their way.

Another hour was now consumed in diving amid cane-brakes and swamps, to which Roaring Ralph evinced a decidedly greater partiality than to the open forest, in which the travellers had found themselves at the dawn; and in this he seemed to show somewhat more of judgment and discretion than would have been argued from his hair-brained conversation; for the danger of stumbling upon scouting Indians, of which the country now seemed so full, was manifestly greater in the open woods than in the dark and almost unfrequented cane-brakes: and the worthy horse-thief, with all his apparent love of fight, was not at all anxious that the angel of his worship should be alarmed or endangered, while entrusted to his zealous safe-keeping.

But it happened in this case, as it has happened with better and wiser men, that Stackpole's cunning over-reached itself, as was fully shown in the event; and it would have been happier for himself and all if his discretion, instead of plunging him among difficult and almost impassable bogs, where a precious hour was wasted in effecting a mere temporary security and concealment from observation, had taught him the necessity of pushing onwards with all possible speed, so as to leave pursuers, if pursuit should be attempted, far behind. At the expiration of that hour, so injudiciously wasted, the fugitives issued from the brake, and stepping into a narrow path worn by the feet of bisons, among stunted shrubs and parched grasses, along the face of a lime-stone bed, sparingly scattered over with a similar barren growth, began to wind their way downward into a hollow vale, in which they could hear the murmurs, and perceive the glimmering waters of the river over which they seemed never destined to pass.

"*Thar*', 'tarnal death to me!" roared Ralph, pointing downwards with triumph, "arn't that old Salt now, looking as sweet and liquorish as a whole trough-full of sugar-tree? We'll just take a dip at him, anngelliferous madam, jist to wash the mud off our shoes; and then, 'tarnal death to me, farewell to old Salt, and the abbregynes together—cock-a-doodle-doo!"

With this comfortable assurance, and such encouragement as he could convey in the lustiest gallicantation ever fetched from lungs of man or fowl, the worthy Stackpole, who had slackened his steps, but without stopping while he spoke, turned his face again to the descent; when—as if that war-cry had conjured up enemies from the very air,—a rifle bullet, shot from a bush not six yards off, suddenly whizzed through his hair, scattering a handful of it to the winds; and while a dozen or more were, at the same instant, poured upon other members of the unfortunate party, fourteen or fifteen savages rushed out from their concealment among the grass and bushes, three of whom seized upon the rein of the unhappy Edith, while twice as many sprang upon Captain Forrester, and, before he could raise an arm in defence, bore him to the earth, a victim or a prisoner.

So much the astounded horse-thief saw with his own eyes; but before he could make good any of the numberless promises he had volunteered, during the morning journey, of killing and eating the whole family of North American Indians, or exemplify the unutterable gratitude and devotion he had as often professed to the fair Virginian, four brawny barbarians, one of them rising at his side and from the very bush whence the bullet had been discharged at his head, rushed against him, flourishing their guns and knives, and yelling with transport, "Got you *now*, Cappin Stackpole, steal-hoss! No go steal no hoss no more! roast on great big fire!"

"'Tarnal death to me!" roared Stackpole, forgetting everything else in the instinct of self-preservation; and firing his piece at the nearest enemy, he suddenly leaped from the path into the bushes on its lower side, where was a precipitous descent, down which he went rolling and crashing with a velocity almost equal to that of the bullets that were sent after him. Three of the four assailants immediately darted after in pursuit, and their shouts growing fainter and fainter as they descended, were mingled with the loud yell of victory, now uttered by a dozen savage voices from the hill-side.

It was a victory, indeed, in every sense, complete, almost bloodless, as it seemed, to the assailants, and effected at a moment when the hopes of the travellers were at the highest: and so sudden was the attack, so instantaneous the change from freedom to captivity, so like the juggling transition of a dream the whole catastrophe, that Forrester, although overthrown and bleeding from two several wounds received at the first fire, and wholly in the power of his enemies, who flourished their knives and axes in his face, yelling with exultation, could scarce appreciate his situation, or understand what dreadful misadventure had happened, until his eye, wandering among the dusky arms that grappled him, fell first upon the body of the negro Emperor, hard by, gored by numberless wounds, and trampled by the feet of his slayers, and then upon the apparition, a thousand times more dismal to his eyes, of his kinswoman snatched from her horse and struggling in the arms of her savage captors. The frenzy with which he was seized at this lamentable sight endowed him with a giant's strength; but it was exerted in vain to free himself from his enemies, all of whom seemed to experience a barbarous delight at his struggles, some encouraging him, with loud laughter and in broken English, to continue them, while others taunted and scolded at him more like shrewish squaws than valiant warriors, assuring him that they were great Shawnee fighting-men, and he a little Long-knife dog, entirely beneath their notice: which expressions, though at variance with all his preconceived notions of the stern gravity of the Indian character, and rather indicative of a roughly jocose than a darkly ferocious spirit, did not prevent their taking the surest means to quiet his exertions and secure their prize, by tying his hands behind him with a thong of buffalo hide, drawn so tight as to inflict the most excruciating pain. But pain of body was then, and for many moments after, lost in agony of mind, which could he conceived only by him who, like the young soldier, has been doomed, once in his life, to see a tender female, the nearest and dearest object of his affections, in the hands of enemies, the most heartless, merciless, and brutal of all the races of men. He saw her pale visage convulsed with terror and despair,—he beheld her arms stretched towards him, as if beseeching the help he no longer had the power to render,—and expected every instant the fall of the hatchet, or the flash of the knife, that was to pour her blood upon the earth before him. He would have called upon the wretches around for pity, but his tongue clove to his mouth, his brain spun round; and such became the intensity of his feelings, that he was suddenly bereft of sense, and fell like a dead man to the earth, where he lay for a time, ignorant of all events passing around, ignorant also of the duration of his insensibility.

CHAPTER XIX

When the soldier recovered his senses, it was to wonder again at the change that had come over the scene. The loud yells, the bitter taunts, the mocking laughs, were heard no more; and nothing broke the silence of the wilderness save the stir of the leaf in the breeze, and the ripple of the river against its pebbly banks below. He glanced a moment from the bush in which he was lying, in search of the barbarians who had lately covered the slope of the hill, but all had vanished; captor and captive had alike fled; and the sparrow twittering among the stunted bushes, and the grasshopper singing in the grass, were the only living objects to be seen. The thong was still upon his wrists, and as he felt it rankling in his flesh, he almost believed that his savage captors, with a refinement in cruelty the more remarkable as it must have robbed them of the sight of his dying agonies, had left him thus bound and wounded, to perish miserably in the wilderness alone.

This suspicion was, however, soon driven from his mind; for making an effort to rise to his feet, he found himself suddenly withheld by a powerful grasp, while a guttural voice muttered in his ear from behind, with accents half angry, half exultant,—"Long-knife no move;—see how Piankeshaw kill Long-knife's brudders!—Piankeshaw great fighting-man!" He turned his face with difficulty, and saw, crouching among the leaves behind him, a grim old warrior plentifully bedaubed over head and breast with the scarlet clay of his native Wabash, his dark shining eyes bent now upon his rifle which he held extended over Roland's body, now turned upon Roland himself, whom he seemed to watch over with a miser's, or a wild-cat's, affection, and now wandering away up the stony path along the hill-side, as if in expectation of the coming of an object dearer even than rifle or captive to his imagination.

In the confused and distracted state of his mind, Roland was as little able to understand the expressions of the warrior as to account for the disappearance of his murderous associates; and he would have marvelled for what purpose he was thus concealed, among the bushes with his grim companion, had not his whole soul been too busily and painfully occupied with the thoughts of his vanished Edith. He strove to ask the wild barbarian of her fate, but the latter motioned him fiercely to keep silence; and the motion and the savage look that accompanied it being disregarded, the Indian drew a long knife from his belt, and pressing the point on Roland's throat, muttered too sternly and emphatically to be misconceived,—"Long-knife speak, Long-knife die! Piankeshaw fight Long-knife's brudders—Piankeshaw great fighting-man!" from which all that Roland could understand was that there was mischief of some kind still in the wind, and that he was commanded to preserve silence on the peril of his life. What that mischief could be he was unable to divine; but he was not kept long in ignorance.

As he lay upon the ground, his cheek pillowed upon it stone which accident, or perhaps the humanity of the old warrior, had placed under his head, he could distinguish a hollow, pattering, distant sound, in which, at first mistaken for the murmuring of the river over some rocky ledge, and then for the clatter of wild beasts approaching over the rocky hill, his practised ear soon detected the trampling of a body of horse, evidently winding their way along the stony road which had conducted him to captivity, and from which he was but a few paces removed. His heart thrilled within him. Was it, could it be, a band of gallant Kentuckians, in pursuit of the bold marauders, whose presence in the neighbourhood of the settlements had been already made known? or could they be (the thrill of expectation grew to transport, as he thought it) his fellow emigrants, summoned by the faithful Nathan to his assistance, and now straining every nerve to overtake the savages, whom they had tracked from the deserted ruin? He could now account for the disappearance of his captors, and the deathlike silence that surrounded him. Too vigilant to be taken at unawares, and perhaps long since apprised of the coming of the band, the Indians had resumed their hiding-places in the grass and among the bushes, preparing for the new-comers an ambuscade similar to that they had so successfully practised against Roland's unfortunate party. "Let them hide as they will, detestable miscreants," he uttered to himself with feelings of vindictive triumph; "they will not, this time, have frightened women and a handful of dispirited fugitives to deal with."

With these feelings burning in his bosom, he made an effort to turn his face towards the top of the hill, that he might catch the first sight of the friendly band, and glut his eyes with the view of the anticipated speedy discomfiture and destruction of his enemies. In this effort he received unexpected aid from the old warrior, who, perceiving his intention, pulled him round with his own hands, telling him, with the grim complacency of one who desired a witness to his bravery, "Now, you hold still, you see,—you see Piankeshaw old Injun,—you see Piankeshaw kill man, take scalp, kill all Long-knife:—debbil great fighting-man, old Piankeshaw!"

which self-admiring assurance, repeated for the third time, the warrior pronounced with extreme earnestness and emphasis.

It was now that Roland could distinctly perceive the nature of the ground on which his captors had formed their ambush. The hill along whose side the bison path went winding down to the river with an easy descent, was nearly bare of trees, its barren soil affording nourishment only for a coarse grass, enamelled with asters and other brilliant flowers, and for a few stunted cedar-bushes, scattered here and there; while, in many places, the naked rock, broken into ledges and gullies, the beds of occasional brooks, was seen gleaming gray and desolate in the sunshine. Its surface being thus broken, was unfit for the operations of cavalry; and the savages being posted, as Roland judged from the position of the old Piankeshaw, midway along the descent, where were but few trees of sufficient magnitude to serve as a cover to assailants, while they themselves were concealed behind rocks and bushes, there was little doubt they could inflict loss upon an advancing body of footmen of equal numbers, and perhaps repel them altogether. But, Roland, now impressed with the belief that the approaching horsemen, whose trampling grew heavier each moment, as if they were advancing at a full trot, composed the flower of his own band, had but little fear of the result of a contest. He did not doubt they would outnumber the savages, who, he thought, could not muster more than fifteen or sixteen guns; and coming from a Station, which he had been taught to believe was of no mean strength it was more than probable their numbers had been reinforced by a detachment from its garrison.

Such were his thoughts, such were his hopes, as the party drew yet nigher, the sound of their hoofs clattering at last on the ridge of the hill; but his disappointment may be imagined, when, as they burst at last on his sight, emerging from the woods above, the gallant party dwindled suddenly into a troop of young men, only eleven in number, who rattled along the path in greater haste than order, as if dreaming of anything in the world but the proximity of an enemy. The leader he recognised at a glance by his tall figure, as Tom Bruce the younger, whose feats of Regulation the previous day had produced a strong though indirect influence on his own fortunes; and the ten lusty youths who followed his heels, he doubted not, made up the limbs and body of that inquisitorial court which, under him as its head, had dispensed so liberal an allowance of border law to honest Ralph Stackpole. That they were now travelling on duty of a similar kind, he was strongly inclined to believe; but the appearance of their horses, covered with foam, as if they had ridden far and fast, their rifles held in readiness in both hands, as if in momentary expectation of being called on to use them, with an occasional gesture from their youthful leader, who seemed to encourage them to greater speed, convinced him they were bent upon more serious business, perhaps in pursuit of the Indians, with whose marauding visitation some accident had made them acquainted.

The smallness of the force, and its almost entire incompetence to yield him any relief, filled the soldier's breast with despair; but, hopeless as he was, he could not see the gallant young men rushing blindly among the savages, each of whose rifles was already selecting its victim, without making an effort to apprize them of their danger. Forgetting, therefore, his own situation, or generously disregarding it, he summoned all his strength, and, as they began to descend the hill, shouted aloud, "Beware the ambush!—Halt"—But before the words were all uttered, he was grasped by the throat with strangling violence, and the old warrior, whose left hand thus choked his utterance, drew his knife a second time, with the other, and seemed for an instant as if he would have plunged it into the soldier's bosom.

But the cry had not been made in vain, and although, from the distance, the words had not been distinguished by the young Kentuckians, enough was heard to convince them the enemy was nigh at hand. They came to an immediate halt, and Roland, whose throat was still held by the warrior and his bosom threatened by the vengeful knife, but whose eyes neither the anguish of suffocation nor the fear of instant death could draw from the little band, saw them leap from their horses, which were given in charge of one of the number, who immediately retired beyond the brow of the hill; while Tom Bruce, a worthy scion of a warlike stock, brandishing his rifle in one hand, and with the other pointing his nine remaining followers down the road, cried, in tones so manly that they came to Roland's ear,—"Now, boys, the women's down *thar*, and the red skins with them! Show fight, for the honour of Kentuck and the love of woman. Every man to his bush, and every bullet to its Injun! Bring the brutes out of their cover!"

This speech, short and homely as it was, was answered by a loud shout from the nine young men, who began to divide, with the intention of obeying its simple final instructions; when the Indians, seeing the design, unwilling to forego the advantage of the first open shot and perhaps hoping by a weak fire to mask their strength, and decoy the young Kentuckians into closer quarters, let fly a volley of six or seven guns from the bushes near to where Roland lay, but without doing much mischief, or even deceiving the young men, as was expected.

"Thar they go, the brutes!" roared Tom Bruce, adding as he sprang with his followers among the bushes, "show 'em your noses, and keep a good squint over your elbows."

"Long-knife big fool,—Piankeshaw eat him up!" cried, the old warrior, now releasing the soldier's throat from durance, but speaking with tones of ire and indignation: "shall see how great Injun fighting-man eat up white man!"

With these words, leaving Roland to endure his bonds, and solace himself as he might, he crept away into the long grass, and was soon entirely lost to sight.

The combat that now ensued was one so different in most of its characteristics from all that Roland had ever before witnessed, that he watched its progress, notwithstanding the tortures of his bonds and the fever of his mind, with an interest even apart from that which he necessarily felt in it, as one whose all of happiness or misery depended upon the issue. In all conflicts in which he had been engaged, the adverse ranks were arrayed face to face, looking upon each other as they fought; but here no man saw his enemy, both parties concealing themselves so effectually in the grass and among the rocks and shrubs, that there was nothing to indicate even their existence, save the occasional discharge of a rifle, and the wreath of white smoke curling up from it into the air. In the battles of regular soldiers, too, men fought in masses, the chief strength of either party arising from the support which individuals thus gave to one another, each deriving additional courage and confidence from the presence of his fellows. Here, on the contrary, it seemed the first object of each individual, whether American or Indian, to separate himself as far from his friends as possible, seeking his own enemies, trusting to his own resources, carrying on the war on his own foundation,—in short, like the enthusiastic Jerseyman, who, without belonging to either side, was found at the battle of Monmouth, peppering away from a fence, at whatever he fancied a foeman—"fighting on his own *hook*" entirely.

It did not seem to Roland as if a battle fought upon such principles, could result in any great injury to either party. But he forget, or rather he was ignorant, that the separation of the combatants, while effecting the best protection not merely to any one individual, but to all his comrades, who must have been endangered, if near him; by every bullet aimed at himself, did not imply either fear or hesitation on his part, whose object, next to that mentioned, was to avoid the shots of the many, while seeking out and approaching a single antagonist, whom he was ever ready singly to encounter.

And thus it happened, that, while Roland deemed the antagonists were manoeuvring over the hill side, dragging themselves from bush to bush and rock to rock, to no profitable purpose, they were actually creeping nigher and nigher to each other every moment, the savages crawling onwards with the exultation of men who felt their superior strength, and the Kentuckians advancing with equal alacrity, as if ignorant of, or bravely indifferent to their inferiority.

It was not a long time, indeed, before the Virginian began to have a better opinion of the intentions of the respective parties; for, by and by, the shots, which were at first fired very irregularly and at long intervals, became more frequent, and, as it seemed, more serious, and an occasional whoop from an Indian, or a wild shout from a Kentuckian, showed that the excitement of actual conflict was beginning to be felt on either side. At the same time, he became sensible, from the direction of the firing, that both parties had gradually extended themselves in a line, reaching, notwithstanding the smallness of their numbers, from the crest of the hill on the one hand, to the borders of the river on the other, and thus perceived that the gallant Regulators, however ignorant of the science of war, and borne by impetuous tempers into a contest with a more numerous foe, were not in the mood to be taken either on the flank or rear, but were resolved, in true military style, to keep their antagonists before them.

In this manner, the conflict continued for many minutes, the combatants approaching nearer and nearer, the excitement waxing fiercer every instant, until shots were incessantly exchanged, and, as it seemed, with occasional effect; for the yells, which grew louder and more frequent on both sides, were sometimes mingled with cries of pain on the one hand, and shouts of triumph on the other; during all which time, nothing whatever was seen of the combatants, at least by Roland, whose mental agonies were not a little increased by his being a compelled spectator, if such he could be called, of a battle in which he was so deeply interested, without possessing the power to mingle in it, or strike a single blow on his own behalf. His fears of the event had been, from the first, much stronger than his hopes. Aware of the greatly superior strength of the savages, he did not doubt that the moment would come when he should see them rush in a body upon the Kentuckians, and overwhelm them with numbers. But that was a measure into which nothing but an uncommon pitch of fury could have driven the barbarians: for with marksmen like those opposed to them, who needed but a glance of an enemy to insure his instant destruction, the first spring from the grass would have been the signal of death to all who attempted it, leaving the survivors, no longer superior in numbers, to decide the contest with men who were, individually, in courage, strength, and skill, at least their equals. Indeed, a proof of the extreme folly of such a course on the part of the Indians was soon shown when the Regulators, fighting their way onwards as if wholly regardless of the superior numbers of the foe, had advanced so nigh the latter as to command (which from occupying the highest ground, they were better able to do) the hiding-places of some of their opponents. Three young warriors, yielding to their fury, ashamed perhaps of being thus bearded by a weaker foe, or inflamed with the hope of securing a scalp of one young Kentuckian who had crept dangerously nigh, suddenly sprung from their lairs, and guided by the smoke of the rifle which he had just discharged, rushed towards the spot, yelling with vindictive exultation. They were the first combatants Roland had yet seen actually engaged in the conflict; and he noted their appearance and act of daring with a sinking heart, as the prelude to a charge from the whole body of Indians upon the devoted Kentuckians. But scarce were their brown bodies seen to rise from the grass, before three rifles were fired from as many points on the hill-side, following each other in such rapid succession that the ear could scarce distinguish the different explosions, each of them telling with fatal effect upon the rash warriors, two of whom fell dead on the spot, while the third and foremost, uttering a faint whoop of defiance and making an effort to throw the hatchet he held in his hand, suddenly staggered and fell in like manner to the earth.

Loud and bold was the shout of the Kentuckians at this happy stroke of success, and laughs of scorn were mingled with their warlike hurrahs, as they prepared to improve the advantage so fortunately gained. Loudest of all in both laugh and hurrah was the young Tom Bruce, whose voice was heard, scarce sixty yards off, roaring, "Hurrah for old Kentuck! Try 'em agin, boys, give it to 'em handsome once more! and then, boys, a rush for the women!"

The sound of a friendly voice at so short a distance fired Roland's heart with hope, and he shouted aloud himself, no Indian seeming nigh, for assistance. But his voice was lost in a tempest of yells, the utterance of grief and fury, with which the fall of their three companions had filled the breasts of the savages. The effect of this fatal loss, stirring up their passions to a sudden frenzy, was to goad them into the very step which they had hitherto so wisely avoided. All sprang from the ground as with one consent, and regardless of the exposure and danger, dashed, with hideous shouts, against the Kentuckians. But the volley with which they were received, each Kentuckian selecting his man, and firing with unerring and merciless aim, damped their short-lived ardour; and quickly dropping again among the grass and bushes, they were fain to continue the combat as they had begun it, in a way which, if it produced less injury to their antagonists, was conducive of greater safety to themselves.

The firing was now hot and incessant on both sides, but particularly on the part of the Regulators, who, inspired by success, but still prudently avoiding all unnecessary exposure of their persons, pressed their enemies with a spirit from which Roland now for the first time drew the happiest auguries. Their stirring hurrahs bespoke a confidence in the result of the fray, infinitely cheering to his spirits; and he forgot his tortures, which from the many frantic struggles he had made to force the thong from his wrists, drawing it at each still further into his flesh, were now almost insupportable, when, amid the din of firing and yelling, he heard Tom Bruce cry aloud to his companions, "Now, boys! one more crack, and then for rifle-butt, knife, and hatchet!" It seemed, indeed, as if the heavy losses the Indians had sustained, had turned the scale of battle entirely in favour of the Kentuckians. It was evident even to Roland, that the former, although yelling and shouting with as much apparent vigour as ever, were gradually giving ground before the latter, and retreating towards their former lairs; while he could as clearly perceive, from Bruce's expressions, that the intrepid Kentuckian was actually preparing to execute the very measure that had caused such loss to his enemies, and which, being thus resolved on, showed his confidence of victory. "Ready, boys!" he heard him shout again, and even nigher than before;—"take the shoot with full pieces, and let the skirmudgeons have it handsome!"

At that conjuncture, and just when Forrester caught his breath with intense and devouring expectation, an incident occurred which entirely changed the face of affairs, and snatched the victory from the hands of the Kentuckians. The gallant Bruce, thus calling upon his followers to prepare for the charge, had scarce uttered the words recorded, before a voice, lustier even than his own, bellowed from a bush immediately on his rear,—"Take it like a butcher's bull-dog, tooth and nail!—knife and skull-splitter, foot and finger, give it to 'em every way,—cock-a-doodle-doo!"

At these words, coming from a quarter and from an ally entirely unexpected, young Bruce looked behind him and beheld, emerging from a hazel bush, through which it had just forced its way, the visage of Roaring Ralph Stackpole, its natural ugliness greatly increased by countless scratches and spots of blood, the result of his leap down the ledge of rocks, when first set upon by the Indians, and his eyes squinting daggers and ratsbane, especially while he was giving utterance to that gallinaceous slogan with which he was wont to express his appetite for conflict, and with which he now concluded his unceremonious salutation.

The voice and visage were alike familiar to Bruce's senses, and neither was so well fitted to excite alarm as merriment. But, on the present occasion, they produced an effect upon the young Regulator's spirits, and through them upon his actions, the most unfortunate in the world; to understand which it must be recollected that the worthy Kentuckian had, twenty-four hours before, with his own hands, assisted in gibbeting honest Ralph on the beech tree, where, he had every reason to suppose, his lifeless body was hanging at that very moment. His astonishment and horror may therefore be conceived, when, turning in some purturbation at the well known voice, he beheld that identical body, the corse of the executed horse-thief, crawling after him in the grass, "winking, and blinking, and squinting," as he was used afterwards to say, "as if the devil had him by the pastern." It was a spectacle which the nerves of even Tom Bruce could not stand; it did what armed Indians could not do,—it frightened him out of his propriety. Forgetting his situation, his comrades, the savages,—forgetting everything but the fact of his having administered the last correction of Lynch-law to the object of his terror, he sprang on his feet, and roaring, "By the etarnal devil, here's Ralph Stackpole!" he took to his heels, running, in his confusion, right in the direction of the enemy, among whom he would have presently found himself, but for a shot, by which, before he had run six yards, the unfortunate youth was struck to the earth.

The exclamation, and the sight of Ralph himself, who also rose to follow the young leader upon what he deemed a rush against the foe, electrified the whole body of the Regulators, who were immediately thrown into confusion; of which the savages took the same advantage they had taken of Bruce's agitation, firing upon them as they rose, and then rushing upon them to end the fray, before they could recover their wits or spirits. It needed but this, and the fall of their leader, to render the disorder of the young men irretrievable; and, accordingly, in less than a moment they were seen,—all, at least, who were not already disabled,—flying in a panic from the field of battle. It was in vain that the captain of horse-thieves, divining at last the cause of their extraordinary flight, roared out that he was a living man, with nothing of a ghost about him whatever; the panic was universal and irremediable, and nothing remained for him to do but to save his own life as quickly as possible.

"'Tarnal death to me!" he bellowed, turning to fly; but a groan from Bruce fell on his ear. He ran to the side of the fallen youth, and catching him by the hand, exclaimed, "Now for the best leg, Tom, and a rush up hill to the bosses!"

"You *ar'n't* hanged then, after all?" muttered the junior; and then fell back as if unable to rise, adding faintly, "Go;—rat it, I'm done for.—As for the—'l—savages, what I have to say—'l—'l—. But I reckon scalping's not much;—'l—'l—one soon gets used to it!"—

And thus the young Kentuckian, his blood oozing-fast, his mind wandering, his utterance failing, muttered, resigning himself to his fate, ignorant that even Stackpole was no longer at his side to hear him. His fate did indeed seem to be inevitable; for while Stackpole had him by the hand, vainly tugging to get him on his feet, three different Indians were seen running with might and main to quench the last spark of his existence, and to finish Stackpole at the same time. But in that very emergency, the ill-luck which seemed to pursue the horse-thief, and all with whom he was associated, found a change; and destiny sent them doth assistance in a way and by means as unexpected as they were unhoped for. The approach of the savages was noticed by Roaring Ralph, who, not knowing how to save his young executioner, against whom he seemed to entertain no feelings of anger whatever, and whose approaching fate he appeared well disposed to revenge beforehand, clapped his rifle to his shoulder, to make sure of one of the number; when his eye was attracted by the spectacle of a horse rushing up the stony road, neighing furiously, and scattering the Indians from before him. It was the charger Briareus, who had broken from the tree where he had been fastened below, and now came dashing up the hill, distracted with terror, or perhaps burning to mingle in the battle, which he had heard and snuffed from afar. He galloped by the three Indians, who leaped aside in alarm, while Stackpole, taking advantage of the moment, ran up and seized him by the bridle. In another moment, he had assisted the fainting Kentuckian upon the animal's back, leaped up behind him, and was dashing with wild speed up the hill, yelling with triumph, and laughing to scorn the bullets that were shot vainly after.

All this the unhappy Roland beheld, and with a revulsion of feelings, that can only be imagined. He saw, without, indeed, entirely comprehending the cause, the sudden confusion and final flight of the little band, at the moment of anticipated victory. He saw them flying wildly up the hill, in irretrievable rout, followed by the whooping victors, who, with the fugitives, soon vanished entirely from view, leaving the field of battle to the dead and to the thrice miserable captives.

CHAPTER XX

The conflict, though sharp and hot, considering the insignificant number of combatants on either side, was of no very long duration, the whole time, from the appearance of the Kentuckians until the flight, scarce exceeding half an hour. But the pursuit, which the victors immediately commenced, lasted a much longer space; and it was more than an hour,—an age of suspense and suffering to the soldier,—before the sound of whooping on the hill apprised him of their return. They brought with them, as trophies of success two horses, on each of which sat three or four different Indians, as many indeed as could get upon the animal's back, where they clung together, shouting, laughing, and otherwise diverting themselves, more like joyous schoolboys than stern warriors who had just fought and won a bloody, battle.

But this semblance of mirth and good humour lasted no longer than while the savages were riding from the hill-top to the battle-ground, which having reached, they sprang upon the ground, and running wildly about, uttered several cries of the most mournful character, laments, as Roland supposed, over the bodies of their fallen companions.

But if such was their sorrow while looking-upon their own dead, the sight of their lifeless foemen—of whom two, besides the negro Emperor, who had been tomahawked the moment after he fell, had been unhappily left lying on the field—soon changed it into a fiercer passion. The wail became a yell of fury, loud and frightful; and Roland could see them gathering around each corpse, striking the senseless clay repeatedly with their knives and hatchets, each seeking to surpass his fellow in the savage work of mutilation. Such is the red man of America, whom courage, an attribute of all lovers of blood, whether man or animal; misfortune, the destiny, in every quarter of the globe, of every barbarous race, which contact with, a civilised one cannot civilise; and the dreams of poets and sentimentalists have invested with a character wholly incompatible with his condition. Individual virtues may be, and indeed frequently are, found among men in a natural state; but honour, justice, and generosity, as characteristics of the mass, are refinements belonging only to an advanced stage of civilisation.

In the midst of this barbarous display of unsatisfied rage, several of the savages approached the unfortunate Roland, and among them the old Piankeshaw, who, flourishing his hatchet, already clotted with blood, and looking more like a demon than a human being, made an effort to dash out the soldier's brains; in which, however, he was restrained by two younger savages, who caught him in their arms, and muttered somewhat in their own tongue, which mollified his wrath in a moment causing him to burst into a roar of obstreperous laughter. "Ees,—good!" he cried, grinning with apparent benevolence and friendship over the helpless youth: "no hurt Long-knife; take him Piankeshaw nation; make good friend squaw, papoose—all brudders, Long-knife." With these expressions, of the purport of which Roland could understand but little, he left him, retiring with the rest, as Roland soon saw, to conceal or bury the bodies of his slain comrades, which were borne in the arms of the survivors to the bottom of the hill, and there, carefully and in silence, deposited among thickets, or in crannies of the rock.

This ceremony completed, Roland was again visited by his Piankeshaw friend, and the two young warriors who had saved his life before, and were perhaps still fearful of trusting it entirely to the tender mercies of the senior. It was fortunate for Roland that he was thus attended; for the old warrior had no sooner approached him than he began to weep and groan, uttering an harangue, which although addressed, as it seemed, entirely to the prostrate captive, was in the Indian tongue, and therefore wholly wasted upon his ears. Nevertheless, he could perceive that the Indian was relating something that weighed very heavily upon his mind, that he was warming with the subject, and even working himself up into a passion; and, indeed, he had not spoken very long before his visage changed from grief to wrath, and from wrath to the extreme of fury, in which he began to handle his hatchet as on the previous occasion, making every demonstration of the best disposition in the world to bury it in the prisoner's brain. He was again arrested by the young savages, who muttered something in his ear as before; and again the effect was to convert his anger into merriment, the change being effected with a facility that might well have amazed the prisoner, had his despair permitted him to feel any lighter emotion. "Good!" cried the old warrior, as if in reply to what the others had said; "Long-knife go Piankeshaw nation,—make great sight for Piankeshaw!" And so saying, he began to dance about, with many grimaces of visage and contortions of body, that seemed to have a meaning for his comrades, who fetched a whoop of admiration, though entirely inexplicable to the soldier. Then seizing the latter by the arm, and setting him on his feet, the warrior led or dragged him a little way down the hill, to a place on the road-side, where the victors were assembled, deliberating doubtless upon the fate of their prisoners.

They seemed to have suffered a considerable loss in the battle, twelve being the whole number now to be seen; and most of these, judging from the fillets of rags and bundles of green leaves tied about their limbs, had been wounded, two of them to all appearance very severely, if not mortally, for they lay upon the earth a little apart from the rest, in whose motions they seemed to take no interest.

As Roland approached, he looked in vain amid the throng for his kinswoman. Neither she nor Telie Doe was to be seen. But casting his eye wildly around, it fell upon a little grove of trees not many yards off, in which he could perceive the figures of horses, as well as of a tall barbarian, who stood on its edge, as if keeping guard, wrapped, notwithstanding the sultriness of the weather, in a blanket, from chin to foot, while his head was as warmly invested in the ample folds of a huge scarlet handkerchief. He stood like a statue, his arms folded on his breast, and lost under the heavy festoons of the blanket; while his eyes were fastened upon the group of Indians on the road-side, from which they wandered only to glare a moment upon the haggard and despairing visage of the soldier. In that copse, Roland doubted not, the savages had concealed a hopeless and helpless captive, the being for whom he had struggled and suffered so long and so vainly, the maid whose forebodings of evil had been so soon and so dreadfully realised.

In the meanwhile, the Indians on the road-side began the business for which they had assembled, that seemed to be, in the first place, the division of spoils, consisting of the guns, horses, and clothes of the dead, with sundry other articles, which, but for his unhappy condition, Roland would have wondered to behold: for there were among them rolls of cloth and calico, heaps of hawks'-bells and other Indian trinkets, knives, pipes, powder and ball, and other such articles, even to a keg or two of the fire-water, enough to stock an Indian trading-house. These, wherever and however obtained, were distributed equally among the Indians by a man of lighter skin than themselves,—a half-breed, as Roland supposed,—who seemed to exercise some authority among them, though ever deferring in all things to an old Indian of exceedingly fierce and malign aspect, though wasted and withered into the semblance of a consumptive wolf, who sat upon a stone, buried in gloomy abstraction, from which, time by time, he awoke, to direct the dispersion of the valuables, through the hands of his deputy, with exceeding great gravity and state.

The distribution being effected, and evidently to the satisfaction of all present, the savages turned their looks upon the prisoner, eyeing him with mingled triumph and exultation; and the old presiding officer, or chief, as he seemed to be, shaking off his abstraction, got upon his feet and made him a harangue, imitating therein the ancient Piankeshaw; though with this difference, that, whereas the latter spoke entirely in his own tongue, the former thought fit, among abundance of Indian phrases, to introduce some that were sufficiently English to enable the soldier to guess, at least, a part of his meaning. His oration, however, as far as Roland could understand it, consisted chiefly in informing him that he was a very great chief, who had killed abundance of white people, men, women, and children, whose scalps had, for thirty years and more, been hanging in the smoke of his Shawnee lodge,—that he was very brave, and loved a white man's blood better than whisky, and that he never spared it out of pity,—adding as the cause, and seeming well pleased that he could boast a deficiency so well befitting a warrior, that he had *"no heart,"*—his interior being framed of stone as hard as the flinty rock under his feet. This exordium finished, he proceeded to bestow sundry abusive epithets upon the prisoner, charging him with having put his young men to a great deal of needless trouble, besides having killed several; for which, he added, the Longknife ought to expect nothing better than to have his face blacked and be burnt alive,—a hint that produced a universal grunt of assent on the part of the auditors. Having received this testimony of approbation, he resumed his discourse, pursuing it for the space of ten minutes or more with considerable vigour and eloquence; but as the whole speech consisted, like most other Indian speeches, of the same things said over and over again, those same things being scarce worth the trouble of utterance, we think it needless to say anything further of it; except that, first, as it seemed to Roland, as far as he could understand the broken expressions of the chief, he delivered a furious tirade against the demon enemy of his race, the bloody Jibbenainosay, the white man's War-Manito, whom he declared it was his purpose to fight and kill, as soon as that destroyer should have the courage to face him, the old Shawnee chief, like a human warrior,—and that it inspired several others to get up and make speeches likewise. Of all these the burden seemed to be the unpardonable crime of killing their comrades, of which the young soldier had been guilty; and he judged by the fury of their countenances, that they were only debating whether they should put him to death on the spot, or carry him to their country to be tortured.

The last speaker of all was the old Piankeshaw, whose meaning could be only guessed at from his countenance and gestures, the one being as angry and wo-begone as the latter were active and expressive. He pointed, at least a dozen times over, to two fresh and gory scalps,—the most highly valued trophies of victory,—that lay at the feet of the Shawnee chief, as many times to the horses, and thrice as often at the person of Roland, who stood now surveying his dark visage with a look of sullen despair, now casting his eyes, with a gaze of inexpressible emotion, towards the little copse, in which he still sought in vain a glimpse of his Edith. But if the old warrior's finger was often bent towards these three attractive objects, innumerable were the times it was pointed at the two or three little whisky-kegs, which, not having been yet distributed, lay untouched upon the grass. The words with which he accompanied these expressive gestures seemed to produce a considerable effect upon all his hearers, even upon the ancient chief; who, at the close of the oration, giving a sign to one of his young men, the latter ran to the copse and in an instant returned, bringing with him one of the horses, which the chief immediately handed over, through his deputy, to the orator, and the orator to one of the two young warriors, who seemed to be of his own tribe. The chief then pointed to a keg of the fire-water, and this was also given to the Piankeshaw, who received it with a grin of ecstacy, embraced it, snuffed at its odoriferous contents, and then passed it in like manner to his second follower. The chief made yet another signal, and the deputy, taking Roland by the arm, and giving him a piercing, perhaps even a pitying, look, delivered him likewise into the hands of the Piankeshaw; who, as if his happiness were now complete, received him with a yell of joy, that was caught up by his two companions, and finally joined in by all the savages present.

This shout seemed to be the signal for the breaking up of the convention. All rose to their feet, iterating and reiterating the savage cry, while the Piankeshaw, clutching his prize, and slipping a noose around the thong that bound his arms, endeavoured to drag him to the horse, on which the young men had already secured the keg of liquor, and which they were holding in readiness for the elder barbarian to mount.

At that conjecture, and while Roland was beginning to suspect that even the wretched consolation of remaining in captivity by his kinswoman's side was about to be denied him, and while the main body of savages were obviously bidding farewell to the little band of Piankeshaws, some shaking them by the hands, while others made game of the prisoner's distress in sundry Indian ways, and all uttering yells expressive of their different feelings, there appeared rushing from the copse, and running among the barbarians, the damsel Telie Doe, who, not a little to the surprise even of the ill-fated Roland himself, ran to his side, caught the rope by which he was held, and endeavoured frantically to snatch it from the hands of the Piankeshaw.

The act, for one of her peculiarly timorous spirit, was surprising enough; but a great transformation seemed to have suddenly taken place in her character, and even her appearance, which was less that of a feeble woman engaged in a work of humanity, than of a tigress infuriated by the approach of hunters against the lair of her sleeping young. She grasped the cord with unexpected strength, and her eyes flashed fire as they wandered around, until they met those of the supposed half-breed, to whom she called with tones of the most vehement indignation,—"Oh, father, father! what are you doing? You won't give him up to the murderers? You promised, you promised—"

"Peace, fool!" interrupted the man thus addressed, taking her by the arm, and endeavouring to jerk her from the prisoner; "away with you to your place, and be silent."

"I will not, father;—I will not be silent, I will not away!" cried the girl, resisting his efforts, and speaking with a voice that mingled the bitterest reproach with imploring entreaty, "you are a white man, father, and not an Indian; yes, father, you are *no* Indian; and you promised no harm should be done,—you did, father, you *did* promise!"

"Away, gal, I tell you!" thundered the renegade parent; and he again strove to drag her from the prisoner. But Telie, as if driven frantic by the act, flung her arms round Roland's body, from which she was drawn only by an effort of strength which her weak powers were unable to resist. But even then she did not give over her purpose; but starting from her father's arms, she ran screaming back to Roland, and would have again clasped him in her own; when the renegade, driven to fury by her opposition, arrested her with one hand, and with the other catching up a knife that lay in the grass, he made as if, in his fit of passion, he would have actually plunged it into her breast. His malevolent visage and brutal threat awoke the terrors of the woman in her heart, and she sank on her knees, crying-with a piercing voice, "Oh, father, don't kill me! don't kill your own daughter!"

"Kill you, indeed!" muttered the outlaw, with a laugh of scorn; "even Injuns don't kill their own children." And taking advantage of her terror, he beckoned to the Piankeshaw, who, as well as all the other Indians, seemed greatly astounded and scandalised at the indecorous interference of a female in the affairs of warriors, to remove the prisoner; which he did by immediately beginning to drag him down the hill. The action was not unobserved by the girl, whose struggles to escape from her father's arms, to pursue, as it seemed, after the soldier, Roland could long see, while her wild and piteous cries were still longer brought to his ears.

As for Roland himself, the words and actions of the girl,—though they might have awakened suspicions, not before-experienced, of her good faith, and even appeared to show that it was less to unlucky accident than to foul conspiracy he owed his misfortunes,—did not, and could not, banish the despair that absorbed his mind, to the exclusion of every other feeling. He seemed even to himself to be in a dream the sport of an incubus, that oppressed every faculty and energy of spirit, while yet presenting the most dreadful phantasms to his imagination. His tongue had lost its function; he strove several times to speak, but tongue and spirit were alike paralysed. The nightmare oppressed mind and body together.

It was in this unhappy condition, the result of overwrought, feelings and intolerable bodily suffering, that he was led by his Piankeshaw masters down the hill to the river, which they appeared to be about to pass; whilst the chief body of marauders were left to seek another road from the field of battle. Here the old warrior descended from his horse, and leaving Roland in charge of the two juniors, stepped a little aside to a place where was a ledge of rocks, in the face of which seemed to be the entrance to a cavern, although carefully blocked up by masses of stone, that had been but recently removed from its foot. The Piankeshaw, taking post directly in front of the hole, began to utter many mournful ejaculations, which were addressed to the insensate rock, or perhaps to the equally insensate corpse of a comrade concealed within. He drew also from a little pouch,—his medicine-bag,—divers bits of bone, wood, and feathers, the most valued idols of his *fetich,* which he scattered about the rock, singing the while, in a highly lugubrious tone, the praises of the dead, and shedding tears that might have been supposed the outpourings of genuine sorrow. But if sorrow it was that thus affected the spirits of the warrior, as it seemed to have done on several previous occasions, it proved to be as easily consolable as before, as the event showed; for having finished his lamentations, and left the rock, he advanced towards Roland, whom he threatened for the third time with his knife; when one of the younger Indians muttering a few words of remonstrance, and pointing at the same time to the keg of fire-water on the horse's back, his grief and rage expired together in a haw-haw, ten times more obstreperous and joyous than any he had indulged before. Then mounting the horse, seemingly in the best humour in the world, and taking the end of the cord by which Roland was bound, he rode into the water, dragging the unfortunate prisoner along at his horse's heels; while the younger Piankeshaws brought up the rear, ready to prevent resistance on the soldier's part, should he prove in any degree refractory.

In this ignominious manner the unhappy Forrester passed the river, to do which had, for twenty-four hours, been the chief object of his wishes. The ford was wide, deep, and rocky, and the current strong, so that he was several times swept from his feet, and being unable to rise would have perished,—happy could he have thus escaped his tormentors—had not the young warriors been nigh to give him assistance. Assistance, in such cases, was indeed always rendered; but his embarrassments and perils only afforded food for mirth to his savage attendants, who, at every fall and dip in the tide, made the hills resound with their vociferous laughter. It is only among children (we mean, of course, *bad* ones) and savages, who are but grown children, after all, that we find malice and mirth go hand in hand,—the will to create misery and the power to see it invested in ludicrous colours.

The river was at last crossed, and the bank being ascended, the three warriors paused a moment to send their last greeting across to their allies, who were seen climbing the hill, taking their own departure from the battle-ground. Even Roland was stirred from his stupefaction, as he beheld the train, some on foot, some on the captured horses, winding up the narrow road to the hill-top. He looked among them for his Edith, and saw her,—or fancied he saw her, for the distance was considerable,—supported on one of the animals, grasped in the arms of a tall savage, the guard of the grove, whose scarlet turban glittering in the sunshine, and his ample white blanket flowing over the flanks of the horse, made the most conspicuous objects in the train. But while he looked, barbarian and captive vanished together behind the hill, for they were at the head of the train. There remained a throng of footmen, who paused an instant on the crest of the ridge to return the farewell whoop of the three Piankeshaws. This being done, they likewise disappeared; and the Piankeshaws, turning their faces towards the west, dragging the prisoner after them, resumed their journey.

CHAPTER XXI

The agony which Roland suffered from the thong so tightly secured upon his wrists, was so far advantageous as it distracted his mind from the subject which had been at first the chief source of his distress: for it was impossible to think long even of his kinswoman, while enduring tortures that were aggravated by every jerk of the rope, by which he was dragged along; these growing more insupportable every moment. His sufferings, however, seemed to engage little of the thoughts of his conductors; who, leaving the buffalo road, and striking into the pathless forest, pushed onward at a rapid pace, compelling him to keep up with them; and it was not until he had twice fainted from pain and exhaustion, that, after some discussion, they thought fit to loosen the thong, which they afterwards removed altogether. Then, whether it was that they were touched at last with compassion, or afraid that death might snatch the prisoner from their hands, if too severely treated, they proceeded even to take other measures of a seemingly friendly kind, to allay his pangs; washing his lacerated wrists in a little brook, on whose banks they paused to give him rest, and then binding them up, as well as the two or three painful, though not dangerous, wounds he had received, with green leaves, which one of the juniors plucked, bruised, and applied with every appearance of the most brotherly interest; while the other, to equal, or surpass him in benevolence, took the keg of whisky from the horse's back, and filling a little wooden bowl that he drew from a pack, insisted that the prisoner should swallow it. In this recommendation the old Piankeshaw also concurred; but finding that Roland recoiled with disgust, after an attempt to taste the fiery liquid, he took the bowl into his own hands, and despatched its contents at a draught. "Good! great good!" he muttered, smacking his lips with high gusto; "white man make good drink!—Piankeshaw great friend white-man's liquor."

Having thus opened their hearts, nothing could be, to appearance, more friendly and affectionate than the bearing of the savages, at least so long as they remained at the brook; and even when the journey was resumed, which it soon was, their deportment was but little less loving. It is true, that the senior, before mounting his horse, proceeded very coolly to clap the noose, which had previously been placed on Roland's arms, around his neck, where it bade fair to strangle him, at the first false step of the horse;

but the young Indians walked at his side, chattering in high good humour; though, as their stock of English extended only to the single phrase, "Bozhoo, brudder," which was not in itself very comprehensible, though repeated at least twice every minute, it may be supposed their conversation had no very enlivening effect on the prisoner.

Nor was the old Piankeshaw much behind the juniors in good humour; though, it must be confessed, his feelings were far more capricious and evanescent. One while he would stop his horse, and dragging Roland to his side, pat him affectionately on the shoulder, and tell him, as well as his broken language could express his intentions, that he would take him to the springs of the Wabash, one of the principal seats of his nation, and make him his son and a great warrior; while at other times, having indulged in a fit of sighing, groaning, and crying, he would turn in a towering rage, and express a resolution to kill him on the spot,—from which bloody disposition, however, he was always easily turned by the interference of the young men.

These capricious changes were perhaps owing in a great measure to the presence of the whisky-keg, which the old warrior ever and anon took from its perch among the packs behind him, and applied to his lips, sorely, as it appeared, against the will of his companion, who seemed to remonstrate with him against a practice so unbecoming a warrior, while in the heart of a foeman's country, and not a little also against his own sense of propriety: for his whole course in relation to the keg was like that of a fish that dallies around the angler's worm, uncertain whether to bite, now looking and longing, now suspecting the hook and retreating, now returning to look and long again, until, finally, unable to resist the temptation, it resolves upon a little nibble, which ends, even against its own will, in a furious bite.

It was in this manner the Piankeshaw addressed himself to his treasure; the effect of which was to render each returning paroxysm of affection and sorrow more energetic than before, while it gradually robbed of their malignity those fits of anger with which he was still occasionally seized. But it added double fluency to his tongue; and, not content with muttering his griefs in his own language, addressing them to his own people, he finally began to pronounce them in English, directing them at Roland; whereby the latter was made acquainted with the cause of his sorrow. This, it appeared, was nothing less than the loss of a son killed in battle with the Kentuckians, and left to moulder, with two or three Shawnee corses, in the cave by the river-side; which loss he commemorated a dozen times over, and with a most piteous voice, in a lament that celebrated the young warrior's virtues: "Lost son," he ejaculated; "good huntaw: kill bear, kill buffalo, catch fish, feed old squaw, and young squaw, and little papoose—good son! mighty good son! Good fighting-man: kill man Virginnee, kill man Kentucky, kill man Injun-man; take scalp, squaw scalp, papoose scalp, man scalp, all kind scalp—debbil good fighting man! No go home no more Piankeshaw nation; no more kill bear; no more kill buffalo; no more catch fish; no more feed old squaw, and young squaw, and little papoose; no more kill man, no more take scalp—lose own scalp, take it Long-knife man Kentucky; no more see old Piankeshaw son,—leave dead, big hole Kentucky; no more see no more Piankeshaw son, Piankeshaw nation!"

With such lamentations, running at times into rage against his prisoner, as the representative of those who had shed the young warrior's blood, the old Piankeshaw whiled away the hours of travel; ceasing them only when seized with a fit of affection, or when some mis-step of the horse sent a louder gurgle, with a more delicious odour, from the cask at his back; which music and perfume together were a kind of magic not to be resisted by one who stood so greatly in need of consolation.

The effect of such constant and liberal visitations to the comforter and enemy of his race, continued for several hours together, was soon made manifest in the old warrior, who grew more loquacious, more lachrymose, and more foolish every moment; until, by and by, having travelled till towards sunset, a period of six or seven hours from the time of setting out, he began to betray the most incontestable evidences of intoxication. He reeled on the horse's back, and finally, becoming tired of the weight of his gun, he extended it to Roland, with a very magisterial, yet friendly nod, as if bidding him take and carry it. It was snatched from him, however, by one of the younger warriors, who was too wise to intrust a loaded carbine in the arms of a prisoner, and who had perhaps noted the sudden gleam of fire, the first which had visited them since the moment of his capture, that shot into Roland's eyes, as he stretched forth his hands to take the weapon.

The old Piankeshaw did not seem to notice who had relieved him of the burden. He settled himself again on the saddle as well as he could, and jogged onwards, prattling and weeping, according to the mood of the moment, now droning out an Indian song, and now nodding with drowsiness; until at last slumber or stupefaction settled so heavily upon his senses that he became incapable of guiding his horse; and the weary animal, checked by the unconscious rider, or stopping of his own accord to browse the green cane-leaves along the path, the Piankeshaw suddenly took a lurch wider than usual, and fell, like a log, to the ground.

The younger savages had watched the course of proceedings on the part of the senior with ill-concealed dissatisfaction. The catastrophe completed their rage, which, however, was fortunately expended upon the legitimate cause of displeasure. They tumbled the unlucky cask from its perch, and assailing it with horrible yells and as much apparent military zeal as could have been exercised upon a human enemy lying in like manner at their feet, they dashed it to pieces with their tomahawks, scattering its precious contents upon the grass.

While they were thus engaged, the senior rose from the earth, staring about him for a moment with looks of stupid inquiry; until beginning at last to comprehend the accident that had happened to him, and perhaps moved by the late of his treasure, he also burst into a fury; and snatching up the nearest gun, he clapped it to his horse's head, and shot it dead on the spot, roaring out, "Cuss' white-man hoss! throw old Piankeshaw! No good nothing! Cuss debbil hoss!"

This act of drunken and misdirected ferocity seemed vastly to incense the young warriors; and the senior waxing as wrathful at the wanton destruction of his liquor, there immediately ensued a battle of tongues betwixt the two parties, who scolded and berated one another for the space of ten minutes or more with prodigious volubility and energy, the juniors expatiating upon the murder of the horse as an act of the most unpardonable folly, while the senior seemed to insist that the wasting of so much good liquor was a felony of equally culpable dye; and it is probable he had the better side of the argument, since he continued to grumble for a long time even after he had silenced the others.

But peace was at last restored, and the savages prepared to resume their journey; but not until they had unanimously resolved that the consequences of the quarrel should be visited upon the head of the captive. Their apparent good-humour vanished, and the old Piankeshaw, staggering up, gave Roland to understand, in an oration full of all the opprobrious epithets he could muster, either in English or Indian, that he, Piankeshaw, being a very great warrior, intended to carry him to his country, to run the gauntlet through every village of the nation, and then to burn him alive, for the satisfaction of the women and children; and while pouring this agreeable intelligence into the soldier's ears, the juniors took the opportunity to tie his arms a second time, heaping on his shoulders their three packs; to which the old man afterwards insisted on adding the saddle and bridle of the horse, though for no very ostensible object, together with a huge mass of the flesh, dug with his knife from the still quivering carcass, which was perhaps designed for their supper.

Under this heavy load, the unhappy and degraded soldier was compelled to stagger along with his masters; but fortunately for no long-period. The night was fast approaching, and having-soon arrived at a little glade in the forest, where a spring of sweet water bubbled from the grass, they signified their intention to make it their camping ground for the night. A fire was struck, the horse flesh stuck upon a fork and roasted, and a share of it tendered to the prisoner; who, sick at heart and feverish in body, refused it with as much disgust as he had shown at the whisky, expressing his desire only to drink of the spring, which he was allowed to do to his liking.

The savages then collected grass and leaves, with which they spread a couch under a tree beside their fire; and here, having compelled the soldier to lie down, they proceeded to secure him for the night with a cruel care, that showed what value the loss of the horse and fire-water, the only other trophies of victory, led them to attach to him. A stake was cut and laid across his breast, and to the ends of this his outstretched arms were bound at both wrist and elbow. A pole was then laid upon his body, to the extremities of which his feet and neck were also bound; so that he was secured as upon, or rather *under*, a cross, without the power of moving hand or foot. As if even this were not enough to satisfy his barbarous companions, they attached an additional cord to his neck; and this, when they lay down beside him to sleep, one of the young warriors wrapped several times round his own arm, so that the slightest movement of the prisoner, were such a thing possible, must instantly rouse the jealous savage from his slumbers.

These preparations being completed, the young men lay down, one on each side of the prisoner, and were soon fast asleep.

The old Piankeshaw, meanwhile, sat by the fire, now musing in drunken revery,—"in cogibundity of cogitation,"—now grumbling a lament for his perished son, which, by a natural licence of affliction, he managed to intermingle with regrets for his lost liquor, and occasionally heaping maledictions upon the heads of his wasteful companions, or soliciting the prisoner's attention to an account, that he gave him at least six times over, of the peculiar ceremonies which would be observed in burning him, when once safely bestowed in the Piankeshaw nation. In this manner, the old savage, often nodding, but always rousing again, succeeded in amusing himself nearly half the night long; and it was not until near midnight that he thought fit, after stirring up the fire, and adding a fresh log to it, to stretch himself beside one of the juniors, and grumble himself to sleep. A few explosive and convulsive snorts, such as might have done honour to the nostrils of a war-horse, marked the gradations by which he sank to repose; then came the deep, long-drawn breath of mental annihilation, such as distinguished the slumber of his companions.

To the prisoner, alone, sleep was wholly denied; for which the renewed agonies of his bonds, tied with the supreme contempt for suffering which usually marks the conduct of savages to their captives, would have been sufficient cause, had there even been no superior pangs of spirit to banish the comforter from his eyelids. Of his feelings during the journey from the river,—which, in consequence of numberless delays caused by the old Piankeshaw's drunkenness, could scarce have been left more than eight or ten miles behind,—we have said but little, since imagination can only picture them properly to the reader. Grief, anguish, despair, and the sense of degradation natural to a man of proud spirit, a slave in the hands of coarse barbarians, kept his spirit for a long time wholly subdued and torpid; and it was not until he perceived the old Piankeshaw's repeated potations, and their effects, that he began to wake from his lethargy, and question himself whether he might not yet escape, and, flying to the nearest settlements for assistance, strike a blow for the recovery of his kinswoman. Weak from exhaustion and wounds, entirely unarmed, and closely watched, as he perceived he was, by the young warriors, notwithstanding their affected friendship, it was plain that nothing could be hoped for, except from caution on his part, and the most besotted folly on that of his captors. This folly was already made perceptible in at least one of the party; and as he watched the oft-repeated visitations of the senior to the little keg, he began to anticipate the period when the young men should also betake themselves to the stupefying draught, and give him the opportunity he longed for with frantic, though concealed, impatience. This hope fell when the cask was dashed to pieces; but hope, once excited, did not easily forsake him. He had heard, and read, of escapes, made by captives like himself, from Indians, when encamped by night in the woods,—nay, of escapes made when the number of captors and the feebleness of the captive (for even women and boys had thus obtained their deliverance), rendered the condition of the latter still more wretched than his own. Why might not *he,* a man and soldier, guarded by only three foemen, succeed, as others had succeeded, in freeing himself?

This question, asked over and over again, and each time answered with greater hope and animation than before, employed his mind until his wary captors had tied him to the stakes, as has been mentioned, leaving him as incapable of motion as if every limb had been solidified into stone. Had the barbarians been able to look into his soul at the moment when he first strove to test the strength of the ligatures, and found them resisting his efforts like bands of brass, they would have beheld deeper and wilder tortures than any they could hope to inflict, ever, at the stake. The effort was repeated once, twice, thrice—a thousand times,—but always in vain: the cords were too securely tied, the stakes too carefully placed, to yield to his puny struggles. He was a prisoner in reality,—without resource, without help, without hope.

And thus he passed the whole of the bitter night, watching the slow progress of moments counted only by the throbbings of his fevered temples, the deep breathings of the Indians, and the motion of the stars creeping over the vista opened to the skies from the little glade, a prey to despair, made so much more poignant by disappointment and self-reproach. Why had he not taken advantage of his temporary release from the cords, to attempt escape by open flight, when the drunkenness of the old Piankeshaw would have increased the chances of success? He had lost his best ally in the cask of liquor; but he resolved,—if the delirious plans of a mind tossed by the most frenzied passions could be called resolutions,—a second day should not pass by without an effort better becoming a soldier, better becoming the only friend and natural protector of the hapless Edith.

In the meanwhile, the night passed slowly away, the moon, diminished to a ghastly crescent, rose over the woods, looking down with a sickly smile upon the prisoner,—an emblem of his decayed fortunes and waning hopes; and a pale streak, the first dull glimmer of dawn, was seen stealing up the skies. But neither moon nor streak of dawn yet threw light upon the little glade. The watch-fire had burned nearly away, and its flames no longer illuminated the scene. The crackling of the embers, with an occasional echo from the wood hard by, as of the rustling of a rabbit, or other small animal, drawn by the unusual appearance of fire near his favourite fountain, to satisfy a timorous curiosity, was the only sound to be heard; for the Indians were in the dead sleep of morning, and their breathing was no longer audible.

The silence and darkness together were doubly painful to Roland, who had marked the streak of dawn, and longed with fierce impatience for the moment when he should be again freed from his bonds, and left to attempt some of those desperate expedients which he had been planning all the night long. In such a frame of mind, even the accidental falling of a half-consumed brand upon the embers, and its sudden kindling into flame, were circumstances of an agreeable nature; and the ruddy glare thrown over the boughs above his head was welcomed as the return of a friend, bringing with it hope, and even a share of his long lost tranquillity.

But tranquillity was not fated to dwell long in his bosom. At that very moment, and while the blaze of the brand was brightest, his ears were stunned by an explosion bursting like a thunderbolt at his very head, but whether coming from earth or air, from the hands of Heaven or the firelock of a human being, he knew not; and immediately after there sprang a huge dark shadow over his body, and there was heard the crash as of an axe falling upon the flesh of the young Indian who slept on his right side. A dismal shriek, the utterance of agony and terror, rose from the barbarian's lips; and then came the sound of his footsteps, as he darted, with a cry still wilder, into the forest, pursued by the sound of other steps; and then all again was silent,—all save groans, and the rustling in the grass of limbs convulsed in the death-throe at the soldier's side.

Astounded, bewildered, and even horror-struck, by these incomprehensible events, the work of but an instant, and all unseen by Roland, who, from his position, could look only upwards towards the boughs and skies, he would have thought himself in a dream, but for the agonised struggles of the young Indian at his side, which he could plainly feel as well as hear: until by and by they subsided, as if in sudden death. Was it a rescue? was that shot fired by a friend? that axe wielded by a human auxiliary? those sounds of feet dying away in the distance, were they the steps of a deliverer? The thought was ecstacy, and he shouted aloud, "Return, friend, and loose me! return!"

No voice replied to the shout; but it roused from the earth a dark and bloody figure, which staggering and falling over the body of the young warrior, crawled like a scotched reptile upon Roland's breast; when the light of the fire shining upon it revealed to his eyes the horrible spectacle of the old Piankeshaw warrior, the lower part of his face shot entirely away, and his eyes rolling hideously, and, as it seemed, sightlessly, in the pangs of death, his hand clutching the knife with which he had so often threatened, and with which he yet seemed destined to take, though in the last gasp of his own, the soldier's life. With one hand he felt along the prisoner's body, as if seeking a vital part, and sustained his own weight, while with the other he made repeated, though feeble and ineffectual, strokes with the knife, all the time rolling, and staggering, and shaking his gory head in a manner most horrible to behold. But vengeance was denied the dying warrior; his blows were offered impotently, and without aim; and becoming weaker at every effort, his left arm at last failed to support him, and he fell across Roland's body; in which position he immediately after expired.

In this frightful condition Roland was left, shocked, although relieved from fear, by the savage's death, crying in vain to his unknown auxiliary for assistance. He exerted his voice, until the woods rang with his shouts; but hollow echoes were the only replies: neither voice nor returning footstep was to be heard; and it seemed as if he had been rescued from the Indians' hands, only to be left, bound and helpless, to perish piecemeal among their bodies. The fear of a fate so dreadful, with the weight of the old Piankeshaw, a man of almost gigantic proportions, lying upon his bosom, was more than his agonised spirits and exhausted strength could endure; and his wounds suddenly bursting out afresh, he lapsed into a state of insensibility, in which, however, it was happily his fate not long to remain.

CHAPTER XXII

When Roland recovered his consciousness, he was no longer a prisoner extended beneath the Indian cross. His limbs were unbound, and he himself lying across the knees of a man who was busily engaged sprinkling his head and breast with water from the little well, to which he had been borne while still insensible. He stared around him with eyes yet filmy and vacant. The first objects they fell on were two lifeless figures, the bodies of his late savage masters, stretched near the half-extinguished fire. He looked up to the face of his deliverer, which could be readily seen, for it was now broad day, and beheld, with such a thrill of pleasure as had not visited his bosom for many weary days, the features of his trusty guide and emissary, honest Nathan Slaughter, who was pursuing the work of resuscitation with great apparent zeal, while little dog Peter stood by wagging his tail, as if encouraging him to perseverance.

"What, Nathan!" he cried, grasping at his hand, and endeavouring, though vainly, to rise from his knee, "do I dream! is it *you*?"

"Verily, thee speaks the truth," replied Nathan;—"it is me,—me and little Peter; and, truly, it is nobody else."

"And I am free again? free, free!—And the savages? the vile, murdering Piankeshaws? Dead! surprised, killed,—every dog of them!"

"Thee speaks the truth a second time," said Nathan Slaughter, snuffling and hesitating in his speech: "thee wicked enemies and captivators will never trouble thee more."

"And who, who was it that rescued me? Hah! there is blood on your face! your hands are red with it! It was *you*, then, that saved me? *you* that killed the accursed cut-throats? Noble Nathan! brave Nathan! true Nathan! how shall I ever requite the act? how shall I ever forget it?" And as he spoke, the soldier, yet lying across Nathan's knees, for his limbs refused to support him, grasped his preserver's hands with a fervour of gratitude that gave new life and vigour to his exhausted spirits.

"And thee does not think then," muttered Nathan, snuffling twice as much as before, but growing bolder as Roland's gratitude reassured him,—"thee does not think,—that is, thee is not of opinion,—that is to say, thee does not altogether hold it to be as a blood-guiltiness, and a wickedness, and a shedding of blood, that I did take to me the weapon of war, and shoot upon thee wicked oppressors, to the saving of thee life? Truly, friend, it was to save thee life,—thee must remember *that*; it was a thing that was necessary, and not to be helped. Truly, friend, it was my desire to help thee in peace and with a peaceful hand; but, of a truth, there was thee enemies at thee side, with their guns and their knives, ready to start up and knock out thee unfortunate brains. Truly, friend, thee sees it couldn't be helped; and, truly, I don't think thee conscience can condemn me."

"Condemn you indeed!" cried the young man; "it was an act to bind my gratitude for ever,—an act to win you the admiration and respect of the whole world, which I shall take care to make acquainted with it."

"Nay, friend," said Nathan, hastily, "the less thee says of it the better: if thee is theeself satisfied in thee conscience of its lawfulness, it is enough. Do thee, therefore, hold thee tongue on this and all other matters wherein thee has seen me do evil; for truly I am a man of a peaceful faith, and what I have done would be but as a grief and a scandal to the same."

"But my friends,—my poor Edith!—wretch that I am to think of myself or of others, while she is still a captive!" cried Roland, again endeavouring to rise. But his limbs, yet paralysed from the tightness with which thongs had been bound around them, tottered beneath him, and but for Nathan, he must have fallen to the earth. "The emigrants," he continued with incoherent haste;—"you brought them? They are pursuing the savages? they have rescued her? Speak, Nathan,—tell me all; tell me that my cousin is free!"

"Truly, friend," muttered Nathan, his countenance losing much of the equanimity that had begun to cover it, and assuming a darker and disturbed expression, "thee doth confuse both theeself and me with many questions. Do thee be content for awhile, till I chafe thee poor legs, which is like the legs of a dead man, and tie up thee wounds. When thee can stand up and walk, thee shall know all I have to tell thee, both good and bad. It is enough thee is theeself safe."

"Alas, I read it all from your looks," cried the soldier; "Edith is still a prisoner: and I lie here a miserable, crushed worm, incapable of aiding, unable even to die for her! But the emigrants, my friends? *they* are at least urging the pursuit? there is a hope they will retake her?"

"Truly, friend," said Nathan, "thee shall know all, if thee will have patience, and hold thee tongue. Truly, the many things thee says doth perplex me. If thee loves thee poor kinswoman, and would save her from cruel bondage and sorrow, thee must be quiet till I have put thee again upon thee legs; which is the first thing to be thought about: and after that, thee shall have my counsel and help to do what is good and proper for the maiden's redeeming."

With these words, Nathan again addressed himself to the task of chafing Roland's half-lifeless limbs, and binding up the several light, though painful wounds, which he had received in the conflict; and the soldier submitting in despair, though still entreating Nathan to tell him the worst, the latter began at last to relate his story.

The bold attempt of Nathan to pass the line of besiegers at the ruin, it seemed, he bad accomplished without difficulty, though not without risk; but this part of the narrative he hurried over, as well as his passage of the river at a solitary and dangerous ford in the wildest recesses of the forest. Then striking through the woods, and aiming for the distant Station, he had arrived within but a few miles of it, when it was his fortune to stumble upon the band of Regulators, who, after their memorable exploit at the beech-tree, had joined the emigrants, then on their march through the woods, and convoyed them to the Station. Here passing the night in mirth and frolic, they were startled at an early hour by the alarming intelligence, brought by a volunteer hunter, who had obtained it none could tell how, of the presence of the Indian army on the north side; and leaving their friends to arm and follow as they could, the visitors immediately mounted their horses to return to Bruce's Station, and thence to seek the field of battle. To these unexpected friends, thus opportunely met in the woods, Nathan imparted his story, acquainting them, in the same words, of the presence of enemies so much nearer at hand than was dreamed, and of the unfortunate dilemma of Forrester and his helpless party,—an account that fired the blood of the hot youths as effectually as it could have done if expressed in the blast of a bugle. A council of war being called on the spot, it was resolved to gallop at once to the rescue of the travellers, without wasting time in seeking additional assistance from the emigrants or their neighbours of the Station just left; which indeed, as from Nathan's observations, it did not seem that the numbers of the foe could be more than double their own, the heroic youths held to be entirely needless. Taking Nathan up, therefore, behind him, and bearing him along, to point out the position of the Indians, the gallant Tom Bruce, followed by his equally gallant companions, dashed through the woods, and succeeded by daybreak in reaching the ruin; where, as Nathan averred, so judiciously had they laid their plans for the attack, the Indians, if still there, might have been surprised, entirely worsted, and perhaps the half of them cut off upon the spot; "which," as he rather hastily observed, "would have been a great comfort to all concerned." But the ruin was deserted, besiegers and besieged had alike vanished, as well as the bodies of those assailants who had fallen in the conflict, to find their graves under the ruins, among the rocks, or in the whirling eddies of the river. The tracks of the horses being discovered in the ravine and at the water's edge, it was inferred that the whole party, too desperate, or too wise, to yield themselves prisoners, had been driven into the river, and there drowned; and this idea inflaming the fury of the Kentuckians to the highest pitch, they sought out and easily discovered among the canes, the fresh trail of the Indians, which they followed, resolving to exact the fullest measure of revenge. Nathan, the man of peace, from whom (for he had not thought proper to acquaint the young men with the warlike part he had himself taken in the battles of the night) no further services were expected, was now turned adrift, to follow or protect himself as he might; and the young men betook themselves to the pursuit with as much speed as the wild character of the woods permitted.

But it formed no part of honest Nathan's designs to be left behind. His feelings were too deeply involved in the fate of the unhappy individuals, whose misadventures he could, or thought he could, so clearly trace to his own indiscretion, to suffer him to rest, while it was yet wrapped in obscurity. He had accepted the charge and responsibility of extricating them from their perils; and his conscience could not be appeased until he had determined for himself whether in truth they were yet beyond the reach of assistance. Making his own observations from the appearance of the different tracts in the ravine, and satisfying himself there was among them one more Christian footprint than could be accounted for, he followed after the young men, examining the Indian trail in places where it had not been effaced by the Kentuckians, until he became convinced that the fugitives had, in some unaccountable way, escaped alive from the river, and were still struggling in retreat, led by some friendly guide, although closely pursued by the foe. This discovery, it was also probable, had been made by the Kentuckians, who had in consequence urged their horses to the utmost, and arriving on the hill where the savages lay in ambush, rushed to the attack, and fought and lost the battle, before Nathan could reach them. He met them indeed retreating in full rout before the victors, many wounded, all overcome by panic, and none willing or able to throw any light on the cause of defeat. One indeed, checking his horse a moment to bid the man of peace look to himself and avoid the savages, who were still urging the pursuit, hastily assured him that the defeat was all owing to Captain Ralph's ghost, which had suddenly got among them, yelling for vengeance on his executioners for which reason the conscience-stricken Regulator called Nathan to witness his oath, which he now made, "that he would never Lynch a man again as long as he lived." And the worthy warrior having added, with another oath, which he called a still superior power to attest, "that he had seen

Stackpole fly off with Tom Brace's soul on the back of a devil, in shape of a big black horse breathing flames and sulphur," struck spur again into his own charger, not, however, until he had first generously invited Nathan to get up be-him, to escape the savage pursuers, who were now seen close behind. Declining the heroic offer, and bidding the youth effect his own escape, Nathan immediately dived, with his inseparable friend and adviser, little Peter, among the canes; where he lay concealed until well assured the victors had abandoned the pursuit, and returned to the field of battle.

"Then, friend," said the man of peace, who may now be permitted to tell his own story, "I took council of Peter as to what we should do; and truly it was our opinion we should creep after the murdering Shawnee creatures—though verily there was more than Shawnees engaged in this wicked business—and see what had become of thee and thee poor women; seeing that we were in a manner, as I may say, the cause of thee troubles, in carrying thee to the very place where we should not, wicked sinners that we are: that is, wicked sinner that *I* am, for truly little Peter had nothing to do with that matter, having done his best to keep us from the ruin. Well, friend, as soon as we thought it safe, we crept to the spot on the hill-side; and safe enough it was, the savages having departed, leaving nothing behind them, save two young Kentuckians and the coloured person, whom they had prevailed over and hewn to pieces with their Hatchets; besides four corpses of their own, which they had stuck in a cave, where Peter snuffed them out: truly, friend, thee don't know what a nose little Peter has! Well, friend, I saw then that thee enemies had divided, the main body departing one way over the hill, while a smaller party had crossed the river with a horse and prisoner. Truly it was Peter's opinion that this prisoner was theeself—thee own very self (a thing I could not be so certain of on my part, seeing that I had never tracked thee, save by thee horse-prints only), and that if we followed thee, we might in some way aid thee to escape, thee captivators being so few in number. And so, friend, we waded the river, and followed thee trail until night came, when little Peter undertook to nose thee on in the dark, which he did very successfully, until we reached the place where the savages had killed their horse, and broken their cask of liquor, when truly the scent of the same did so prevail over Peter's nose, that I was in fear he never would smell right again in all his life, which was a great grief to me; for truly Peter's nose is, as I may say, the staff of my life, my defence, and my succour: truly thee don't know the value of little Peter's nose. And, moreover, the savour of the dead horse did somewhat captivate his attention; for truly little Peter is but a dog, and he loves horse-flesh. Well, friend, this was a thing that perplexed me; until, by and by, having brought little Peter to reason in the matter of the horse, and washed his nose in a brook which it was my fortune to discover, he did bethink him what he was after, and so straightway hunt for the track, which being recovered we went on our way until we lighted right on thee captivators' camp-fire, and truly we lighted upon it much sooner than we expected. Well, friend," continued the narrator, "having crept up as near as I durst, I could see how thee was fixed, tied to the poles so thee could not help theeself; and the three savages lying beside thee, with their guns in the hollows of their arms, ready to be seized in a moment. Truly, friend, the sight threw me into another perplexity; and I lay watching thee and thee cruel oppressors for more than an hour, marvelling in what way I could give thee help."

"An hour!" cried Roland; "a friend lying by me during that hour, the most wretched and distracted of my whole existence? Had you but cut the rope, and given me the knife to strike a blow for myself!"

"Truly," said the man of peace, "I did so desire to do, seeing that then thee might have killed the Injuns theeself; which would have been more seemly, as being a thing thee conscience would not disapprove of; whereas mine, as thee may suppose, was quite averse to any such bloody doings on my own part. But, truly, I durst not adventure upon the thing thee speaks of; for, first, I saw by the stick on thee breast, thee was tied so tight and fast, it would be an hour's work to cut thee loose—thee captivators lying by all the while; and, secondly, I knew, by the same reason, thee limbs would be so numb thee could neither stand upon thee legs, nor hold a weapon in thee hand, for just as long a time; and, besides, I feared, in case thee should discover there was help nigh at hand, thee might cry out in thee surprise, and so alarm these sleeping captivators. And so, friend, I was in what thee may call a pucker, not knowing what to do; and so I lay hard by thee, with Peter at the back of me, watching and revolving the matter for that whole hour, as I told thee; when suddenly down fell a stick into the fire, and the same blazing up brightly, I saw two of the savages lying beside thee, their heads so close together thee might have supposed they both grew from the same pair of shoulders, and so nigh to me withal, that, verily, I might have poked them with the muzzle of my gun. Truly, friend," continued Nathan, looking both bewildered and animated, as he arrived at this period of his story, "I can't tell thee how it then happened,—whether it was a sort of nervousness in my fingers' ends, or whether it was all an accident; but, truly, as it happened, my gun went off in my hands, as it might be of its own accord, and, truly, it blew the two evil creatures' brains out! And then, friend, thee sees, there was no stopping, there being the third of thee captivators to look after; and, truly, as I had done so much, I thought I might as well do all,—the killing of three men being but a little worse than the killing of two; and, besides, the creature would have hurt thee, as thee lay at his mercy. And so, friend, I did verily spring upon him, sinner that I am, and strike him a blow with my hatchet, which I had taken from my belt to be ready; whereupon he fled, and I after him, being in great fear lest, if he escaped, he should return upon thee and kill thee, before I could get back to cut thee loose And so, friend, it happened that—that I killed him likewise!—for which I don't think thee can, in thee heart, blame me, seeing that it was all, over and over again, on *thee* account, and nobody else's. Truly, friend, it is quite amazing, the ill things thee has brought me to!"

"Had there been twenty of the villains, and you had killed them all, I should have held it the noblest and most virtuous act you could have performed," said Roland, too fiercely agitated by his own contending passions to note the strange medley of self-accusing and exculpatory expressions, the shame-faced, conscience-stricken looks, alternating with gleams of military fire and self-complacency, with which the man of peace recounted his bloody exploit, or the adroit attempt, with which he concluded it, to shuffle the responsibility of the crime, if crime it were, from his own to the young Virginian's shoulders. At another moment, the latter might have speculated with as much surprise as approval on the extraordinary metamorphosis of Nathan, the man of amity and good will, into a slayer of Indians, double-dyed in gore; but at that juncture, he had little inclination to dwell on anything save his own liberation and the hapless fate of his cousin.

CHAPTER XXIII

By dint of chafing and bathing in the spring, still foul and red with the blood of the Piankeshaws, the limbs of the soldier soon recovered their strength, and he was able to rise, to survey the scene of his late sufferings and liberation, and again recur to the harassing subject of his kinswoman's fate. Again he beset Nathan with questions, which soon recalled the disturbed looks which his deliverer had worn when first assailed with interrogatories. He adjured him to complete the good work he had so bravely begun, by leaving himself to his fate, and making his way to the emigrants, or to the nearest inhabited Station, whence assistance might be procured to pursue the savages and their captives, before it might be too late. "Lead the party first to the battleground," he said: "I am now as a child in strength, but I can crawl thither to meet you; and once on a horse again, be assured no one shall pursue better or faster than I."

"If thee thinks of rescuing the maiden," said Nathan—

"I will do so, or die," exclaimed Roland, impetuously; "and would to Heaven I could die twice over, so I might snatch her from the murdering monsters. Alas! had you but followed them, instead of these three curs; and done that service to Edith you have done to me!"

"Truly," said Nathan, "thee talks as if ten men were as easily knocked on the head as ten rabbits. But, hearken, friend, and do thee have patience for a while! There is a thing in this matter that perplexes me; and, verily, there is two or three. Why did thee desert the ruin? and who was it led thee through the canes? Let me know what it was that happened thee; for, of a truth, there is more in this same matter than thee thinks."

Thus called upon, Roland acquainted Nathan with the events that had succeeded his departure from the ruin,—the appearance of Ralph Stackpole, and the flight of the party by the river,—circumstances that moved the wonder and admiration of Nathan,—and with all the other occurrences up to the moment of the defeat of the Kentuckians, and the division of the plunder among the victorious Indians. The mention of these spoils, the rifles, rolls of cloth, beads, bells, and other gewgaw trinkets, produced an evident impression on Nathan's mind; which was greatly increased when Roland related the scene betwixt Telie Doe and her reprobate father, and repeated those expressions which seemed to show that the attack upon the party was by no means accidental, but the result of a previously formed design, of which she was not ignorant.

"Where Abel Doe is, there, thee may be sure, there is knavery!" said Nathan; demanding earnestly if Roland had seen no other white man in the party.

"I saw no other," he replied: "but there was a tall man in a blanket, wearing a red turban, who looked at me from a distance; and I thought he was a half-breed, like Doe,—for so, at first, I supposed the latter to be."

"Well, friend! And he seemed to command the party, did he not?" demanded Nathan, with interest.

"The leader," replied Roland, "was a vile, grim old rascal, that they called Kenauga, or Kenauga, or—"

"Wenonga!" cried Nathan, with extraordinary vivacity, his whole countenance, in fact, lighting up with the animation of intense interest,—"an old man tall and raw-boned, a scar on his nose and cheek, a halt in his gait, his left middle-finger short of a joint, and a buzzard's beak and talons tied to his hair?—It is Wenonga, the Black-Vulture. Truly, little Peter! thee is but a dolt and a dog, that thee told me nothing about it!"

The soldier remarked, with some surprise, the change of Nathan's visage, and with still more, his angry reproaches of the trusty animal, the first he had heard him utter.

"And who then is the old Black-Vulture," he asked, "that he should drive from your mind even the thought of my poor wretched Edith?"

"Thee is but a boy in the woods, if thee never heard of Wenonga, the Shawnee," replied Nathan hastily,—"a man that has left the mark of his axe on many a ruined cabin along the frontier, from the Bloody Run of Bedford to the Kenhawa and the Holston. He is the chief that boasts he has no heart: and, truly, he has none, being a man that has drunk the blood of women and children—Friend! thee kinswoman's scalp is already hanging at his girdle!"

This horrible announcement, uttered with a fierce earnestness that proved the sincerity of the speaker, froze Roland's blood in his veins, and he stood speechless and gasping; until Nathan, noting his agitation, and recovering in part from his own ferment of spirits, exclaimed, even more hastily than before—"Truly, I have told thee what is false—thee kinswoman is safe,—a prisoner, but alive and safe."

"You have told me she is dead—murdered by the foul assassins," said Roland; "and if it be so, it avails not to deny it. If it be so, Nathan," he continued, with a look of desperation, "I call Heaven and earth to witness, that I will pursue the race of the slayers with thrice the fury of their own malice,—never to pause, never to rest, never to be satisfied with vengeance, while an Indian lives with blood to be shed, and I with strength to shed it."

"Thee speaks like a man!" said Nathan, grasping the soldier's hand, and fairly crushing it in his gripe,—"that is to say," he continued, suddenly letting go his hold, and seeming somewhat abashed at the fervour of his sympathy, "like a man, according to thee own sense of matters and things. But do thee be content; thee poor maid is alive, and like to be so; and that thee may be assured of it, I will soon tell thee the thing that is on my mind. Friend, do thee answer me a question,—Has thee any enemy among the Injuns?—that is to say, any reprobate white man like this Abel Doe,—who would do thee a wrong?"

The soldier started with surprise, and replied in the negative.

"Has thee no foe, then, at home, whom thee has theeself wronged to that point that he would willingly league with murdering Injuns to take thee life?"

"I have my enemies, doubtless, like all other men," said Roland, "but none so basely, so improbably malignant."

"Verily, then, thee makes me in a perplexity as before," said Nathan; "for as truly as thee stands before me, so truly did I see, that night when I left thee at the ruins, and crawled through the Injun lines, a white man that sat at a fire with Abel Doe, the father of the maid Telie, apart from the rest, and counselled with him how best to sack the cabin, without killing the two women. Truly, friend, it was a marvel to myself, there being so many of the murdering villains, that they did us so little mischief: but, truly, it was because of the women. And, truly, there was foul knavery between these two men; for I heard high words and chaffering between them, as concerning a price or reward which Abel Doe claimed of the other for the help he was rendering him, in snapping thee up, with thee kinswoman. Truly, thee must not think I was mistaken; for seeing the man's red shawl round his head gleaming in the fire, and not knowing there was any one nigh him (for Abel Doe lay flat upon the earth), a wicked thought came into my head; 'for, truly,' said I, 'this man is the chief, and, being alone, a man might strike him with a knife from behind the tree he rests against, and being killed, his people will fly in fear, without any more blood-shed;' but creeping nearer, I saw that he was but a white man in disguise; and so, having listened awhile, to hear what I could, and hearing what I have told thee, I crept away on my journey."

The effect of this unexpected revelation upon the young Virginian was as if an adder had suddenly fastened upon his bosom. It woke a suspicion, involving indeed an improbability such as his better reason revolted at, but full of pain and terror. But wild and incredible as it seemed, it received a kind of confirmation from what Nathan added.

"The rifle-guns, the beads, and the cloth," he said, "that were distributed after the battle,—does thee think they were plunder taken from the young Kentuckians they had vanquished? Friend, these things were a price with which the white man in the red shawl paid the assassin villains for taking thee prisoner,—thee and thee kinswoman. His hirelings were vagabonds of all the neighbouring tribes, Shawnees, Wyandots, Delawares, and Piankeshaws, as I noted well when I crept among them; and old Wenonga is the greatest vagabond of all, having long since been degraded by his tribe for bad luck, drunkenness, and other follies, natural to an Injun. My own idea is, that that white man thirsted for thee blood, having given thee up to the Piankeshaws, who, thee says, had lost one of their men in the battle; for which thee would certainly have been burned alive at their village: but what was his design in captivating thee poor kinswoman that thee calls Edith, truly I cannot divine, not knowing much of thee history."

"You shall hear it," said Roland, with hoarse accents,—"at least so much of it as may enable you to confirm or disprove your suspicions. There is indeed one man whom I have always esteemed my enemy, the enemy also of Edith,—a knave capable of any extremity, yet never could I have dreamed of a villany so daring, so transcendent as this!"

So saying, Roland, smothering his agitation as he could, proceeded to acquaint his rude friend, now necessarily his confidant, with so much of his history as related to Braxley, his late uncle's confidential agent and executor;—a man whom Roland's revelations to the gallant and inquisitive Colonel Bruce, and still more, perhaps, his conversations with Edith in the wood, may have introduced sufficiently to the reader's acquaintance. But of Braxley, burning with a hatred he no longer chose to subdue, the feeling greatly exasperated, also, by the suspicion Nathan's hints had infused into his mind, he now spoke without restraint; and assuredly, if one might have judged by the bitterness of his invectives, the darkness of the colours with which he traced the detested portrait, a baser wretch did not exist on the whole earth. Yet to a dispassionate and judicious hearer it might have seemed that there was little in the evidence to bear out an accusation so sweeping and heavy. Little, indeed, had the soldier to charge against him save his instrumentality in defeating hopes and expectations which had been too long indulged to be surrendered without anger and pain. That this instrumentality, considering all the circumstances, was to be attributed to base and fraudulent motives, it was natural to suspect; but the proofs were far from being satisfactory, as they rested chiefly on surmises and assumptions.

It will be recollected, that on the death of Major Forrester, Braxley had brought to light a testament of undoubted authenticity, but of ancient date, in which the whole estate of the deceased was bequeathed to his own infant child,—an unfortunate daughter, who, however, it had never been doubted, had perished many years before among the flames of the cabin of her foster-mother, but who Braxley had made oath was, to the best of his knowledge, still alive. His oath was founded, he averred, upon the declaration of a man, the husband of the foster-mother, a certain Atkinson, whom tory principles and practices, and perhaps crimes and outrages—for such were charged against him—had long since driven to seek refuge on the frontier, but who had privily returned to the major's house, a few weeks before the latter's death, and made confession that the girl was still living; but, being recognised by an old acquaintance, and dreading the vengeance of his countrymen, he had immediately fled again to the frontier, without acquainting any one with the place of the girl's concealment. The story of Atkinson's return was confirmed by the man who had seen and recognised him, but who knew nothing of the cause of his visit; and Braxley declared he had already taken steps to ferret him out, and had good hopes through his means of recovering the lost heiress.

This story Roland affected to believe a vile fabrication, the result of a deep-laid, and, unfortunately, too successful design on Braxloy's part to get possession, in the name of an imaginary heiress, of the rich estates of his patron. The authenticity of the will, which had been framed at a period when the dissensions between Major Forrester and his brothers were at the highest, Roland did not doubt; it was the non-existence of the individual in whose favour it had been executed, a circumstance which he devoutly believed, that gave a fraudulent character to its production. He even accused Braxley of having destroyed a second will (by which the former was of course annulled, even supposing the heiress were still living), a testament framed a few months before his uncle's death; in which the latter had bequeathed all his possessions to Edith, the child of his adoption. That such a second will had been framed, appeared from the testator's own admissions; at least, he had so informed Edith, repeating the fact on several different occasions. The fact, indeed, even Braxley did not deny; but he averred, that the second instrument had been destroyed by the deceased himself, as soon as the confession of Atkinson had acquainted him with the existence of his own unfortunate daughter. This explanation Roland rejected entirely, insisting that during the whole period of Atkinson's visit, and for some weeks before, his uncle had been in a condition of mental imbecility and unconsciousness, as incapable of receiving and understanding the supposed confession as he was of acting on it. The story was only an additional device of Braxley to remove from himself the suspicion of having destroyed the second will.

But whatever might have been thought of these imputations, it was evident that the young soldier had another cause for his enmity,—one, indeed, that seemed more operative on his mind and feelings than even the loss of fortune. The robber and plunderer, for these were the softest epithets he had for his rival, had added to his crimes the enormity of aspiring to the affections of his kinswoman; whom the absence of Roland and the helpless imbecility of her uncle left exposed to his presumption and his arts. Had the maiden smiled upon his suit, this indeed might have seemed a legitimate cause of hatred on the part of Roland; but Edith had repelled the lover with firmness, perhaps even with contempt. The presumption of such a rival Roland might perhaps have pardoned; but he saw in the occurrences that followed, a bitter and malignant revenge of the maiden's scorn, which none but the basest of villains could have attempted. It was this consideration which gave the sharpest edge to the young man's hatred: and it was his belief that a wretch capable of such a revenge, was willing to add to it any other measure of villany, however daring and fiendish, that had turned his thoughts upon Braxley, when Nathan's words first woke the suspicion of a foeman's design and agency in the attack on his party. How Braxley, a white man and Virginian, and therefore the foe of every western tribe, could have so suddenly and easily thrown himself into the arms of the savages, and brought them to his own plans, it might have been difficult to say. But anger is credulous, and fury stops not at impossibilities. "It is Braxley himself!" he cried, at the close of his narration; "how can it be doubted? He announced publicly his intention to proceed to the frontier, to the Kenhawa settlements, in search of the fabulous heiress, and was gone before our party had all assembled in Fincastle. Thus, then, he veiled his designs, thus concealed a meditated villany. But his objects—it was not my miserable life he sought—what would that avail him?—they aimed at my cousin,—and she is now in his power!"

"Truly, then," said Nathan, who listened to the story with great interest, and now commented on Roland's agitation with equal composure, "thee doth make a great fuss for nothing; for, truly, the maid will not be murdered—Truly, thee has greatly relieved my mind. Thee should not think the man, being a white man, will kill her."

"Kill her!" cried Roland—"Would that twenty bullets had pierced her heart, rather than she should have fallen alive into the hands of Braxley! Miserable wretch that I am! what can I do to save her? We will rescue her,

Nathan; we will seek assistance; we will pursue the ravisher;—it is not yet too late. Speak to me—I shall go distracted: what must we do?—what *can* we do?"

"Truly," said Nathan, "I fear me, we can do nothing.—Don't thee look so frantic, friend; I don't think thee has good sense. Thee talks of assistance—what is thee thinking about? where would thee seek assistance? Has thee forgot the Injun army is on the north side, and all the fighting-men of the Stations gone to meet them? There is nobody to help thee."

"But the emigrants, my friends? they are yet nigh at hand—"

"Truly," said Nathan, "thee is mistaken. The news of the Injuns, that brought friend Thomas the younger into the woods, did greatly dismay them, as the young men reported; and, truly, they did resolve to delay their journey no longer, but start again before the break of day, that they might the sooner reach the Falls, and be in safety with their wives and little ones. There is no help for thee. Thee and me is alone in the wilderness, and there is no friend with us. Leave wringing thee hands, for it can do thee no good."

"I am indeed friendless, and there is no hope," said Roland, with the accents of despair; "while we seek assistance, and seek it vainly, Edith is lost,—lost for ever! Would that we had perished together! Hapless Edith! wretched Edith!—Was ever wretch so miserable as I?"

With such expressions, the young man gave a loose to his feelings, and Nathan surveyed, first with surprise and then with a kind of gloomy indignation, but never, as it seemed, with anything like sympathy, the extravagance of his grief.

"Thee is but a madman!" he exclaimed at last, and with a tone of severity that arrested Roland's attention: "does thee curse thee fate, and the Providence that is above thee, because the maid of thee heart is carried into captivity unharmed? Is thee wretched, because thee eyes did not see the Injun axe struck into her brain? Friend, thee does not know what such a sight is; but *I* do—yes, I have looked upon such a thing, and I will tell thee what it is; for it is good thee should know. Look, friend," he continued, grasping Roland by the arm, as if to command his attention, and surveying him with a look both wild and mournful, "thee sees a man before thee who was once as young and as happy as thee,—yea, friend, happier, for I had many around me to love me,—the children of my body, the wife of my bosom, the mother that gave me birth. Thee did talk of such things to me in the wood,—thee did mention them one and all,—wife, parent, and child! Such things had I; and men spoke well of me—But thee sees what I am! There is none of them remaining,—none only but *me*; and thee sees me what I am! Ten years ago I was another man,—a poor man, friend, but one that was happy. I dwelt upon the frontiers of Bedford—thee may not know the place; it is among the mountains of Pennsylvania, and far away. *There* was the house that I did build me; and in it there was all that I held dear, 'my gray old mother,'—(that's the way thee did call her, when thee spoke of her in the wood!)—'the wife of my bosom,' and 'the child of my heart,'—the *children*, friend,—for there was five of them, sons and daughters together,—little innocent babes that had done no wrong; and, truly, I loved them well. Well, friend, the Injuns came around us: for being bold, because of my faith that made me a man of peace and the friend of all men, I sat me down far on the border. But the Shawnees came upon me, and came as men of war, and their hands were red with the blood of my neighbours, and they raised them against my little infants. Thee asked me in the wood, what I would do in such case, having arms in my hand? Friend, I *had* arms in my hand, at that moment,—a gun that had shot me the beasts of the mountain for food, and a knife that had pierced the throats of bears in their dens. I gave them to the Shawnee chief, that he might know I was a friend.—Friend! if thee asks me now for my children, I can tell thee—With my own knife he struck down my eldest boy! with my own gun he slew the mother of my children!—If thee should live till thee is gray, thee will never see the sight I saw that day! When thee has children that Injuns murder, as thee stands by,—a wife that clasps thee legs in the writhing of death,—her blood, spouting up to thee bosom, where she has slept,—an old mother calling thee to help her in the death-struggle:—then, friend, *then* thee may see—then thee may know—then thee may feel—then thee may call theeself wretched, for thee will be so! Here was my little boy,—does thee see? there his two sisters—thee understands?—there—Thee may think I would have snatched a weapon to help them *then*! Well, thee is right:—but it was too late!—All murdered, friend!—all—all,—all cruelly murdered!"

It is impossible to convey an idea of the extraordinary vehemence, the wild accents, the frantic looks, with which Nathan ended the horrid story, into which he had been betrayed by his repining companion. His struggles to subdue the passions that the dreadful recollections of a whole family's butchery awoke in his bosom, only served to add double distortion to his changes of countenance, which, a better index of the convulsion within than were his broken, incoherent, half-inarticulate words, assumed at last an appearance so wild, so hideous, so truly terrific, that Roland was seized with horror, deeming himself confronted with a raging maniac. He raised his hand to remove that of Nathan, which still clutched his arm, and clutched it with painful force; but while in the act, the fingers relaxed of themselves, and Nathan dropped suddenly to the earth, as if struck down by a thunderbolt, his mouth foaming, his eyes distorted, his hands clenched, his body convulsed,—in short, exhibiting every proof of an epileptic fit, brought on by overpowering agitation of mind. As he fell, little Peter sprang to his side, and throwing his paws on his unconscious master's breast, stood over him as if to protect him, growling at Roland; who, though greatly shocked at the catastrophe, did not hesitate to offer such relief as was in his power. Disregarding the menace of the dog, which seemed at last to understand the purpose was friendly, he raised Nathan's head upon his knee, loosened the neckcloth that bound his throat, and sprinkled his face with water from the spring. While thus engaged, the cap of the sufferer fell from his head, and Roland saw that Nathan carried with him a better cause for the affliction than could be referred to any mere temporary emotion, however overwhelming to the mind. A horrible scar disfigured the top of his head, which seemed to have been, many years before, crushed by the blows of a heavy weapon; and it was equally manifest that the savage scalping-knife had done *its* work on the mangled head.

The soldier had heard that injuries to the head often resulted in insanity of some species or other; he could now speculate, on better grounds, and with better reason, upon some of those singular points of character which seemed to distinguish the houseless Nathan from the rest of his fellow-men.

CHAPTER XXIV

The convulsion was but momentary, and departed with almost the same suddenness that marked its accession. Nathan started half up, looked wildly around him, surveying the bodies of the two Piankeshaws, and the visage of the sympathising soldier. Then snatching up and replacing his hat with one hand, and grasping Roland's with the other, he exclaimed, as if wholly unconscious of what had happened him,—

"Thee has heard it, and thee knows it,—thee knows what the Shawnees have done to me—they have killed them all, all that was of my blood! Had they done so by thee, friend," he demanded with eagerness, "had they done so by *thee*, what would thee have done to them?"

"Declared eternal war upon them and their accursed race!" cried Roland, greatly excited by the story; "I would have sworn undying vengeance, and I would have sought it,—ay, sought it without ceasing. Day and night, summer and winter, on the frontier and in their own lands and villages, I would have pursued the wretches, and pursued them to the death."

"Thee is right," cried Nathan, wringing the hand he still held, and speaking with a grin of hideous approval;—"by night and by day, in summer and in winter, in the wood and in the wigwam, thee would seek for their blood, and thee would shed it;—thee would think of thee wife and thee little babes, and thee heart would be as stone and fire within thee—thee would kill, friend, thee would kill, thee would kill!" And the monosyllable was breathed over and over again with a ferocity of emphasis that showed how deep and vindictive was the passion in the speaker's mind. Then,—with a transition of feeling as unexpected as it was abrupt, he added, still wringing Roland's hand, as if he had found in him a sympathizing friend, whose further kindness he was resolved to deserve, and to repay,—"Thee is right; I have thought about what thee has said—Thee shall have assistance. Thee is a brave man, and thee has not mocked at me because of my faith. Thee enemies shall be pursued, and the maid thee loves shall be restored to thee arms."

"Alas," said Roland, almost fearing from the impetuosity, as well as confidence, with which Nathan now spoke, that his wits were in a state of distraction, "where shall we look for help, since there are none but ourselves in this desert, of whom to ask it?"

"From our two selves it must come, and from none others," said Nathan, briskly. "We will follow the murdering thieves that have robbed thee of thee treasure, and we will recover the maid Edith from their hands."

"What! unaided? alone?"

"Alone, friend, with little Peter to be our guide, and Providence our hope and our stay. Thee is a man of courage, and thee heart will not fail thee, even if thee should find theeself led into the heart of the Injun nation. I have thought of this thing, friend, and I perceive there is good hope we shall prevail, and prevail better than if we had an hundred men to follow at our backs; unless we had them ready with us, to march this very day. Does thee hear me, friend? The Shawnee fighting-men are now in Kentucky, assembled in a great army, scalping and murdering as they come: their villages are left to be guarded by women and children and old men no longer fit for war. Thee understands me? If thee waits till thee collects friends, thee will have to cut thee way with them through fighting-men returned to their villages before thee; if thee proceeds as thee is, thee has nothing to fear that thee cannot guard against with thee own cunning,—nothing to oppose thee that thee cannot conquer with thee own strength and courage."

"And how," cried Roland, too ardent of temper, too ready to snatch at any hope, to refuse his approbation to the enterprise, though its difficulties immediately crowded before his eyes, "how shall we follow a trail so long and cold? where shall we find arms? where—"

"Friend," said Nathan, interrupting him, "thee speaks without thought. For arms and ammunition, thee has thee choice among the spoils of these dead villains, thee captivators. For the trail, thee need think nothing of that: lost or found, thee may be certain it leads to the old Vulture's town on the Miami: there thee will find thee cousin, and thither I can lead thee."

"Let us go then, in Heaven's name," cried Roland, "and without further delay; every moment is precious."

"Thee speaks the truth; and if thee feels thee limbs strong enough—"

"They are nerved by hope; and while that remains, I will neither faint nor falter. Edith rescued, and one blow—one good blow struck at the villain that wrongs her;—then let them fail me, if Heaven wills it, and fail me for ever!"

Few more words were required to confirm Roland's approval of the project so boldly, and indeed, as it seemed, so judiciously advised by his companion. To seek assistance was, as Nathan had justly said, to cast away the opportunity which the absence of the warriors from their towns opened to his hopes,—an opportunity in which craft and stratagem might well obtain the success not to be won, at a later period, and after the return of the marauders, even by a band of armed men.

Turning to the corses that still lay on the couch of leaves where they expired, Nathan began with little ceremony, and none of the compunction that might have been expected, to rob them of their knives, guns, and ammunition, with which Roland, selecting weapons to his liking, was soon well armed. The pouches of the warriors, containing strips of dried venison and stores of parched corn, Nathan appropriated in the same way, taking care, from the superabundance, to reward the services of little Peter, who received with modest gratitude, but despatched with energetic haste, the meal which his appearance, as well as his appetite, showed was not a blessing of every-day occurrence.

These preparations concluded, Nathan signified his readiness to conduct the young soldier on his way. But as he stepped to the edge of the little glade, and turned to take a last look of the dead Indians, the victims of his own warlike hand, a change came over his appearance. The bold and manly look which he had for a moment assumed, was exchanged for an air of embarrassment and almost timidity, such as marked his visage of old, at the Station. He hesitated, paused, looked at the bodies again, and then at Roland; and finally muttered aloud, though with doubting accents,—

"Thee is a man of war, friend,—a man of war and a soldier! and thee fights Injuns even as the young men of Kentucky fights them; and thee may think it but right and proper, as they do, in such case made and provided, to take the scalps off the heads of these same dead vagabonds! Truly, friend, if thee is of that mind, truly, I won't oppose thee!"

"Their scalps? *I* scalp them!" cried Boland, with a soldier's disgust; "I am no butcher: I leave them to the bears and wolves, which the villains in their natures so strongly resembled. I will kill Indians wherever I can; but no scalping, Nathan, no scalping from me!"

"Truly, it is just as thee thinks proper," Nathan mumbled out; and without further remark he strode into the wood, following the path which the Piankeshaws had travelled the preceding evening, until, with Roland, he reached the spot where had happened the catastrophe of the keg,—a place but a few hundred paces distant from the glade. Along the whole way he had betrayed symptoms of dissatisfaction and uneasiness, for which Roland could not account; and now, having arrived at this spot, he came to a pause, and revealed the source of his trouble.

"Do thee sit down here and rest thee weary limbs, friend," he said. "Truly, I have left two Injun guns lying open to the day; and, truly, it doth afflict me to think so; for if other Injuns should chance upon this place, they must needs find them, and perhaps use them in killing poor white persons. Truly, I will hide them in a hollow tree, and return to thee in a minute."

With these words, he immediately retraced his path, leaving Roland to wonder and speculate at leisure over the singular intermixture of humane and ferocious elements of which his character seemed compounded. But the speculation was not long indulged; in a few moments Nathan's footsteps were heard ringing along the arched path, and he again made his appearance, but looking a new man. His gait was fierce and confident, his countenance bold and expressive of satisfaction. "Things should never be done by halves," he muttered, but more as if speaking to his own thoughts than to his companion.

With this brief apology, he again led the way through the forest; but not until Roland had observed, or thought he observed, a drop of blood fall from his tattered knife-sheath to the earth. But the suspicion that this little incident, coupled with the change in Nathan's deportment, awoke in Roland's mind, he had no leisure to pursue, Nathan now striding forward at a pace which soon brought his companion to a painful sense of his own enfeebled and suffering condition.

"Thee must neither faint nor flag," said Nathan; "thee enemies have the start of thee by a whole day; and they have thee horses also. Truly, it is my fear, that, with these horses and thee kinswoman, Abel Doe and the man Braxley, thee foeman, may push on for the Injun town with what speed they can, leaving their Injun thieves the footmen, to follow on as they may, or perhaps to strike through the woods for the north side, to join the ramping villains that are there burning and murdering! Thee must keep up thee strength till night-fall; when thee shall have good meat to eat and a long sleep to refresh thee; and, truly, on the morrow thee will be very well, though a little feverish."

With such encouragement, repeated time by time as seemed to him needful, Nathan continued to lead through wood and brake, with a vigour and freshness of step that moved the wonder and envy of Roland, who knew that, like himself, Nathan had been without sleep for two nights in succession; besides, having employed the intervening days in the most laborious exertions. Such an example of untiring energy and zeal, and the reflection that they were displayed in his cause—in the cause of his hapless Edith—supported Roland's own flagging steps; and he followed without murmuring, until the close of the day found him again on the banks of the river that had witnessed so many of his sufferings. He had been long aware that Nathan had deserted the path of the Piankeshaws; but not doubting his superior knowledge of the woods had led him into a shorter path, he was both surprised and concerned, when, striking the river at last, he found himself in a place entirely unknown, and apparently many miles below the scene of conflict of the previous day.

"He that would follow upon the heels of Wenonga," said Nathan, "must walk wide of his footsteps, for fear lest he should suddenly tread on the old reptile's tail. Thee don't know the craft of an old Injun that expects to be followed,—as, truly, it is like the Black-Vulture may expect it now. Do thee be content, friend; there is more paths to Wenonah's town than them that Wenonga follows; and, truly, we may gain something by taking the shortest."

Thus satisfying Roland he had good reasons for choosing his own path, Nathan led the way to the verge of the river; where, leaving the broad buffalo-trace by which he descended the banks, and diving through canes and rocks, until he had left the ford to which the path led, a quarter-mile or more behind, he stopped at last under a grim cliff overgrown with trees and brambles, where a cove or hollow in the rock, of a peculiarly wild, solitary, and defensible character, invited him to take up quarters for the night.

Nor did this seem the first time Wandering Nathan had sought shelter in the place, which possessed an additional advantage in a little spring that trickled from the rock, and collected its limpid stores in a rocky basin hard by; there were divers half-burned brands lying on its sandy floor, and a bed of fern and cane-leaves, not yet dispersed by the winds, that had evidently been once pressed by a human form.

"Thee will never see a true man of the woods," said Nathan, with much apparent self-approval, "build his camp-fire on a roadside, like that unlucky foolish man, Ralph Stackpole by name, that ferried thee down the river. Truly, it was a marvel he did not drown thee all, as well as the poor man Dodge! Here, friend, we can sleep in peace; and, truly, sleep will be good for thee, and me, and little Peter."

With these words, Nathan set about collecting dried logs and branches, which former floods had strown in great abundance along the rocks; and dragging them into the cove, he soon set them in a cheerful blaze. He then drew forth his stores of provender—the corn and dried meat he had taken from the Piankeshaws' pouches,—the latter of which, after a preliminary sop or two in the spring, for the double purpose of washing off the grains of gunpowder, tobacco, and what not, the usual scrapings of an Indian's pocket,—and of restoring its long vanished juices,—he spitted on twigs of cane, and roasted with exceeding patience and solicitude at the fire. To these dainty viands he added certain cakes and lumps of some nondescript substance, as Roland supposed it, until assured by Nathan it was good maple-sugar, and of his own making. "Truly," said he, "it might have been better, had it been better made. But, truly, friend, I am, as thee may see, a man that lives in the woods, having neither cabin nor wigwam, the Injuns having burned down the same, so that it is tedious to rebuild them; and having neither pots nor pans, the same having been all stolen, I did make my sugar in the wooden troughs, boiling it down with hot stones; and, truly, friend, it doth serve the purpose of salt, and is good against hunger in long journeys."

There was little in the dishes, set off by Nathan's cookery, or in his own feelings, to dispose the sick and weary soldier to eat; and having swallowed but a few mouthfuls, he threw himself upon the bed of leaves, hoping to find that refreshment in slumber which neither food nor the conversation of his companion could supply. His body being as much worn and exhausted as his mind, the latter was not doomed to be long tossed by grief and fear; and before the last hues of sunset had faded in the west, slumber had swept from his bosom the consciousness of his own sufferings, with even the memory of his Edith.

In the meanwhile, Nathan had gathered more wood to supply the fire during the night, and added a new stock of cane-leaves for his own bed; having made which to his liking, disposed his arms where they could be seized at a moment's warning, and, above all, accommodated little Peter with a couch at his feet, he also threw himself at length, and was soon sound asleep.

CHAPTER XXV

The morning-star, peeping into the hollow den of the wanderers, was yet bright on the horizon, when Roland was roused from his slumbers by Nathan, who had already risen and prepared a hasty meal resembling in all respects that of the preceding evening. To this the soldier did better justice than to the other: for, although feeling sore and stiff in every limb, he experienced none of the feverish consequences Nathan had predicted from his wounds; and his mind, invigorated by so many hours of rest, was more tranquil and cheerful. The confidence Nathan seemed to feel in the reasonableness and practicability of their enterprise, however wild and daring it might have seemed to others, was his own best assurance of its success; and hope thus enkindled and growing with his growing strength, it required no laborious effort to summon the spirits necessary to sustain him during the coming trials.

This change for the better was not unnoticed by Nathan, who exhorted him to eat freely, as a necessary prelude to the labours of the day; and the rude meal being quickly and satisfactorily despatched, and little Peter receiving his due share, the companions, without further delay, seized their arms, and recommenced their journey. Crossing the river at the buffalo-ford above, and exchanging the road to which it led for wilder and lonelier paths traced by smaller animals, they made their way through the forest, travelling with considerable speed, which was increased, as the warmth of exercise gradually restored their native suppleness to the soldier's limbs.

And now it was, that, as the opening of a glorious dawn, flinging sunshine and life over the whole wilderness, infused still brighter hopes into his spirit, he began to divide his thoughts between his kinswoman and his guide, bestowing more upon the latter than he had previously found time or inclination to do. His strange appearance, his stranger character, his sudden metamorphosis from a timid and somewhat over-conscientious professor of the doctrines of peace and good-will, into a highly energetic and unremorseful, not to say, valiant man of war, were all subjects to provoke the soldier's curiosity; which was still further increased when he pondered over the dismal story Nathan had so imperfectly told him on the past day. Of those dreadful calamities which, in Nathan's own language, "had made him what he was," a houseless wanderer of the wilderness, the Virginian would gladly have known more; but his first allusion to the subject produced such evident disorder in Nathan's mind, as if the recollection were too harrowing to be borne, that the young man immediately repressed his inquiries, and diverted his guide's thoughts into another channel. His imagination supplied the imperfect links in the story: he could well believe that the same hands which had shed the blood of every member of the poor borderer's family, might have struck the hatchet into the head of the resisting husband and father; and that the effects of that blow, with the desolation of heart and fortune which the heavier ones, struck at the same time, had entailed, might have driven him to the woods, an idle, and perhaps aimless, wanderer.

How far these causes might have operated in leading Nathan into those late acts of blood which were at such variance with his faith and professions, it remained also for Roland to imagine; and, in truth, he imagined they had operated deeply and far; though nothing in Nathan's own admissions could be found to sanction any belief save that they were the results, partly of accident, and partly of sudden and irresistible impulse.

At all events, it was plain that his warlike feats, however they might at first have shocked his sense of propriety, now sat but lightly on his conscience; and, indeed, since his confession at the Piankeshaw camp, he ceased even to talk of them, perhaps resting upon that as an all-sufficient explanation and apology. It is certain from that moment he bore himself more freely and boldly, entered no protest whatever against being called on to do his share of such fighting as might occur—a stipulation made with such anxious forethought when he first consented to accompany the lost travellers—nor betrayed any tenderness of invective against the Indians, whom, having first spoken of them only as "evil-minded poor Shawnee creatures," he now designated, conformably to established usage among his neighbours of the Stations, as "thieves and dogs," "bloody villains, and rapscallions;" all which expressions he bestowed with as much ease and emphasis as if he had been accustomed to use them all his life.

With this singular friend and companion Roland pursued his way through the wilderness, committing life, and the hopes that were dearer than life, to his sole guidance and protection; nor did anything happen to shake his faith in either the zeal or ability of Nathan to conduct to a prosperous issue the cause he had so freely and disinterestedly espoused.

As they thridded the lonely forest-paths together, Nathan explained at length the circumstances upon which he founded his hopes of success in their project; and, in doing so, convinced the soldier, not only that his sagacity was equal to the enterprise, but that his acquaintance with the wilderness was by no means confined to the region south of the Ohio; the northern countries, then wholly in the possession of the Indian tribes, appearing to be just as well known to him, the Miami country in particular, in which lay the village of the Black-Vulture. How this knowledge had been obtained was not so evident; for, although he averred he hunted the deer or trapped the beaver on either side the river, as appeared to him most agreeable, it was hardly to be supposed he could carry on such operations in the heart of the Indian nation. But it was enough for Roland that the knowledge so essential to his own present plans, was really possessed by his conductor, and he cared not to question how it had been arrived at; it was an augury of success, of which he felt the full influence.

The evening of that day found him upon the banks of the Kentucky, the wild and beautiful river from which the wilderness around derived its name; and the next morning, crossing it on a raft of logs speedily constructed by Nathan, he trod upon the soil of the north side, famous even then for its beauty and for the deeds of bloodshed almost daily enacted among its scattered settlements, and destined, unhappily, to be rendered still more famous for a tragedy which that very day witnessed, far off among the barren ridges of the Licking, where sixty of the district's best and bravest sons fell the victims less of Indian subtlety than of their own unparalleled rashness. But of that bloody field the travellers were to hear thereafter; the vultures were winging their flight towards the fatal scene; but they alone could snuff, in that silent desert, the scent of the battle that vexed it.

Sleeping that night in the woods, the next day, being the fourth since they left the Piankeshaw camp, beheld the travellers upon the banks of the Ohio; which, seen, for the first time, in the glory of summer, its crystal waters wheeling placidly along amid hills and forests, ever reflected in the bright mirror below, and with the air of virgin solitude which, through so many leagues of its course, it still presents, never fails to fill the beholder's mind with an enchanting sense of its loveliness.

Here a raft was again constructed; and the adventurers pushing boldly across, were soon upon the opposite shore. This feat accomplished, Nathan took the precaution to launch their frail float adrift in the current, that no tell-tale memorial of a white man's visit should remain to be read by returning warriors. The next moment, ascending the bank of the river, he plunged with his companion into the midst of brake and forest; neither of them then dreaming that upon the very spot where they toiled through the tangled labyrinths, a few years should behold the magic spectacle of a fair city, the Queen of the West, uprisen with the suddenness, and almost the splendour, of the *Fata-Morgana*, though, happily, doomed to no such evanescent existence. Then handling their arms, like men who felt they were in a foe-man's country, and knew that every further step was to be taken in peril, they resumed their journey, travelling with such speed and vigour (for Roland's strength had returned apace), that at the close of the day they were, according to Nathan's account, scarce twenty miles distant from the Black-Vulture's village, which they might easily reach the following day. On the following day, accordingly, they resumed their march, avoiding all paths, and stealing through the most unfrequented depths of the woods, proceeding with a caution which was every moment becoming more obviously necessary to the success of their enterprise.

Up to this period their journey had presented nothing of interest, being a mere succession of toil, privation, and occasional suffering, naturally enough to be expected in such an undertaking; but it was now about to be varied by an adventure of no little interest in itself, and, in its consequences, destined to exercise a powerful influence on the prospects of the travellers.

Laying their plans so as to reach the Indian village only about nightfall, and travelling but slowly and with great circumspection, they had not, at mid-day, accomplished much more than half the distance; when they came to a halt in a little dell, extremely wild and sequestered, where Nathan proposed to rest a few hours, and recruit their strength with a warm dinner—a luxury they had not enjoyed for the last two days, during which they had subsisted upon the corn and dried meat from the Indian wallets. Accident had, a few moments before, provided them materials for a more palatable meal. They had stumbled upon a deer that had just fallen under the attack of a catamount; which, easily driven from its yet warm and palpitating quarry, surrendered the feast to its unwelcome visitors. An inspection of the carcass showed that the animal had been first struck by the bullet of some wandering Indian hunter—a discovery that somewhat concerned Nathan, until, after a more careful examination of the wound, which seemed neither severe nor mortal, he was convinced the poor beast had run many long miles, until, in fact, wholly exhausted, before the panther had finished the work of the huntsman. This circumstance removing his uneasiness, he helped himself to the choicest portion of the animal, amputated a hind leg without stopping to flay it, and clapping this upon his shoulder in a very business-like way, left the remainder of the carcass to be despatched by the wild-cat at her leisure.

The little dell, in which Nathan proposed to cook and enjoy his savoury treasure, at ease and in safety, was enclosed by hills; of which the one by which they descended into it fell down in a rolling slope densely covered with trees; while the other, rocky, barren, and almost naked, rose precipitously up, a grim picture of solitude and desolation. A scanty brook, oozing along through the swampy bottom of the hollow, and supplied by a spring near its head, at which the two friends halted to prepare their meal, ran meandering away among alders and other swampy plants, to find exit into a larger vale that opened below, though hidden from the travellers by the winding of the rocky ridge before them.

In this lonely den, Nathan and Roland began straightway to disencumber themselves of arms and provisions, seeming well satisfied with its convenience. But not so little Peter; who, having faithfully accompanied them so far, now following numbly at his master's heels, and now, in periods of alarm or doubt, taking post in front, the leader of the party, uplifted his nose, and fell to snuffing about him in a way that soon attracted his master's notice. Smelling first around the spring, and then giving a look both up and down the glen, as if to satisfy himself there was nothing wrong in either of those quarters, he finally began to ascend the rocky ridge, snuffing as he went, and ever and anon looking back to his master and soliciting his attention by a wag of his tail.

"Truly, thee did once wag to me in vain!" said Nathan, snatching up his gun, and looking volumes of sagacious response at his brute ally, "but thee won't catch me napping again; though, truly, what thee can smell here, where is neither track of man nor print of beast, truly, Peter, I have no idea!"

With these words, he crept up the hill himself, following in little Peter's wake; and Roland, who also grasped his rifle, as Nathan had done, though without perhaps attaching the same importance to Peter's note of warning, thought fit to imitate his example.

In this manner, cautiously crawling up, the two friends reached the crest of the hill; and peering over a precipice of fifty or more feet sheer descent, with which it suddenly dipped into a wild but beautiful little valley below, beheld a scene that, besides startling them somewhat out of their tranquillity, caused both to bless their good fortune they had not neglected the warning of their brute confederate.

The vale below, like that they had left, opened into a wider bottom-land, the bed of a creek, which they could see shining among the trees that overshadowed the rich alluvion; and into this poured a rivulet that chattered along through the glen at their feet, in which it had its sources. The hill on the other side of the little vale, which was of an oval figure, narrowest at its outlet, was rough and precipitous, like that on which they lay; but the two uniting above, bounded the head of the vale with a long, bushy, sweeping slope—a fragment of a natural amphitheatre—which was evidently of an easy ascent, though abrupt and steep. The valley thus circumscribed, though broken, and here and there deeply furrowed by the water-course, was nearly destitute of trees, except at its head, where a few young beeches flung their silver boughs and rich green foliage abroad over the grassy knolls, and patches of papaws drooped their loose leaves and swelling fruit over the stream. It was in this part of the valley, at the distance of three or four hundred paces from them, that the eyes of the two adventurers, directed by the sound of voices, which they had heard the instant they reached the crest of the ridge, fell, first, upon the smoke of a huge fire curling merrily up into the air, and then upon the bodies of no less than five Indian warriors, all zealously and uproariously engaged in an amusement highly characteristic of their race. There was among them a white man, an unfortunate prisoner, as was seen at a glance, whom they had bound by the legs to a tree; around which the savages danced and leaped, yelling now with rage, now in merriment, but all the while belabouring the poor wretch with rods and switches, which, at every turn round the tree, they laid about his head and shoulders with uncommon energy and zest. This was a species of diversion better relished, as it seemed, by the captors than their captive; who, infuriated by his pangs, and perhaps desiring, in the desperation of the moment, to provoke them to end his sufferings with the hatchet, retaliated with his fists, which were at liberty, striking fiercely at every opportunity, and once with such effect as to tumble one of the tormentors to the earth—a catastrophe, however, that the others rewarded with roars of approving laughter, though without for a moment intermitting their own cruelties.

This spectacle, it may be well supposed, produced a strong effect upon the minds of the travellers, who, not without alarm on their own account at the discovery of such dangerous neighbours, could not view without emotion a fellow white man and countryman helpless in their hands, and enduring tortures perhaps preliminary to the more dreadful one of the stake. They looked one another in the face: the Virginian's eyes sparkled with a meaning which Nathan could not misunderstand; and clutching his rifle tighter in his hands, and eyeing the young man with an ominous stare, he muttered,—"Speak, friend,—thee is a man and a soldier—what does thee think, in the case made and provided?"

"We are but two men, and they five," replied Roland, firmly, though in the lowest voice; and then repeated, in the same energetic whisper,—"we are but two men, Nathan; but there is no kinswoman now to unman me!"

Nathan took another peep at the savages before speaking. Then looking upon the young man with an uneasy countenance, he said,—"We are but two men, as thee says, and they five; and, truly, to do what thee thinks of, in open day, is a thing not to be thought on by men that have soft places in their bosoms. Nevertheless, I think, according to thee own opinion, we being strong men that have the wind of the villains, and a good cause to help us, truly, we might snap the poor man they have captivated out of their hands, with considerable much damage to them besides, the murdering rapscallions!—But, friend," he added, seeing Roland give way to his eagerness,—"thee spoke of the fair maid, thee cousin—If thee fights this battle, truly, thee may never see her more."

"If I fall," said Roland,—but he was interrupted by Nathan:

"It is not *that* thee is to think of. Truly, friend, thee may fight these savages, and thee may vanquish them; but unless thee believes in thee conscience thee can kill them every one—truly, friend, thee can hardly expect it?"

"And why should we? It is enough if we can rescue the prisoner."

"Friend, thee is mistaken. If thee attacks the villains, and but one of them escapes alive to the village, sounding the alarm, thee will never enter the same in search of the maid, thee kinswoman. Thee sees the case: thee must choose between the captive there and thee cousin!"

This was a view of the case, and as Roland felt, a just one, well calculated to stagger his resolutions, if not entirely to abate his sympathy for the unknown sufferer. As his hopes of success in the enterprise for which he had already dared and endured so much, evidently depended upon his ability to approach the Indian village without awakening suspicion, it was undeniable that an attack upon the party in the vale, unless resulting in its complete destruction, must cause, to be borne to the Black-Vulture's town, and on the wings of the wind, the alarm of white men in the woods; and thus not only cut him off from it, but actually bring upon himself all the fighting men who might be remaining in the village. To attack the party with the expectation of wholly destroying it, was, or seemed to be, an absurdity. But to desert a wretched prisoner whom he had it perhaps in his power to rescue from captivity, and from a fate still more dreadful, was a dereliction of duty, of honour, of common humanity, of which he could scarce persuade himself to be guilty. He cast his eyes up the glen, and once more looked upon the captive, who had sunk to the ground, as if from exhaustion, and whom the savages, after beating him awhile longer, as if to force him again on his feet, that they might still enjoy their amusement, now fell to securing with thongs. As Roland looked, he remembered his own night of captivity, and hesitated no longer. Turning to Nathan, who had been earnestly reading the struggles of his mind, as revealed in his face, he said, and with unfaltering resolution,—"You say we *can* rescue that man.—I was a prisoner, like him, bound too,—a helpless, hopeless captive—three Indians to guard me, and but one friend to look upon me; yet did not that friend abandon me to my fate.—God will protect my poor cousin—we must rescue him!"

"Thee is a man, every inch of thee!" said Nathan, with a look of uncommon satisfaction and fire: "thee shall have thee will in the matter of these murdering Shawnee dogs; and, it may be, it will be none the worse for thee kinswoman."

With that he motioned Roland to creep with him beyond the crest of the hill, where they straightway held a hurried consultation of war to determine upon the plan of proceedings in the prosecution of an adventure so wild and perilous.

The soldier, burning with fierce ardour, proposed that they should take post respectively the one at the head, the other at the outlet of the vale, and creeping as nigh the enemy as they could, deliver their fire, and then rushing on, before the savages could recover from their surprise, do their best to finish the affair with their hatchets,—a plan, which, as he justly said, offered the only prospect of cutting off the retreat of those who might survive the fire. But Nathan had already schemed the matter otherwise: he had remarked the impossibility of approaching the enemy from below, the valley offering no concealment which would make an advance in that quarter practicable; whereas the bushes on the slope, where the two walls of the glen united, afforded the most inviting opportunity to creep on the foe without fear of detection. "Truly," said he, "we will get us as nigh the assassin thieves as we can; and, truly, it may be our luck, each of us, to get a brace of them in range together, and so bang them beautiful!"—an idea that was manifestly highly agreeable to his imagination, from which he seemed to have utterly banished all those disgusts and gaingivings on the subject of fighting, which had formerly afflicted it; "or perhaps, if we can do nothing better," he continued, "we may catch the vagabonds wandering from their guns, to pick up sticks for their fire; in which case, friend, truly, it may be our luck to help them to a second volley out of their own pieces: or, if the worst must come, truly, then, I do know of a device that may help the villains into our hands, even to their own undoing!"

With these words, having first examined his own and Roland's arms, to see that all were in proper battle condition, and then directed little Peter to ensconce in a bush, wherein little Peter straightway bestowed himself, Tiger Nathan, with an alacrity of motion and ardour of look that indicated anything rather than distaste to the murderous work in hand, led the way along the ridge, until he had reached the place where it dipped down to the valley, covered with the bushes through which he expected to advance to a desirable position undiscovered.

But a better auxiliary even than the bushes was soon discovered by the two friends. A deep gully, washed in the side of the hill by the rains, was here found running obliquely from its top to the bottom, affording a covered way, by which, as they saw at a glance, they could approach within twenty or thirty yards of the foe entirely unseen; and, to add to its advantages, it was the bed of a little water-course, whose murmurs, as it leaped from rock to rock, assured them they could as certainly approach unheard.

"Truly," muttered Nathan, with a grim chuckle, as he looked, first, at the friendly ravine, and then at the savages below, "the Philistine rascals is in our hands, and we will smite them hip and thigh!"

With this inspiring assurance he crept into the ravine; and Roland following, they were soon in possession of a post commanding, not only the spot occupied by the enemy, but the whole valley.

Peeping through the fringe of shrubs that rose, a verdant parapet, on the brink of the gully, they looked down upon the savage party, now less than forty paces from the muzzle of their guns, and wholly unaware of the fate preparing for them. The scene of diversion and torment was over; the prisoner, a man of powerful frame but squallid appearance, whose hat,—a thing of shreds and patches,—adorned the shorn pate of one of the Indians, while his coat, equally rusty and tattered, hung from the shoulders of a second, lay bound under a tree, but so nigh that they could mark the laborious heavings of his chest. Two of the Indians sat near him on the grass keeping watch, their hatchets in their hands, their guns resting within reach against the trunk of a tree overthrown by some hurricane of former years, and now mouldering away. A third was engaged with his tomahawk, lopping away the few dry boughs that remained on the trunk. Squatting at the fire, which the third was thus labouring to replenish with fuel, were the two remaining savages, who, holding their rifles in their hands, divided their attention betwixt a shoulder of venison roasting on a stick in the fire, and the captive, whom they seemed to regard as destined to be sooner or later disposed of in a similar manner.

The position of the parties precluded the hope Nathan had ventured to entertain of getting them in a cluster, and so doing double execution with each bullet; but the disappointment neither chilled his ardour nor embarrassed his plans. His scheme of attack had been framed to embrace all contingences; and he wasted no further time in deliberation. A few whispered words conveyed his last instructions to the soldier; who, reflecting that he was fighting in the cause of humanity, remembering his own heavy wrongs, and marking the fiery eagerness that flamed from Nathan's visage, banished from his mind whatever disinclination he might have felt at beginning the fray in a mode so seemingly treacherous and ignoble. He laid his axe on the brink of the gully at his side, together with his foraging cap; and then, thrusting his rifle through the bushes, took aim at one of the savages at the fire, Nathan directing his piece against the other.

Both of them presented the fairest marks, as they sat wholly unconscious of their danger, enjoying in imagination the tortures yet to be inflicted on the prisoner. But a noise in the gully,—the falling of a stone loosened by the soldier's foot, or a louder than usual plash of water,—suddenly roused them from their dreams; they started up, and turned their eyes towards the hill.—"Now, friend!" whispered Nathan;—"if thee misses, thee loses thee maiden and thee life into the bargain.—Is thee ready?"

"Ready," was the reply.

"Right, then, through the dog's brain,—fire!"

The crash of the pieces, and the fall of the two victims, both marked by a fatal aim, and both pierced through the brain, were the first announcement of peril to their companions; who, springing up, with yells of fear and astonishment, and snatching at their arms, looked wildly around them for the unseen foe. The prisoner, also, astounded out of his despair, raised his head from the grass, and glared around. The wreaths of smoke curling over the bushes on the hill-side, betrayed the lurking place of the assailants; and savages and prisoner turning together, they all beheld at once the spectacle of two human heads,—or, to speak more correctly, two human caps, for the heads were far below them,—rising in the smoke, and peering over the bushes, as if to mark the result of the volley. Loud, furious, and exulting were the screams of the Indians, as with the speed of thought, seduced by a stratagem often practised among the wild heroes of the border, they raised and discharged their pieces against the imaginary foes so incautiously exposed to their vengeance. The caps fell, and with them the rifles that had been employed to raise them; and the voice of Nathan thundered through the glen, as he grasped his tomahawk and sprang from the ditch,—"Now, friend! up with thee axe, and do thee duty!"

With these words, the two assailants at once leaped into view, and with a bold hurrah, and bolder hearts, rushed towards the fire, where lay the undischarged rifles of their first victims. The savages yelled also in reply, and two of them bounded forward to dispute the prize. The third, staggered into momentary inaction by the suddenness and amazement of the attack, rushed forward but a step; but a whoop of exultation was on his lips, as he raised the rifle which *he* had not yet discharged, full against the breast of Tiger Nathan. But, his triumph was short-lived; the blow, so fatal as it must have proved to the life of Nathan, was averted by an unexpected incident. The prisoner, near whom he stood, putting all his vigour into one tremendous effort, burst his bonds, and, with a yell ten times louder and fiercer than had yet been uttered, added himself to the combatants. With a furious cry of encouragement to his rescuers,—"Hurrah for Kentucky!—

give it to 'em good!" he threw himself upon the savage, beat the gun from his hands, and grasping him in his brawny arms, hurled him to the earth, where, rolling over and over in mortal struggle, growling and whooping, and rending one another like wild beasts, the two, still locked in furious embrace, suddenly tumbled down the banks of the brook, there high and steep, and were immediately lost to sight.

Before this catastrophe occurred, the other Indians and the assailants met at the fire; and each singling out his opponent, and thinking no more of the rifles, they met as men whose only business was to kill or to die. With his axe flourished over his head, Nathan rushed against the tallest and foremost enemy, who, as he advanced, swung his tomahawk, in the act of throwing it. Their weapons parted from their hands at the same moment, and with perhaps equal accuracy of aim; but meeting with a crash in the air, they fell together to the earth, doing no harm to either. The Indian stooped to recover his weapon; but it was too late: the hand of Nathan was already upon his shoulder: a single effort of his vast strength sufficed to stretch the savage at his feet; and holding him down with knee and hand, Nathan snatched up the nearest axe. "If the life of thee tribe was in thee bosom," he cried, with a look of unrelenting fury, of hatred deep and ineffaceable, "thee should die the dog's death, as thee does!" And with a blow furiously struck, and thrice repeated, he despatched the struggling savage as he lay.

He rose, brandishing the bloody hatchet, and looked for his companion. He found him upon the earth, lying upon the breast of his antagonist, whom it had been his good fortune to over-master. Both had thrown their hatchets, and both without effect, Roland because skill was wanting, and the Shawnee because, in the act of throwing, he had stumbled over the body of one of his comrades, so as to disorder his aim, and even to deprive him of his footing. Before he could recover himself, Roland imitated Nathan's example, and threw himself upon the unlucky Indian,—a youth, as it appeared, whose strength, perhaps at no moment equal to his own, had been reduced by recent wounds,—and found that he had him entirely at his mercy. This circumstance, and the knowledge that the other Indians were now overpowered, softened the soldier's wrath; and when Nathan, rushing to assist him, cried aloud to him to move aside, that he might "knock the assassin knave's brains out," Roland replied by begging Nathan to spare his life. "I have disarmed him," he cried—"he resists no more—Don't kill him."

"To the last man of his tribe!" cried Nathan, with unexampled ferocity; and, without another word, drove the hatchet into the wretch's brain.

The victors now leaping to their feet, looked round for the fifth savage and the prisoner; and directed by a horrible din under the bank of the stream, which was resounding with, curses, groans, heavy blows, and the plashing of water, ran to the spot, where the last incident of battle was revealed to them in a spectacle as novel as it was shocking. The Indian lay on his back suffocating in mire and water; while astride his body sat the late prisoner, covered from head to foot with mud and gore, furiously plying his fists, for he had no other weapons, about the head and face of his foe, his blows falling like sledge-hammers or battering-rams, with such strength and fury that it seemed impossible any one of them could fail to crush the skull to atoms; and all the while garnishing them with a running accompaniment of oaths and maledictions little less emphatic and overwhelming. "You switches gentlemen, do you, you exflunctified, perditioned rascal? Ar'n't you got it, you niggur-in-law to old Satan? you 'tarnal half-imp, you? H'yar's for you, you dog, and thar's for you, you dog's dog! H'yar's the way I pay you in a small-change of sogdologers!"

And thus he cried, until Roland and Nathan seizing him by the shoulders, dragged him by main force from the Indian, who was found, when they came to examine the body afterwards, actually pommelled to death, the skull having been beaten in as with bludgeons.—The victor sprang upon his feet, and roared his triumph aloud:—"Ar'n't I lick'd him handsome!—Hurrah for Kentucky and old Salt—Cock-a-doodle-doo!"

And with that, turning to his deliverers, he displayed to their astonished eyes, though disfigured by blood and mire, the never-to-be-forgotten features of the captain of horse-thieves, Soaring Ralph Stackpole.

CHAPTER XXVI

The amazement of Stackpole at finding to whom he owed his deliverance, was not less than that of the travellers; but it was mingled, in his case, with feelings of the most unbounded and clamorous delight. Nathan he grasped by the hands, being the first upon whom he set his eyes; but no sooner had they wandered to the soldier, than throwing his arms around him, he gave him a hug, neither tender nor respectful, but indicative of the intensest affection and rapture.

"You cut the rope, stranger, and you cut the tug," he cried, "on madam's beseeching! but h'yar's the time you holped me out of a fix without axing! Now, strannger, I ar'n't your dog, 'cause how, I'm anngelliferous madam's: but if I ar'n't your dog, I'm your man, Ralph Stackpole, to be your true-blue through time and etarnity, any way you'll ax me; and if you wants a sodger, I'll 'list with you, I will, 'tarnal death to me!"

"But how, in heaven's name, came you here a prisoner? I saw you escape with my own eyes," said Roland, better pleased, perhaps, at the accession of such a stout auxiliary than with his mode of professing love and devotion.

"Strannger," said Ralph, "if you war to ax me from now till doomsday about the why and the wharfo' I couldn't make you more nor one answer: I come to holp anngelliferous madam out of the hands of the abbregynes, according to my sworn duty as her natteral-born slave and redemptioner! I war hard on the track, when the villians here caught me."

"What!" cried Roland, his heart for the first time warming towards the despised horse-thief, while even Nathan surveyed him with something like complacency, "you are following my poor cousin then? You were not brought here a prisoner?"

"If I war, I wish I may be shot," said Ralph: "it warn't a mile back on the ridge, whar the Injuns snapped me; 'causa how, I jist bang'd away at a deer, and jist then up jumps the rascals on me, afo' I had loaded old speechifier; and so they nabb'd me! And so, sodger, h'yar's the way of it all: You see, d'you see, as soon as Tom Bruce comes to, so as to be able to hold the hoss himself—"

"What," said Roland, "was he not mortally wounded?"

"He ar'n't much hurt to speak on, for all of his looking so much like coffin-meat at the first jump: it war a kind of narvousness come over him that men feels when they gets the thwack of a bullet among the narves. And so, you see, d'you see, says I, 'Tom Bruce, do you stick to the critter, and he'll holp you out of the skrimmage;' and, says I, 'I'll take the back-track, and foller atter madam.' And, says he, says he—But, 'tarnal death to me, let's scalp these h'yar dead villians, and do the talking atter! Did you see the licking I gin this here feller? It war a reggular fair knock-down-and-drag-out, and I licked him! Thar's all sorts of ways of killing Injuns; but, I reckon, I'm the only gentleman in all Kentuck as ever took a scalp in the way of natur'! Hurrah for Kentuck! and hurrah for Ralph Stackpole, for he ar' a screamer!"

The violation of the dead bodies was a mode of crowning their victory which Roland would have gladly dispensed with; but such forbearance, opposed to all border ideas of manly spirit and propriety, found no advocate in the captain of horse-thieves, and none, we are sorry to say, even in the conscientious Nathan; who, having bathed his peaceful sword too deep in blood to boggle longer at trifles, seemed mightily inclined to try his own hand at the exercise. But this addition to the catalogue of his backslidings was spared him, Roaring Ralph falling to work with an energy of spirit and rapidity of execution, which showed he needed no assistance, and left no room for competition.—Such is the practice of the border, and such it has been ever since the mortal feud, never destined to be really ended but with the annihilation, or civilisation, of the American race, first began between the savage and the white intruder. It was, and is, essentially a measure of retaliation, compelled, if not justified, by the ferocious example of the red man. Brutality ever begets brutality; and magnanimity of arms can be only exercised in the case of a magnanimous foe. With such, the wildest and fiercest rover of the frontier becomes a generous and even humane enemy.

The Virginian was yet young in the war of the wilderness: and turning in disgust from a scene he could not prevent, he made his way to the fire, where the haunch of venison, sending forth a savoury steam through the whole valley, was yet roasting on the rude Indian spit,—a spectacle which (we record it with shame) quite banished from his mind not only all thoughts of Ralph's barbarism, but even the sublime military ardour awakened by the din and perils of the late conflict. Nor were its effects less potential upon Nathan and Ralph, who, having first washed from their hands and faces the stains of battle, now drew nigh, snuffing the perfume of a dinner with as much ardour as they could have bestowed on the scent of battle. The haunch, cooked to their hands, was straightway removed to a convenient place, where all, drawing their knives, fell foul with an energy of appetite and satisfaction that left them oblivious of most sublunary affairs. The soldier forgot his sorrows, and Nathan forgot little Peter,—though little Peter, by suddenly creeping out of the bushes on the hill, and crawling humbly to the table, and his master's side, made it apparent he had not forgot himself. As for the captain of horse-thieves, he forgot everything save the dinner itself, which he attacked with an appetite well nigh ravenous, having, as he swore, by way of grace over the first mouthful, eaten nothing save roots and leaves for more than three days. It was only when, by despatching at least twice his share of the joint, he began to feel, as he said, "summat like a hoss and a gentleman," that the others succeeded in drawing from him a full account of the circumstances which had attended his solitary inroad into the Indian country and his fall into the clutches of the Shawnee party.

But little had the faithful fellow to impart, beyond what he had already told. Galloping from the fatal hill, the scene of defeat to the young Kentuckians, he sustained Tom Bruce in his arms, until the latter, reviving, had recovered strength enough to provide for his own safety; upon which Ralph, with a degree of Quixotism, that formed a part of his character, and which was, in this instance, strengthened by his grateful devotion to Edith, the saver of his life, declared he would pursue the trail of her captors, even if it led him to their village, nor cease his efforts until he had rescued her out of their hands, or laid down his life in her service. In this resolution he was encouraged by Bruce, who swore on his part, that he would instantly follow with his father, and all the men he could raise, recover the prisoners, and burn the towns of the whole Shawnee nation about their ears; a determination he was perhaps the more readily driven to by the reflection that the unlucky captives were his father's individual guests, and had been snatched away while still, in a manner, under, or relying on, his father's protection. So much he promised, and so much there was no doubt he would, if able, perform; nevertheless, he exhorted Ralph to do his best, in the meanwhile, to help the strangers, vowing, if he succeeded in rendering them any assistance, or in taking a single scalp of the villains that had borne them off, he would not only never Lynch him, himself, but would not even allow others to do it, though he were to steal all the horses in Kentucky, his father's best bay mare included.

Thus encouraged, the valiant horse-thief, bidding farewell to Tom Bruce and Brown Briareus together, commenced making good his words by creeping back to the battle-field; when, arriving before Nathan, he struck the trail of the main party, and immediately pursued it with zeal and courage, but still with the necessary caution and circumspection; his hopes of being able to do something to the advantage of his benefactress, resting principally on his knowledge of several of the outer Indian towns, in every one of which, he boasted, he had stolen horses. Being but poorly provided with food, and afraid to hunt while following so closely on the heels of the marauders, he was soon reduced to want and suffering, which he bore for three days with heroic fortitude; until at last, on the morning of the present day, being in a state of utter starvation, and a buck springing up in his path, he could resist the temptation no longer, and so fired upon it. The animal being wounded, and apparently severely, he set off in pursuit, too eager to lose time by recharging his piece; and it was while he was in that defenceless condition that the five Indians, a detachment and rear-guard, as it proved, of the very party he was dogging, attracted by the sound of his gun, stole upon him unawares and made him a prisoner. This, it seems, had happened but a short distance behind; and there was every reason to suppose that the buck, from whose loins the travellers had filched the haunch that destiny had superseded by a better, was the identical animal whose seducing appearance had brought Stackpole into captivity. He was immediately recognised by his captors, whose exultation was boundless, as indeed was their cruelty; and he could only account for their halting with him in that retired hollow, instead of pushing on to display their prize to the main body, by supposing they could not resist their desire to enjoy a snug little foretaste of the joys of torturing him at the stake, all by themselves,—a right they had earned by their good fortune in taking him. In the valley, then, they had paused, and tying him up, proceeded straightway to flog him to their hearts' content; and they had just resolved to intermit the amusement awhile, in favour of their dinner, when the appearance of his bold deliverers rushing into their camp, converted the scene of brutal merriment into one of retributive vengeance and blood.

The discovery that the five human beings he had contributed so much to destroy, were part and parcel of the very band, the authors of all his sufferings, the captors of his kinswoman, abated some little feelings of compunction with which Roland had begun occasionally to look upon the gory corses around him.

The main body of marauders, with their prisoner, there seemed good reason to suppose, were yet upon their march to the village, though too far advanced to leave any hope of overtaking them, were that even desirable. It is true, that Roland, fired by the thought of being so near his kinswoman, and having before his eyes a proof of what might be done by craft and courage, even against overwhelming numbers, urged Nathan immediately to recommence the pursuit; the Indians would doubtless halt to rest and refresh, as the luckless five had done, and might be approached and destroyed, now that they themselves had increased their forces by the rescue of Ralph, in the same way: "we can carry, with us," he said, "these Indians' guns, with which we shall be more than a match for the villains;" and he added other arguments, such, however, as appeared much more weighty to himself than to honest Nathan. That the main party should have halted, as he supposed, did not appear at all probable to Nathan: they had no cause to arrest them in their journey, and they were but a few miles removed from the village, whither they would doubtless proceed without delay, to enjoy the rewards of their villany, and end the day in revel and debauch. "And truly, friend," he added, "it will be better for thee, and me, and the maid, Edith, that we steal her by night from out of a village defended only by drowsy squaws and drunken warriors, than if we were to aim at taking her out of the camp of a war-party. Do thee keep thee patience; and, truly, there is no telling what good may come of it." In short, Nathan had here, as in previous instances, made up his mind to conduct affairs his own way; and Roland, though torn by impatience, could do nothing better than submit.

And now, the dinner being at last despatched, Nathan directed that the bodies of the slain Indians should be tumbled into a gully, and hidden from sight; a measure of such evident precaution as to need no explanation. This was immediately done; but not before Ralph and the man of peace had well rummaged the pouches of the dead, helping themselves to such valuables and stores of provender and ammunition as they could lay hands on; in addition to which, Nathan stripped from one a light Indian hunting-shirt, from another a blanket, a woman's shawl, and a medicine bag, from a third divers jingling bundles of brooches and hawk-bells, together with a pouch containing vermilion and other paints, the principal articles of savage toilet; which he made up into a bundle, to be used for a purpose he did not conceal from his comrades. He then seized upon the rifles of the dead (from among which Stackpole had already singled out his own), and removing the locks, hid them away in crannies of the cliffs, concealing the locks in other places;—a disposition which he also made of the knives and tomahawks; remarking, with great justice, that "if honest Christian men were to have no good of the weapons, it was just as well murdering Injuns should be no better off."

These things concluded, the dead covered over with boughs and brambles, and nothing left in the vale to attract a passing and unobservant eye, he gave the signal to resume the march, and with Roland and Captain Ralph, stole from the field of battle.

CHAPTER XXVII

The twilight was darkening in the west, when the three adventurers, stealing through tangled thickets, and along lonely ridges, carefully avoiding all frequented paths, looked out at last, from a distant hill, upon the valley in which lay the village of the Black-Vulture. The ruddy light of evening, bursting from clouds of crimson and purple, and shooting down through gaps of the hills in cascades of fire, fell brightly and sweetly on the little prairies, or natural meadow-lands; which, dotted over with clumps of trees, and watered by a fairy river, a tributary of the rapid Miami, winding along from side to side, now hiding beneath the shadow of the hills, now glancing into light, gave an air of tender beauty to the scene better befitting, as it might have seemed, the retreat of the innocent and peaceful sons of Oberon, than the wild and warlike children of the wilderness. Looking further up the vale, the eye fell upon patches of ripening maize, waving along the river; and beyond these, just where the valley winded away behind the hills, at the distance of a mile or more, thin wreaths of smoke creeping from roofs of bark and skins, indicated the presence of the Indian village.

Thus arrived at the goal and haven of their hopes, the theatre in which was to be acted the last scene in the drama of their enterprise, the travellers surveyed it for awhile from their concealment, in deep silence, each speculating in his own mind upon the exploits still to be achieved, the perils yet to be encountered, ere success should crown their exertions, already so arduous and so daring. Then creeping back again into a deep hollow, convenient for their purpose, they held their last consultation, and made their final preparations for entering the village. This Nathan at first proposed to do entirely alone, to spy out the condition of the village, and to discover, if possible, in what quarter the marauders had bestowed the unhappy Edith; and this being a duty requiring the utmost secrecy and circumspection, he insisted it could not be safely committed to more than one person.

"In that case," said valiant Ralph, "I'm your gentleman! Do you think, old Tiger Nathan (and, 'tarnal death to me, I do think you're 'ginnin' to be a peeler of the rale ring-tail specie,—I do, old Rusty, and thar's my fo'paw on it: you've got to be a man at last, a feller for close locks and fighting Injuns that's quite cu'rous to think on, and I'll lick any man that says a word agin you, I will, 'tarnal death to me): But I say, do you think I'm come so far atter madam, to gin up the holping her out of bondage to any mortal two-legg'd crittur whatsomever? I'm the person what knows this h'yar town better nor ar another feller in all Kentucky; and that I stick on,—for, cuss me, I've stole hosses in it!"

"Truly," said Nathan, after reflecting awhile, "thee might make theeself of service to the maid, even in thee own way; but, verily, thee is an unlucky man, and thee brings bad luck wheresoever thee goes; and so I'm afeard of thee."

"Afeard of your nose!" said Ralph, with great indignation; "ar'n't I jist been slicked out of the paws of five mortal abbregynes that had me in the tugs? and ar'n't that luck enough for any feller? I tell you what, Nathan, me and you will snuff the track together: you shall hunt up anngelliferous madam, and gin her my compliments; and, while you're about it, I'll steal her a hoss to ride off on!"

"Truly," said Nathan, complacently, "I was thinking of that; for, they says, thee is good in a horse-pound; and it needs the poor maid should have something better to depend on, in flight, than her own poor innocent legs. And so, friend, if thee thinks in thee conscience thee can help her to a strong animal, without fear of discovery, I don't care if thee goes with me: and, truly, if thee could steal two or three more of the creatures for our own riding, it might greatly advantage the maid."

"Thar you talk like a feller of gumption," said Ralph: "only show me the sight of a bit of skin-rope for halters, and you'll see a sample of hoss-stealing to make your ha'r stand on eend!"

"Of a truth," said Nathan, "thee shan't want for halters, if leather can make them. There is that on my back which will make thee a dozen; and, truly, as it needs I should now put me on attire more suitable to an Injun village, it is a satisfaction thee can put the old garment to such good use."

With these words, Nathan stripped off his coat of skins, so aged and so venerable, and gave it to the captain of horse-thieves; who, vastly delighted with the prize, instantly commenced cutting it into strips, which he twisted together, and fashioned into rude halters; while Nathan supplied its place by the loose calico shirt he had selected from among the spoils of the Indian party, throwing over it, mantle-wise, the broad Indian blanket. His head he bound round with the gaudy shawl which he had also taken from the brows of a dead foe-man; and he hung about his person various pouches and ornamented belts, provided for the purpose. Then, daubing over his face, arms, and breast with streaks of red, black, and green paint, that seemed designed to represent snakes, lizards, and other reptiles; he was, on a sudden, converted into a highly respectable-looking savage, as grim and awe-inspiring as these barbaric ornaments and his attire, added to his lofty stature, could make him. Indeed, the metamorphosis was so complete, that Captain Ralph, as he swore, could scarce look at him without longing, as this worthy personage expressed it, "to be at his top-knot."

In the meanwhile, Forrester had not deferred with patience to an arrangement which threatened to leave him, the most interested of all, in inglorious activity, while his companions were labouring in the cause of his Edith. He remonstrated, and insisted upon accompanying them to the village, to share with them all the dangers of the enterprise.

"If there was danger to none but ourselves, truly, thee should go with us and welcome," said Nathan; representing, justly enough, the little service that Roland, destitute of the requisite knowledge and skill, could be expected to render, and the dangers he must necessarily bring upon the others, in case of any, the most ordinary, difficulties arising in their progress through the village. Everything must now depend upon address, upon cunning and presence of mind; the least indiscretion (and how many might not the soldier, his feelings wound up to a pitch of the intensest excitement, commit?) must of necessity terminate in the instant destruction of all. In short, Roland was convinced, though sorely against his will, that wisdom and affection both called on him to play the part Nathan had assigned him; and he submitted to be ruled accordingly,—with the understanding, however, that the rendezvous, in which he was to await the operations of the others, should be upon the very borders of the village, whence he might, in any pressing emergency, in case of positive danger and conflict, be immediately called to their assistance.

When the twilight had darkened away, and the little river, rippling along on its course, sparkled only in the light of the stars, the three friends crept from their retreat, and descended boldly into the valley; where, guided by the barking of dogs, the occasional yells of a drunken or gamesome savage, and now and then the red glare of a fire flashing from the open crannies of a cabin, they found little difficulty in approaching the Indian village. It was situated on the further bank of the stream, and, as described, just behind the bend of the vale, at the bottom of a rugged, but not lofty hill; which, jutting almost into the river, left yet space enough for the forty or fifty lodges composing the village, sheltering them in winter from the bitter blasts that rush, at that season, from the northern lakes. Beyond the river, on the side towards the travellers, the vale was broader; and it was there the Indians had chiefly planted their corn-fields,—fields enriched by the labour, perhaps also by the tears, of their oppressed and degraded women.

Arriving at the borders of the cultivated grounds, the three adventurers crossed the river, which was neither broad nor deep, and stealing among logs and stumps at the foot of the hill, where some industrious savage had, in former years, begun to clear a field, which, however, his wives had never planted, they lay down in concealment, waiting until the subsiding of the unusual bustle in the village, a consequence manifestly of the excesses which Nathan predicted the victors would indulge in, should render their further advance practicable. But this was not the work of a moment. The savage can drink and dance through the night with as lusty a zeal as his white neighbour; the song, the jest, the merry tale, are as dear to his imagination; and in the retirement of his own village, feeling no longer the restraint of stolid gravity,—assumed in the haunts of the white man, less to play the part of a hero than to cover the nakedness of his own inferiority,—he can give himself up to wild indulgence, the sport of whim and frolic; and, when the fire-water is the soul of the feast, the feast only ends with the last drop of liquor.

It could be scarcely doubted that the Indians of the village were, this night, paying their devotions to the Manito of the rum-keg, and drinking folly and fury together from the enchanted draught, which one of the bravest of the race—its adorer and victim, like Logan the heroic, and Red-Jacket the renowned,—declared could only have been distilled "from the hearts of wild-cats and the tongues of women,—it made him so fierce and so foolish;" nor could it, on the other hand, be questioned that many a sad and gloomy reminiscence, the recollection of wrong, of defeat, of disaster, of the loss of friends and of country, was mingled in the joy of the debauch. From their lurking-place near the village, the three friends could hear many a wild whoop, now fierce and startling, now plaintive and mourning,—the one, as Nathan and Ralph said, the halloo for revenge, the other the whoop of lamentation,—at intervals chiming strangely in with unmeaning shrieks and roaring laughter, the squeaking of women and the gibbering of children, with the barking of curs, the utterance of obstreperous enjoyment, in which the whole village, brute and human, seemed equally to share. For a time, indeed, one might have deemed the little hamlet an outer burgh of Pandemonium itself; and the captain of horse-thieves swore, that, having long been of opinion "the red abbregynes war the rule children of Sattan, and niggers only the grand-boys, he should now hold the matter to be as settled as if booked down in an almanac,—he would, 'tarnal death to him."

But if the festive spirit of the barbarians might have lasted for ever, there was, it appeared, no such exhaustless quality in their liquor; and, that failing at last, the uproar began gradually to decrease; although it was not until within an hour of midnight that Nathan declared the moment had arrived for entering the village.

He then rose from his lair, and repeating his injunctions to Roland to remain where he was, until the issue of his own visit should be known, added a word of parting counsel, which, to Roland's imagination, bore somewhat an ominous character. "The thing that is to come," he said, "neither thee nor me knows anything about; for, truly, an Injun village is a war-trap, which one may sometimes creep into easy enough; but, truly, the getting out again is another matter. And so, friend, if it should be my luck, and friend Ralph's, to be killed or captivated, so that we cannot return to thee again, do thee move by the first blink of day, and do thee best to save thee own life; and, truly, I have some hope that thee may succeed, seeing that, if I should fall, little Peter (which I will leave with thee, for, truly, he would but encumber me among the dogs of the village, having better skill to avoid murdering Injuns than the creatures of his own kind), will make thee his master,—as verily, he can no longer serve a dead one,—and show thee the way back again from the wilderness. Truly, friend, he hath an affection for thee, for thee has used him well; which he can say of no other persons, save only thee and me excepted."

With that, having laid aside his gun, which, as he represented, could be, in such an undertaking, of no service, and directed Stackpole to do the same, he shook Roland by the hand, and, waiting an instant till Ralph had followed his example, and added his farewell in the brief phrase,—"Sodger, I'm atter my mistress; and, for all Nathan's small talk about massacree and captivation, we'll fetch her, with a most beautiful lot of hosses; so thar's no fawwell about it,"—turned to little Peter, whom he addressed quite as gravely as he had done the Virginian. "Now, little dog Peter," said he, "I leave thee to take care of theeself and the young man that is with thee; and do thee be good, and faithful, and obedient, as thee always has been, and have a good care thee keeps out of mischief."

With these words, which Peter, doubtless, perfectly understood, for he squatted himself down upon the ground, without any attempt to follow his master, Nathan departed, with Roaring Ralph at his side, leaving Roland to mutter his anxieties and fears, his doubts and impatience, into the ears of the least presuming of counsellors.

CHAPTER XXVIII

The night was brilliantly clear, the stars shining with an excess of lustre, with which Nathan would perhaps, at that moment, have gladly dispensed, since it was by no means favourable to the achievement he was now so daringly attempting. Fortunately, however, the Indian village lay, for the most part, in the shadow of the hill, itself covered with majestic maples and tulip-trees, that rose in dark and solemn masses above it, and thus offered the concealment denied in the more open parts of the valley. With Ralph still at his side, he crept round the projecting corner of the hill, and, shrouded in its gloom, drew nigh the village, wherein might be still occasionally heard the halloo of a drunken savage, followed by an uproarious chorus of barking and howling curs.

Whether it was that these sounds, or some gloomy forebodings of his own, awoke the anxieties of Nathan, he did not deign to reveal; but, by and by, having arrived within but a few paces of a wretched pile of skins and boughs, the dwelling of some equally wretched and improvident barbarian, he came to a sudden halt, and withdrawing the captain of horse-thieves aside from the path, addressed him in the following terms:—

"Thee says, friend, thee has taken horses from this very Village, and that thee knows it well?"

"As well," replied Ralph, "as I know the step-mothers on my own thumbs and fingers,—I do, 'tarnal death to me,—that is to say, all the parts, injacent and outjacent, circum-surrounding the boss-stamp; for thar's the place of my visiting. The way to fetch it, old boy, is jist to fetch round this h'yar old skin-pot, whar thar's a whole bee's-nest of young papooses, the size of bull-toads,—from that, up—(I know it, 'cause how, I heerd 'em squallin'; and thar war some one a lickin' 'em); or, if you don't favour taking it so close to the skirmudgeons, then you must claw up the knob h'yar, and then take and take the shoot, till you fetch right among the hosses, whar you h'ar them whinnying down the holler; and thar—"

"Friend," said Nathan, cutting him short, "it is on *thee* doings, more than on them of any others, that the hopes of the maid Edith—"

"Call her anngelliferous madam," said Ralph, "for I can't stand any feller being familiar with her,—I can't, no how."

"Well, friend," said Nathan, "it is on thee doings that her escaping the Shawnee villains this night depends. If thee does well, it may be we shall both discover and carry her safe away from captivation: if thee acts as a foolish imprudent man,—and, truly, friend, I have my fears of thee,—thee will both fail to help her theeself, and prevent others doing it, who, it may be, has the power."

"Old boy," said the captain of horse-thieves, with something like a gulp of emotion, "you ar'n't respectable to a feller's feelings. But I'll stand anything from you, 'cause how, you down'd my house in a fa'r tussle, and you helped the captain thar that helped me out of trouble. If you're atter ginning me a bit of wisdom, and all on madam's account, I'm jist the gentleman that h'ars you. State the case, and h'yar stands I confawmable."

"Well, friend," said Nathan, "what I have to advise thee is, that thee stops where thee is, leaving the rest of this matter entirely to me; seeing that, as thee knows nothing of this Injun village, excepting the horse-pound thereof, it will not be safe for thee to enter. Do thee rest where thee is, and I will spy out the place of the maiden's concealing."

"Old feller," said Captain Ralph, "you won't pretend you knows more of the place than me? You don't go for to say you ever stole a hoss here?"

"Do thee be content, friend," said Nathan, "to know there is not a cabin in all the village that is unbeknown to me: do thee be content with that. Thee must not go near the pound, until thee knows for certain the maid thee calls madam can be saved. Truly, friend, it may be we cannot help her to-night, but may do so to-morrow night."

"I see what you're up to," said Ralph: "and thar's no denying it war a natteral piece of nonsense to steal a hoss, afo' madam war ready to ride him. And so, old Nathan, if it ar' your qualified opinion I'll sarve madam better by snuggin' under a log, than by snuffin' atter her among the cabins, I'm jist the gentleman to knock under, accordin' to reason."

This declaration seemed greatly to relieve the uneasiness of Nathan, who recommending him to be as good as his word, and ensconce among some logs lying near the path, awaiting the event of his own visit to the heart of the village, immediately took his leave; though not with the timid and skulking step of a spy. Wrapping his blanket about his shoulders, and assuming the gait of a savage, he stalked boldly forwards; jingling under his mantle the bundle of hawk's-bells which he carried in his hand, as if actually to invite the observation of such barbarians as were yet moving through the village.

But this stretch of audacity, as the listening horse-thief was at first inclined to esteem it, was soon seen to have been adopted with a wise foreknowledge of its effects in removing one of the first and greatest difficulties in the wanderer's way. At the first cabin was a troop of yelling curs, that seemed somewhat disturbed by the stranger's approach, and disposed to contest his right of passing scot-free; but a jerk of the bells settled the difficulty in a moment; and the animals, mute and crest-fallen, slunk nastily away, as if expecting the crash of a tomahawk about their ears, in the usual summary Indian way, to punish their presumption in baying a warrior.

"A right-down natteral, fine conceit!" muttered Captain Ralph, approvingly: "the next time I come a-grabbin' hosses, if I don't fetch a bushel of the jinglers, I wish I may be kicked! Them thar Injun dogs is always the devil."

In the meanwhile, Nathan, though proceeding with such apparent boldness, and relying upon his disguise as all-sufficient to avert suspicion, was by no means inclined to court any such dangers as could be really avoided. If the light of a fire still burning in a wigwam, and watched by wakeful habitants, shone too brightly from its door, he crept by with the greatest circumspection; and he gave as wide a berth as possible to every noisy straggler who yet roamed through the village.

There was indeed necessity for every precaution. It was evident, that the village was by no means so destitute of defence as he had imagined,—that the warriors of Wenonga had not generally obeyed the call that carried the army of the tribes to Kentucky, but had remained in inglorious ease and sloth in their own cabins. There was no other way, at least, of accounting for the dozen or more male vagabonds, whom he found at intervals stretched here before a fire, where they had been carousing in the open air, and there lying asleep across the path, just where the demon of good cheer had dropped them. Making his own inferences from their appearance, and passing them with care, sometimes even, where their slumbers seemed unsound, crawling by on his face, he succeeded at last in reaching the central part of the village; where the presence of several cabins of logs, humble enough in themselves, but far superior to the ordinary hovels of an Indian village, indicated the abiding place of the superiors of the clan, or of those apostate white men, renegades from the States, traitors to their country and to civilisation, who were, at that day, in so many instances, found uniting their fortunes with the Indians, following, and even leading them, in their bloody incursions upon the frontiers. To one of those cabins Nathan made his way with stealthy step; and peeping through a chink in the logs, beheld a proof that here a renegade had cast his lot, in the appearance of some half a dozen naked children, of fairer hue than the savages, yet not so pale as those of his own race, sleeping on mats round a fire, at which sat, nodding and dozing, the dark-eyed Indian mother.

One brief, earnest look Nathan gave to this spectacle; then, stealing away, he bent his steps towards a neighbouring cabin, which he approached with even greater precautions than before. This was a hovel of logs, like the other, but of still better construction, having the uncommon convenience of a chimney, built of sticks and mud, through whose low wide top ascended volumes of smoke, made ruddy by the glare of the flames below. A cranny here also afforded the means of spying into the doings within; and Nathan, who approached it with the precision of one not unfamiliar with the premises, was not tardy to avail himself of its advantages. Bare naked walls of logs, the interstices rudely stuffed with moss and clay,—a few uncouth wooden stools,—a rough table,—a bed of skins,—and implements of war and the chase hung in various places about the room, all illuminated more brilliantly by the fire on the hearth than by the miserable tallow candle, stuck in a lamp of humid clay, that glimmered on the table,—were not the only objects to attract the wanderer's eye. Sitting by the fire were two men, both white; though the blanket and calico shirt of one, and the red shawl which he was just in the act of removing from his brows, as Nathan peeped through the chink, with an uncommon darkness of skin and hair, might have well made him pass for an Indian. His figure was very tall, well proportioned, and athletic; his visage manly, and even handsome; though the wrinkles of forty winters furrowed deeply in his brows, and perhaps a certain repelling gleam, the light of smothered passions shining from the eyes below, might have left that merit questionable with the beholder.

The other was a smaller man, whom Roland, had he been present, would have recognised as the supposed half-breed, who, at the partition of spoils, after the capture of his party, and the defeat of the young Kentuckians, had given him a prisoner into the hands of the three Piankeshaws,—in a word, the renegade father of Telie Doe. Nor was his companion less familiar to Nathan, who beheld in his sombre countenance the features of that identical stranger, seen with Doe at the fire among the assailants at the memorable ruin, whose appearance had awakened the first suspicion that there was more in the attack than proceeded from ordinary causes. This was a discovery well fitted to increase the interest, and sharpen the curiosity, of the man of peace: who peering in upon the pair from the chink, gave all his faculties to the duty of listening and observing. The visage of Doe, dark and sullen at the best, was now peculiarly moody; and he sat gazing into the fire, apparently regardless of his companion, who, as he drew the shawl from his head, and threw it aside, muttered something into Doe's ears, but in a voice too low for Nathan to distinguish what he said. The whisper was repeated once and again, but without seeming to produce any impression upon Doe's ears; at which the other growing impatient, gave, to Nathan's great satisfaction, a louder voice to his discourse:

"Hark, you, Jack,—Atkinson,—Doe,—Shanogenaw,—Rattlesnake,—or whatever you may be pleased to call yourself," he cried, striking the muser on the shoulder, "are you mad, drunk, or asleep? Get up, man, and tell me, since you will tell me nothing else, what the devil you are dreaming about?"

"Why, curse it," said the other, starting up somewhat in anger, but draining, before he spoke, a deep draught from an earthen pitcher that stood on the table,—"I was thinking, if you must know, about the youngster, and the dog's death we have driven him to—Christian work for Christian men, eh?"

"The fate of war!" exclaimed the renegade's companion, with great composure; "we have won the battle, boy;—the defeated must bear the consequences."

"Ondoubtedly," said Doe,—"up to the rack, fodder or no fodder: that's the word; there's no 'scaping them consequences; they must be taken as they come,—gantelope, fire-roasting, and all. But, I say, Dick—saving your pardon for being familiar," he added, "there's the small matter to be thought on in the case,—and that is, it was not Injuns, but rale right-down Christian men that brought the younker to the tug. It's a bad business for white men, and it makes me feel oncomfortable."

"Pooh," said the other, with an air of contemptuous commiseration, "you are growing sentimental. This comes of listening to that confounded whimpering Telie."

"No words agin the gal!" cried Doe, sternly; "you may say what you like of me, for I'm a rascal that desarves it; but I'll stand no barking agin the gal."

"Why, she's a good girl and a pretty girl,—too good and too pretty to have so crusty a father,—and I have nothing against her, but her taking on so about the younker, and so playing the devil with the wits and good-looks of my own bargain."

"A dear bargain she is like to prove to all of us," said Doe, drowning his anger, or remorse, in another draught from the pitcher. "She has cost us eleven men already: it is well the bulk of the whelps was Wabash and

Maumee dogs, or you would have seen her killed and scalped, for all of your guns and whisky,—you would, there's no two ways about it. Howsomever, four of 'em was dogs of our own, and two of them was picked off by the Jibbenainosay. I tell you what, Dick, I'm not the man to skear at a raw-head-and-bloody-bones; but I do think the coming of this here cursed Jibbenainosay among us, jist as we was nabbing the girl and sodger, was as much as to say there was no good could come of it; and so the Injuns thought too—you saw how hard it was to bring 'em up to the scratch, when they found he had been knifing a feller right among 'em! I do believe the crittur's Old Nick himself!"

"So don't I," said the other; "for it is quite unnatural to suppose the devil would ever take part against his own children."

"Perhaps," said Doe, "you don't believe in the crittur?"

"Good Jack, honest Jack," replied his companion, "I am no such ass."

"Them that don't believe in hell, will natterly go agin the devil," muttered the renegade, with strong signs of disapprobation; and then added earnestly,—"Look you, Squire, you're a man that knows more of things than me, and the likes of me. You saw that 'ere Injun, dead, in the woods under the tree, where the five scouters had left him a living man?"

"Ay," said the man of the turban; "but he had been wounded by the horseman you so madly suffered to pass the ambush at the ford, and was obliged to stop from loss of blood and faintness. What so natural as to suppose the younker fell upon him (we saw the tracks of the whole party where the body lay), and slashed him in your devil's style, to take advantage of the superstitious fear of the Indians?"

"There's nothing like being a lawyer, sartain!" grumbled Doe. "But the warrior right among us, there at the ruin?—you seed him yourself,—marked right in the thick of us! I reckon you won't say the sodger, that we had there trapped up fast in the cabin, put the cross on that Injun too?"

"Nothing more likely," said the sceptic;—"a stratagem a bold man might easily execute in the dark."

"Well, Squire," said Doe, waxing impatient, "you may jist as well work it out according to law that this same sodger younker, that never seed Kentucky afore in his life, has been butchering Shawnees there, ay, and in this d—d town too, for ten years agone. Ay, Dick, it's true, jist as I tell you: there has been a dozen or more Injun warriors struck and scalped in our very wigwams here, in the dead of the night, and nothing, in the morning, but the mark of the Jibbenainosay to tell who was the butcher. There's not a cussed warrior of them all that doesn't go to his bed at night in fear; for none knows when the Jibbenainosay,—the Howl of the Shawnees,—may be upon him. You must know, there was some bloody piece of business done in times past (Injuns is the boys for them things!)—the murdering of a knot of innocent people—by some of the tribe, with the old villain Wenonga at the head of 'em. Ever since that, the Jibbenainosay has been murdering among them; and they hold that it's a judgment on the tribe, as ondoubtedly it is. And now, you see, that's jist the reason why the old chief has turned such a vagabond; for the tribe is rifled at him, because of his bringing such a devil on them, and they won't follow him to battle no more, except some sich riff-raff, vagabond rascals as them we picked up for this here rascality, no how. And so, you see, it has a sort of set the old feller mad: he thinks of nothing but the Jibbenainosay,—(that is, when he's sober, though, cuss him, I believe it's all one when he's drunk, too.)—of hunting him up and killing him, for he's jist a feller to fight the devil, there's no two ways about it. It was because I told him we was going to the woods on Salt, where the crittur abounds, and where he might get wind of him, that he smashed his rum-keg, and agreed to go with us."

"Well, well," said Doe's associate, "this is idle talk. We have won the victory, and must enjoy it. I must see the prize."

"What good can come of it?" demanded Doe, moodily: "the gal's half dead and whole crazy,—or so Telie says. And as for your gitting any good-will out of her, cuss me if I believe it. And Telie says—"

"That Telie will spoil all! I told you to keep the girl away from her."

"Well, and didn't I act accordin'? I told her I'd murder her, if she went near her agin—a full-blooded, rale-grit rascal to talk so to my own daughter, an't I? But I should like to know where's the good of keeping the gal from her, since it's all she has for comfort?"

"And that is the very reason she must be kept away," said the stranger, with a look malignly expressive of self-approving cunning: "there must be no hope, no thought of security, no consciousness of sympathy, to make me more trouble than I have had already. She must know where she is, and what she is, a prisoner among wild savages: a little fright, a little despair, and the work is over. You understand me, eh? There is a way of bringing the devil himself to terms; and as for a woman, she is not much more unmanageable. One week of terrors, real and imagined, does the work; and then, my jolly Jack, you have won your wages."

"And I have desarved 'em," said Doe, striking his fist upon the table with violence; "for I have made myself jist the d——dest rascal that was ever made of a white man. Lying, and cheating, and perjuring, and murdering—it's nothing better nor murder, that of giving up the younker that never did harm to me or mine, to the Piankeshaws,—for they'll burn him, they will, d—n 'em! there's no two ways about it.—There's what I've done for you; and if you were to give me had the plunder, I reckon 'twould do no more than indamnify me for my rascality. And so, here's the end on't;—you've made me a rascal, and you shall pay for it."

"It is the only thing the world ever does pay for," said the stranger, with edifying coolness; "and so, don't be afflicted. To be a rascal is to be a man of sense,—provided you are a rascal in a sensible way,—that is, a profitable one."

"Ay," said Doe, "that's the doctrine you have been preaching ever since I knowed you; and *you* have made a fortun' by it. But as for me, though I've toed the track after your own leading, I'm jist as poor as ever, and ten times more despisable,—I am, d—n me; for I'm a white Injun, and there's nothing more despisable. But here's the case," he added, working himself into a rage,—"I won't be a rascla for nothing,—I'm sworn to it: and this is a job you must pay for to the full vally, or you're none the better on it."

"It will make your fortune," said his companion in iniquity: "there was bad luck about us before; but all is now safe—The girl will make us secure."

"I don't see into it a bit," said Doe, morosely: "you were secure enough without her. The story of the other gal you know of gave you the grab on the lands and vall'ables; and I don't see what's the good to come of this here other one, no how."

"Then have you less brains, my jolly Jack, then I have given you credit for," said the other. "The story you speak of is somewhat too flimsy to serve us long. We must have a better claim to the lands than can come of possession in trust for an heir not to be produced, till we can find the way to Abraham's bosom. We have now obtained it: the younker, thanks to your Piankeshaw cut-throats, is on the path to Paradise; the girl is left alone, sole claimant, and heiress at law. In a word, Jack, I design to marry her;—ay, faith will-she nill-she, I will marry her: and thereby, besides gratifying certain private whims and humours not worth mentioning, I will put the last finish to the scheme, and step into the estate with a clear conscience."

"But the will, the cussed old will?" cried Doe. "You've got up a cry about it, and there's them that won't let it drop so easy. What's an heir at law agin a will? You take the gal back, and the cry is, 'Where's the true gal, the major's daughter?' I reckon, you'll find you're jist got yourself into a trap of your own making!"

"In that case," said the stranger, with a grin, "we must e'en act like honest men, and find (after much hunting and rummaging, mind you!) the major's *last* will."

"But you burned it!" exclaimed Doe: "you told me so yourself."

"I told you so, Jack; but that was a little bit of innocent deception, to make you easy. I told you so; but I kept it, to guard against accidents. And here it is, Jack," added the speaker, drawing from amid the folds of his blanket a roll of parchment, which he proceeded very deliberately to spread upon the table: "The very difficulty you mention occurred to me; I saw it would not do to raise the devil, without retaining the power to lay him. Here then is the will, that settles the affair to your liking. The girl and the younker are co-heirs together; but the latter dying intestate, you understand, the whole falls into the lap of the former. Are you easy now, honest Jack? Will this satisfy you all is safe?"

"It is jist the thing to an iota," ejaculated Doe, in whom the sight of the parchment seemed to awaken cupidity and exultation together: "there's no standing agin it in any court in Virginnee!"

"Right, my boy," said his associate. "But where is the girl? I must see her."

"In the cabin with Wenonga's squaw, right over agin the Council-house," replied Doe; adding with animation, "but I'm agin your going nigh her, till we settle up accounts jist as honestly as any two sich d—d rascals can. I say, by G—, I must know how the book stands, and how I'm to finger the snacks: for snacks is the word, or the bargain's no go."

"Well,—we can talk of this on the morrow."

"To-night's the time," said Doe: "there's nothing like having an honest understanding of matters afore-hand. I'm not going to be cheated,—not meaning no offence in saying so; and I've jist made up my mind to keep the gal out of your way, till we've settled things to our liking."

"Spoken like a sensible rogue," said the stranger, with a voice all frankness and approval, but with a lowering look of impatience, which Nathan, who had watched the proceedings of the pair with equal amazement and interest, could observe from the chink, though it was concealed from Doe by the position of the speaker, who had risen from his stool, as if to depart, but who now sat down again, to satisfy the fears of his partner in villany. To this he immediately addressed himself, but in tones lower than before, so that Nathan could no longer distinguish his words.

But Nathan had heard enough. The conversation, as far as he had distinguished it, chimed strangely in with all his own and Roland's suspicions; there was, indeed, not a word uttered that did not confirm them. The confessions of the stranger, vague and mysterious as they seemed, tallied in all respects with Roland's account of the villanous designs imputed to the hated Braxley; and it was no little additional proof of his identity, that, in addressing Doe, whom he styled throughout as Jack, he had, once at least, called him by the name of Atkinson,—a refugee, whose connection with the conspiracy in Roland's story Nathan had not forgotten. It was not, indeed, surprising that Abel Doe should possess another name; since it was a common practice among renegades like himself, from some sentiment of shame or other obvious reasons, to assume an *alias* and *nom de guerre*, under which they acquired their notoriety: the only wonder was, that he should prove to be that person whose agency in the abduction of Edith would, of all other men in the world, go furthest to sustain the belief of Braxley being the principal contriver of the outrage.

Such thoughts as these may have wandered through Nathan's mind; but he took little time to con them over. He had made a discovery at that moment of more stirring importance and interest. Allowing that Edith Forrester was the prisoner of whom the disguised stranger and his sordid confederate spoke, and there was little reason to doubt it, he had learned, out of their own mouths, the place of her concealment, to discover which was the object of his daring visit to the village. Her prison-house was the wigwam of Wenonga, the chief,—if chief he could still be called, whom the displeasure of his tribe had robbed of almost every vestige of authority; and thither Nathan, to whom the vile bargaining of the white-men no longer offered interest, supposing he could even have overheard it, instantly determined to make his way.

But how was Nathan to know the cabin of the chief from the dozen other hovels that surrounded the Council-house. That was a question which, perhaps Nathan did not ask himself: for creeping softly from Doe's hut, and turning into the street (if such could be called the irregular winding space that separated the two lines of cabins composing the village), he stole forward, with nothing of the hesitation or doubt which might have been expected from one unfamiliar with the village.

CHAPTER XXIX

While Nathan lay watching at the renegade's hut, there came a change over the aspect of the night, little less favourable to his plans and hopes than even the discovery of Edith's place of concealment, which he had so fortunately made. The sky became suddenly overcast with clouds, and deep darkness invested the Indian village; while gusts of wind, sweeping with a moaning sound over the adjacent hills, and waking the forests from their repose, came rushing over the village, whirring and fluttering aloft like flights of the boding night-raven, or the more powerful bird of prey that had given its name to the chieftain of the tribe.

In such darkness, and with the murmur of the blasts and the rustling of boughs to drown the noise of his footsteps, Nathan no longer feared to pursue his way; and rising boldly to his feet, drawing his blanket close around him, and assuming, as before, the gait of a savage, he strode forwards, and in less than a minute, was upon the public square,—if such we may call it,—the vacant area in the centre of the village, where stood the rude shed of bark and boughs, supported by a circular range of posts, all open, except at top, to the weather, which custom had dignified with the title of Council-house. The bounds of the square were marked by clusters of cabins placed with happy contempt of order and symmetry, and by trees and bushes that grew among and behind them, particularly at the foot of the hill on one side, and, on the other, along the borders of the river; which, in the pauses of the gusts, could be heard sweeping hard by over a broken and pebbly channel. Patches of bushes might even be seen growing in places on the square itself; and here and there were a few tall trees, remnants of the old forest which had once overshadowed the scene towering aloft, and sending forth on the blast such spiritual murmurs, and wild oraculous whispers, as were wont, in ancient days, to strike an awe through soothsayers and devotees in the sacred groves of Dodona.

Through this square, looking solitude and desolation together, lay the path of the spy; and he trode it without fear, although it offered an obstruction that might well have daunted the zeal of one less crafty and determined. In its centre, and near the Council-house, he discovered a fire, now burning low, but still, as the breeze, time by time, fanned the decaying embers into flame, sending forth light enough to reveal the spectacle of at least a dozen savages stretched in slumber around it, with as many ready rifles stacked round a post hard by. Their appearance, without affrighting, greatly perplexed the man of peace; who, though at first disposed to regard them as a kind of guard, to whom had been committed the charge of the village and the peace of the community, during the uproar and terrors of the debauch, found reason, upon more mature inspection, to consider them a band from some neighbouring village, perhaps an out-going war party, which, unluckily for himself, had tarried at the village to share the hospitalities, and take part in the revels, of its inhabitants. Thus, there was near the fire a huge heap of dried corn-husks and prairie-grass, designed for a couch,—a kind of, luxury which Nathan supposed the villagers would have scarce taken the trouble to provide, unless for guests whose warlike pride and sense of honour would not permit them to sleep under cover until they had struck the enemy in his own country, and were returning victorious to their own; and as a proof that they had shared as guests in all the excesses of their hosts, but few of them were seen huddled together on the couch, the majority lying about in such confusion and postures as could only have been produced by the grossest indulgence.

Pausing awhile, but not deterred by the discovery of such undesirable neighbours, Nathan easily avoided them by making the circuit of the square; creeping along from tree to tree, and bush to bush, until he had left the whole group on the rear, and arrived in the vicinity of a cabin, which, from its appearance, might with propriety be supposed the dwelling of the most distinguished demagogue of the tribe. It was a cottage of logs very similar to those of the renegades, who had themselves, perhaps, built it for the chief, whose favour it was so necessary to purchase by every means in their power; but as it consisted of only a single room, and that by no means spacious, the barbarian had seen fit to eke it out by a brace of summer apartments, being tents of skins, which were pitched at its ends like wings, and, perhaps, communicated directly with the interior, though each had its own particular door of mats looking out upon the square.

All these appearances Nathan could easily note, in occasional gleams from the fire, which, falling upon the rude and misshapen lodge, revealed its features obscurely to the eye. It bore an air of solitude that became the dwelling of a chief. The soil around it, as if too sacred to be invaded by the profane feet of the multitude, was left overgrown with weeds and starveling bushes; and an ancient elm, rising among them, and flinging its shadowy branches wide around, stood like a giant watchman, to repel the gaze of the curious.

This solitude, these bushes through which he could crawl unobserved, and the shadows of the tree, offering a concealment equally effectual and inviting, were all circumstances in Nathan's favour; and giving one backward glance to the fire on the square, and then fixing his eye on one of the tents, in which, as the mat at the door shook in the breeze, he could detect the glimmering of a light, and fancied he could even faintly hear the murmur of voices, he crawled among the bushes, scarcely doubting that he was now within but a few feet of the unhappy maid in whose service he had toiled so long and so well.

But the path to the wigwam was not yet free from obstructions. He had scarce pushed aside the first bush in his way, opening a vista into the den of leaves, where he looked to find his best concealment, before a flash of light from the fire, darting through the gap, and falling upon a dark grim visage almost within reach of his hand, showed him that he had stumbled unawares upon a sleeping savage,—a man that had evidently staggered there in his drunkenness, and falling among the bushes, had straightway given himself up to sottish repose.

For the first time, a thrill smote through the bosom of the spy; but it was not wholly a thrill of dismay. There was little indeed in the appearance of the wretched sleeper, at that moment, to inspire terror; for apart from the condition of helpless impotence, to which his ungovernable appetites had reduced him, he seemed to be entirely unarmed,—at least Nathan could see neither knife nor tomahawk about him. But there was that in the grim visage, withered with age, and seamed with many a scar,—in the mutilated, but bony and still nervous hand lying on the broad naked chest,—and in the recollections of the past they recalled to Nathan's brain, which awoke a feeling not less exciting, if less unworthy, than fear. In the first impulse of surprise, it is true, he started backwards, and grovelled flat upon his face, as if to beat an instant retreat in the only posture which could conceal him, if the sleeper should have been disturbed by his approach. But the savage slept on, drugged to stupefaction by many a deep and potent draught; and Nathan, preserving his snake-like position only for a moment, rose slowly upon his hands, and peered over again upon the unconscious barbarian.

But the bushes had closed again around him, and the glimmer of the dying fire no longer fell upon the barbarian. With an audacity of daring that marked the eagerness and intensity of his curiosity, Nathan with his hands pushed the bushes aside, so as again to bring a gleam upon the swarthy countenance; which he perused with such feelings as left him for a time unconscious of the object of his enterprise, unconscious of everything save the spectacle before him, the embodied representation of features which events of former years had painted in indelible hues on his remembrance. The face was that of a warrior, worn with years, and covered with such scars as could be boasted only by one of the most distinguished men of the tribe. Deep seams also marked the naked chest of the sleeper; and there was something in the appearance of his garments of dressed hides, which, though squalid enough, were garnished with multitudes of silver brooches and tufts of human hair, with here and there a broad Spanish dollar looped ostentatiously to the skin, to prove he was anything but a common brave. To each ear was attached a string of silver coins, strung together in regular gradation from the largest to the smallest,—a profusion of wealth which could appertain only to a chief. To prove, indeed, that he was no less, there was visible upon his head, secured to the tiara, or *glory*, as it might be called (for such is its figure) of badgers' hairs, which is so often found woven around the scalp-lock of a North-western Indian, an ornament consisting of the beaks and claws of a buzzard, and some dozen or more of its sable feathers. These, as Nathan had previously told the soldier, were the distinguishing badges of Wenonga, or the Black-Vulture (for so the name is translated); and it was no less a man than Wenonga himself, the oldest, most famous, and, at one time, the most powerful chief of his tribe, who thus lay, a wretched, squalid sot, before the doors of his own wigwam, which he had been unable to reach. Such was Wenonga; such were many of the bravest and most distinguished of his truly unfortunate race, who exchanged their lands, their fathers' graves, and the lives of their people, for the doubtful celebrity which the white man is so easily disposed to allow them.

The spy looked upon the face of the Indian; but there was none at hand to gaze upon his own, to mark the hideous frown of hate, and the more hideous grin of delight, that mingled on, and distorted his visage, as he gloated, snake-like, over that of the chief. As he looked, he drew from its sheath in his girdle his well-worn, but still bright and keen knife,—which he poised in one hand, while feeling, with what seemed extraordinary fearlessness or confidence of his prey, with the other along the sleeper's naked breast, as if regardless how soon he might wake. But Wenonga still slept on, though the hand of the white man lay upon his ribs, and rose and fell with the throbs of his warlike heart. The knife took the place of the hand, and one thrust would have driven it through the organ that had never beaten with pity or remorse; and that thrust Nathan, quivering through every fibre with nameless joy and exultation, and forgetful of everything but his prey, was about to make. He nerved his hand for the blow; but it trembled with eagerness. He paused an instant, and before he could make a second effort, a voice from the wigwam struck upon his ear, and the strength departed from his arm. He staggered back, and awoke to consciousness; the sound was repeated; it was the wail, of a female voice, and its mournful accents, coming to his ear in an interval of the gust, struck a new feeling into his bosom. He remembered the captive, and his errand of charity and mercy.

He drew a deep and painful breath, and muttering, but within the silent recesses of his breast, "Thee shall not call to me in vain!" buried the knife softly in its sheath. Then crawling silently away, and leaving the chief to his slumbers, he crept through the bushes until he had reached the tent from which the mourning voice proceeded. Still lying upon his face, he dragged himself to the door, and looking under the corner of the mat that waved before it in the wind, he saw at a glance that he had reached the goal of his journey.

The tent was of an oval figure, and of no great extent; but being lighted only by a fire burning dimly in the centre of its earthen floor, and its frail walls darkened by smoke, the eye could scarcely penetrate to its dusky extremity. It consisted, as has been said, of skins, which were supported upon poles, wattled together like the framework of a crate or basket; the poles of the opposite sides being kept asunder by cross-pieces, which, at the common centre of intersection or radiation, were themselves upheld by a stout wooden pillar. Upon this pillar, and on the slender rafters, were laid or suspended sundry Indian utensils of the kitchen and the field, wooden bowls, earthen pans and Irazen pots, guns, hatchets, and fish-spears, with ears of corn, dried roots, smoked meats, blankets and skins, and many articles that had perhaps been plundered from the Long-knives, such as halters and bridles, hats, coats shawls, and aprons, and other such gear; among which was conspicuous a bundle of scalps, some of them with long female tresses, the proofs of the prowess of a great warrior, who, like the other fighting-men of his race, accounted the golden ringlets of a girl as noble a trophy of valour as the grizzled locks of a veteran soldier.

On the floor of the tent, piled against its sides and farthest extremity, was the raised platform of skins, with rude partitions and curtains of mats, which formed the sleeping-couch, or, perhaps we might say, the sleeping-apartments, of the lodge. But these were in a great measure hidden under heaps of blankets, skins, and other trumpery articles, that seemed to have been snatched in some sudden hurry from the floor, which they had previously cumbered. In fact, there was every appearance that the tent had been for a long time used as a kind of store-room, the receptacle of a bandit's omnium-gatherum, and had been hastily prepared for unexpected inmates. But these particulars, which he might have noted at a glance, Nathan did not pause to survey. There were objects of greater attractions for his eyes in a group of three female figures: in one of whom, standing near the fire, and grasping the hands and garments of a second, as if imploring pity or protection, her hair dishevelled, her visage bloodless, her eyes wild with grief and terror, he beheld the object of his perilous enterprise, the lovely and unhappy Edith Forrester. Struggling in her grasp, as if to escape, yet weeping, and uttering hurried expressions that were meant to soothe the agitation of the captive, was the renegade's daughter, Telie, who seemed herself little less terrified than the prisoner. The third person of the group was an Indian beldam, old, withered, and witch-like, who sat crouching over the fire, warming her skinny hands, and only intermitting her employment occasionally to eye the more youthful pair with looks of malignant hatred and suspicion.

The gale was still freshening, and the elm-boughs rustled loudly in the wind; but Nathan could overhear every word of the captive, as, still grasping Telie by the hand, she besought her, in the language of desperation, "not to leave her, not to desert her, at such a moment;" while Telie, shedding tears, which seemed to be equally those of shame and sorrow, entreated her to fear nothing, and permit her to depart.

"They won't hurt you,—no, my father promised that," she said: "it is the chief's house, and nobody will come nigh to hurt you. You are safe, lady; but, oh! my father will kill me, if he finds me here."

"It was your father that caused it all!" cried Edith, with a vehement change of feeling; "it was *he* that betrayed us, *he* that killed, oh! killed my Roland! Go!—I hate you! Heaven will punish you for what you have done; Heaven will never forgive the treachery and the murder—Go, go! they will kill me, and then all will be well,—yes, all will be well!"

But Telie, thus released, no longer sought to fly. She strove to obtain and kiss the hand that repelled her, sobbing bitterly, and reiterating her assurances that no harm was designed the maiden.

"No,—no harm! Do I not know it all?" exclaimed Edith, again giving way to her fears, and grasping Telie's arm. "*You* are not like your father; if you betrayed me once, you will not betray me again. Stay with me,—yes, stay with me, and I'll forgive you,—forgive you all. That man—that dreadful man! I know him well: he will come—he has murdered my cousin, and he is,—oh Heaven, how black a villain! Stay with me, Telie, to protect me from that man; stay with me, and I'll forgive all you have done."

It was with such wild entreaties Edith, agitated by an excitement that seemed almost to have unsettled her brain, still urged Telie not to abandon her; while Telie, repeating again and again her protestations that no injury was designed or could happen, and that the old woman at the fire was specially deputed to protect her, and would do so, begged to be permitted to go, insisting, with every appearance of sincere alarm, that her father would kill her if she remained,—that he had forbidden her to come near the prisoner, which, nevertheless, she had secretly done, and would do again, if she could this time avoid discovery.

But her protestations were of little avail in moving Edith to her purpose; and it was only when the latter, worn out by suffering and agitation, and sinking helpless on the couch at her feet, had no longer the power to oppose her, that Telie hurriedly, yet with evident grief and reluctance, tore herself away. She pressed the captive's hand to her lips, bathed it in her tears, and then, with many a backward glance of sorrow, stole from the lodge. Nathan crawled aside as she passed out, and watching a moment until she had fled across the square, returned to his place of observation. He looked again into the tent, and his heart smote him with pity as he beheld the wretched Edith sitting in a stupor of despair, her head sunk upon her breast, her hands clasped, her ashy lips quivering, but uttering no articulate sound. "Thee prays Heaven to help thee, poor maid!" he muttered to himself: "Heaven denied the prayer of them that was as good and as lovely; but thee is not yet forsaken!"

He took his knife from its sheath, and turned his eyes upon the old hag, who sat at the fire with her back partly towards him, but her eyes fastened upon the captive, over whom they wandered with the fierce and unappeasable malice, that was in those days seen rankling in the breast of many an Indian mother, and expended upon prisoners at the stake with a savage, nay, a demoniacal zeal that might have put warriors to shame. In truth, the unlucky captive had always more to apprehend from the squaws of a tribe than from its warriors; and *their* cries for vengeance often gave to the torture wretches whom even their cruel husbands were inclined to spare.

With knife in hand, and murderous thoughts in his heart, Nathan raised a corner of the mat, and glared for a moment upon the beldam. But the feelings of the white-man prevailed; he hesitated, faltered, and dropping the mat in its place, retreated silently from the door. Then restoring his knife for a second time to its sheath, listening awhile to hear if the drunken Wenonga yet stirred in his lair, and taking a survey of the sleepers at the nearly extinguished fire, he crept away, retraced his steps through the village, to the place where he had left the captain of horse-thieves, whom,—to the shame of that worthy be it spoken,—he found fast locked in the arms of Morpheus, and breathing such a melody from his upturned nostrils as might have roused the whole village from its repose, had not that been at least twice as sound and deep as his own.

"Tarnal death to me!" said he, rubbing his eyes when Nathan shook him from his slumbers, "I war nigh gone in a dead snooze!—being as how I ar'n't had a true reggelar mouthful of snortin' this h'yar no-time,—considering I always took it with my hoptical peepers right open. But, I say, Nathan, what's the last news from the abbregynes and anngelliferous madam?"

"Give me one of thee halters," said Nathan, "and do thee observe now what I have to say to thee."

"A halter!" cried Ralph, in dudgeon; "you ar'n't for doing all, and the hoss-stealing too?"

"Friend," said Nathan, "with this halter I must bind one that sits in watch over the maiden; and, truly, it is better it should be so, seeing that these hands of mine have never been stained with the blood of woman."

"And you have found my mistress?" said Ralph, in a rapture. "Jist call the Captain, and let's be a doing!"

"He is a brave youth, and a youth of a mighty heart," said Nathan; "but this is no work for them that has never seen the ways of an Injun village. Now, friend, does thee hear me? The town is alive with fighting-men, and there is a war-party of fourteen painted Wyandotts sleeping on the Council-square. But don't thee be dismayed thereupon; for, truly, these assassin creatures is all besotted with drink; and were there with us but ten stout young men of Kentucky, I do truly believe we could knock every murdering dog of an on the head, and nobody the wiser. Does thee hear, friend? Do but thee own part in this endeavour well, and we will save the young and tender maid thee calls madam. Take theeself to the pound, which thee may do safely, by following the hill: pick out four good horses, fleet and strong, and carry them safely away, going up the valley,—mind, friend, thee must go *up*, as if thee was speeding thee way to the Big Lake, instead of to Kentucky: then, when thee has ridden a mile, thee may cross the brook, and follow the hills, till thee has reached the hiding-place that we did spy from out upon this village. Thee hears, friend? There thee will find the fair maid, Edith; which I will straightway fetch out of her bondage. And, truly, it may be, I have learned *that*, this night, which will make both her and the young man thee calls Captain, which is a brave young man, both rich and happy. And now, friend, thee has heard me; and thee must do thee duty."

"If I don't fetch her the beautifullest hoss that war ever seed in the woods," said Ralph, "thar's no reason, except because the Injuns ar'n't had good luck this year in grabbing! And I'll fetch him round up the holler, jist as you say too, and round about till I strike the snuggery, jist the same way; for thar's the way you show judgematical, and I'm cl'ar of your way of thinking. And so now, h'yar's my fo'-paw, in token thar's no two ways about me, Ralph Stackpole, a hoss to my friends, and a niggur to them that sarves me!"

With these words, the two associates, equally zealous in the cause in which they had embarked, parted, each to achieve his own particular share of the adventure, in which they had left so little to be done by the young Virginian.

But, as it happened, neither Roland's inclination nor fate was favourable to his playing so insignificant a part in the undertaking. He had remained in the place of concealment assigned him, tortured with suspense, and racked by self-reproach, for more than an hour: until, his impatience getting the better of his judgment, he resolved to creep nigher the village, to ascertain, if possible, the state of affairs. He had arrived within earshot of the pair, and without overhearing all, had gathered enough of their conversation to convince him that Edith was at last found, and that the blow was now to be struck for her deliverance. His two associates separated before he could reach them; Ralph plunging among the bushes that covered the hill, while Nathan, as before, stalked boldly into the village. He called softly after the latter, to attract his notice; but his voice was lost in the gusts sweeping along the hill; and Nathan proceeded onwards, without heeding him. He hesitated a moment whether to follow, or return to his station, where little Peter, more obedient, or more prudent than himself, still lay, having resolutely refused to stir at the soldier's invitation to accompany him; until finally, surrendering his discretion to his anxiety, he resolved to pursue after Nathan,—a measure of imprudence, if not of folly, which, at a less exciting moment, no one would have been more ready to condemn than himself. But the image of Edith in captivity, and perhaps of Braxley standing by, the master of her fate, was impressed upon his heart, as if pricked into it with daggers; and to remain longer at a distance, and in inaction, was impossible. Imitating Nathan's mode of advance as well as he could, guided by his dusky figure, and hoping soon to overtake him, he pushed forward and was soon in the dreaded village.

CHAPTER XXX

In the meanwhile, Edith sat in the tent abandoned to despair, her mind not yet recovered from the stunning effect of her calamity, struggling confusedly with images of blood and phantasms of fear, the dreary recollections of the past mingling with the scarce less dreadful anticipations of the future. Of the battle on the hill-side she remembered nothing save the fall of her kinsman, shot down at her feet,—all she had herself witnessed, and all she could believe; for Telie Doe's assurances, contradicted in effect by her constant tears and agitation, that he had been carried off to captivity like herself, conveyed no conviction to her mind: from that moment, events were pictured on her memory as the records of a feverish dream, including all the incidents of her wild and hurried journey to the Indian village. But with these broken and dream-like reminiscences, there were associated recollections, vague, yet not the less terrifying, of a visage that had haunted her presence by day and by night, throughout the whole journey, watching, over her with the pertinacity of an evil genius; and which, as her faculties woke slowly from their trance, assumed every moment a more distinct and dreaded appearance in her imagination.

It was upon these hated features, seen side by side with the blood-stained aspect of her kinsman, she now pondered in mingled grief and terror; starting occasionally from the horror of her thoughts only to be driven back to them again by the scowling eyes of the old crone; who, still crouching over the fire, as if its warmth could never strike deep enough into her frozen veins, watched every movement and every look with the vigilance, and as it seemed, the viciousness of a serpent. No ray of pity shone even for a moment from her forbidding, and even hideous countenance; she offered no words, she made no signs, of sympathy; and, as if to prove her hearty disregard, or profound contempt for the prisoner's manifest distress, she by and by, to while the time, began to drone out a succession of grunting sounds, such as make up a red-man's melody, and such indeed as any village urchin can drum with his heels out of an empty hogshead. The song, thus barbarously chanted, at first startled and affrighted the captive; but its monotony had at last an effect which the beldam was far from designing. It diverted the maiden's mind in a measure from its own harassing thoughts, and thus introduced a kind of composure where all had been before painful agitation. Nay, as the sounds, which were at no time very loud, mingled with the piping of the gale without and the rustling of the old elm at the door, they lost their harshness, and were softened into a descant that was lulling to the senses, and might, like a gentler nepenthe, have, in time, cheated the over-weary mind to repose. Such, perhaps, was beginning to be its effect. Edith ceased to bend upon the hag the wild, terrified looks that at first rewarded the music; she sunk her head upon her bosom, and sat as if gradually giving way to a lethargy of spirit, which, if not sleep, was sleep's most beneficent substitute.

From this state of calm she was roused by the sudden cessation of the music; and looking up, she beheld, with a renewal of all her alarms, a tall man, standing before her, his face and figure both enveloped in the folds of a huge blanket, from which, however, a pair of gleaming eyes were seen riveted upon her own countenance. At the same time, she observed that the old Indian woman had risen, and was stealing softly from the apartment. Filled with terror, she would have rushed after the hag, to claim her protection: but she was immediately arrested by the visitor, who, seizing her by the arm firmly, yet with an air of respect, and suffering his blanket to drop to the ground, displayed to her gaze features that had long dwelt, its darkest phantoms, upon her mind. As he seized her, he muttered, and still with an accent of the most earnest respect,—"Fear me not, Edith; I am not yet an enemy."

His voice, though one of gentleness, and even of music, completed the terrors of the captive, who trembled in his hand like a quail in the clutches of a kite, and would, but for his grasp, as powerful to sustain as to oppose, have fallen to the floor. Her lips quivered, but they gave forth no sound; and her eyes were fastened upon his with a wildness and intensity of glare that showed the fascination, the temporary self-abandonment of her spirit.

"Fear me not, Edith Forrester," he repeated, with a voice even more soothing than before: "You know me;—I am no savage;—I will do you no harm."

"Yes,—yes,—yes," muttered Edith at last, but in the tones of an automaton, they were, at first, so broken and inarticulate, though they gathered force and vehemence as she spoke—"I know you,—yes, yes, I do know you, and know you well. You are Richard Braxley,—the robber, and now the persecutor of the orphan; and this hand that holds me is red with the blood of my cousin. Oh, villain! villain! are you not yet content?"

"The prize is not yet won," replied the other, with a smile that seemed intended to express his contempt of the maiden's invectives, and his ability to forgive them: "I am indeed Richard Braxley,—the friend of Edith

Forrester, though she will not believe it,—a rough and self-willed one, it may be, but still her true and unchangeable friend. Where will she look for a better? Anger has not alienated, contempt has not estranged me: injury and injustice still find me the same. I am still Edith Forrester's friend; and such, in the sturdiness of my affection, I will remain, whether my fair mistress will or no. But you are feeble and agitated: sit down and listen to me. I have that to say which will convince my thoughtless fair the day of disdain is now over."

All these expressions, though uttered with seeming blandness, were yet accompanied by an air of decision and even command, as if the speaker were conscious the maiden was fully in his power, and not unwilling she should know it. But his attempt to make her resume her seat upon the pile of skins from which she had so wildly started at his entrance, was resisted by Edith; who, gathering courage from desperation, and shaking his hand from her arm, as if snatching it from the embraces of a serpent, replied with even energy,—"I will not sit down,—I will not listen to you. Approach me not—touch me not. You are a villain and murderer, and I loathe, oh! unspeakably loathe, your presence. Away from me, or—"

"Or," interrupted Braxley with the sneer of a naturally mean and vindictive spirit, "you will cry for assistance! From whom do you expect it? From wild, murderous, besotted Indians, who, if roused from their drunken slumbers, would be more like to assail you with their hatchets than to weep for your sorrows? Know, fair Edith, that you are now in their hands;—that there is not one of them, who would not rather see those golden tresses hung blackening in the smoke from the rafters of his wigwam, than floating over the brows they adorn—Look aloft: there are ringlets of young and fair, the innocent and tender, swinging above you!—Learn, moreover, that from these dangerous friends there is none who can protect you, save *me*. Ay, my beauteous Edith," he added, as the captive, overcome by the representation of her perils so unscrupulously, nay, so sternly made, sank almost fainting upon the pile, "it is even so; and you must know it. It is needful you should know what you have to expect, if you reject my protection. But that you will not reject; in faith, you *cannot!* The time has come, as I told you it would, when your disdainful scruples—I speak plainly, fair Edith!—are to be at an end. I swore to you—and it was when your scorn and unbelief were at the highest—that you should yet smile upon the man you disdained, and smile upon no other. It was a rough and uncouth threat for a lover; but my mistress would have it so. It was a vow breathed in anger: but it was a vow not meant to be broken. You tremble! I am cruel in my wooing; but this is not the moment for compliment and deception. You are *mine*, Edith: I swore it to myself—ay, and to you. You cannot escape. You have driven me to extremities; but they have succeeded. You are mine; or you are—nothing."

"Nothing let it be," said Edith, over whose mind, prone to agitation and terror, it was evident the fierce and domineering temper of the individual could exercise an irresistible control, and who, though yet striving to resist, was visibly sinking before his stern looks and menacing words;—"let it be nothing! Kill me, if you will, as you have already killed my cousin. Oh! mockery of passion, of humanity, of decency, to speak to me thus;—to *me*, the relative, the more than sister of him you have so basely and cruelly murdered!"

"I have murdered no one," said Braxley, with stony composure: "and if you will but listen patiently, you will find I am stained by no crime save that of loving a woman who forces me to woo her like a master, rather than a slave. Your cousin is living and in safety."

"It is false," cried Edith, wringing her hands; "with my own eyes I saw him fall, and fall covered with blood!"

"And from that moment you saw nothing more," rejoined Braxley. "The blood came from the veins of others; he was carried away alive, and almost unhurt. He is a captive,—a captive like yourself. And why? Shall I remind my fair Edith how much of her hostility and scorn I owed to her hot and foolish kinsman? how he persuaded her the love she so naturally bore so near a relative was reason enough to reject the affection of a suitor? how impossible she should listen to the dictates of her own heart, or the calls of her interest, while misled by a counsellor so indiscreet, and yet so trusted? Before that unlucky young man stepped between me and my love, Edith Forrester could listen,—ay, and could smile. Nay, deny it if you will; but hearken. Your cousin is safe; rely upon that; but, rely, also, he will never again see the home of his birth, or the kinswoman whose fortunes he has so opposed, until she is the wife of the man he misjudges and hates. He is removed from my path: it was necessary to my hopes. His life is, at all events, safe; his deliverance rests with his kinswoman. When she has plighted her troth, and surely she *will* plight it—"

"Never! never!" cried Edith, starting up, her indignation for a moment getting the better of her fears: "with one so false and treacherous, so unprincipled and ungrateful, so base and revengeful,—with such a man, with such a villain, never! no, never!"

"I *am* a villain indeed, Edith," said Braxley, but with exemplary coolness; "all men are so. Good and evil are sown together in our natures, and each has its season and its harvest. In this breast, as in the breast of the worst and the noblest, Nature set, at birth, an angel and a devil, either to be the governor of my actions, as either should be best encouraged. If the devil be now at work, and have been for months, it was because your scorn called him from his slumbers. Before that time Edith, I was under the domination of my angel; who then called, or who deemed me, a villain? Was I then a robber and persecutor of the orphan? Am I *now*? Perhaps so,—but it is yourself that have made me so. For you, I called up my evil genius to my aid; and my evil-genius aided me. He bade me woo no longer like the turtle but strike like the falcon. Through plots and stratagems, through storms and perils, through battle and blood, I have pursued you, and I have conquered at last. The captive of my sword and spear, you will spurn my love no longer; for, in truth, you cannot. I came to the wilderness to seek an heiress for your uncle's wealth; I have found her. But she returns to her inheritance the wife of the seeker! In a word, my Edith,—for why should I, who am now the master of your fate, forbear the style of a conqueror? why should I longer sue, who have the power to command?—you are *mine*,—mine beyond the influence of caprice or change,—mine beyond the hope of escape. This village you will never leave but as a bride."

So spoke the bold wooer, elated by the consciousness of successful villany, and perhaps convinced from long experience of the timorous, and doubtless, feeble, character of the maid, that a haughty and overbearing tone would produce an impression, however painful it might be to her, more favourable to his hopes than the soft hypocrisy of sueing. He was manifestly resolved to wring from her fears the consent not to be obtained from her love. Nor had he miscalculated the power of such a display of bold, unflinching energetic determination in awing, if not bending, her youthful spirit. She seemed indeed, stunned, wholly overpowered by his resolved and violent manner; and she had scarcely strength to mutter the answer that rose to her lips:

"If it be so," she faltered out, "this village, then, I must never leave; for here I will die, die even by the hands of barbarians, and die a thousand times, ere I look upon you, base and cruel man, with any but the eyes of detestation. I hated you ever,—I hate you yet."

"My fair mistress," said Braxley, with a sneer that might have well become the lip of the devil he had pronounced the then ruler of his breast, "knows not all the alternative. Death is a boon the savages may bestow, when the whim takes them. But before that, they must show their affection for their prisoner. There are many that can admire the bright eyes and ruddy cheeks of the white maiden; and some one, doubtless, will admit the stranger to a corner of his wigwam and his bosom! Ay, madam, I will speak plainly,—it is as the wife of Richard Braxley or of a pagan savage you go out of the tent of Wenonga. Or why go out of the tent of Wenonga at all? Is

Wenonga insensible to the beauty of his guest? The hag that I drove from the fire, seemed already to see in her prisoner the maid that was to rob her of her husband."

"Heaven help me!" exclaimed Edith, sinking again to her seat, wholly overcome by the horrors it was the object of the wooer to accumulate on her mind. He noted the effect of his threat, and stealing up, he took her trembling, almost lifeless hand, adding, but in a softer voice,—

"Why will Edith drive one who adores her to these extremities? Let her smile but as she smiled of yore, and all will yet be well. One smile secures her deliverance from all that she dreads, her restoration to her home and to happiness. With that smile, the angel again awakes in my bosom, and all is love and tenderness."

"Heaven help me!" iterated the trembling girl, struggling to shake off Braxley's hand. But she struggled feebly and in vain; and Braxley, in the audacity of his belief that he had frightened her into a more reasonable mood, proceeded the length of throwing an arm around his almost insensible victim.

But heaven was not unmindful of the prayer of the desolate and helpless maid. Scarce had his arm encircled the waist of the captive, when a pair of arms, long and brawny, infolded his body as in the hug of an angry bear, and in an instant he lay upon his back on the floor, a knee upon his breast, a hand at his throat, and a knife, glittering blood-red in the light of the fire, flourished within an inch of his eyes: while a voice, subdued to a whisper, yet distinct as if uttered in tones of thunder, muttered in his ear,—"Speak, and thee dies!"

The attack, so wholly unexpected, so sudden and so violent, was as irresistible as astounding; and Braxley, unnerved by the surprise and by fear, succumbing as to the stroke of an avenging angel, the protector of innocence, whom his villany had conjured from the air, lay gasping upon the earth without attempting the slightest resistance, while the assailant, dropping his knife and producing a long cord of twisted leather, proceeded, with inexpressible dexterity and speed, to bind his limbs, which he did in a manner none the less effectual for being so hasty. An instant sufficed to secure him hand and foot; in another, a gag was clapped in his mouth and secured by a turn of the rope round his neck; at the third, the conqueror, thrusting his hand into his bosom, tore from it the stolen will, which he immediately after buried in his own. Then, spurning the baffled villain into a corner, and flinging over his body a pile of skins and blankets, until he was entirely hidden from sight, he left him to the combined agonies of fear, darkness, and suffocation.

Such was the rapidity, indeed, with which the whole affair was conducted, that Braxley had scarce time to catch a glimpse of his assailant's countenance; and that glimpse, without abating his terror, took but little from his amazement. It was the countenance of an Indian,—or such it seemed,—grimly and hideously painted over with figures of snakes, lizards, skulls, and other savage devices, which were repeated upon the arms, the half-naked bosom, and even the squalid shirt of the victor. One glance, in the confusion and terror of the moment, Braxley gave to his extraordinary foe; and then the mantles piled upon his body concealed all objects from his eyes.

In the meanwhile, Edith, not less confounded, sat cowering with terror, until the victor, having completed his task, sprang to her side,—a movement, however, that only increased her dismay,—crying, with warning gestures, "Fear not and speak not;—up and away!" when, perceiving she recoiled from him with all her feeble strength, and was indeed unable to rise, he caught her in his arms, muttering, "Thee is safe—thee friends is nigh!" and bore her swiftly, yet noiselessly, from the tent.

CHAPTER XXXI

The night was even darker than before, the fire of the Wyandotts on the square had burned so low as no longer to send even a ray to the hut of Wenonga, and the wind, though subsiding, still kept up a sufficient din to drown the ordinary sound of footsteps. Under such favourable circumstances, Nathan (for, as may be supposed, it was this faithful friend who had snatched the forlorn Edith from the grasp of the betrayer) stalked boldly from the hut, bearing the rescued maiden in his arms, and little doubting that, having thus so successfully accomplished the first and greatest step in the enterprise, he could now conclude it in safety, if not with ease.

But there were perils yet to be encountered, which the man of peace had not taken into anticipation, and which, indeed, would not have existed, had his foreboding doubts of the propriety of admitting either of his associates, and honest Stackpole especially, to a share of the exploit, been suffered to influence his counsels to the exclusion of that worthy but unlucky personage altogether. He had scarce stepped from the tent-door before there arose on the sudden, and at no great distance from the square over which he was hurrying his precious burden, a horrible din,—a stamping, snorting, galloping and neighing of horses, as if a dozen famished bears or wolves had suddenly made their way into the Indian pinfold, carrying death and distraction into the whole herd. And this alarming omen was almost instantly followed by an increase of all the uproar, as if the animals had broken loose from the pound, and were rushing, mad with terror, towards the centre of the village.

At the first outbreak of the tumult, Nathan had dropped immediately into the bushes before the wigwam; but perceiving that the sounds increased, and were actually drawing nigh, and that the sleepers were waking on the square, he sprang again to his feet, and, flinging his blanket around Edith, who was yet incapable of aiding herself, resolved to make a bold effort to escape, while darkness and the confusion of the enemy permitted. There was, in truth, not a moment to be lost. The slumbers of the barbarians, proverbially light at all times, and readily broken even when the stupor of intoxication has steeped their faculties, were not proof against sounds at once so unusual and so uproarious. A sudden yell of surprise, bursting from one point, was echoed by another, and another voice; and, in a moment, the square resounded with these signals of alarm, added to the wilder screams which some of them set up, of "Long-knives! Long-knives!" as if the savages supposed themselves suddenly beset by a whole army of charging Kentuckians.

It was at this moment of dismay and confusion, that Nathan rose from the earth, and, all other paths being now cut off, darted across a corner of the square towards the river, which was in a quarter opposite to that whence the sounds came, in hopes to reach the alder-thicket on its banks, before being observed. And this, perhaps, he would have succeeded in reaching, had not Fortune, which seemed this night to give a loose to all her fickleness, prepared a new and greater difficulty.

As he rose from the bushes, some savage, possessed of greater presence of mind than his fellows, cast a decaying brand from the fire into the heap of dried grass and maize-husks, designed for their couches, which, bursting immediately into a furious flame, illuminated the whole square and village, and revealed, as it was designed to do, the cause of the wondrous uproar. A dozen or more horses were instantly seen galloping into the square, followed by a larger and denser herd behind, all agitated by terror, all plunging, rearing, prancing, and kicking, as if possessed by a legion of evil spirits, though driven, as was made apparent by the yells which the Indians set up on seeing him, by nothing more than the agency of a human being.

At the first flash of the flames seizing upon the huge bed of straw, and whirling up in the gust in a prodigious volume, Nathan gave up all for lost, not doubting that he would be instantly seen and assailed. But the spectacle of their horses dashing madly into the square, with the cause of the tumult seen struggling among them, in the apparition of a white man, sitting aloft, entangled inextricably in the thickest of the herd, and evidently borne forward with no consent of his own, was metal more attractive for Indian eyes; and Nathan perceived that he was not only neglected in the confusion by all, but was likely to remain so, long enough to enable him to put the thicket betwixt him and the danger of discovery.

"The knave has endangered us, and to the value of the scalp on his own foolish head;" muttered Nathan, his indignation speaking in a voice louder than a whisper: "but, truly, he will pay the price: and, truly, his loss is the maiden's redeeming!"

He darted forwards as he spoke; but his words had reached the ears of one, who, cowering like himself among the weeds around Wenonga's hut, now started suddenly forth, and displayed to his eyes the young Virginian, who, rushing eagerly up, clasped the rescued captive in his arms, crying,—"Forward now, for the love of Heaven! forward, forward!"

"Thee has ruined all!" cried Nathan, with bitter reproach, as Edith, rousing from insensibility at the well known voice, opened her eyes upon her kinsman, and, all unmindful of the place of meeting, unconscious of everything but his presence—the presence of him whose supposed death she had so long lamented,—sprang to his embrace with a cry of joy that was heard over the whole square, a tone of happiness, pealing above the rush of the winds and the uproar of men and animals. "Thee has ruined all,—theeself and the maid! Save thee own life!"

With these words, Nathan strove to tear Edith from his grasp, to make one more effort for her rescue; and Roland, yielding her to his superior strength, and perceiving that a dozen Indians were running against them, drew his tomahawk, and, with a self-devotion which marked his love, his consciousness of error, and his heroism of character, waved Nathan away, while he himself rushed, back upon the pursuers, not so much, however, in the vain hope of disputing the path, as, by laying down his life on the spot, to purchase one more hope of escape to his Edith.

The act, so unexpectedly, so audaciously bold, drew a shout of admiration from throats which had before only uttered yells of fury: but it was mingled with fierce laughter, as the savages, without hesitating at, or indeed seeming at all to regard his menacing position, ran upon him in a body, and avoiding the only blow they gave him the power to make, seized and disarmed him,—a result that, notwithstanding his fierce and furious struggles, was effected in less space than we have taken to describe it. Then, leaving him in the hands of two of their number, who proceeded to bind him securely, the others rushed after Nathan, who, though encumbered by his burden, again inanimate, her arms clasped around his neck, as they had been round that of her kinsman, made the most desperate exertions to bear her off, seeming to regard her weight no more than if the burden had been a cushion of thistle-down. He ran for a moment with astonishing activity, leaping over bush and gully, where such crossed his path, with such prodigious strength and suppleness of frame, as to the savages appeared little short of miraculous; and, it is more than probable he might have effected his escape, had he chosen to abandon the helpless Edith. As it was, he, for a time, bade fair to make his retreat good. He reached the low thicket that fringed the river, and one more step would have found him in at least temporary security. But that step was never to be taken. As he approached, two tall barbarians suddenly sprang from the cover, where they had been taking their drunken slumbers; and, responding with exulting whoops to the cries of the others, they leaped forward to secure him. He turned aside, running downwards to where a lonely wigwam, surrounded by trees, offered the concealment of its shadow. But he turned too late; a dozen fierce wolf-like dogs, rushing from the cabin, and emboldened by the cries of the pursuers, rushed upon him, hanging to his skirts, and entangling his legs, rending and tearing all the while, so that he could fly no longer. The Indians were at his heels: their shouts were in his ears; their hands were almost upon his shoulders. He stopped, and turning towards them with a gesture and look of desperate defiance, and still more desperate hatred, exclaimed,—"Here, devils! cut and hack! your time has come, and I am the last of them!" And holding Edith at the length of his arm, he pulled open his garment, as if to invite the death-stroke.

But his death, at least at that moment, was not sought after by the Indians. They seized him, and, Edith being torn from his hands, dragged him, with endless whoops, towards the fire, whither they had previously borne the captured Roland, over whom, as over himself, they yelled their triumph; while screams of rage from those who had clashed among the horses after the daring white man who had been seen among them, and the confusion that still prevailed, showed that *he* also had fallen into their hands.

The words of defiance which Nathan breathed at the moment of yielding, were the last he uttered. Submitting passively to his fate, he was dragged onwards by a dozen hands, a dozen voices around him vociferating their surprise at his appearance even more energetically than the joy of their triumph. His Indian habiliments and painted body evidently struck them with astonishment, which increased as they drew nearer the fire, and could better distinguish the extraordinary devices he had traced so carefully on his breast and visage. Their looks of inquiry, their questions jabbered freely in broken English as well as in their own tongue, Nathan regarded no more than their taunts and menaces, replying to these, as to all, only with a wild and haggard stare, which seemed to awe several of the younger warriors, who began to exchange looks of peculiar meaning. At last, as they drew nearer the fire, an old Indian staggered among the group, who made way for him with a kind of respect, as was, indeed, his due,—for he was no other than the old Black-Vulture himself. Limping up to the prisoner, with as much ferocity as his drunkenness would permit, he laid one hand upon his shoulder, and with the other aimed a furious hatchet-blow at his head. The blow was arrested by the renegade Doe, or Atkinson, who made his appearance at the same time with Wenonga, and muttered some words in the Shawnee tongue, which seemed meant to soothe the old man's fury.

"Me Injun-man!" said the chief, addressing his words to the prisoner, and therefore in the prisoner's language,—"Me kill all white-man! Me

Wenonga: me drink white-mans blood! me no heart!" And to impress the truth of his words on the prisoner's mind, he laid his right hand, from which the axe had been removed, as well as his left, on Nathan's shoulder, in which position supporting himself, he nodded and wagged his head in the other's face, with as savage a look of malice as he could infuse into his drunken features. To this the prisoner replied by bending upon the chief a look more hideous than his own, and indeed so strangely unnatural and revolting, with lips so retracted, features so distorted by some nameless passion, and eyes gleaming with fires so wild and unearthly, that even Wenonga, chief as he was, and then in no condition to be daunted by anything, drew slowly back, removing his hands from the prisoner's shoulder, who immediately fell down in horrible convulsions, the foam flying from his lips, and his fingers clenching like spikes of iron into the flesh of two Indians that had hold of him.

Taunts, questions, and whoops were heard no more among the captors, who drew aside from their wretched prisoner, as if from the darkest of their Manitoes, all looking on with unconcealed wonder and awe. The only person, indeed, who seemed undismayed at the spectacle, was the renegade, who, as Nathan shook and writhed in the fit, beheld the corner of a piece of parchment projecting from the bosom of his shirt, and looking vastly like that identical instrument he had seen but an hour or two before in the hands of Braxley. Stooping down, and making as if he would have raised the convulsed man in his arms, he drew the parchment from its hiding-place, and, unobserved by the Indians, transferred it to a secret place in his own garments. He then rose up, and stood like the rest, looking upon the prisoner, until the fit had passed off, which it did in but a few moments, Nathan starting to his feet, and looking around him in the greatest wildness, as if, for a moment, not only unconscious of what had befallen him, but even of his captivity.

But unconsciousness of the latter calamity was of no great duration, and was dispelled by the old chief saying, but with looks of drunken respect, that had succeeded his insane fury—"Me brudder great-medicine white-man! great white-man medicine! Me Wenonga, great Injun-captain, great kill-man-white-man, kill-all-man, man-man, squaw-man, little papoose-man! Me make medicine-man brudder-man! Medicine-man tell Wenonga all Jibbenainosay?—where find Jibbenainosay? How kill Jibbenainosay? kill white-man's devil-man! Medicine-man tell Injun-man why medicine-man come Injun town? steal Injun prisoner? steal Injun hoss? Me Wenonga,—me good brudder medicine-man."

This gibberish, with which he seemed, besides expressing much new-born good will, to intimate that his cause lay in the belief that the prisoner was a great white conjuror, who could help him to a solution of sundry interesting questions, the old chief pronounced with much solemnity and suavity; and he betrayed an inclination to continue it, the captors of Nathan standing by and looking on with vast and eager interest. But a sudden and startling yell from the Indians who had charge of the young Virginian, preceded by an exclamation from the renegade who had stolen among them, upset the curiosity of the party,—or rather substituted a new object for admiration, which set them all running towards the fire, where Roland lay bound. The cause of the excitement was nothing less than the discovery which Doe had just made, of the identity of the prisoner with Roland Forrester, whom he had with his own hands delivered into those of the merciless Piankeshaws, and whose escape from them and sudden appearance in the Shawnee village were events just as wonderful to the savages as the supposed powers of the white medicine-man, his associate.

But there was still a third prodigy to be wondered at. The third prisoner was dragged from among the horses to the fire, where he was almost immediately recognised by half a dozen different warriors, as the redoubted and incorrigible horse-thief, Captain Stackpole. The wonderful conjuror, and the wonderful young Long-knife, who was one moment a captive in the hands of Piankeshaws on the banks of the Wabash, and, the next, an invader of a Shawnee village in the valley of the Miami, were both forgotten: the captain of horse-thieves was a much more wonderful person,—or, at least, a much more important prize. His name was howled aloud and in a moment became the theme of every tongue; and he was instantly surrounded by every man in the village,—we may say, every woman and child, too, for the alarm had brought the whole village into the square; and the shrieks of triumph, the yells of unfeigned delight with which all welcomed a prisoner so renowned and so detested, produced an uproar ten times greater than that which gave the alarm.

It was indeed Stackpole, the zealous and unlucky slave of a mistress whom it was his fate to injure and wrong in every attempt he made to serve her; and who had brought himself and his associates to their present bonds by merely toiling on the present occasion too hard in her service. It seems,—for so he was used himself to tell the tale,—that he entered the Indian pound with the resolution to fulfil Nathan's instructions to the letter; and he accordingly selected four of the best animals of the herd, which he succeeded in haltering without difficulty or noise. Had he paused here, he might have retreated with his prizes without fear of discovery. But the excellence of the opportunity,—the best he had ever had in his life,—the excellence, too, of the horses, thirty or forty in number, "the primest and beautifullest critturs," he averred, "what war ever seed in a hoss-pound," with a notion which now suddenly beset his grateful brain, namely, that by carrying off the whole herd he could "make anngelliferous madam rich in the item of hoss-flesh," proved too much for his philosophy and his judgment; and after holding a council of war in his own mind, he came to a resolution "to steal the lot."

This being determined upon, he imitated the example of magnanimity lately set him by Nathan, stripped off and converted his venerable wrap-rascal into extemporary halters, and so made sure of half a dozen more of the best horses; with which, and the four first selected, not doubting that the remainder of the herd would readily follow at their heels, he crept from the fold, to make his way up the valley, and round among the hills, to the rendezvous. But that was a direction in which, as he soon learned to his cost, neither the horses he had in hand, nor those that were to follow in freedom, had the slightest inclination to go; and there immediately ensued a struggle between the stealer and the stolen, which, in the space of a minute or less, resulted in the whole herd making a demonstration towards the centre of the village, whither they succeeded both in carrying themselves and the vainly resisting horse-thief, who was borne along on the backs of those he had haltered, like a land-bird on the bosom of a torrent, incapable alike of resisting or escaping the flood.

In this manner he was taken in a trap of his own making, as many a better and wiser man of the world has been, and daily is; and it was no melioration of his distress to think he had whelmed his associates in his ruin, and defeated the best and last hopes of his benefactress. It was with such feelings at his heart, that he was dragged up to the fire, to be exulted over and scolded at as long as it should seem good to his captors. But the latter, exhausted by the day's revels, and satisfied with their victory, so complete and so bloodless, soon gave over tormenting him, resolving, however, that he should be soundly beaten at the gantelope on the morrow, for the especial gratification, and in honour, of the Wyandott party, their guests.

This resolution being made, he was, like Roland and Nathan, led away bound, each being bestowed in a different hut, where they were committed to safer guards than had been appointed to watch over Edith; and, in an hour after, the village was again wrapped in repose. The last to betake themselves to their rest were Doe, and his confederate, Braxley, the latter of whom had been released from his disagreeable bonds, when Edith was carried back to the tent. It was while following Doe to his cabin, that he discovered the loss of the precious document upon the possession of which he had built so many stratagems, and so many hopes of success. His agitation and confusion were so great at the time of Nathan's assault, that he was wholly unaware it had been taken from him by this assailant; and Doe, to whom its possession opened newer and bolder prospects, and who had already formed a design for using it to his own advantage, effected to believe that he had dropped it on the way, and would easily recover it on the morrow, as no Indian could possibly attach the least value to it.

Another subject of agitation to Braxley, was the reappearance of his rival; who, however, Doe assured him, was "now as certainly a dead man, as if twenty bullets had been driven through his body."—"He is in the hands of the Old Vulture," said he, grimly, "and he will burn in fire jist as sure as *we* will, Dick Braxley, when the devil gits us!—that is, unless we ourselves save him!"

"We, Jack!" said the other, with a laugh: "and yet who knows how the wind may blow *you*? But an hour ago you were as remorseful over the lad's supposed death as you are now apparently indifferent what befalls him."

"It is true," replied Doe, coolly: "but see the difference! When the Piankeshaws were burning him,—or when I thought the dogs were at it,—it was a death of *my* making for him: it was *I* that helped him to the stake. But here the case is altered. He comes here on his own hook; the Injuns catch him on his own hook; and, d—n them, they'll burn him on his own hook! and so it's no matter of my consarning. There's the root of it!"

This explanation satisfied his suspicious ally; and having conversed a while longer on what appeared to them most wonderful and interesting in the singular attempt at the rescue, the two retired to their repose.

CHAPTER XXXII

The following day was one of unusual animation and bustle in the Indian village, as the prisoners could distinguish even from their several places of confinement, without, however, being sensible of the cause. Prom sunrise until after mid-day, they heard, at intervals, volleys of fire-arms shot off at the skirts of the town, which, being followed by shrill halloos as from those who fired them, were immediately re-echoed by all the throats in the village—men, women, children, and dogs uniting in a clamour that was plainly the outpouring of savage exultation and delight. It seemed as if parties of warriors, returning victorious from the lands of the Long-knife, were, time after time, marching into and through the village, proclaiming the success of their arms, and exhibiting the trophies of their triumph. The hubbub increased, the shouts became more frequent and multitudinous, and the village for a second time seemed given up to the wildest and maddest revelry, to the sway of unchained demons, or of men abandoned to all the horrible impulses of lycanthropy.

During all this time, the young Virginian lay bound in a wigwam, guarded by a brace of old warriors, who occasionally varied the tedium of watching by stalking to the door, where, like yelping curs paying their respects to passers-by, they up-lifted their voices and vented a yell or two in testimony of their approbation of what was going on without. Now and then, also, they even left the wigwam, but never for more than a few moments at a time; when, having thus amused themselves, they would return, squat themselves down by the prisoner's side, and proceed to entertain him with sundry long-winded speeches in their own dialect, of which, of course, he understood not a word. Wrapped in his own bitter thoughts, baffled in his last hope, and now grown indifferent what might befall him, he lay upon the earthen floor during the whole day, expecting almost every moment to behold some of the shouting crew of the village rush into the hovel and drag him away to the tortures which, at that period, were so often the doom of the prisoner.

But the solitude of his prison-house was invaded only by his two old jailers; and it was not until nightfall that he beheld a third human countenance. At that period, Telie Doe stole trembling into the hut, bringing him food, which she set before him, but with looks of deep grief and deeper abasement, which he might have attributed to shame and remorse for a part played in the scheme of captivity, had not all her actions shown that, although acquainted with the meditated outrage, she was sincerely desirous to avert it.

Her appearance awakened his dormant spirits, and recalled the memory of his kinswoman, of whom he besought her to speak, though well aware she could speak neither hope nor comfort. But scarce had Telie, more abashed and more sorrowful at the question, opened her lips to reply, when one of the old Indians interposed, with a frown of displeasure, and, taking her by the arm, led her angrily to the door, where he waved her away, with gestures that seemed to threaten a worse reception should she presume to return.

Thus thwarted and driven back again upon his own reflections, Roland gave himself up to despondency, awaiting with sullen indifference the fate which he had no doubt was preparing for him. But he was doomed once more to experience the agitations of hope, the tormentor not less than the soother of existence.

Soon after nightfall, and when his mind was in a condition resembling the hovel in which he lay—a cheerless ruin, lighted only by occasional flickerings from a fire of spirit fast smouldering into ashes—he heard a step enter the door, and, by and by, a jabbering debate commenced between the newcomer and his guards, which resulted in the latter presently leaving the cabin. The intruder then stepped up to the fire, which he stirred into a flame; and seating himself full in its light, revealed, somewhat to Roland's surprise, the form and visage of the renegade, Abel Doe, whose acts on the hill-side had sufficiently impressed his lineaments on the soldier's memory. He eyed the captive for awhile very earnestly, but in deep silence, which Roland himself was the first to break.

To the soldier, however, bent upon preserving the sullen equanimity which was his best substitute for resignation, there was enough in the appearance of this man to excite the fiercest emotions of indignation. Others might have planned the villany which had brought ruin and misery upon his head; but it was Doe who, for the bravo's price, and with the bravo's baseness, had set the toils around him, and struck the blow. It was, indeed, only through the agency of such an accomplice that Braxley could have put his schemes into execution, or ventured even to attempt them. The blood boiled in his veins as he surveyed the mercenary and unprincipled hireling, and strove, though in vain, to rise upon his fettered arms, to give energy to his words of denunciation.

"Villain!" he cried, "base, wretched, dastardly caitiff! have you come to boast the fruits of your rascally crime?"

"Right, captain!" replied Doe, with a consenting nod of the head, "you have nicked me on the right p'int: villain's the true word to begin on; and, perhaps, 'twill be the one to end on: but that's as we shall conclude about it, after we have talked the matter over."

"Begone, wretch,—trouble me not," said Roland, "I have nothing to say to you, but to curse you."

"Well, I reckon that's natteral enough, too, that cussing of me," said Doe, "seeing as how I've in a manner deserved it. But there's an end to all things, even to cussing; and, may be, you'll jist take a jump the other way, when the gall's over. A friend to-day, an enemy to-morrow, as the saying is; and you may jist as well say it backwards; for, as things turn up, I'm no sich blasted enemy, jist now, no-way no-how. I'm for holding a peace talk, as the Injuns say, d—n 'em, burying the axe, and taking a whiff or two at the kinnikinick of friendship. So cuss away, if it will do you good; and I'll stand it. But as for being off, why I don't mean it noway. I've got a bargain to strike with you, and it is jist a matter to take the tiger-cat out of you,—it is, d—n it: and when you've heard it, you'll be in no sich hurry to get rid of me. But, afore we begin, I've jist got a matter to ax you: and that is,—how the h— — you cleared the old Piankeshaw and his young uns?"

"If you have anything to propose to me," said Roland, smothering his wrath as well as he could, though scarce hoping assistance or comfort of any kind from the man who had done him so much injury, "propose it, and be brief, and trouble me with no questions."

"Well now," said Doe, "a civil question might as well have a civil answer! If you killed the old feller and the young-uns, you needn't be ashamed of it; for cuss me, I think all the better of you for it; for it's not every feller can kill three Injuns that has him in the tugs, by no means no-how. But, I reckon, the ramscallions took to the liquor? (Injuns will be Injuns, there's no two ways about it!) and you riz on 'em, and so paid 'em up scot and lot, according to their desarvings? You couldn't have done a better thing to make me beholden: for, you see, I had the giving of you up to 'em, and I felt bad,—I did, d—n me, for I knew the butchers would burn you, if they got you to the Wabash—I did, captain, and I had bad thoughts about it. But it was a cussed mad notion of you, following us, it was, there's no denying! Howsomever, I won't talk of that. I jist want to ax you where you picked up that Injun-looking feller that was lugging off the gal, and what his natur'? The Injuns say, he's a conjuror: now I never heerd of conjurors among the whites, like as among the Injuns, afore I cut loose from 'em, and I'm cur'ous on the subject!—I jist ax you a civil question, and I don't mean no harm in it. There's nobody can make the feller out; and, as for Ralph Stackpole, blast him, he says he never seed the crittur afore in his life!"

"If you would have me answer *your* question," said Roland, in whom Doe's discourse was beginning to stir up many a former feeling, "you must first answer mine. This person you speak of,—what is to be his fate?"

"Why, burning, I reckon: but that's according as he pleases the old Vulture: for, if he can find out what never an Injun Medicine has been able to do, it may be, the old chief will feed him up and make him his conjuror. They say, he's conjuring with the crittur now."

"And Stackpole, what will they do with him?"

"Burn him, sartin! They're jist waiting till the warriors come in from the Licking, where, you must know, they have taken a hundred scalps, or so, at one grab: and then the feller will roast beyond all mention."

"And I, too," said the Virginian, with such calmness us he could, "I, too, am to meet the same fate?"

"Most ondoubtedly," said Doe, with an ominous nod of assent. "There's them among us that speak well of you, as having heart enough to be made an Injun: but there's them that have sworn you shall burn; and burn you *must!*—That is, onless—" But he was interrupted by Roland, exclaiming hurriedly,—

"There is but one more to speak of—my cousin? my poor friendless cousin?"

"There," said Doe, "you needn't be afeard of burning, by no means whatsomever. We didn't catch the gal to make a roast of. She is safe enough; there's one that will take care of her."

"And that one is the villain Braxley! Oh, knave that you are, could you have the heart,—you who have a daughter of your own, could you have committed *her* into the arms of such a villain?"

"No, by G——, I couldn't!" said Doe, with great earnestness: "but another man's daughter is quite another thing. Howsomever, you needn't take on for nothing; for he means to marry her and take her safe back to Virginny: and, you see, I bargained with him agin all rascality; for I had a gal of my own, and I couldn't think of his playing foul with the poor creatur'. No, we had an understanding about all that, when we was waiting for you on old Salt. All Dick wants is jist a wife that will help him to them lands of the old major. And that, you see, is jist the whole reason of our making the grab on you."

"You confess it, then!" cried Roland, too much excited by the bitterest of passions to be surprised at the singular communicativeness of his visitor: "you sold yourself to the villain for gold! for gold you hesitated not to sacrifice the happiness of one victim of his passions, the life of another! Oh, basest of all that bear the name of man, how could you do this villany?"

"Because," replied Doe, with as much apparent sincerity as emphasis, "because I am a d—d rascal: there's no sort of doubt about it; and we won't be tender the way we talk of it. I was an honest man once, captain, but I am a rascal now; warp and woof, skin-deep and heart-deep, ay, to the bones and marrow,—I am all the way a rascal! But don't look as if you was astonished already. I come to make a clean breast of all sorts of matters, jist, captain, for a little bit of your advantage and my own: and there's things coming that will make you look a leetle of a sight wilder! And, first and foremost, to begin. Have you any particular longing to be out of this here Injun town, and well shut of the d—d fire torture?"

"Have I any desire to be free! Mad question!"

"Well, captain, I'm jist the man, and the only one, that can help you; for them that would, can't, and them that can, won't. And, secondly and lastly, captain, as the parsons say in the settlements, have you any hankering to be the master of the old major, your uncle's lands and houses?"

"If you come to mock and torture me,"—said Roland, but was interrupted by the renegade.

"It is jist to save you from the torture," said he, "that I'm now speaking; for, cuss me, the more I think of it, the more I can't stand it no-how. I'm a rascal, captain, but I'm no tiger-cat, especially to them that hasn't misused me, and there's the grit of a man about you that strikes my feelings exactly. But, you see, captain, there's a bargain first to be struck between us, afore I comes up to the rack—but I'll make tarms easy."

"Make them what you will, and But, alas! where shall I find means to repay you? I who am robbed of everything?"

"Didn't I say I could help you to the major's lands and houses? and a'n't they a fortun' for an emperor?"

"You! *you* help me? help me to *them*?"

"Captain," said the renegade, with sundry emphatic nods of the head, "I'm a sight more of a rascal than you ever dreamed on! and this snapping of you up by Injun deviltry, that you think so hard of, is but a small part of my misdoings: I've been slaving agin you this sixteen years, more of less, *slaving* (that's the word, for I made a niggur of myself) to rob you of these here very lands that I'm now thinking of helping you to! You don't believe me, captain! Well, did you ever hear of a certain honest feller of old Augusta, called John Atkinson?"

"Hah!" cried the soldier, looking with new eyes upon the renegade; "you are then the fellow upon whose perjured testimony Braxley relied to sustain his frauds?"

"The identical same man, John Atkinson, or Jack, as they used to call me; but now Abel Doe, for convenience sake," said the refugee, with great composure; "and so, now, you can see into the whole matter. It was *me* that had the keeping of the major's daughter that you knows of. Well, I was an honest feller in them days, I was, captain, by G——!" repeated the fellow with something that sounded like remorseful utterance, "and jist as contented in my cabin on the mountain as the old major himself in his big house at Felhallow. But Dick Braxley came, d—n him, and there was an end of all honest doings: for Dick was high with the old major, and the major was agin his brothers; and says Dick, says he, 'Put but this little gal,'—meaning the major's daughter,—'out of the way and I'm jist as good as the major's heir; and I'll make your fortun'"—

"Ay! and it was *he* then, the villain himself," cried Roland, "who devised this horrible iniquity, which, by innuendo at least, he charged upon my father!—You are a rascal indeed! And you murdered the poor child?"

"Murdered! No, rat it, there was no murdering in the case: it was jist hiding in a hole, as you may call it. We burned down the wigwam, and made on as if the gal was burned in it; and then I stumped off to the Injun border, among them that didn't know me, and according to Dick's advice, helped myself to another name, and jist passed off the gal for my own daughter."

"Your own daughter!" cried Roland, starting half up, but being unable to rise on account of his bonds: "the story then is true! and Telie Doe is my uncle's child, the lost heiress?"

"Well, supposing she is?" said Atkinson, "I reckon you'd not be exactly the man to help her to her rights?"

"Ay, by Heaven, but I would though!" said Roland, "if rights they be. If my uncle, upon knowledge that she was still alive, thought fit to alter his intentions with regard to Edith and myself, he would have found none more ready to acknowledge the poor girl's claims than ourselves, none more ready to befriend and assist her."

"Well! there's all the difference between being an honest feller and a rascal!" muttered Atkinson, casting his eyes upon the fire, which he fell to studying for a moment with great earnestness. Then starting up hastily, and turning to the prisoner he exclaimed—

"There's not a better gal in the etarnal world! You don't know it, captain; but that Telie, that poor critter that's afeard of her own shadow, did run all risks, and play all manner of fool's tricks, to save you from this identical same captivation; and the night you was sleeping at Bruce's fort, and we waiting for you at the ford, she cried, and begged, and prayed that I would do you no more mischief; and, cuss her, she threatened to tell you and Bruce, there, the whole affair of the ambush; till I scared her with my tomahawk, like a d——d rascal as I am (but there's nothing will fetch her round but fear of murdering); and so swore her to keep silence. And then, captain, her running away after you in the woods,—why, it was jist to circumvent us,—to lead you to the t'other old road, and so save you; it was, captain, and she owned it: and if you'd a' taken to her leading, as she axed you, she'd 'a' got you out of the snarl altogether. Howsomever, captain," he continued, after making those admissions, which solved all the enigmas of Telie's conduct, "I won't lie in this matter no-how. The gal is no gal of the major's, but my own flesh and blood: the major's little critter sickened on the border, and died off in less than a year; and so there was all our rascally burning and lying for nothing; for, if we had waited a while, the poor thing would have died of her own accord. Well, captain, I'm making a long story about nothing: but the short of it is, I didn't make a bit of a fortun' at all, but fell into troubles; and the end was, I turned Injun, jist as you see me; and a feller there, Tom Bruce, took to my little gal out of charity; and so she was bred up a beggar's brat, with everybody a jeering of her, because of her d——d rascally father. And, you see, this made a wolf of me; for I couldn't bring her among the Injuns, to marry her to a cussed niggur of a savage,—no, captain, I couldn't; for she's my own natteral flesh and blood, and, captain, I love her! And so I goes back to Virginny, to see what Braxley could do for her; and there, d——n him, he puts me up to a new rascality; which was nothing less than setting up my gal for the major's daughter, and making her a great heiress, and marrying of her. Howsomever, this wouldn't do, this marrying; for, first, Dick Braxley was a bigger rascal than myself, and it was agin my conscience to give him the gal, who was a good gal, deserving of an honest husband; and, next the feller was mad after young madam, and there was no telling how soon he might p'ison my gal, to marry the other. And so we couldn't fix the thing then to our liking, no way; but by and by we did. For when the major died, he sends for me in a way I told him of; and here's jist the whole of our rascality. We was, in the first place, jist to kill you off—"

"To kill me, villain!" cried Roland, whose interest was already excited to the highest pitch by the renegade's story.

"Not exactly with our own hands; for I bargained agin that: but it was agreed you should be put out of the way of ever returning agin to Virginny. Well, captain, Dick was then to marry the young lady; and then jist step into the major's estate by virtue of the major's will,—the second one you must know, which Dick took good care to hide away, pretending to suppose the major had destroyed it."

"And that will," exclaimed Roland, "the villain, the unparalleled villain is still possessed of!"

"No, rat him,—the devil has turned upon him at last, and it is in better hands!" said Atkinson; and without more ado, he drew the instrument from his bosom and unfolded it before Roland's astonished eyes. "Read it," said Doe, with exulting voice: "I can make nothing of the cursed pot-hooks myself, having never been able to stand the flogging of a school-house; but I know the fixings of it, the whole estate devised equally to you and the young woman, to be divided according as you may agree of yourselves, a monstrous silly way, that; but there's no helping it."

And holding it before the Virginian, in the light of the fire, the latter satisfied himself at a glance that Atkinson had truly reported its contents. It was written with his uncle's own hand, briefly but clearly; and while manifesting throughout, the greatest affection on the part of the testator toward his orphan niece, it contained no expressions indicative either of ill-will to his nephew or disapprobation of the part the young man had chosen to play in the great drama of revolution. And this was the more remarkable as it was dated at a period soon after Roland had so wilfully, or patriotically, fled to fight the battles of his country, and when it might have been supposed the stern old loyalist's anger was at its height. A better and more grateful proof that the young man had neither lost his regard nor confidence, was shown in a final codicil, dated in the year of Roland's majority, in which he was associated with Braxley as executor, the latter worthy having been made to figure in that capacity alone, in the body of the will.

"This is indeed a discovery!" cried Roland, with the agitation of joy and hope. "Cut my bonds, deliver me, with my cousin and companions,—and the best farm in the manor shall reward you:—nay, you shall fix your own terms for your daughter and yourself."

"Exactly," said Atkinson, who, although the prisoner was carefully bound, exhibited a jealous disinclination to let the will come near his hands, and now restored it carefully to his own bosom; "we must talk over that matter of tarms, jist to avoid mistakes. And to begin, captain, I will jist observe, as before, that if you don't take my offer, and close with me hard and fast, you will roast at an Injun stake jist as sartainly as you are now snugging by an Injun fire; you will, d——n me, there's no two ways about it!"

"The terms, the terms?" cried Roland, eagerly: "name them; I will not dispute them."

But the renegade was in no such hurry.

"You see," said he, "I'm a d——d rascal, as I said; and in this matter, I am just as much a rascal as before, for I'm playing foul with Braxley, having bargained to work out the whole thing in his sarvice. Howsomever, there is a kind of fair play in cheating *him*, seeing it was him that made a rascal of me. And moresomever, I have my doubts of him, and there's no way I can hold him up to a bargain. And, lastly, captain, I don't see how he can be of any sarvice to my gal! He can't marry her if he would; and if he could, he shouldn't have her; and as for leaving her to his tender mercies, I would jist as soon think of hunting her up quarters in a bear's den. And as for keeping her among these d——d brutes, the Injuns—for brutes they are captain, there's no denying it—"

"Why need you speak of it more? I will find her a home and protection,—a home and protection for both of you."

"As for *me*, captain, thanking' you for the favour, you won't do me no sich thing, seeing as how I don't look for it. There's two or three small matters agin me in the Settlements, which it is no notion of mine to bring up for reckoning. The gal's the crittur to be protected; and I'll take my pay out chiefly in the good you do to her; and for the small matters, not meaning no offence, I can trust best to her; for she's my daughter, and she won't cheat me. Now, captain, a better gal than Telie—her true name's Matilda, but she never heard anything of it but Telie—a better gal was never seen in the woods, for all she's young and timorsome; and it's jist my notion and my desire, that, whatever may become of me, nothing but good shall become of her. And now, captain, here's my tarms; I'll cut you loose from Injun tugs and Injun fires, carry you safe to the Settlements, and give you this here precious sheepskin,—which is jist as much as saying I'll make you the richest man, in farms, flocks, and niggurs, in all Virginny; and you shall marry the gal, and make a lady of her!"

"Marry her!" cried Roland, in amazement and consternation,—"marry her!"

"Ay, captain! that's the word," said Atkinson: "I have an idea you'll make her a good husband, for you're an honest feller, and a brave one—I'll say that for you; and she'll make you a good wife, or I'll give you my scalp on it. I reckon the crittur has a liking for you already; for I never did see any body so beg, and plead, and take on for mortal feller. Marry her's the tarms; and, I reckon, you'll allow, they're easy ones?"

"My good friend, you are surely jesting!" said the Virginian. "I will do for her whatever you can wish, or demand. The best farm in the whole estate shall be hers, and the protection of my kinswoman will be cheerfully and gratefully granted."

"As for jesting, captain," said the renegade, with a lowering brow, "there's not one particle of it about me, from top to toe. I offer you a bargain that has all the good on your side; and I reckoned you'd 'a' jumped at it with a whole hoss-load of thank'ees. I offer you a gal that's the best gal in the whole eternal wood; and I reckon you may count all that this here sheepskin will bring you as jist so much dowry of my giving. A'n't that making tarms easy?—for, as for the small matters for myself, them is things I will come upon the gal for, without troubling you for 'em. Now you see, captain, I'll 'jist argue the matter. You may reckon it strange I should make you such an offer; and ondoubtedly, so it is. But here's the case. First, captain, I'm agin burning you; it makes. me oneasy, to think of it—for you ha'n't done me no harm, and you're a young feller of the rale Virginny grit, jist after my own heart, and I takes to you. And, next, captain, there's the gal—a good gal, captain, that's desarving of all I can do for her, and a heap more. But, captain, what's to become of the crittur when I'am done for? You see, some of these cussed Injuns—or it may be the white men, for they're all agin me—will take the scalp off me some day, sooner or later, there's no two ways about it. Well, then, what's to become of the poor gal, that ha'n't no friend in the big world to care for her? Now, you see, I'm thinking of the gal, and I'm making the bargain for her; and I made it in my own mind jist the minute I seed you were a captive among us, and laid my hand on this here will. Said I to myself, 'I'll save the youngster, and I'll marry my gal to him, and there's jist two good things I'll do for the pair of 'em!' And so, captain, there's exactly the end of it. If you'll take the gal, you shall have her, and you'll make three different critturs greatly beholden to you:—first, the gal, who's a good gal, and a comely gal, and will love and honor you jist as hard as the best madam in the land; next, myself, that am her father, and longs to give her to an honest feller, that won't misuse her, and, last, your own partickelar self;—for the taking of her is exactly the only way you have of gitting hack the old major's lands, and what I hold to be jist as agreeable, dragging clear of a hot Injun fire that will roast you to cinders if you remain in this d—d village two days longer!"

"My friend," cried Roland, driven to desperation, for he perceived Atkinson was making his extraordinary proposal in perfectly good faith and simplicity, as a regular matter of matter of business, "you know not what you ask. Free me and my kinswoman—"

"As for young madam there," interrupted the renegade, "don't be at all oneasy. She's in good hands, I tell you; and Braxley'll fetch her straight off to Virginny as soon as he has brought her to reason."

"And your terms," said Roland, smothering his fury as he could, "imply an understanding that my cousin is to be surrendered to him?"

"Ondoubtedly," replied Doe; "there's no two ways about it. I work on my own hook, in the matter of the fortun'—'cause how, Dick's not to be trusted where the play's all in his own hands; but as for cheating him out of the gal, there's no manner of good can come of it, and it's clear agin my own interest. No, captain, here's the case; you takes my gal Telie, and Braxley takes the t'other; and so it's all settled fair between you."

"Hark you, rascal!" cried Roland, giving way to his feelings; "if you would deserve a reward, you must win it, not by saving *me,* but my cousin. My own life I would buy at the price of half the lands which that will makes me master of—for the rescue of Edith from the vile Braxley I would give *all.* Save her—save her from Braxley—and then ask me what you will."

"Well," said Atkinson, "and you'll marry my gal?"

"Death and furies! are you besotted? I will enrich her—ay, with the best of my estate—with all—she shall have it all."

"And you won't have her, then?" cried the renegade, starting up in anger: "you don't think her good enough for you, because you're of a great quality stock, and she's come of nothing but me, John Atkinson, a plain back-woods feller? Or mayhap," he added, more temperately, "you're agin taking her because of my being sich a d—d notorious rascal? Well, now, I reckon that's a thing nobody will know of in Virginny, unless you should tell it yourself. You can jist call her Telie Jones, or Telie Small, or any nickname of that natur', and nobody'll be the wiser; and I shall jist say nothing about it myself—I won't, captain, d—n me; for it's the gal's good I'm hunting after, and none of my own."

"You are mad, I tell you," cried the soldier. "Fix your own terms for her: I will execute any instrument, I will give you any bond—"

"None of your cussed bonds for me," said Doe, with great contempt; "I knows the worth of 'em, and I'm jist lawyer enough to see how you could git out of 'em, by swearing they were written under compulsion, or whatsomever you call it. And, besides, who's to stop your cheating the gal that has nobody to take care of her, when you gits her in Virginny, where I darn't follow her? No, captain, there's jist but the one way to make all safe and fair; and that's by marrying her. So marry her, captain; and jist to be short, captain, you must marry her or burn, there's no two ways about it. I make you the last offer; there's no time for another; for to-morrow you must be help'd off, or it's too late for you. Come, captain, jist say the word—marry the gal, and I'll save you."

"You are mad, I tell you again. Marry her I neither can nor will. But—"

"There's no occasion for more," interrupted Doe, starting angrily up. "You've jist said the word, and that's enough. And now, captain, when you come to the stake, don't say *I* brought you there: no, d—n it, don't—for I've done jist all I could do to help you to life and fortun'—I have, d—n me, you can't deny it."

And with these words, uttered with sullen accents and looks, the renegade stole from the hut, disregarding all Roland's entreaties to him to return, and all the offers of wealth with which the latter, in a frenzy of despair, sought to awaken his eupidity and compassion. The door-mats had scarce closed upon his retreating figure before they were parted to give entrance to the two old Indians, who immediately assumed their positions at his side, preserving them with vigilant fidelity throughout the remainder of the night.

CHAPTER XXXIII

In the meantime, and at the very moment when the renegade was urging his extraordinary proposals to the young Virginian, a scene was passing in the hut of Wenonga, in which one of Roland's fellow-prisoners was destined to play an important and remarkable part. There, in the very tent in which he had struck so daring a blow for the rescue of Edith, but in which Edith appeared no more, lay the luckless Nathan, a victim not so much of his own rashness as of the excessive zeal, not to say folly, of his coadjutors. And thither he had been conducted but a few hours before, after having passed the previous night and day in a prison-house less honoured, but fated, as it proved, to derive peculiar distinction from the presence of such a guest.

His extraordinary appearance, partaking so much of that of an Indian juggler arrayed in the panoply of legerdemain, had produced, as was mentioned, a powerful effect on the minds of his captors, ever prone to the grossest credulity and superstition; and this was prodigiously increased by the sudden recurrence of his disease,—a dreadful infliction, whose convulsions seem ever to have been proposed as the favourite exemplars for the expression of prophetic fury and the demoniacal orgasm, and were aped alike by the Pythian priestess on her tripod and the ruder impostor of an Indian wigwam. The foaming lips and convulsed limbs of the prisoner, if they did not "speak the god," to the awe-struck barbarians, declared at least the presence of the mighty fiend who possessed his body; and when the fit was over, though they took good care to bind him with thongs of bison-hide, like his companions, and led him away to a place of security, it was with a degree of gentleness and respect that proved the strength of their belief in his supernatural endowments. This belief was still further indicated, the next day, by crowds of savages who flocked into the wigwam where he was confined, some to stare at him, some to inquire the mysteries of their fate, and some, as it seemed, with credulity less unconditional, to solve the enigma of his appearance before yielding their full belief. Among these last were the renegade and one or two savages of a more sagacious or sceptical turn than their fellows, who beset the supposed conjuror with questions calculated to pluck out the heart of his mystery.

But questions and curiosity were in vain. The conjuror was possessed by a silent devil; and whether it was that the shock of his last paroxysm had left his mind benumbed and stupefied, whether his courage had failed at last, leaving him plunged in despair, or whether, indeed, his frigid indifference was not altogether assumed to serve a peculiar purpose, it was nevertheless certain that he bestowed not the slightest attention upon any of his questioners, not even upon Doe, who had previously endeavoured to unravel the riddle by seeking the assistance of Ralph Stackpole,—assistance, however, which Ralph, waxing sagacious of a sudden, professed himself wholly unable to give. This faithful fellow, indeed, professed to be just as ignorant of the person and character of the young Virginian; swearing, with a magnanimous resolve, to assume the pains and penalties of Indian ire on his own shoulders, that "the hoss-stealing" (which, he doubted not, would be held the most unpardonable feature in the adventure,) "was jist a bit of a private speculation of his own,—that there was nobody with him,—that he had come on his expedition alone, and knew no more of the other fellers than he did of the 'tarnal tempers of Injun hosses,—not he!" In short, the skeptics were baffled, and the superstitious were left to the enjoyment of their wonder and awe.

At nightfall, Nathan was removed to Wenonga's cabin, where the chief, surrounded by a dozen or more warriors, made him a speech in such English phrases as he had acquired, informing the prisoner, as before, that "he, Wenonga, was a great chief and warrior, that the other, the prisoner, was a great medicine-man; and, finally, that he, Wenonga, required of his prisoner, the medicine-man, by his charms, to produce the Jibbenainosay, the unearthly slayer of his people and curse of his tribe, in order that he, the great chief, who feared neither warrior nor devil, might fight him, like a man, and kill him, so that he, the aforesaid destroyer, should destroy his young men in the dark no longer."

Not even to this speech, though received by the warriors with marks of great approbation, did Nathan vouchsafe the least notice; and the savages despairing of moving him to their purpose at that period, but hoping perhaps to find him in a more reasonable mood at another moment, left him—but not until they had again inspected the thongs and satisfied themselves they were tied in knots strong and intricate enough to hold even a conjuror. They, also, before leaving him to himself, placed food and water at his side, and in a way that was perhaps designed to show their opinion of his wondrous powers; for as his arms were pinioned tightly behind his back, it was evident he could feed himself only by magic.

The stolid indifference to all sublunary matters which had distinguished Nathan throughout the scene, vanished the moment he found himself alone. In fact, the step of the savage the last to depart was yet rustling among the weeds at the Black-Vulture's door, when, making a violent effort, he succeeded in placing himself in a sitting posture, and glared with eager look around the apartment, which was, as before, dimly lighted by a fire on the floor. The piles of skins and domestic utensils were hanging about, as on the preceding night; and indeed, nothing seemed to have been disturbed, except the weapons, of which there had been so many when Edith occupied the den, but of which not a single one now remained. Over the fire,—the long tresses that depended from it swinging and fluttering in the currents of smoke and heated air,—was the bundle of scalps, to which Braxley had so insidiously directed the gaze of Edith, and which was now one of the first objects that met Nathan's eyes.

Having reconnoitered every corner and cranny, and convinced himself that there was no lurking savage watching his movements, he began straightway to test the strength of the thong by which his arms were bound; but without making the slightest impression on it. The cord was strong, the knots were securely tied; and after five or six minutes of struggling in which he made the most prodigious efforts to tear it asunder, without hesitating at the anguish it caused him, he was obliged to give over his hopes, fain could he have, like Thomson's demon in the net of the good Knight, enjoyed that consolation of despair,—to

"Sit him felly down, and gnaw his bitter nail."

He summoned his strength, and renewed his efforts again and again, but always without effect; and being at last persuaded of his inability to aid himself, and leaned back against a bundle of skins, to counsel with his own thoughts what hope, if any, yet remained.

At that instant, and while the unuttered misery of his spirit might have been read in his haggard and despairing eyes, a low whining sound, coming from a corner of the tent, but on the outside, with a rustling and scratching, as if some animal were struggling to burrow its way betwixt the skins and the earth, into the lodge, struck his ear. He started, and he stared round with a wild but joyous look of recognition.

"Hist, hist!" he cried, or rather whispered, for his voice was not above his breath; "hist, hist! If thee ever was wise, now do thee show it!"

The whining ceased, the scratching and rustling were heard a moment longer; and, then, rising from the skin wall, under which he had made his way, appeared—no bulky demon, indeed, summoned by the conjuror to his assistance—but little dog Peter, his trusty, sagacious, and hitherto inseparable friend, creeping with stealthy step, but eyes glistening with affection, towards the bound and helpless prisoner.

"I can't hug thee, little Peter!" cried the master, as the little animal crawled to him, wagging his tail, and, throwing his paws upon Nathan's knee, looked into his face with a most meaning stare of inquiry; "I can't hug thee, Peter! Thee sees how it is! the Injuns have ensnared me. But where *thee* is, Peter, there is hope. Quick, little Peter!" he cried, thrusting his arms out from his back; "thee has teeth, and thee knows how to use them—thee has gnawed me free before—Quick, little Peter, quick! The teeth is thee knives; and with them thee can cut me free!"

The little animal, whose remarkable docility and sagacity have been instanced before, seemed actually to understand his master's words, or, at least, to comprehend, from his gestures the strange duty that was now required of him; and, without more ado, he laid hold with his teeth upon the thong round Nathan's wrists, tugging and gnawing at it with a zeal and perseverance that seemed to make his master's deliverance, sooner or later, sure; and his industry was quickened by Nathan, who all the while encouraged him with whispers to continue his efforts.

"Thee gnawed me loose, when the four Shawnees had me bound by their fire, at night, on the banks of the Kenhawa. (Does thee remember *that*, Peter?) Ay, thee did, while the knaves slept; and from that sleep they never waked, the murdering villains—no, not one of them! Gnaw, little Peter, gnaw hard and fast; and care not if thee wounds me with thee teeth; for, truly, I will forgive thee, even if thee bites me to the bone. Faster, Peter, faster! Does thee boggle at the skin, because of its hardness? Truly, I have seen thee a hungered, Peter, when thee would have cracked it like a marrow-bone! Fast, Peter, fast; and thee shall see me again in freedom!"

With such expressions Nathan inflamed the zeal of his familiar, who continued to gnaw for the space of five minutes or more, and with such effect, that Nathan, who ever and anon tested the brute's progress by a violent jerk at the rope, found, at the fourth or fifth effort, that it yielded a little, and cracked, as if its fibres were already giving way.

"Now, Peter! tug, if thee ever tugged!" he cried, his hopes rising almost to ecstacy: "A little longer, one bite more, a little, but a little longer, Peter, if thee loves thee master! Yea, Peter, and we will walk the woods again in freedom! Now, Peter, now for the last bite!"

But the last bite Peter, on the sudden, betrayed a disinclination to make. He ceased his toil, jostled against his master's side, and uttered a whine, the lowest that could be made audible.

"Hah!" cried Nathan, as, at the same instant, he heard the sound of footsteps approaching the wigwam, "thee speaks the truth, and the accursed villains is upon us! Away with thee, dog—thee shall finish thee work by and by!"

Faithful to his master's orders, or perhaps to his own sense of what was fitting and proper in such a case, little Peter leaped hastily among the skins and other litter that covered half the floor and the sleeping-berths of the lodge, and was immediately out of sight, having left the apartment, or concealed himself in its darkest corner. The steps approached; they reached the door: Nathan threw himself back, reclining against his pile of furs, and fixed his eye upon the mats at the entrance. They were presently parted; and the old chief Wenonga came halting into the apartment,—halting, yet with a step that was designed to indicate all the pride and dignity of a warrior. And this attempt at state was the more natural and proper, as he was armed and painted as if for war, his grim-countenance hideously bedaubed on one side with vermillion, and the other with black; a long scalping-knife, without sheath or cover, swinging from his wampum belt; while a hatchet, the blade and handle both of steel, was grasped in his hand. In this guise, and with a wild and demoniacal glitter of eye, that seemed the result of mingled drunkenness and insanity, the old chief stalked and limped up to the prisoner, looking as if bent upon his instant destruction. That his passions were up in arms, that he was ripe for mischief and blood, was, indeed, plain and undeniable; but he soon made it apparent that his rage was only conditional and alternative, as regarded the prisoner. Pausing within three or four feet of him, and giving him a look that seemed designed to freeze his blood, it was so desperately hostile and savage, he extended his arm and hatchet,—not, however, to strike, as it appeared, but to do what might be judged almost equally agreeable to nine-tenths of his race,—that is, to deliver a speech.

"I am Wenonga!" he cried, in his own tongue, being perhaps too much enraged to think of any other, "I am Wenonga, a great Shawnee chief. I have fought the Longknives, and drunk their blood: when they hear my voice they are afraid; they run howling away, like dogs when the squaws beat them from the fire—who ever stood before Wenonga? I have fought my enemies, and killed them. I never feared a white man: why should I fear a white man's devil? Where is the Jibbenainosay, the curse of my tribe?—the Shawneewannaween, the howl of my people? He kills them in the dark, he creeps upon them while they sleep; but he fears to stand before the face of a warrior! Am I a dog? or a woman? The squaws and the children curse me, as I go by: they say *I* am the killer of their husbands and fathers; they tell me it was the deed of Wenonga, that brought the white man's devil to kill them; 'if Wenonga is a chief, let him kill the killer of his people!' I am Wenonga; I am a man; I fear nothing: I have sought the Jibbenainosay. But the Jibbenainosay is a coward; he walks in the dark, he kills in the time of sleep, he fears to fight a warrior! My brother is a great medicine-man; he is a white man, and he knows how to find the white man's devils. Let my brother speak for me; let him show me where to find the Jibbenainosay; and he shall be a great chief, and the son of a chief: Wenonga will make him his son, and he shall be a Shawnee!"

"Does Wenonga, at last, feel he has brought a devil upon his people?" said Nathan, speaking for the first time since his capture, and speaking in a way well suited to strike the interrogator with surprise. A sneer, as it seemed, of gratified malice crept over his face, and was visible even through the coat of paint that still invested his features; and to crown all, his words were delivered in the Shawnee tongue, correctly and unhesitatingly pronounced; which was itself, or so Wenonga appeared to hold it, a proof of his superhuman acquirements.

The old chief started, as the words fell upon his ear, and looked around him in awe, as if the prisoner had already summoned a spirit to his elbow.

"I have heard the voice of the dead!" he cried. "My brother is a great Medicine! But I am a chief;—I am not afraid."

"The chief tells me lies," rejoined Nathan, who, having once unlocked his lips, seemed but little disposed to resume his former silence;—"the chief tells me lies: there is no white-devil hurts his people!"

"I am an old man, and a warrior,—I speak the truth!" said the chief, with dignity; and then added, with sudden feeling,—"I am an old man: I had sons and grandsons—young warriors, and boys that would soon have blacked their faces for battle[12]—where are they? The Jibbenainosay has been in my village, he has been in my wigwam—there are none left—the Jibbenainosay killed them!"

[Footnote 12: The young warriors of many tribes are obliged to confine themselves to black paint, during their probationary campaigns.]

"Ay!" exclaimed the prisoner, and his eyes shot fire as he spoke, "they fell under his hand, man and boy—there was not one of them spared—they were of the blood of Wenonga!"

"Wenonga is a great chief!" cried the Indian: "he is childless; but childless he has made the Long-knife."

"The Long-knife, and the son of Onas!" said Nathan.

The chief staggered back, as if struck by a blow, and stared wildly upon the prisoner.

"My brother is a medicine-man,—he knows all things!" he exclaimed. "He speaks the truth: I am a great warrior; I took the scalp of the Quakel[13]—"

[Footnote 13: *Quakels*—a corruption of Quakers, whom the Indians of Pennsylvania originally designated as the sons of *Onos*, that being one of the names they bestowed upon Penn.]

"And of his wife and children—you left not one alive!—Ay!" continued Nathan, fastening his looks upon the amazed chief, "you slew them all! And he that was the husband and father was the Shawnees' friend, the friend even of Wenonga!"

"The white-men are dogs and robbers!" said the chief: "the Quakel was my brother; but I killed him. I am an Indian—I love white-man's blood. My people have soft hearts; they cried for the Quakel: but I am a warrior with no heart. I killed them: their scalps are hanging to my fire-post! I am not sorry; I am not afraid."

The eyes of the prisoner followed the Indian's hand, as he pointed, with savage triumph, to the shrivelled scalps that had once crowned the heads of childhood and innocence, and then sank to the floor, while his whole frame shivered as with an ague-fit.

"My brother is a great medicine-man," iterated the chief: "he shall show me the Jibbenainosay, or he shall die."

"The chief lies!" cried Nathan, with a sudden and taunting laugh: "he can talk big things to a prisoner, but he fears the Jibbenainosay!"

"I am a chief and warrior. I will fight the white-man's devil!"

"The warrior shall see him then," said the captive, with extraordinary fire. "Cut me loose from my bonds, and I will bring him before the chief."

And as he spoke, he thrust out his legs, inviting the stroke of the axe upon the thongs that bound his ankles.

But this was a favour, which, stupid or mad as he was, Wenonga hesitated to grant.

"The chief," cried Nathan, with a laugh of scorn, "would stand face to face with the Jibbenainosay, and yet fears to loose a naked prisoner!"

The taunt produced its effect. The axe fell upon tho thong, and Nathan leaped to his feet. He extended his wrists. The Indian hesitated again. "The chief shall see the Jibbenainosay!" cried Nathan; and the cord was cut.

The prisoner turned quickly round; and while his eyes fastened with a wild but joyous glare upon his jailer's, a laugh that would have become the jaws of a hyena lighted up his visage, and sounded from his lips. "Look!" he cried, "thee has thee wish! Thee sees the destroyer of thee race,—ay, murdering villain, the destroyer of thee people, and theeself!"

And with that, leaping upon the astounded chief with rather the rancorous ferocity of a wolf than the enmity of a human being, and clutching him by the throat with one hand, while with the other he tore the iron tomahawk from his grasp, he bore him to the earth, clinging to him as he fell, and using the wrested weapon with such furious haste and skill that, before they had yet reached the ground, he had buried it in the Indian's brain. Another stroke, and another, he gave with the same murderous activity and force; and Wenonga trode the path to the spiritland, bearing the same gory evidences of the unrelenting and successful vengeance of the white-man that his children and grand-children had borne before him.

"Ay, dog, thee dies at last! at last I have caught thee!"

With these words, Nathan, leaving the shattered skull, dashed the tomahawk into the Indian's chest, snatched the scalping-knife from the belt, and with one grinding sweep of the blade, and one fierce jerk of his arm, the gray scalp-lock of the warrior was torn from the dishonoured head. The last proof of the slayer's ferocity was not given until he had twice, with his utmost strength, drawn the knife over the dead man's breast, dividing skin, cartilage, and even bone, before it, so sharp was the blade and so powerful the hand that urged it.

Then, leaping to his feet, and snatching from the post the bundle of withered scalps—the locks and ringlets of his own murdered family,—

which he spread a moment before his eyes with one hand, while the other extended, as if to contrast the two prizes together, the reeking scalp-lock of the murderer, he sprang through the door of the lodge, and fled from the village; but not until he had, in the insane fury of the moment, given forth a wild, ear-piercing yell, that spoke the triumph, the exulting transport, of long-baffled but never-dying revenge. The wild whoop, thus rising in the depth and stillness of the night, startled many a wakeful warrior and timorous mother from their repose. But such sounds in a disorderly hamlet of barbarians were too common to create alarm or uneasiness; and the wary and the timid again betook themselves to their dreams, leaving the corse of their chief to stiffen on the floor of his own wigwam.

CHAPTER XXXIV

From an uneasy slumber, into which, notwithstanding his sufferings of mind and body, he had at last fallen, Roland was roused at the break of day by a horrible clamour, that suddenly arose in the village. A shrill scream, that seemed to come from a female voice, was first heard; then a wild yell from the lungs of a warrior, which was caught up and repeated by other voices; and, in a few moments, the whole town resounded with shrieks dismal and thrilling, and expressing astonishment mingled with fear and horror.

The prisoner, incapable of comprehending the cause of such a commotion, looked to his guards, who had started up at the first cry, grasped their arms, and stood gazing upon one another with perturbed looks of inquiry. The shriek was repeated, by one,—twenty,—a hundred throats; and the two warriors, with hurried exclamations of alarm, rushed from the wigwam, leaving the prisoner to solve the riddle as he might. But he tasked his faculties in vain. His first idea—and it sent the blood leaping to his heart—that the village was suddenly attacked by an army of white men,—perhaps by the gallant Bruce, the commander of the Station where his misfortunes had begun,—was but momentary; no lusty hurrahs were heard mingling with the shrieks of the savages, and no explosions of fire-arms denoted the existence of conflict. And yet he perceived that the cries were not all of surprise and dismay. Some voices were uplifted in rage, which was evidently spreading among the agitated barbarians, and displacing the other passions in their minds.

In the midst of the tumult, and while he was yet lost in wonder and speculation, the renegade Doe suddenly rushed into the wigwam, pale with affright and agitation.

"They'll murder you, captain!" he cried, "there's no time for holding back now—Take the gal, and I'll save you. The village is up—they'll have your blood, they're crying for it already—squaws, warriors and all—ay, d——n 'em, there's no stopping 'em now!"

"What in Heaven's name is the matter?" demanded the soldier.

"All etarnity's the matter!" replied Doe, with vehement utterance: "the Jibbenainosay has been in the village, and killed the chief—ay, d——n him,—struck him in his own house, marked him at his own fire! he lies, dead and scalped—ay, and crossed too—on the floor of his own wigwam;—the conjuror gone, snapped up by his devil, and Wenonga stiff and gory! Don't you hear 'em yelling? The Jibbenainosay, I tell you—he has killed the chief; we found him dead in his cabin; and the Injuns are bawling for revenge—they are, d——n 'em, and they'll murder you, burn you, tear you to pieces;—they will, there's no two ways about it: they're singing out to murder the white men, and they'll be on you in no time!"

"And there is no escape!" cried Roland, whose blood curdled, as he listened to the thrilling yells that were increased in number and loudness, as if the enraged barbarians, rushing madly through the village, were gathering arms to destroy the prisoners,—"there is no escape?"

"Take the gal! jist say the word, and I'll save you, or die with you, I will, d——n me!" exclaimed Doe, with fierce energy. "There's hosses grazing in the pastures; there's halters swinging above us: I'll mount you and save you. Say the word, captain, and I'll cut you loose and save you—say it, and be quick; your life depends on it—Hark! the dogs is coming! Hold out your arms till I cut the tug—"

"Anything for my life!" cried the Virginian; "but if it can be only bought at the price of marrying the girl, it is lost."

And the soldier would have resisted the effort Doe was making for his deliverance.

"You'll be murdered, I tell you!" re-echoed Doe, with increased vehemence, holding the knife ready in his hand: "they're coming on us: I don't want to see you butchered like an ox. One word, captain!—I'll take your word; you're an honest fellow, and I'll believe in you;—jist one word, captain; I'll help you; I'll fight the dogs for you; I'll give you weapons. The gal, captain! life and the fortun, captain!—The gal! the gal!"

"Never, I tell you, never!" cried Roland, who, faithful to the honour and integrity of spirit which conducted the men of that day, the mighty fathers of the republic, through the vicissitudes of revolution to the rewards of liberty, would not stoop to the meanness of falsehood and deception even in that moment of peril and fear;—"anything but that—but that, never!"

But, whilst he spoke, Doe, urged on by his own impetuous feelings, had cut the thong from his wrists, and was even proceeding to divide those that bound his ankles, disregarding all his protestations and averments, or perhaps drowning them in his own eager exclamations of "The gal, captain,—the word, jist one word!" when a dozen or more savages burst into the hut, and sprang upon the Virginian, yelling, cursing, and flourishing their knives and hatchets, as if they would have torn him to pieces on the spot. And such, undoubtedly, was the aim of some of the younger men, who struck at him several furious blows, that were only averted by the older warriors at the expense of some of their own blood shed in the struggle, which was, for a moment, as fiercely waged over the prisoner as the conflict of enraged hounds over the body of a disabled panther, that are all emulous to worry and tear. One instant of dreadful confusion, of shrieks, blows, and maledictions, and the Virginian was snatched up in the arms of two or three of the strongest men, and dragged from the hut; but only to find himself surrounded by a herd of villagers, men, women, and children, who fell upon him with as much fury as the young warriors had done, beating him with bludgeons, wounding him with their knives, so that it seemed impossible the older braves could protect him much longer. But others ran to their assistance; and forming a circle around him, so as to exclude the mob, he was borne onwards, in temporary security, but destined to a fate to which murder on the spot would have been gentleness and mercy.

The tumult had roused Edith also from her painful slumbers; and the more necessarily, since, although removed from the tent in which she was first imprisoned, she was still confined in Wenonga's wigwam. It was the scream of the hag, the chieftain's wife, who had discovered his body, that first gave the alarm; and the villagers all rushing to the cabin, and yelling their astonishment and terror, there arose an uproar, almost in her ears, that was better fitted to fright her to death than to lull her again to repose. She started from her couch of furs, and with a woman's weakness, cowered away in the furthest corner of the lodge, to escape the pitiless fees, whom her fears represented as already seeking her life. Nor was this chimera banished from her mind when a man, rushing in, snatched her from her ineffectual concealment and hurried her towards the door. But her terrors ran in another channel, when the ravisher, conquering the feeble resistance she attempted, replied to her wild entreaties "not to kill her," in the well-remembered voice of Braxley:

"Kill you, indeed!" he muttered, but with agitated tones; "I come to save you; even *you* are in danger from the maddened villains: they are murdering all! We must fly,—ay, and fast. My horse is saddled,—the woods are open—I will yet save you."

"Spare me!—for my uncle's sake, who was your benefactor, spare me!" cried Edith, struggling to free herself from his grasp. But she struggled in vain. "I aim to save you," cried Braxley; and without uttering another word, bore her from the hut; and, still grasping her with an arm of iron, sprang upon a saddled horse,—the identical animal that had once sustained the weight of the unfortunate Pardon Dodge,—which stood under the elm-tree, trembling with fright at the scene of horror then represented on the square.

Upon this vacant space was now assembled the whole population of the village, old and young, the strong and the feeble, all agitated alike by those passions, which, when let loose in a mob, whether civilised or savage, almost enforce the conviction that there is something essentially demoniac in the human character and composition; as if, indeed, the earth of which man is framed had been gathered only after it had been trodden by the foot of the Prince of Darkness.

Even Edith forgot for a moment her fears of Braxley,—nay, she clung to him for protection,—when her eye fell upon the savage herd, of whom the chief number were crowded together in the centre of the square, surrounding some object rendered invisible by their bodies, while others were rushing tumultuously hither and thither, driven by causes she could not divine, brandishing weapons, and uttering howls without number. One large party was passing from the wigwam itself, their cries not less loud or ferocious than the others, but changing occasionally into piteous lamentations. They bore in their arms the body of the murdered chief,—an object of such horror, that when Edith's eye; had once fallen upon it, it seemed as if her enthralled spirit would never have recovered strength to remove them.

But there was a more fearful spectacle yet to be seen. The wife of Wenonga suddenly rushed from the lodge, bearing a fire-brand in her hand. She ran to the body of the chief, eyed it, for a moment, with such a look as a tigress might cast upon her slaughtered cub, and then, uttering a scream that was heard over the whole square, and whirling the brand round her head, until it was in a flame, fled with frantic speed towards the centre of the area, the mob parting before her, and replying to her shrieks, which were uttered at every step, with outcries scarce less wild and thrilling. As they parted thus, opening a vista to the heart of the square, the object which seemed the centre of attraction to all was fully revealed to the maiden's eyes. Bound to two strong posts near the Council-house, their arms drawn high above their heads, a circle of brush-wood, prairie-grass, and other combustibles heaped around them, were two wretched captives,—white men, from whose persons a dozen savage hands were tearing their garments, while as many more were employed heaping additional fuel on the pile. One of these men, as Edith could see full well, for the spectacle was scarce a hundred paces removed, was Roaring Ralph, the captain of horse-thieves. The other—and *that* was a sight to rend her eye-balls from their sockets,—was her unfortunate kinsman, the playmate of her childhood, the friend and lover of maturer years,—her cousin,—brother,—her all,—Roland Forrester. It was no error of sight, no delusion of mind: the spectacle was too palpable to be doubted: it was Roland Forrester whom she saw, chained to the stake, surrounded by yelling and pitiless barbarians, impatient for the commencement of their infernal pastime, while the wife of the chief, kneeling at the pile, was already endeavouring, with her brand, to kindle it into flame.

The shriek of the wretched maiden, as she beheld the deplorable, the maddening sight, might have melted hearts of stone, had there been even such among the Indians. But Indians, engaged in the delights of torturing a prisoner, are, as the dead chief had boasted himself, *without* heart. Pity, which the Indian can feel at another moment, as deeply, perhaps, and benignly as a white man, seems then, and is, entirely unknown, as much so, indeed, as if it had never entered into his nature. His mind is then voluntarily given tip to the drunkenness of passion; and cruelty, in its most atrocious and fiendish character, reigns predominant. The familiar of a Spanish Inquisition has sometimes moistened the lips of a heretic stretched upon the rack,—the Buccaneer of the tropics has relented over the contumacious prisoner gasping to death under his lashes and heated pincers; but we know of no instance where an Indian, torturing a prisoner at the stake, the torture once begun, has ever been moved to compassionate, to regard with any feelings but those of exultation and joy, the agonies of the thrice-wretched victim.

The shriek of the maiden was unheard, or unregarded; and Braxley,—himself so horrified by the spectacle that, while pausing to give it a glance, he forgot the delay was also disclosing it to Edith,—grasping her tighter in his arms, from which she had half leaped in her frenzy, turned his horse's head to fly, without seeming to be regarded or observed by the savages, which was perhaps in part owing to his having resumed his Indian attire. But, as he turned, he could not resist the impulse to snatch one more look at his doomed rival. A universal yell of triumph sounded over the square; the flames were already bursting from the pile, and the torture was begun.

The torture was begun,—but it was not destined long to endure. The yell of triumph was yet resounding over the square, and awakening responsive echoes among the surrounding hills, when the explosion of at least fifty rifles, sharp, rattling, and deadly, like the war-note of the rattle-snake, followed by a mighty hurrah of Christian voices, and the galloping of horse into the village from above, converted the whole scene into one of amazement and terror. The volley was repeated, and by as many more guns; and in an instant there was seen rushing into the square a body of at least a hundred mounted white men, their horses covered with foam and staggering with exhaustion, yet spurred on by their riders with furious ardour; while twice as many footmen were beheld rushing after, in mad rivalry, cheering and shouting, in reply to their leader, whose voice was heard in front of the horsemen thundering out,—"Small change for the Blue Licks! Charge 'em, the brutes! give it to 'em handsome!"

The yells of dismay of the savages, taken thus by surprise, and, as it seemed, by a greatly superior force, whose approach, rapid and tumultuous as it must have been, their universal devotion to the Saturnalia of blood had rendered them incapable of perceiving; the shouts of the mounted assailants, as they dashed into the square and among the mob, shooting as they came, or handling their rifles like maces, and battle-axes; the trampling and neighing of the horses; and the thundering hurrahs of the footmen charging into the town with almost the speed of the horse, made a din too horrible for description. The shock of the assault was not resisted by the Indians even for a moment. Some rushed to the neighbouring wigwams for their guns, but the majority, like the women and children, fled to seek refuge among the rocks and bushes of the overhanging hill; from which, however, as they approached it, a deadly volley was shot upon them by foemen who already occupied its tangled sides. Others again fled towards the meadows and corn-fields, where, in like manner, they were intercepted by bands of mounted Long-knives, who seemed pouring into the valley from every hill. In short, it was soon made apparent that the village of the Black-Vulture was assailed from all sides, and by such an army of avenging white men as had never before penetrated into the Indian territory.

All the savages,—all, at least, who were not shot or struck down in the square,—fled from the village; and among the foremost of them was Braxley, who, as much astounded as his Indian confederates, but better prepared for flight, struck the spurs into his horse, and still retaining his helpless prize, dashed across the river, to escape as he might.

In the meanwhile, the victims at the stake, though roused to hope and life by the sudden appearance of their countrymen, were neither released from bonds nor perils. Though the savages fled, as described, from the charge of the white men, there were some who remembered the prisoners, and were resolved that they should never taste the sweets of liberty. The beldam, who was still busy kindling the pile, roused from her toil by the shouts of the enemy and the shrieks of her flying people, looked up a moment, and then snatching at a knife dropped by some fugitive, rushed upon Stackpole, who was nearest her, with a wild scream of revenge. The horse-thief, avoiding the blow as well as he could, saluted the hag with a furious kick, his feet being entirely at liberty; and such was its violence that the woman was tossed into the air, as if from the horns of a bull, and then fell, stunned and apparently lifeless, to perish in the flames she had kindled with her own breath.

A tall warrior, hatchet in hand, with a dozen more at his back, rushed upon the Virginian. But before he could strike, there came leaping with astonishing bounds over the bodies of the wounded and dying, and into the circle of fire, a figure that might have filled a better and braver warrior with dread. It was the medicine-man, and former captive, the Indian habiliments and paint still on his body and visage, though both were flecked and begrimed with blood. In his left hand was a bundle of scalps, the same he had taken from the tent of Wenonga; the grizzled scalp-lock of the chief, known by the vulture-feathers, beak, and talons, still attached to it, was hanging to his girdle; while the steel battle-axe, so often wielded by Wenonga, was gleaming aloft in his right hand.

The savage recoiled, and with loud yells of "The Jibbenainosay! the Jibbenainosay!" turned to fly, while even those behind him staggered back at the apparition of the destroyer, thus tangibly presented to their eyes; nor was their awe lessened, when the supposed fiend, taking one step after the retreating leader of the gang, drove the fatal hatchet into his brain, with as lusty a whoop of victory as ever came from the lungs of a warrior. At the same moment he was hidden from their eyes by a dozen horsemen that came rushing up, with tremendous huzzas, some darting against the band, while others sprung from their horses to liberate the prisoners. But this duty had been already rendered, at least in the case of Captain Forrester. The axe of Wenonga, dripping with blood to the hilt, divided the rope at a single blow, and then Roland's fingers were crushed in the grasp of his preserver, as the latter exclaimed, with a strange, half-frantic chuckle of triumph and delight,—

"Thee sees, friend! Thee thought I had deserted thee? Truly, truly, thee was mistaken!"

"Hurrah for old Tiger Nathan! I'll never say Q to a quaker agin as long as I live!" exclaimed another voice, broken, feeble, and vainly aiming to raise a huzza; and the speaker, seizing Nathan with one hand, while the other grasped tremulously at Captain Forrester's, displayed to the latter's eyes the visage of Tom Bruce the younger, pale, sickly, emaciated, his once gigantic proportions wasted away, and his whole appearance indicating anything but fitness for a field of battle.

"Strannger!" cried the youth, pressing the soldier's hand with what strength he could, and laughing faintly, "we've done the handsome thing by you, me and dad, thar's no denying! But we went your security agin all sorts of danngers in our beat; and thar's just the occasion. But h'yar's dad to speak for himself: as for me, I rather think breath's too short for wasting."

"Hurrah for Kentucky!" roared Colonel Bruce, as he sprang from his horse, and seized the hand of Roland, wringing and twisting it with a fury of friendship and gratulation, which, at another moment, would have caused the soldier to grin with pain. "H'yar we are, captain!" he cried: "picked you out of the yambers!—Swore to follow you and young madam to the end of creation,—beat up for recruits, sung out 'Blue Lick' to the people, roused the General from the Falls,—whole army, a thousand men; double quick step; found Tiger Nathan in the woods—whar's the creatur'? told of your fixin'; beat to arms, flew ahead, licked the enemy,—and ha'n't we extarminated 'em?"

With these hurried, half-incoherent expressions, the gallant Kentuckian explained, or endeavoured to explain, the mystery of his timely and most happy appearance; an explanation, however, of which the soldier, bewildered by the whirl of events, the tumult of his own feelings, and not less by the uproarious congratulations of his friends, of whom the captain of horse-thieves, released from his post of danger, was not the least noisy or affectionate, heard, or understood not a word. To these causes of confusion were to be added the din and tumult of conflict, the screams of the flying Indians, and the shouts of pursuing and opposing white-men, rising from every point of the compass; for from every point they seemed rushing in upon the foe, whom they appeared to have completely environed. Was there no other cause for the distraction of mind which left the young soldier, while thus beset by friendly hands and voices, incapable of giving them his whole attention? His thoughts were upon his kinswoman, of whose fate he was still in ignorance. But before he could ask the question prompted by his anxieties, it was answered by a cheery hurrah from Bruce's youngest son, Richard, who came galloping into the square and up to the place of torture, whirling his cap into the air, in a frenzy of boyish triumph and rapture. At his heels, and mounted upon the steed so lately bestridden by Braxley, the very animal, which, notwithstanding its uncommon swimming virtues, had left its master, Pardon Dodge, at the bottom of Salt River, was—could Roland believe his eyes?—the identical Pardon Dodge himself, looking a hero, he was so begrimed with blood and gunpowder, and whooping and hurrahing, as he came, with as much spirit as if he had been born on the border, and accustomed all his life to fighting Indians. But Roland did not admire long at the unlooked-for resurrection of his old ally of the ruin. In his arms, sustained with an air of infinite pride and exultation, was an apparition that blinded the Virginian's eyes to every other object;—it was Edith Forrester; who, extending her own arms, as the soldier sprang to meet her, leaped to his embrace with such wild cries of delight, such abandonment of spirit to love and happiness, as stirred up many a womanish emotion in the breast of the surrounding Kentuckians.

"There!" cried Dodge, "there, capting! Seed the everlasting Injun feller carrying her off on the hoss; knowed the crittur at first sight; took atter, and brought the feller to: seed it was the young lady, and was jist as glad to find her as to find my hoss,—if I wa'n't, it a'n't no matter."

"Thar, dad!" cried Tom Bruce, grasping his father's arm, and pointing, but with unsteady finger and glistening eye, at the two cousins,—"that, that's a sight worth dying for!" with which words he fell suddenly to the earth.

"Dying, you brute!" cried the father in surprise and concern: "you ar'n't had a hit, Tom?"

"Not an iota," replied the youth, faintly, "except them etarnal slugs I fetched from old Salt; but, I reckon, they've done for me: I felt 'em a dropping, a dropping inside, all night. And so, father, if you'll jist say I've done as much as my duty, I'll not make no fuss about going."

"Going, you brute!" iterated the father, clasping the hand of his son, while the others, startled by the young man's sudden fall, gathered around, to offer help, or to gaze with alarm on his fast changing countenance; "why, Tom, my boy, you don't mean to make a die of it?"

"If—if you think I've done my duty to the strannger and the young lady," said the young man; and added, feebly pressing the father's hand,—"and to *you*, dad, to you, and mother, and the rest of 'em."

"You have, Tom," said the colonel, with somewhat a husky voice—"to the travelling strannger, to mother, father, and all—"

"And to Kentucky?" murmured the dying youth,

"To Kentucky," replied the father.

"Well, then, it's no great matter—You'll jist put Dick in my place: he's the true grit; thar'll be no mistake in Dick, for all he's only a young blubbering boy; and then it'll be jist all right, as before. And it's my notion, father—"

"Well, Tom, what is it?" demanded Bruce, as the young man paused as if from mingled exhaustion and hesitation.

"I don't mean no offence, father," said he,—"but it's my notion, if you'll never let a poor traveller go into the woods without some dependable body to take care of him—"

"You're right, Tom; and I an't mad at you for saying so; and I won't."

"And don't let the boys abuse Nathan,—for, I reckon he'll fight, if you let him take it in his own way. And,—and, father, don't mind Captain Ralph's stealing a hoss or two out of our pound!"

"He may steal the lot of 'em, the villain!" said Bruce, shaking his head to dislodge the tears that were starting in his eyes; "and he shall be none the wuss of it."

"Well, father,—" the young man spoke with greater animation, and with apparently reviving strength,—"and you think we have pretty considerably licked the Injuns h'yar, jist now?"

"We have, Tom,—thar's no doubting it. And we'll lick 'em over and over again, till they've had enough of it."

"Hurrah for Kentucky!" cried the young man, exerting his remaining strength to give energy to the cry, so often uplifted, in succeeding years, among the wild woodlands around. It was the last effort of his sinking powers. He fell back, pressed his father's and his brother's hands, and almost immediately expired,—a victim not so much of his wounds, which were not in themselves necessarily fatal, nor perhaps even dangerous, had they been attended to, as of the heroic efforts, so overpowering and destructive in his disabled condition, which he had made to repair his father's fault; for such he evidently esteemed the dismissing the travellers from the Station without sufficient guides and protection.

CHAPTER XXXV

Thus fell the young Kentuckian,—a youth endeared to all who knew him, by his courage and good humour; and whose fall would, at a moment of less confusion, have created a deep and melancholy sensation. But he fell amid the roar and tempest of battle, when there was occasion for other thoughts and other feelings than those of mere individual grief.

The Indians had been driven from their village, as described, aiming not to fight, but fly; but being intercepted at all points by the assailants, and met, here by furious volleys poured from the bushy sides of the hill, there by charges of horsemen galloping through the meadows and cornfields, they were again driven back into the town, where, in sheer desperation, they turned upon their foes to sell their lives as dearly as they might. They were met at the edge of the village by the party of horse and footmen that had first dislodged them, with whom, being driven pell-mell among them by the shock of the intercepting bands, they waged a fierce and bloody, but brief conflict; and still urged onwards by the assailants behind, fought their way back to the square, which, deserted almost entirely at the period of young Bruce's fall, was now suddenly seen, as he drew his last gasp, scattered over with groups of men flying for their lives, or struggling together in mortal combat; while the screams of terror-struck women and children gave a double horror to the din.

The return of the battle to their own immediate vicinity produced its effects upon the few who had remained by the dying youth. It fired, in especial, the blood of Captain Ralph, who, snatching up a fallen axe, rushed towards the nearest combatants, roaring, by way of consolation, or sympathy, to the bereaved father, "Don't take it hard, Cunnel,—I'll have a scalp for Tom's sake in no time!" As for Tiger Nathan, he had disappeared long before, with most of the horsemen, who had galloped up to the stake with the younger Bruce and his father, being evidently too fiercely excited to remain idle any longer. The father and brother of the deceased, the two cousins and Pardon Dodge, who lingered by the latter, still on his horse, as if old companionship with the soldier and the service just rendered the maid had attached him to all their interests, were all that remained on the spot. But all were driven from a contemplation of the dead, as the surge of battle again tossed its bloody spray into the square.

"Thar's no time for weeping," muttered Bruce, softly laying the body of the youth (for Tom had expired in his arms) upon the earth: "he died like a man, and thar's the end of it,—Up, Dick, and stand by the lady—Thar's more work for us."

"Everlasting bad work, Cunnel!" cried Dodge; "they're a killing the squaws! hark, dunt you hear 'em squeaking? Now, Cunnel, I can kill your tarnal *man* fellers, for they've riz my ebenezer, and I've kinder got my hand in; but, I rather calkilate, I han't no disposition to kill wimming!"

"Close round the lady!" shouted Bruce, as a sudden movement in the mass of combatants, and the parting from it of a dozen or more wild Indian figures, flying in their confusion, for they were pursued by thrice their number of white men, right towards the little party at the stake, threatened the latter with unexpected danger.

"I'm the feller for 'em, now that my hand's in!" cried Pardon Dodge; and taking aim with his rifle,—the only one in the group that was charged, at the foremost of the Indians, he shot him dead on the spot,—a feat that instantly removed all danger from the party; for the savages, yelling at the fall of their leader and the discovery of antagonists thus drawn up in front, darted off to the right hand at the wildest speed, as wildly pursued by the greater number of Kentuckians.

And now it was, that, as the wretched and defeated barbarians, scattering at Dodge's fire, fled from the spot, the party at the stake beheld a sight well fitted to turn the alarm they had for a moment felt on their own account, into horror and pity. The savage shot down by Dodge was instantly scalped by one of the pursuers, of whom five or six others rushed upon another man—for a second of the fugitives had fallen at the same moment, but only wounded,—attacking him furiously with knives and hatchets, while the poor wretch was seen with raised arms vainly beseeching for quarter. As if this spectacle was not in itself sufficiently pitiable, there was seen a girlish figure at the man's side, struggling with the assailants, as if to throw herself between them and their prey, and uttering the most heart-piercing shrieks.

"It is Telie Doe!" shouted Forrester, leaping from his kinswoman's side, and rushing with the speed of light to her assistance.—He was followed, at almost as fleet a step, by Colonel Bruce, who recognised the voice at the same instant, and knew by the ferocious cries of the men,—"Kill the cursed tory! kill the renegade villain!" that it was the girl's apostate father, Abel Doe, who was dying under their vengeful weapons.

"Hold, friends, hold!" cried Roland, as he sprang amid the infuriated Kentuckians. His interposition was for a moment successful: surprise arrested the impending weapons; and Doe, taking advantage of the pause, leaped to his feet, ran a few yards, and then fell again to the ground.

"No quarter for turn-coats and traitors! no mercy for white Injuns!" cried the angry men, running again at their prey. But Roland was before them; and as he bestrode the wounded man, the gigantic Bruce rushed up, and, catching the frenzied daughter in his arms, exclaimed, with tones of thunder, "Off, you perditioned brutes! would you kill the man before the eyes of his own natteral-born daughter? Kill Injuns, you brutes,—thar's the meat for you!"

"Hurrah for Cunnel Tom Bruce!" shouted the men in reply; and satisfying their rage with direful execrations, invoked upon "all white Injuns and Injun white men," they rushed away in pursuit of more legitimate objects of hostility, if such were still to be found,—a thing not so certain, for few Indian whoops were now mingled with the white man's cry of victory.

In the meanwhile, Roland had endeavoured to raise the bleeding and mangled renegade to his feet; but in vain, though assisted by the efforts of the unhappy wretch himself; who, raising his hands, as if still to avert the blows of an unrelenting enemy, ejaculated wildly,—"It a'n't nothing,—its only for the gal. Don't murder a father before his own child!"

"You are safe,—fear nothing," said Roland, and at the same moment, poor Telie herself rushed into the dying man's arms, crying, with tones that went to the Virginian's heart,—"They're gone, father, they're gone! Now get up, father, and they won't hurt you no more; the good captain has saved you, father; they won't hurt you, they won't hurt you no more!"

"Is it the Captain?" cried Doe, struggling again to rise, while Bruce drew the girl gently from his arms. "Is it the captain?" he repeated, bending his eager looks and countenance ghastly with wounds upon the Virginian. "They han't murdered you then? I'm glad on it, captain;—I'll die the easier, captain! And the gal, too?" he exclaimed, as his eyes fell upon Edith, who, scarce knowing in her horror what she did, but instinctively seeking the protection of her kinsman, had crept up to the group now around the dying wretch. "It's all right, captain!—But where's Dick? where's Dick Braxley? You han't killed him among you?"

"Think not of the villain," said Roland; "I know naught of him."

"I'm a dying man, captain," exclaimed Doe; "I know'd this would be the end of it. If Dick's a prisoner, jist bring him up and let me speak with him. It will be for your good, captain."

"I know nothing of the scoundrel. Think of yourself," said the Virginian.

"Why, there, don't I see his red han'kercher," cried Doe, pointing to Dodge, who, from his horse, which he had not yet deserted, perhaps, from fear of again losing him, sat looking with soldier-like composure on the expiring renegade, until made conscious that the shawl which he had tied round his waist somewhat in manner of an officer's sash, had become an object of interest to Doe and all others present.

"I took it from the Injun feller," said he, with great self-complacency, "the everlasting big rascal that was a carrying off madam on my own hoss, and madam was jist as dead as a piece of rock. I know'd the crittur, and sung out to the feller to stop, and he wouldn't; and so I jist blazed away at him, right bang at his back,—knocked him over jist like a streak o' lightning, and had the scalp off his 'tarnal ugly head afore you could say John Robinson,—and all the while madam was jist as dead as a piece of rock. Here's the top-knot, and an ugly dirty top-knot it is!" With which words, the valiant Dodge displayed his trophy, a scalp of black hair, yet reeking with blood.

A shiver passed through Edith's frame, she grasped her cousin's arm to avoid falling, and with a countenance as white and ghastly as countenance could be, exclaimed,—

"It was Braxley!—It was he carried me off;—but I knew nothing. It was he! Yes, it was *he*!"

"It war'n't a white man?" cried Dodge, dropping his prize in dismay; while even Roland staggered with horror at the thought of a fate so sudden and dreadful overtaking his rival and enemy.

"Ha, ha!" cried the renegade, with a hideous attempt at laughter; "I told Dick the devil would have us; but I had no idea Dick would be the first afore him! Shot,—scalped,—sarved like a mere dog of an Injun! Well, the game's up at last, and we've both made our fortun's! Captain, I've been a rascal all my life, and I die no better. You wouldn't take my offer, captain;—it's no matter." He fumbled in his breast, and presently drew to light the will, with which he so vainly strove the preceding night to effect his object with Roland; it was stained deeply with his blood. "Take it, captain," he cried, "take it; I give it to you without axing tarms; I leave it to yourself, captain. But you'll remember her, captain? The gal, captain! the gal! I leave it to yourself—"

"She shall never want friend or protector," said Roland.

"Captain," murmured the renegade, with his last breath, and grasping the soldier's hand with his last convulsive effort—"you're an honest feller; I'll—yes, captain, I'll trust you!"

These were the renegade's last words; and before Bruce, who muttered, half in reproach, half in kindness, "The gal never wanted friend or protector, till she fled from me, who was as a father to her," could draw the sobbing daughter away, the wretched instrument of a still more wretched principal in villany, had followed his employer to his last account.

In the meanwhile, the struggle was over, the battle was fought and won. The army, for such it was, being commanded in person by the hero of Kaskaskias,[14] the great protector, and almost founder of the West,—summoned in haste to avenge the slaughter at the Blue Licks,—a lamentable disaster, to which we have several times alluded, although it was foreign to our purpose to venture more than an allusion,—and conducted with unexampled speed against the Indian towns on the Miami, had struck a blow which was destined long to be remembered by the Indians, thus for the first time assailed in their own territory. Consisting of volunteers well acquainted with the woods, all well mounted and otherwise equipped, all familiar with battle, and all burning for revenge, it had reached within but ten or twelve miles of Wenonga's town, and within still fewer of a smaller village, which it was the object of the troops first to attack, at sunset of the previous day, and encamped in the woods to allow man and horse, both well nigh exhausted, a few hours' refreshment, previous to marching upon the neighbouring village; when Nathan, flying with the scalp and arms of Wenonga in his hand, and looking more like an infuriated madman than the inoffensive man of peace he had been so long esteemed, suddenly appeared amidst the vanguard, commanded by the gallant Bruce, whom he instantly apprised of the condition of the captives at Wenonga's town, and urged to attempt their deliverance.

[Footnote 14: General George Rogers Clark.]

This was done, and with an effect which has been already seen. The impetuosity of Bruce's men, doubly inflamed by the example of the father and his eldest son, to whom the rescue of their late guests was an object of scarce inferior magnitude even compared with the vengeance for which they burned in common with all others, had in some measure defeated the hopes of the General, who sought, by a proper disposition of his forces, completely to invest the Indian village, so as to ensure the destruction or capture of every inhabitant. As it was, however, very few escaped; many were killed, and more, including all the women and children (who, honest Dodge's misgivings to the contrary notwithstanding, were in no instance designedly injured), taken prisoners. And this, too, at an expense of but very few lives lost on the part of the victors; the Indians attempting resistance only when the fall of more than half their numbers, and the presence of foes on every side, convinced them that flight was wholly impracticable.

The victory was, indeed, so complete, and—as it appeared that several bands of warriors from more distant villages were in the town at the time of the attack—the blow inflicted upon the tribe so much severer than was anticipated even from a series of attacks upon several different towns, as was at first designed, that the victors, satisfied that they had done enough to convince the red-man of the irresistible superiority of the Long-knife, satisfied, too, perhaps, that the cheapness of the victory rendered it more valuable than a greater triumph achieved at a greater loss, gave up at once their original design of carrying the war into other villages, and resolved to retrace their march to the Settlements.

But the triumph was not completed until the village, with its fields of standing corn, had been entirely destroyed—a work of cruel vengeance, yet not so much of vengeance as of policy; since the destruction of their crops, by driving the savages to seek a winter's subsistence for their families in the forest, necessarily prevented their making warlike inroads upon their white neighbours during that season. The maize-stalks, accordingly, soon fell before the knives and hatchets of the Kentuckians; while the wigwams were given to the flames. When the last of the rude habitations had fallen, crashing, to the earth, the victors began their retreat towards the frontier; so that within a very few hours after they first appeared, as if bursting from the earth, amid the amazed barbarians, nothing remained upon the place of conflict and site of a populous village, save scattered ruins and mangled corses.

Their own dead the invaders bore to a distance, and interred in the deepest dens of the forest; and then, with their prisoners, carried with them as the surest means of inducing the tribe to beg for peace, in order to effect their deliverance, they resumed the path, which, in good time, led them again to the Settlements.

CHAPTER XXXVI

With the battle at the Black-Vulture's town, the interest of our history ceases; and there it may be said to have its end. The deliverance of the cousins, the one from captivity and death, the other from a fate to her more dreadful than death; the restoration of the will of their uncle; and the fall of the daring and unprincipled villain to whose machinations they owed all their calamities, had changed the current of their fortunes, which was now to flow in a channel where the eye could no longer trace obstructions. The last peal of thunder had dissipated the clouds of adversity, and the star of their destiny shone out with all its original lustre. The future was no longer one of mere hope; it presented all the certainty of happiness of which human existence is capable.

Such being the case, it would be a superfluous and unprofitable task to pursue our history further, were it not that other individuals, whose interests were so long intermingled with those of the cousins, have a claim upon our notice. And first, before speaking of the most important of all, the warlike man of peace, the man-slaying hater of blood, the redoubtable Nathan Slaughter, let us bestow a word upon honest Pardon Dodge, whose sudden re-appearance on the stage of life so greatly astonished the young Virginian.

This resuscitation, however, as explained by Dodge himself, was, after all, no such wonderful matter. Swept from his horse by the violence of the flood, in the memorable flight from the ruin, a happy accident had flung him upon the raft of timber that bordered the fatal *chute*; where, not doubting that, from the fury of the current, all his companions had perished, and that he was left to contend alone against the savages, he immediately sought a concealment among the logs, in which he remained during the remainder of the night and the greater part of the following day, until pretty well assured the Indians were no longer in his vicinity. Then, scaling the cliffy banks of the river, and creeping through the woods, it was his good fortune at last to stumble upon the clearings around Brace's Station, at which he arrived soon after the defeated Regulators had effected their return. Here—having now lost his horse, arms, everything but life; having battled away also in the midnight siege some of those terrors that made Indians and border life so hateful to his imagination, and being perhaps seduced by the hope of repairing his losses, and revenging the injuries he had suffered—he was easily persuaded to follow Colonel Bruce and the army of Kentuckians to the Indian territory, where Fate, through his arm, struck a blow so dreadfully yet retributively just at the head of the long-prospering villain, the unprincipled and unremorseful Braxley.

It was mentioned, that when Nathan first burst upon the astonished Bruce, where he lay with his vanguard encamped in the woods, his appearance and demeanour were rather those of a truculent madman than of the simple-minded, inoffensive creature he had so long appeared to the eyes of all who knew him. His Indian garments and decorations contributed somewhat to this effect; but the man, it was soon seen, was more changed in spirit, than in outward attire. The bundle of scalps in his hand, the single one, yet reeking with blood, at his belt, and the axe of Wenonga, gory to the helve, and grasped with a hand not less blood-stained, were not more remarkable evidences of transformation than were manifested in his countenance, deportment, and expressions. His eye beamed with a wild excitement, with exultation, mingled with fury; his step was fierce, active, firm, and elastic, like that of a warrior leaping through the measures of the war-dance; and when he spoke, his words were of battle and bloodshed. He flourished the axe of Wenonga, pointed grimly toward the village, and while recounting the number of warriors who lay therein waiting to be knocked on the head, he seemed, judging his thoughts from his gestures, to be employed in imagination in despatching them with his own hands.

When the march, after a hasty consultation, was agreed upon and resumed, he, although on foot, maintained a position at the head of the army, guiding it along with a readiness and precision which argued extraordinary familiarity with all the approaches to the village; and when the assault was actually commenced, he was still among the foremost, as the reader has seen, to enter the village and the square. To cut the bonds of the Virginian, and utter a fervent expression of delight at his rescue, was not enough to end the ferment in Nathan's mind. Leaving the Virginian immediately to the protection of the younger Bruce, he rushed after the flying Indians, among whom he remained fighting wherever the conflict was hottest, until there remained no more enemies to encounter, achieving such exploits as filled all who beheld him with admiration and amazement.

Nor did the fervour of his fury end altogether even with the battle. He was among the most zealous in destroying the Indian village, applying the fire with his own hands to at least a dozen different wigwams, shouting with the most savage exultation, as each burst into flames.

It was not indeed until the work of destruction was completed, the retreat commenced, and the army once more buried in the woods, that the demon which had thus taken possession of his spirit, seemed inclined to relax its hold, and restore him once more to his wits. It was then, however, that the remarks which all had now leisure to make on his extraordinary transformation, the mingled jests and commendations of which he found himself the theme, began to make an impression on his mind, and gradually wake him as from a dream that had long mastered and distracted his faculties. The fire of military enthusiasm flashed no more from his eyes, his step lost its bold spring and confidence, he eyed those who so liberally heaped praise on his lately acquired courage and heroic actions, with uneasiness, embarrassment, and dismay; and cast his troubled eyes around, as if in search of some friend capable of giving counsel and comfort in such case made and provided. His looks fell upon little Peter, who had kept ever at his side from the moment of his escape from the village, and now trotted along with the deferential humility which became him, while surrounded by so gallant and numerous an assemblage; but even little Peter could not relieve him from the weight of eulogy heaped on his head, nor from the prickings of the conscience which every word of praise and every encomiastic huzza seemed stirring up in his breast.

In this exigency, he caught sight of the Virginian,—mounted once more upon his own trusty Briareus, which the younger Bruce had brought with him to the field of battle,—and remembered on the sudden that he had not yet acquainted the former with the important discovery of the will, which he had so unexpectedly made in the village. The young soldier was riding side by side with his cousin, for whom a palfrey had been easily provided from the Indian pound, and indulging with her many a joyous feeling which their deliverance was so well suited to inspire; but his eye gleamed with double satisfaction as he marked the approach of his trusty associate and deliverer.

"We owe you life, fortune, everything," he cried, extending his hand; "and be assured neither Edith nor myself will forget it. But how is this, Nathan?" he added, with a smile, as he perceived the bundle of scalps, which Nathan, in the confusion or absence of his mind, yet dangled in his hands,—"you were not used so freely to display the proofs of your prowess!"

"Friend," said Nathan, giving one look, ghastly with sorrow and perturbation, to the shaking ringlets, another to the youth, "thee looks upon locks that was once on the heads of my children!" He thrust the bundle into his bosom, and pointed with a look of inexpressible triumph to that of Wenonga, hanging to his belt. "And here," he muttered, "is the scalp of him that slew them! It is enough, friend: thee has had my story,—thee will not censure me. But, friend," he added, hastily, as if anxious to revert to another subject; "I have a thing to say to thee, which it concerns thee and the fair maid, thee cousin, to know. There was a will, friend,—a true and lawful last will and testament of thee deceased uncle, in which theeself and thee cousin was made the sole heirs of the same. Truly, friend, I did take it from the breast of the villain that plotted thee ruin; but, truly, it was taken from me again, I know not how."

"I have it safe," said Roland, displaying it for a moment, with great satisfaction, to Nathan's eyes. "It makes me master of wealth, which you, Nathan, shall be the first to share. You must leave this wild life of the border, go with me to Virginia,—"

"I, friend!" exclaimed Nathan, with a melancholy shake of the head; "thee would not have me back in the Settlements, to scandalise them that is of my faith! No, friend; my lot is cast in the woods, and thee must not ask me again to leave them. And, friend, thee must not think I have served thee for the lucre of money or gain: for, truly, these things is now to me as nothing. The meat that feeds me, the skins that cover, the leaves that make my bed, are all in the forest around me, to be mine when I want them; and what more can I desire? Yet, friend if thee thinks theeself obliged by whatever I have done for thee, I would ask of thee one favour, that thee can grant."

"A hundred!" said the Virginian, warmly.

"Nay, friend," muttered Nathan, with both a warning and beseeching look, "all that I ask is, that thee shall say nothing of me that should scandalise and disparage the faith to which I was born."

"I understand you," said Roland, "and will remember your wish."

"And now, friend," continued Nathan, "do thee take theeself to the haunts of thee fellows, the habitations of them that is honest and peaceful,—thee, and the good maiden, thee cousin; for, truly, it is not well, neither for thee nor for her,—and especially for her, that is feeble and fearful,—to dwell nigh to where murdering Injuns abound."

"Yet go with us, good Nathan," said Edith, adding her voice to the entreaties of her kinsman: "there shall be none to abuse or find fault with you."

"Thee is a good maid," said Nathan, surveying her with, an interest that became mournful as he spoke. "When thee goes back to thee father's house, thee will find them that will gladden at thee coming; and hearts will yearn with joy over thee young and lovely looks. Thee will smile upon them, and they will be happy. Such," he added, with deep emotion, "such might have been *my* fate, had the Injun axe spared me but a single child. But it is not so; there is none left to look upon me with smiles and rejoicing,—none to welcome me from the field and the forest with the voice of love—no, truly, truly,—there is not one,—not one." And as he spoke, his voice faltered, his lip quivered, and his whole countenance betrayed the workings of a bereaved and mourning spirit.

"Think not of this," said Roland, deeply affected, as his cousin also was, by this unexpected display of feeling in the rude wanderer: "the gratitude of those you have so well served, shall be to you in place of a child's affection. We will never forget our obligations. Come with us, Nathan,—come with us."

But Nathan, ashamed of the weakness which he could not resist, had turned away to conceal his emotion; and, stalking silently off, with the ever-faithful Peter at his heels, was soon hidden from their eyes.

The Virginian never saw his wild comrade again. Neither Nathan's habits nor inclinations carried him often into the society of his fellow-men, where reproaches and abuse were sure to meet him. Insult and contumely were, indeed, no longer to be dreaded by the unresisting wanderer, after the extraordinary proofs of courage which he had that day given. But, apparently, he now found as little to relish in encomiums passed on his valour as in the invectives to which he had been formerly exposed. He stole away, therefore, into the woods, abandoning the army altogether, and was no more seen during the march.

But Roland did not doubt be should behold him again at Bruce's Station, where he soon found himself, with his kinswoman, in safety; and where,—now happily able to return to the land of his birth and the home of his ancestors,—he remained during a space of two or three weeks, waiting the arrival of a strong band of Virginia rangers, who (their term of military service on the frontier having expired) were on the eve of returning to Virginia, and with whom he designed seeking protection for his own little party. During all this period he impatiently awaited the re-appearance of Nathan, but in vain; and as he was informed, and indeed, from Nathan's own admissions, knew, that the latter had no fixed place of abode, he saw that it was equally vain to attempt hunting him up in the forest. In short, he was compelled to depart on his homeward journey,—a journey happily accomplished in safety,—without again seeing him; but not until he had left with the commander of the Station a goodly store of such articles of comfort and necessity as he thought would prove acceptable to his solitary friend.

Nor did he take leave without making others of his late associates acquainted with his bounty. The pledge he had given the dying renegade he offered to redeem to the daughter, by bearing her with him to Virginia, and providing her a secure home, under the protection of his cousin; but Telie preferring rather to remain in the family of Colonel Bruce, who seemed to entertain for her a truly parental affection, he took such steps as speedily converted the poor dependent orphan into a person of almost wealth and consequence. His bounty-grants and land-warrants he left in the hands of Bruce, with instructions to locate them to the best advantage in favour of the girl, to whom he assigned them with the proper legal formalities; a few hundred acres, however, being conveyed to Captain Ralph and the worthy Dodge,—of whom the latter had given over all thought of returning to the Bay-State, having, as he said, "got his hand in to killing Injuns, and not caring a fourpence-ha'penny for the whole everlasting set of them."

Thus settling up his accounts of gratitude, he joyously, and with Edith still more joyous at his side, turned his face towards the East and Virginia,—towards Fell-hallow and home: to enjoy a fortune of happiness to which the memory of the few weeks of anguish and gloom passed in the desert only served to impart additional zest.

Nor did he, even in the tranquil life of enjoyment which he was now enabled to lead, lose his interest in the individuals who had shared his perils and sufferings. His inquiries, made wherever, and whenever, intelligence could be obtained, were continued for many years, until, in fact, the District and Wilderness of Kentucky existed no more, but were both merged in a State, too great and powerful to be longer exposed to the inroads of savages. The information which he was able to glean in relation to the several parties, was, however, uncertain and defective, the means of intelligence being, at that early period, far from satisfactory: but such as it was, we lay it before the reader.

The worthy Colonel Bruce continued to live and flourish with his Station, which soon grew into a town of considerable note. The colonel himself, when last heard from, was no longer a colonel, his good stars, his military services, and perhaps the fervent prayers of his wife, having transformed him, one happy day, into a gallant Brigadier. His son Dick trode in the footsteps, and grew into the likeness of his brother Tom, being as brave and good-humoured, and far more fortunate; and Roland heard, a few years after his own departure from Kentucky, with much satisfaction, that the youth was busily occupied, during such intervals of peace as the Indians allowed, in clearing and cultivating the lands bestowed on Telie Doe, whom he had, though scarce yet out of his teens, taken to wife.

No very certain information was ever obtained in regard to the fate of Pardon Dodge; but there was every reason to suppose he remained in Kentucky, fighting Indians to the last, having got so accustomed to that species of pastime as to feel easy while practising it. We are the more inclined to think that such was the case, as the name is not yet extinct on the frontier; and one individual bearing it, has very recently, in one of the fiercest, though briefest of Indian wars, covered it with immortal lustre.

Of Ralph Stackpole, the invader of Indian horse-pounds, it was Captain Forrester's fortune to obtain more minute, though, we are sorry to say, scarce more satisfactory intelligence. The luck, good and bad together, which had distinguished Roaring Ralph, in all his relations with Roland, never, it seems, entirely deserted him. His improvident, harum-scarum habits had very soon deprived him of all the advantages that might have resulted from the soldier's munificent gift, and left him a landless good-for-nothing, yet contented vagabond as before. With poverty returned sundry peculiar propensities which he had manifested in former days; so that Ralph again lost savour in the nostrils of his acquaintance; and the last time that Forrester heard of him, he had got into a difficulty in some respects similar to that in the woods of Salt River from which Roland, at Edith's intercession, had saved him. In a word, he was one day arraigned before a county-court in Kentucky, on a charge of horse-stealing, and matters went hard against him, his many offences in that line having steeled the hearts of all against him, and the proofs of guilt, in this particular instance, being both strong and manifold. Many an angry and unpitying eye was bent upon the unfortunate fellow, when his counsel rose to attempt a defence;—which he did in the following terms: "Gentlemen of the Jury," said the man of law,—"here is a man, Captain Ralph Stackpole, indicted before you on the charge of stealing a horse; and the affa'r is pretty considerably proved on him."—Here there was a murmur heard throughout the court, evincing much approbation of the counsel's frankness. "Gentlemen of the Jury," continued the orator, elevating his voice, "what I have to say in reply, is, first, that that man thar', Captain Ralph Stackpole, did, in the year seventeen seventy-nine, when this good State of Kentucky, and particularly those parts adjacent to Bear's Grass, and the mouth thereof, where now stands the town of Louisville, were overrun with yelping Injun-savages,—did, I say, gentlemen, meet two Injun-savages in the woods on Bear's Grass, and take their scalps, single-handed—a feat, gentlemen of the jury, that a'n't to be performed every day, even in Kentucky!" Here there was considerable tumult in the court, and several persons began to swear. "Secondly, gentlemen of the jury," exclaimed the attorney-at-law, with a still louder voice, "what I have to say, *secondly*, gentlemen of the jury, is, that this same identical prisoner at the bar, Captain Ralph Stackpole, did, on another occasion, in the year seventeen eighty-two, meet another Injun-savage in the woods—a savage armed with rifle, knife, and tomahawk—and met him with—you suppose, gentlemen, with gun, axe, and scalper, in like manner!—No, gentlemen of the jury!—

with his *fists*, and" (with a voice of thunder) "licked him to death in the natural way!—Gentlemen of the jury, pass upon the prisoner—guilty or not guilty?" The attorney resumed his seat: his arguments were irresistible. The jurors started up in their box, and roared out, to a man, "*Not guilty!*" From that moment, it may be supposed, Roaring Ralph could steal horses at his pleasure. Nevertheless, it seems, he immediately lost his appetite for horse-flesh; and leaving the land altogether, he betook himself to a more congenial element, launched his broad-horn on the narrow bosom of the Salt, and was soon afterwards transformed into a Mississippi alligator; in which amphibious condition, we presume, he roared on to the day of his death.

As for the valiant Nathan Slaughter—the last of the list of worthies, after whom the young Virginian so often inquired—less was discovered in relation to his fate than that of the others. A month, or more, perhaps, after Roland's departure, he re-appeared at Bruce's Station, where he was twice or thrice again seen. But, whether it was that, as we have once before hinted, he found the cheers and hearty hurrahs, in token of respect for his valiant deeds at Wenonga's town, with which Bruce's people received him, more embarrassing and offensive than the flings and sarcasms with which they used in former days to greet his appearance, or whether he had some still more stirring reason for deserting the neighbourhood, it is certain that he, in a short time, left the vicinity of Salt River altogether, going no man knew whither. He went, and with him his still inseparable friend, little dog Peter.

From that moment the Jibbenainosay ceased to frequent his accustomed haunts in the forest; the phantom Nick of the Woods was never more beheld stalking through the gloom; nor was his fearful cross ever again seen traced on the breast of a slaughtered Indian.